I0618315

Curse of the Cuda

By Brent Story

This book is a work of fiction. Names, characters, businesses, organizations, places, events, and incidents either are the product of the author's imagination or are used fictitiously. Any resemblance to actual persons, living or dead, events, or locales is entirely coincidental.

Copyright © 2012 Brent Story

All rights reserved.

ISBN: 0615644147

ISBN-13:978-0-615-64414-1

Dedication

To my wife Laura who put up with everything associated with
producing this novel

Chapter 1

A ringing phone brought Trevor's drunken sleep to an end. Groggily, he pawed at the handset to end its infernal noise. It was just beyond reach because his other arm was pinned to the bed by his latest conquest. The noise had not made her stir. The alcohol they consumed late into the night was probably the culprit.

Carefully, he eased his arm from beneath her torso and massaged it to restore the blood flow. At last, he got the handset in his hand and was making his way into the other room so he wouldn't wake his guest. He shook his head thinking about how he was going to get her to leave without hurting her feelings. He had gotten what he needed last night and didn't want to have that "day after" conversation about where things were going.

"Dad," the voice on the other side of the phone said.

"Hi son," he replied, barely audible, the first words being blocked by an overabundance of phlegm in his throat.

"I didn't wake, you did I? I thought 11:00 a.m. would be safe."

"No, no, I was just about to get up," Trevor lied.

Just then, Trevor's friend, Crystal, a waitress at Sloppy Joe's, asked, "Who's on the phone?"

"My son, can you give me some privacy?" he said in an irritated tone.

"Oh, okay. Do you mind if I use your shower?"

"No, go ahead."

Trevor's son, Jack, heard the feminine voice and asked, "Who's the lady?"

"Just a friend."

"Anything serious?"

"No. There hasn't been anything serious since your mother. I think she ruined me."

"Come on dad, I know mom wasn't the easiest to get along with at times, but you weren't exactly an angel, off fishing all the time and leaving her alone to take care of me and Emily."

"Touché' son, I deserved that. I'm sorry son. I know how much you love your mother. Why, I even get along with her now that my alimony payments are over."

"That's great dad, the reason I called is to tell you that I won't be able to make it next week.

Disappointed, Trevor asked, "What's up?"

"My company wants me to fix some problems with a new chip I designed. They've asked me to cancel my vacation."

"That sucks, but I understand. Maybe you can reschedule."

"Yeah, maybe we can do it next year."

"Love you son."

There was a pause on the other line. "Yeah, love you too."

Crystal finished her shower and approached Trevor wearing only a towel barely covering her nakedness.

"How about a little morning wake me up?" she said, opening the towel to reveal her full breasts.

Even though Trevor considered it for a minute, he decided it would be best to end the tryst now, and replied, "I'm sorry Crystal, but it's late and I have to get some work done today. Give me a minute to shower and I'll run you back to town."

Trevor could see the disappointment in her face as she turned to get dressed. Once in the bathroom, he reflected on his life as he peered into the mirror. The eyes looking back at him were puffy with the beginnings of crow's feet. His hair was full, but had started to gray around his temples and mustache. How many times had he been staring at this hung-over face promising to change his ways? Too many to think about, he concluded.

Chapter 2

Trevor Callaway bought the 45-foot Chris-Craft sport fishing boat five years ago. He named it Child Support because he would have owned it sooner if he hadn't been paying so much. Trevor wasn't bitter about having children, but was bitter about paying for kids without the joy of being with them on a daily basis. Also, it infuriated him knowing that he paid his ex-wife much more money than she needed and she pissed it away on new clothes, jewelry, and lavish vacations.

His children were always excited to see him while growing up; they acted like the weeks or months since his last visit were meaningless, but he knew better. Divorce had created a distance from them Trevor knew could never be erased.

That part of his life was over. No need to torment himself—that was the way it was. The kids were all grown up now. His son Jack had managed to marry a nice girl, move to Silicon Valley, and pursue a career in computers. In addition, his daughter Emily was engaged, living in Chicago and working as a reporter for the Chicago Tribune.

Life dealt its cards and Trevor often wondered how much influence he actually had over the game. Was his destiny written in the stars – or did his actions control it? It was a shame that most of his learning occurred after he made mistakes, and it depressed him knowing that he might never get the opportunity to correct them. What the hell--this was his life now! No sense worrying about the past because it couldn't be changed.

Trevor was a successful author and able to arrange his schedule to include days and sometimes weeks of fishing. But periodically, he would have to park the Child Support in the Key West Marina and return to his house on White Street to write. He would rather fish than write, but his writing paid the bills.

Many of his publishers compared him to Ernest Hemingway. Although this didn't hurt his marketability--he couldn't agree. Hemingway's writings were often viewed as depressing; Trevor wrote romance novels for all those women missing something in their lives that most men would never understand. He understood after a failed marriage, but was too bitter and hurt to ever expose his soul to any woman again. Women had become toys in his life, something to play with and then discard when he tired of them.

Trevor first met his boat crew, Dave and Richie, while in Vietnam. With a journalism background, he was commissioned as a spokesperson to the press. He reported body counts, battle victories, and whatever other propaganda his superiors ordered him to.

On one of his assignments, Trevor was sent to interview Dave Pritchard and Richard (Richie) Randall, the only survivors of a platoon sent to take a meaningless North Vietnamese stronghold. He was told they were heroes and that news of their valor should be shared with the world.

While conducting the interview, Trevor found that Richie and Dave had been practically slaughtered during the assault. The pair watched while their friends were blown to pieces, body parts flying through the air, often striking them and splattering blood on their uniforms. If not for a last minute air strike by some F-16's with Napalm, there would not have been any heroes.

Within minutes the foliage on the hill was turned into a giant bonfire incinerating the Vietnamese and anything else in its path. The smell of burning flesh filled the air as Dave and Richie were found by a reconnaissance platoon, shell-shocked, huddled together and crying.

Now they were surprised that the Army was calling them heroes, and they weren't real crazy about being labeled as such. The two men were livid as they entered Trevor's office.

"We ain't no fucking heroes!" Dave said angrily, when questioned about the incident.

"Yeah, we're fucking assholes" Richie chimed in, and then added, "assholes for not running to Canada!"

Trevor refused to write the propaganda about the reluctant heroes and was transferred to an artillery division. Dave and Richie wrote to him periodically while they were in Vietnam, but from their letters he knew they would never be normal again.

Fortunately, after a while, Richard Nixon and the United States government realized the war in Vietnam was a mistake and called for the return of American troops. Trevor made it home with only a few scars on his calves, caused by some shrapnel sprayed from an exploding mortar shell. As luck would have it, this happened only a few weeks before he was being sent home. Now he had physical scars to remind him of the mental scars he would carry for life.

After Vietnam, Trevor lost touch with Dave and Richie until years later. During a short break from one of his novels, while playing golf at the only course in Key West (something he had to do from time to time to cure writer's block), he was summoned to the perimeter fence on the fifteenth hole by two pitiful looking characters. They were homeless by appearance, longhaired with beards; one was wearing sandals, his feet filthy, and the other was wearing Nikes so dirty you almost couldn't make out the swoosh logo.

"Hey man, you wanna buy some quality used golf balls? I have Pinnacles, Titlest, Max Flies, Top Flites, and even a few of the new Titaniums," the man in Nikes asked.

He held up an old bread bag filled with golf balls and gave his sales pitch saying, "Six balls for five bucks or a dozen for eight."

Trevor could smell beer on the guy's breath, though it was only 9:00 a.m. However, despite their rough appearance, there was something different about these two street people that Trevor couldn't quite put his finger on.

"I'll take two dozen," Trevor replied.

"Thanks man," the one in sandals said.

Trevor pulled out his wallet and handed Nike a twenty and said, "Keep the change." The man leaned forward to hand Trevor the golf balls over the fence. As he moved, his dog tags rattled against the fence. Trevor's eyes studied the clinking objects, while he read the name, Randall, Richard. It took a minute for the cobwebs to clear. Richard Randall, he thought to himself. He knew that name! Richard Randall...."Richie?" Trevor said, his voice ending in a high pitch.

"How do you know my name?" Nike asked.

"Richie, it's me, Trevor. You know, from Nam."

The man in sandals spoke up, "Wow this is really freaky. Trevor! I'm Dave Pritchard."

"Richie and Dave, what the hell are you two doing here selling used golf balls?" Trevor questioned.

"It's a long story," Richie said, his eyes cast toward the ground.

Trevor knew the story. Countless numbers of young men had returned from Vietnam with their lives forever changed, and they had a hard time fitting back into the society that sent them there.

"Richie and I tried to work when we got home, but would you believe some people wouldn't hire us because we're Vietnam Vets? After that we found that we just didn't give a shit about anything. Our families didn't understand, and the only people we felt comfortable around were each other. During the summer we live in a shack on the Upper Peninsula of Michigan. We hunt, fish, and can our own vegetables. When winter approaches, we hop a train to Florida to look for golf balls and work the fish houses to survive. Right now we're staying in a lean-to on Cudjoe Key, and sometimes we crash with a couple of friends that own an old houseboat in Key West Harbor."

"How'd you guys like to work for me?"

"Doin' what?" Richie questioned.

"I've got a 45-foot sport fishing boat, the Child Support, docked in the Key West Marina and I need a crew."

"I don't know if I can commit to a steady job," Dave replied.

"What more could you want? You'd have a place to live, and the only work would be some maintenance and crewing when we fish. You can drink on the job as long as you don't stay drunk."

"Let's give it a shot Dave," Richie said. "Remember, we can trust Trevor. They sent him to artillery when he wouldn't write that bullshit about us."

"Yeah," Dave said, "I guess you're right."

"Get your stuff together and I'll meet you on US 1 when I'm done with my round," Trevor yelled as he headed back to the golf cart.

Trevor's game lacked concentration after his meeting with Richie and Dave. He wondered whether he made the right decision to enlist two homeless Vietnam Vets to crew his boat. Oh well, he thought, this may be another learning experience.

On the next tee shot he sliced one onto US 1 and cringed while he waited for the sound of shattering glass. It never happened, so he decided to give himself a mulligan and teed up another ball. His second shot was short, but safe, lying just on the right fringe of the fairway.

As he walked up to the ball his mind began wandering as it did sometimes while he was writing, but this time it was different. Seeing Richie and Dave had triggered thoughts he had attempted to hide from for years. Most of the time he was successful, but their faces had summoned visions that seem to travel up from a dark place in his mind, a place like the bottom of a well, a cold place, a forbidding place.

Suddenly there were choppers on the golf course and mortars too. Trevor clamped his hands over his ears and crouched down to avoid being hit. He closed his eyes, but he could still see his platoon members being shot by the Vietnamese snipers. He couldn't take it any more so he yelled, "Stop it you fucking bastards!" As he stood there trembling someone put a hand on his shoulder. He turned to punch the assailant in the throat since he had no weapon—something they had taught him in basic training. Seconds before he delivered the lethal blow, he snapped out of it and saw a bewildered man in his sixties wearing plaid Bermuda shorts standing before him.

"Are you all right?"

"Yeah, yeah, I think the heat made me feel a little faint."

During the next few miserable holes Trevor tried to forget about what had happened, but couldn't focus on anything else.

"Damn, I thought that shit was gone forever," he said out loud, then looked around to see if anyone was around to see him talking to himself. The old man was on the tee box standing with his hands on his hips, his body language telling Trevor hurry up. Trevor waved to let the old man know he would hurry, made his shot and then moved on to the eighteenth hole.

After that terrible round, he decided that he better keep writing because he would never make it as a professional golfer. Trevor tipped the cart attendant, threw his clubs into the bed of his fifteen year old 1985 Ford Pick-up and turned onto US 1 to head toward Key West.

On the right-hand side of the road, close to where the third hole is, stood those two unsavory looking individuals with their right pant legs pulled up and their thumbs pointing toward Key West.

"Going our way, big guy?" Richie said.

Both Richie and Dave laughed as they threw their duffel bags in the back of the pick-up. They squeezed themselves into the truck's cab and suddenly the gagging smell of old beer and body odor permeated the air inside. Trevor had to breathe through his mouth to keep from becoming ill. He never could understand how street people could live with such filth.

Trevor's house was built in the 1800's. It was a three-bedroom, and two-bath. The second bathroom was added by one of the previous owners in the 1950's. The outside was typical of the older houses in the neighborhood; they all had large porches that wrapped around the exterior with ornate wooden railings. Purple and pink bougainvilleas were scattered about the landscape, somehow thriving in the poor soil conditions.

Key West had become a chic place to have winter homes, with the Calvin Kleins of the fashion world and numerous movie stars now residing there during the cooler months. The onslaught of these rich inhabitants was sending property taxes through the roof. It was getting so the Conchs (native Key Westers) couldn't afford to live where they had grown up. They learned to keep their taxes down by letting the exterior of their houses deteriorate because the tax assessor could only make his appraisal by viewing the property from the front walk.

Trevor had decided that this was a good strategy, and had not fixed up the outside of his house for the same reason. If not for his planning, the tax assessors would probably have hiked up his taxes even more than they already had. However, inside the house was beautiful with its refinished hardwood floors and walls decorated with various maritime antiques, old fishing reels, lures, and ship models. Living in this house helped Trevor to write by sparking his imagination. The surroundings reminded him of years gone past where heroes, villains, and lovely women were caught up in dangerous situations.

Trevor handed Richie and Dave clean towels and suggested they bathe.

"Man, it's not Saturday night," Richie kidded.

"You kind of get used to the smell of body odor when you live on the street," Dave said, sniffing at his armpits.

"Kind of like those Europeans and their women with hairy armpits," Richie added.

"You guys have to take at least three showers a week if you're going to crew for me," Trevor said, letting them know that his nose couldn't tolerate anything less.

"I think we can handle that, don't you Richie?"

"I guess so."

Dave went into the bathroom to shower and Richie sat in the living room in awe of its many interesting artifacts.

"Hey Trevor, where did you find all of this stuff?

"I picked up a little here, a little there. A lot of it I bought on US 1 in Dania, an area they call antique row. Some of it's from the

Boston Harbor area. Whenever I have to travel for a book signing, I usually have some time to myself and I use it to go antique shopping."

"Where did you get that wooden figure of a mermaid?"

"Do you like her? She's one of my favorites. She came from the bow of an ancient schooner that used to transport tea and spices to the U.S. from the Far East."

"She's got a nice rack!"

"Yeah, that's what caught my eye when I saw her in an antique store in San Francisco. She cost me five thousand dollars, but I had to have her."

Richie gulped when he heard how much the figurine cost and said, "Man, that's a lot of Budweiser."

"Oh well, you can't spend it when you're gone"

Trevor guessed the guys were about his size, so he searched his dresser drawers for some used Sportiff fishing shorts and T-shirts for them. He found two pairs of shorts, one navy blue and the other tan, both still in good condition. In his T-shirt drawer he found an old Fantasy Fest 1997 shirt and a Nautica shirt with a couple of small holes in it, but still presentable. The Nautica shirt did have a little sentimental value in it as he had received it from one of his past loves, but the shirt had faded and so had the memories. He didn't bother looking for underwear, because he guessed that they probably didn't wear any.

After Richie and Dave showered, Trevor fixed them a lunch of peanut butter and jelly sandwiches on Bahama bread, his specialty. They washed down the sandwiches with some Budweiser, and then Trevor suggested they go check out their new home.

As they walked outside, a musty odor reminded Trevor that Richie and Dave's things were piled by the door. He had asked them earlier to please leave them outside until they could be washed.

"Why don't you guys throw your things in the washer while we're gone?"

"Sure thing boss, just show us how to use the washer and it's a done deal," Richie said.

Trevor took them around to the utility room located at the rear of the house and started to show them how to operate the washer.

"Where do you put the quarters?" Dave kidded.

As they piled into the cab of the truck Trevor inhaled and thought, much better. Someone smelled like Tommy Hilfiger cologne, so he remarked, "Somebody smells good!"

Richie turned to Trevor, "Sorry, I hope you don't mind me borrowing some. I forgot what it's like to smell good."

"Help yourself, even Tommy Hilfiger couldn't have saved you before."

They all laughed knowing the truth of that statement.

It was always interesting driving through Key West. There were pink skinned tourists crowded onto noisy little mopeds putting their lives at risk, women on bicycles wearing bikini tops just large enough to cover the essential parts and gay men and women walking down the street holding hands and kissing. Yes, Key West is a city where practically anything goes

"Hey, look at that Dumpster!" Richie pointed and said. Someone had taken hours to glue shells and different items to the dumpster's surface creating an ornate piece of artwork. "Only in Key West!" Dave added.

Key West Marina was less than three miles from Trevor's house, so it took only minutes to get there. The marina's location made things very convenient for Trevor when approaching storms demanded that he check his boat's lines or when he stopped by routinely just to check on his pride and joy.

"Wow, she's a beaut!" Richie exclaimed. Trevor had the boat fully refinished after he bought her. All of her painted areas were primed and repainted with special marine epoxy paints. The teak had been meticulously sanded and varnished, her engines pulled and skillfully rebuilt. She had radar, depth finder, GPS and a radio – all of the latest technologies. Trevor spared no expense on her fishing equipment either. The inventory included four Penn International reels with custom rods, a downrigger, and two of the best outriggers money could buy. You see, as with Ernest Hemingway, one of Trevor's passions in life was fishing.

Chapter 3

It was a clear sunny day and the sky and sea competed to see which could draw your eyes into its brilliant blue and expansive depths. Only the intermittent screeching of seagulls looking for a free meal interrupted the drone of the boat's engines. The air was pure except for those times when the boat's direction, or a shift in the wind, caused the diesel fumes to invade the crew's lungs.

Captain Trevor and his mates, Richie and Dave, had been out for days fishing for blue marlin off the coast of Chub Cay in the Bahamas. This was day three, and so far there had been only one true marlin knock down. The fish had come up to the trailing bait and toyed with it as if to say not today fellas. Yes, there had been plenty of mahi mahi, big bulls over forty pounds, enough to make any fisherman jealous. But they weren't fishing for mahi--they were fishing for marlin.

The time was 9:30 a.m. and they had been trolling for an hour and forty-five minutes. Trevor usually liked to start earlier, but the Mount Gay Rum and Coke from the night before had taken its toll. The heat was stifling, adding to their misery. If not for the movement of the boat, it would be unbearable. Large sweat rings appeared on their shirts under their necklines and armpits. With eyes squinting and heads pounding, they trolled their baits hoping to find the elusive marlin.

All of a sudden Dave heard a snapping sound and the alarming buzz of line being peeled off the Penn International reel. Something big and fast had taken the bait, but after days of disappointment they had learned to withhold judgment until a marlin fin was spotted ripping through the water.

Whatever took the bait was swimming and turning like a runaway torpedo. Suddenly, the action stopped as Dave reeled in the line. Years of experience told him what he'd find. As he turned the crank toward its last few rotations, he saw what he'd expected; the three hundred-pound leader wire had been cut as if wire cutters had been used.

"What do you think it was?" Trevor asked.

"Might have been an extremely large cuda or a shark," Richie guessed.

"Figures," Trevor said. "The first knockdown of the day had to be a cuda."

"I don't know how it got through that 300 lb. leader so fast," Dave added while holding up the damaged line.

"There's some big cuda around here because of all the prey available in these waters," Trevor stated, and then began his story.

"I remember fishing for grouper and mutton snapper off the ledge in the bahamas. I got hooked up with a big snapper and had him halfway up to the boat, and then bam! A huge cuda swam up and cut him off leaving only the head. After that happened a few times, I got a little pissed off, so I tried to catch the bastard. I took a live pinfish and back hooked him, and then floated him out with a balloon bobber. You think that son-of-a-bitch took the bait? Too smart! I think God gave the cuda extra brains and balls for some reason."

Trevor realized they had been cruising without any baits in the water and said, "So much for all this talking shit about trash fish – let's get our lines back in the water and catch what we really came out here for!"

Dave unsnapped the broken leader and opened the bait box to retrieve one of several pre-rigged ballyhoos and clipped it on. He then threw the bait over the stern and began to peel out line until it was far enough behind the boat.

After that, he secured the line in the outrigger and took a minute to watch the bait, making sure it was skipping across the water like a live fish. Dave chuckled to himself remembering what one fisherman had once said about outriggers. "Outriggers can be compared to a woman's bra – they lift, separate and make the bait more appealing."

Once the lines were in place, he yelled to the rest of the crew, "Who wants a Kalik?"

The men loved the potent beer brewed in the Bahamas.

"Starting kind of early aren't we?" Trevor remarked.

"Better than drinking Mount Gay, which is probably what I should do. You know 'the hair of the dog that bit you' I think is how the saying starts," Dave replied.

Thinking a beer might help his hangover Trevor remarked, "All right. I'll have one, but let's take it easy, I want a full day of fishing and I don't want you falling overboard and becoming cuda bait.

Remember, there's one out there probably pissed off because he's got your hook in him!"

The sun was straight up and the heat was even more intense. Three Kaliks later, the captain and crew were feeling a little groggy. They had caught two mahis: a cow 32 lbs, and a bull 47 lbs. A wahoo weighing 51 lbs. was also hooked and they spent forty-five minutes landing him – but still no marlin. Dave made some peanut butter and jelly sandwiches for lunch, which they washed down with more Kaliks. After lunch, Trevor asked Dave to replace the baits with fresh ones because he planned on trolling for a few more hours.

Two hours later, Trevor and Dave were slipping in and out of consciousness, while Richie piloted the boat. Richie turned to check the baits and something caught his eye – something gigantic. He squinted and saw a large sail fin moving through the water towards the skipping bait. He screamed, "Fish on the bait!" Trevor and Dave jumped up so fast they almost passed out. They ran to the stern trying to see what Richie was screaming about, and watched as the fish passed by, slowing to tap at one of the baits with his sword. He appeared to be massive at least 600 lbs. or more. They all waited in anticipation to see what this giant of the seas next move would be.

Trevor made his way to the fighting chair and strapped himself in, wishing he had taken time to urinate first. The restraining belt caused even more pressure on his bladder making matters worse. The sail fin was on the surface again and moving towards the bait. Wham! The fish hit like a freight train. Dave picked up the Penn International rod and reel and awkwardly handed the rod to Trevor, with both men struggling to place the butt of the rod in the gimbal of the fighting chair.

It was now time to set the hook. Too soon, and he'd pull the bait from the fish's mouth. Too late, and he'd swallow the bait, belly hooking him, and possibly killing the fish. The latter would upset Trevor terribly because he believed in conservation and always tried to tag and release all of the billfish that he'd caught in recent years. He even belonged to a game-fishing club whose members all agreed to tag and release, so that future generations could enjoy this type of fishing.

Trevor counted to ten and pulled back on the rod screaming, "He's hooked!" The huge fish jumped ten feet in the air and shook his head violently from side to side.

"Get ready to follow him!" Trevor screamed at the mate.

Richie had already pulled both levers back to put the boat in reverse. As the boat traveled backwards, the water slapped up against the transom. The crew had to so react fast because a fish that size could empty a reel in a matter of minutes. The reel was screaming like a pissed off woman with PMS as the fish dove deeper and deeper, trying to free itself from its unknown bondage.

When the marlin turned upward, the pressure on his mouth slackened and he charged to the surface with his new felt freedom. Trevor heard the reel go silent and noticed the reel had stopped turning. The line began to slacken. He yelled, "He's coming up!" Frantically, he turned the crank like he never had before, hoping to take up the line before the fish could throw the hook.

"Take up the slack!" Trevor yelled to Richie. The mate threw both levers towards the bow and the vessel lurched forward. Between Trevor's frantic reeling and the forward movement of the boat, the line had tightened and Trevor was now able to feel that his prey was still at hand.

The fish, sensing the tension of the line once again as it approached the surface, jumped violently shaking his head from side to side trying to throw the hook. He then dove again hoping that the dark depths of the ocean could provide a safe haven. The same scene took place several times over the next few hours.

The sun had turned a brilliant orange and had slipped rapidly toward the horizon. The sky, once clear blue, was now violet and filled with purple clouds whose tips were bright orange from the light being reflected from the setting sun. Trevor, his bladder hurting more than his hands and arms, had urinated in his pants. The sickening smell of urine and sweat was flowing off his body. However, it didn't seem to bother his crew after their years of living on the street.

The marlin was tiring, although it was still making small runs. Trevor had managed to bring the huge fish closer and closer to the boat. Then suddenly, while making a run, the action came to a stop. Trevor, fearing the fish had gotten off, began to reel in the line hoping to feel some evidence of the fish. After a couple of cranks, it began to feel as though he was keeping the fish from sinking to the ocean's depths.

"It's on but not fighting – feels like it's dead," he said while turning the handle. He reeled in the line wondering what could have happened. Sometimes a billfish's stomach can pop out of its mouth and kill it – maybe it had a heart attack, he thought. Trevor cranked and cranked, the line seemed endless even though he had been able to reel in half the line while the fish was still alive.

Finally the massive carcass came into sight, a huge silver-bellied monolith from the deep.

"My God, his tail's missing!" Trevor cried.

As the fish was pulled alongside the boat, the captain and crew stared in horror as they viewed this deformed majestic giant. The tail looked as though it had been surgically removed.

Whatever did this had some sharp teeth, Trevor thought to himself.

"What are we going to do now?" Trevor asked.

"He's only good for smokin' now," Dave suggested.

"Better tie him on the stern dive platform and beat feet to Bimini before it starts rotting," Dave suggested.

"They won't believe this at the Game Fishing Club," he added.

Richie went to the storage locker to get some line to secure the fish to the transom. While rooting around in the locker, he spied a block and tackle and brought it to haul the fish onto the dive platform. Dave took the line and tied a noose, and then slipped it over the fish's bill pushing it until it came to rest behind the gills. Next, he slipped another noose over the tail stump high enough so that it wouldn't slip off. Using the block and tackle they eased one end at a time onto the dive platform, making sure the lines and not the platform supported most of the fish's weight. They tied some extra lines around the marlin just in case the seas picked up. Richie also laid some bags of ice along the top of the fish to keep it cool.

The marlin's lifeblood dripped from the tail arteries that had been severed during the attack. The blood entered the water in thick dark red drops, and then quickly joined the water molecules leaving small pinkish patches.

The predator lay 10 feet below the surface, silent and hidden from view by the large vessel. The marlin's tail had temporarily satisfied his hunger, but the dripping blood was arousing his predatory senses.

It was dark now and the crew was tired from the day's activities. The stars sparkled like diamonds against the pitch-black sky, their visibility improved by the lack of city lights. There was a warm ocean breeze blowing, but the seas were relatively calm. Way off on the horizon, lightning flashes could be seen, but fortunately in the opposite direction of their travel. Richie switched on the navigation lights and started the engines. The boat was pointed toward Bimini and their journey began.

In the depths of the darkening seas, the cuda also turned and began to follow the trail of dripping blood. Normally territorial, this huge barracuda was now being controlled by its primal instincts.

Chapter 4

Carla Morgan was born and raised in Palm Beach. The daughter of an oil tycoon, she led the good life while growing up. The family's large Victorian mansion was built on the Palm Beach coast of Florida overlooking the Atlantic Ocean. Carla had spent many days of her childhood frolicking along the beach shore collecting seashells and sea creatures, especially when the wind blew clumps of Sargasso seaweed to shore.

On her eighteenth birthday, two days before high school graduation, Carla was informed that both her parents had died in a plane crash. The engines on the family's Cessna had sputtered and died shortly after take-off from Cat Cay. Carla's father, the pilot, should have kept flying straight, to maintain airspeed, belly-landing the plane in the ocean. Instead, he did what they tell you not to do in flight school; he turned and tried to land back at the airport. With full fuel tanks, turning the plane slowed its air speed and caused it to drop like a rock. Perhaps the fact that he knew his wife didn't know how to swim is why he attempted this tragic maneuver.

After the incident Carla's life was in turmoil. With no brothers or sisters – she was alone now. Her parents had set up a trust as many wealthy people do to keep the Feds and State from getting rich. Carla was eighteen now and considered old enough to make her own decisions, but at this time in her life, she didn't want that pressure.

Neil, the family's butler, was a kind and honest man. He was the one who received the call from the authorities and given the responsibility of telling her about her parent's demise. When Neil walked into her room with tears in his eyes, Carla knew that something was terribly wrong. She had never seen him cry in the eighteen years that she had known him.

"Neil, what's wrong?"

He grabbed her hand and spoke softly, "Carla my dear, it's your parents."

"Neil, what do you mean?"

"There's been a terrible accident."

"But they're all right aren't they?"

Neil had to force out the words that followed, "I'm afraid they've both been killed."

"No, you're lying! Neil, tell me it isn't true!"

"I wish it weren't my dear sweet child, but it is."

"What happened?"

Neil recounted the grim details to Carla, while hugging her tightly to comfort her.

The next day, after a long night of reminiscing with Neil about all of those wonderful years they had spent with her parents, she asked him to remain at the estate and manage her affairs. Neil told her there was nothing in the world that he would rather do. Being single his whole life, Carla was the daughter he never had.

Carla decided it would be best to keep busy. The trust fund was able to supply more money than she could ever spend, but she needed a purpose in life. All those years of writing poetry on the beach and keeping a detailed journal of her life helped her discover a love for written words. Carla decided she would get a formal education and major in English, hoping to be a successful author or in the worst-case scenario, an English professor. She chose to attend the University of Florida, even though she could have afforded any private school.

Carla had begun to ripen as a woman. All of her baby fat was gone, and she was left with a voluptuous body. Five foot six, one hundred twenty pounds; she was the type of woman every other woman hates. The Italian in her father's bloodline had given her olive skin. The Nordic ancestry in her mother's genes bestowed upon her light blonde hair, which she kept cut short. This made it easy to wash and fix every day after swimming. Each morning for the last four years she had gotten up and jogged three miles to the college pool, put on her suit and swam laps for half an hour.

She loved the freedom of swimming naked and many times as a little girl her mother had scolded her for removing her suit. However, her mother, Elaine, usually would give up after repeated warnings, and let little Carla run around nude. It really didn't matter because the family owned a large part of the beachfront where visitors rarely appeared. Carla enjoyed skinny-dipping well into her teens, especially during the summer months around dusk while the water was still warm.

Before 8:00 a.m. only some of the lights in the U.F. Coliseum were turned on to conserve electricity, so many times when no one was around, Carla would remove her suit and let it fall to the bottom of the deep end. Carla figured that if anyone showed up while she was skinny-dipping, she would swim underwater to the deep end and put her suit back on. But, so far she hadn't had to deal with any other early swimmers.

Chapter 5

Kit Hanson spent his adolescence on Dania Beach as a lifeguard. He loved having a job that allowed him to be near the sea and its inhabitants.

At the ripe age of thirteen he used to ride his bike to Spoils Island (a sand bar on the north side of Port Everglades in Fort Lauderdale) to collect specimens for his salt-water aquarium. Unfortunately, by the time the fish were sucked up in a slurp gun (a device that could be described as a giant hypodermic plunger) and transported home seven bumpy miles by bike, their chance of survival was slim. Nonetheless, these activities helped influence his decision to become a marine biologist.

Kit Hanson was in his last year at the University of Florida and was almost finished earning a BA in Marine Biology. He loved his field of study and during his summer breaks he worked at Sea World in Orlando helping to maintain the large aquariums. He was an excellent free diver, and had even been able to spear grouper at forty feet while holding his breath. However, a bad experience with scuba gear at age eighteen had given him a scuba diving phobia. This fear was something he knew that he had to overcome.

The incident occurred when his brother, Dirk, invited him to go scuba diving knowing that Kit hadn't been certified. Kit knew that it wasn't smart to dive without proper training but his brother laughed and said, "There's nothing to it. All you have to do is keep breathing, and never swim up faster than your bubbles."

It was 9:00 a.m. when they met at Dirk's house on the water in Boca Raton and loaded the diving gear into the 40-foot Sea Ray pleasure craft. The weather was nice, but it looked like some clouds were looming on the horizon. The trip down the Intracoastal and out of Boca Inlet was pleasant. Once offshore, they found the reef and anchored, but decided not to get in the water right away because the weather had starting clouding up. The stereo on the yacht was blasting 80's rock-n-roll, while everyone hung out waiting to see what the weather was going to do. The seas were fairly calm, but they could see ominous looking clouds gathering offshore.

Kit was sitting on the back area of the boat when he heard a strange buzzing sound. He traced the noise to some fishing poles. They had brought along some fishing poles just in case someone felt like fishing. He reached over to touch one and received a small electrical shock. It was a static shock like the ones you get from touching a doorknob after walking on wool carpet during cold weather.

Kit yelled, "Hey man, check this out!" He grabbed a rod from the rod holder and found that if he lowered it to the deck the buzzing stopped. If the process was reversed, the buzzing became louder. Dirk watched Kit do this several times and then said, "Hey bro', I wouldn't do that too much because the rod is made out of graphite, making it a perfect lightening rod."

Kit said, "Yeah, I guess you're right," and placed the rod on the deck. They decided that it would be a good idea to take the rest of the fishing poles and place them on the deck also. Each person received a small static shock as they grabbed the rods.

After experiencing intense lightening strikes in the vicinity, they decided to anchor at Boca Bay inside the Inlet and wait out the weather. Kit drank three beers in two hours. Not many under normal circumstances, but drinking one beer is taboo while scuba diving. And, if certified, he would have known this. His nose was also slightly stuffy that day, which made two strikes against him.

After the sky cleared, they anchored off shore on a reef in about thirty-five feet of water. As Dirk helped him put on his dive gear, Kit started to feel claustrophobic from the weight of the equipment. Dirk gave him some last minute instructions, "Remember, never swim up faster than your bubbles or you'll get the bends."

After Kit entered the water, his equipment became weightless and with his buoyancy compensator, he could even float. This wasn't as comfortable as free diving, but he knew he must learn to enjoy scuba diving if he was to function as a Marine Biologist.

Dirk entered the water and began his descent. Kit pushed the air release button on his buoyancy compensator and followed. At fifteen feet, the pain in Kit's ears told him to equalize the pressure in his nasal and ear canals. He reached up, pinched his nose, and pushed with his lungs to increase the air pressure in his head. Only one ear popped. Kit repeated the procedure, applying even more pressure, and then finally, the other ear popped. He was now at twenty-five feet and watched as Dirk swam off into the distance.

I guess he forgot about the buddy system, Kit thought.

He had heard that no one should dive alone. One should always have a buddy in case he or she should run out of air or get into some kind of trouble. He was pissed and a little nervous that his brother had taken off without him.

Thirty feet down Dirk saw a large grouper ahead and realized that his brother was now out of sight. Kit felt it slowly coming on, a dizziness spreading throughout his whole body. He knew he must not panic. It must be the beer or the nasal condition causing this, he thought. But right now that didn't matter. He must remain calm. It wasn't easy, because Kit looked to the surface and watched as it began to sway back and forth. It was as if someone had grabbed his head and was pushing it from side to side.

"I am conscious – all I have to do is make it to the surface before I pass out."

Back and forth the surface swayed on the way up.

Not too fast. Let the bubbles rise ahead of you, he thought to himself. His class ring from high school slid off his finger due to the narrowing caused by the water's coolness and pressure on his finger. He turned and watched it fall into the depths, thinking momentarily about chasing after it, but then deciding that his life was more important than a ring.

Moments later his head pierced the surface. The swaying had stopped, but was replaced by a severe headache and earache. Dirk's girlfriend, Tina, was sunning herself on the bow. She noticed Kit surface and wondered where Dirk was.

"Kit, is something wrong?"

"I'm all right."

"Would you mind helping me in the boat?"

Still a little shaky, Kit climbed up the dive ladder assisted by Tina.

"I saw Dirk's bubbles about two hundred feet off the bow," Tina said, as Kit removed his gear.

"How come you came up?"

"I started getting dizzy and thought I was going to pass out."

"You're lucky you didn't!"

When Dirk joined them later he apologized for leaving Kit and said he would pay more attention next time.

"I didn't even notice you drinking beer. I thought you knew better," said Dirk.

It would be four years before Kit considered trusting his life to scuba gear. So far he had managed to collect specimens free diving, but knew he must overcome his fear of scuba diving to conduct certain types of research properly.

Kit decided it was time to become certified, so he enrolled at a local dive shop in Gainesville. At first he thought it was unusual to find a dive shop so far inland, but later discovered that Gainesville and surrounding areas had many springs and rivers with numerous underwater caverns and caves that required scuba gear for exploration.

Kit was at the end of the course and the last step was an open water dive to a depth of forty feet in the waters off St. Augustine. He was still nervous because so far they had only done ditch and don exercises in the instructor's private pool. This is an exercise where the diver has to swim to the bottom of the pool, remove all of his or her gear, then surface, take a breath, and return to the bottom putting all of the gear back on while submerged.

Kit decided that the best way to overcome his phobia was to go someplace that he felt comfortable with fairly deep water and stay down for a long time.

I've got it! I'll take my scuba gear and go to the college pool. If I go early, no one will be around and I'll be able to sit on the bottom of the deep end until I run out of air.

The day before his open water dive, Kit took his scuba gear and headed to the college pool. As he entered the college sports complex he thought, perfect not a soul in sight!

Hurriedly, he donned his scuba gear and slid into the deep end of the pool. It was a little scary because only half the lights were on due to it being so early. He equalized pressure only once this time and experienced no dizziness. I must try to slow my breathing to conserve air, he thought as he headed for the bottom.

Kit was lying on the bottom of the pool and beginning to enjoy life underwater, when he heard a splash on the surface. Even in the dim light he could make out the body of a young woman, in a one-piece bathing suit, swimming across the surface. Kit hoped he had enough air to remain on the bottom until the swimmer left the pool. Lap after lap, he watched the graceful swimmer pass by on the surface. At one point, she paused directly overhead and Kit, fearing she had seen him, held his breath. He resumed breathing only after she swam away to continue her laps.

Suddenly, his world became dark and fear began to set in. He felt something on his head and without thinking, reached up and took hold of it. Instantly, the light returned and he began to laugh underwater because he was holding a navy blue, one-piece women's Speedo. It had dropped from the surface and landed squarely on the top his head, draping itself over his mask and blocking his vision. Kit knew this would complicate things a little. He'd have to have to explain to this woman why he was in the deep end of the pool wearing scuba gear and holding her bathing suit while she's swimming laps naked overhead.

...

Carla loved the way the bubbles tickled her breasts as she glided naked through the water. However, today there seemed to be more bubbles than usual, especially in the deep end. Just after her turn, the bubbles seemed to engulf her whole body. She noticed that this phenomenon seemed to happen only in the deep end, but she told herself that she must have imagined it.

On Carla's last lap she would hold her breath and swim underwater from the shallow end to her swimsuit at the bottom of the deep end and put it back on. This was the plan to be carried out in the event of an unexpected visitor.

Kit watched as Carla's naked body passed overhead several times. He noticed that she was indeed a true blonde, and was simply one of the most beautiful women he had ever seen. She had exquisite breasts that swayed from side to side as she swam, being propelled elegantly through the water by firm legs and buttocks. Kit decided that she must exercise daily to maintain such a muscular physique.

What would she do when she discovered him at the bottom of the pool lusting over her? Little did he know he was about to find out!

During Carla's last lap, as she swam rapidly towards the deep end of the pool, a strange, dark, figure was beginning to take shape where she had dropped her bathing suit. As she got closer, fear overtook her. Whatever it was didn't belong there, so she turned and swam to the side of the pool. Carla flew from the water barely using the ladder to help herself out and retrieved a towel to cover her naked body.

Embarrassed, Kit knew he must confront the swimmer, apologize, return her suit and explain why he was wearing scuba gear and hanging out in the deep end of the pool at 6:45 a.m.

Carla, wearing a towel and feeling a little more comfortable, watched as the dark shape approached reminiscent of The Creature from the Black Lagoon. As Kit neared, her fear turned into anger as Carla wondered just how long he had been down there. Kit climbed the ladder carefully, holding the woman's Speedo in his right hand.

"I'll take that," Carla said, as she snatched it from his hand. Kit removed his facemask and Carla saw for the first time the creature that had been watching her.

"I'm really sorry"

"You should be!"

"What are you, some kind of pervert?"

"Hey, who expected some 'nature woman' to be swimming in the college pool at 6:45 in the morning?" Kit said indignantly.

They both looked at each other, realizing how silly this scene looked, and began laughing uncontrollably. He isn't a creature after all. In fact he is kind of a hunk, Carla thought as she surveyed the man in front of her. Kit was at least six-foot tall with a lean, muscular, tanned body, like that of a swimmer. He had hair the color of beach sand and big, round, hazel eyes with long eyelashes. When he smiled, his dimples could probably melt even the coldest woman's heart.

Carla excused herself and retreated behind some bleachers to put her suit back on while Kit removed his scuba gear. Upon Carla's return, Kit extended his hand and introduced himself.

"Kit Hanson, marine biology student." "Carla Morgan, 'nature woman' and English major."

They both broke into laughter once more. Kit told her why he was scuba diving in the pool and Carla told of how she had developed the bad habit of swimming nude.

There was electricity between them. They both felt it. Wanting to extend this feeling, they agreed to continue their conversation over breakfast at the Rainbow Bridge, a local health food restaurant.

Carla was first to arrive at the restaurant and picked a secluded booth in the back section. Several minutes later Kit walked through the door. Carla stared as he approached the booth. Kit was even more gorgeous than she had remembered. She was still staring when he arrived. He smiled at Carla, and at that point, she realized she hadn't acknowledged his presence.

"Hi," Kit said, "are you okay?"

"Oh yeah, I'm fine," she returned feeling a bit embarrassed.

Kit slid into the booth and they talked for over an hour forgetting about the world around them. Carla talked about her life careful not to let on that she was filthy rich. If their relationship continued, Carla hoped it would be for love and not for money. Kit also shared tales of his life and Carla found it fascinating. After he was finished, she realized that she had met someone that loved the sea even more than she did.

After a while, Kit said that he hated to go, but that he had to finish typing a 25 page research paper titled, "The Mating Habits of the Atlantic Nurse Shark." He explained that his typing left something to be desired because he had always been a key peeker in his high school keyboarding classes, and for this reason, had never achieved any typing speed. Therefore, it took him twice as long as most people to produce his research papers.

"Shame on you," Carla said, and offered to edit and type his paper.

"Remember, I have to do a lot of writing as an English major. I type over a 100 words per minute because I didn't look at my fingers during keyboarding class!"

Kit looked down at the table with his bottom lip protruding like a scolded child. Carla thought that his little act was funny and laughed at him.

When they finished lunch, Carla suggested that Kit come over that night so that she could begin typing his paper. She took out a pen and wrote directions to her apartment on a napkin.

Carla spent most of the afternoon making the place look presentable by picking up dirty clothes, changing the kitty litter, and dusting. She suggested that her roommate, Jan, get lost so that she and her new acquaintance could be alone. After a short protest, Jan agreed to go visit one of her friends while Kit was over.

Carla was a little nervous because this was the first man that she had carried on an intelligent conversation with since she moved to Gainesville. Sure, she had been approached by plenty of cute guys in the last few months, but she always felt like all they wanted to do is get into her pants. Kit was different she could feel it.

Later that day, around 6:30 p.m., Kit showed up at Carla's apartment with his research notes. He had on a pair of tight jean shorts that were form-fitting. His long, tanned legs seemed to stretch for miles. The orange and blue tank top with "Go Gators!" printed on the front showed his muscular upper torso.

"Hi," was all that she could say when Kit noticed her looking at his crotch.

Kit, feeling a little embarrassed, said, "Hi, I brought my stuff."

Carla regained her composure, then said, "Yes, I can see that," then chuckled inside and thought, I like your stuff!

"Come on in. I ordered a pizza in case we get hungry"

Kit said, "You'll have to let me pay for it. After all, you're the one doing me a favor."

"Don't be silly, you're my guest."

"No, I insist."

Carla actually liked the fact that Kit insisted on paying. It showed good character. Although, she wondered how he'd feel if he knew she was worth millions.

Carla took the notes from Kit and suggested that they get started.

"We'll have to go to my bedroom. That's where my computer is," she said as she walked down the hallway to her room. Kit followed Carla enjoying the slight jiggle in her bottom and the VPL's (visible panty lines) caused by the clinging spandex shorts that she was wearing. First date and I'm already in her bedroom, he thought to himself as he entered her room. They sat on the bed and went over the material. Kit had already written a rough draft by hand, including his works cited. Carla went over the text and was quite impressed with Kit's writing abilities.

"I only see a couple of awkward sentences and some missing or misplaced commas," she said after reading it.

"Commas seem to be a problem area with me," Kit admitted.

Carla replied, "Don't worry. They seem to be the biggest problem for most people. You wouldn't believe how many mistakes I catch in books all the time."

Carla sat down at the computer and began hammering away at the keys. Kit was amazed at her typing skills. This could be a relationship made in heaven for a crappy typist like myself, he thought.

Kit walked over and stood behind Carla just to see what his paper looked like jumping onto the monitor's screen as she typed. He hadn't realized how low-cut Carla's top was when he entered the apartment, but now his eyes were exploring every nook and cranny of her exposed flesh. Carla started hitting the backspace key one too many times and said, "I'm sorry, but I can't work with someone looking over my shoulder."

"Ugh, I'm sorry," Kit said, as he returned to the bed like a good boy.

He picked up a copy of Cosmopolitan magazine from her nightstand and studied the scantily clad model on the cover and thought to himself, this girl has nothing on Carla. Soon he started thinking about what he had seen earlier that day while peering up from the bottom of the college pool. He felt a stirring in his shorts and decided that he had better think of something else just in case he had to stand up and walk over to the computer where Carla was sitting.

Shortly thereafter, the doorbell rang and Kit offered to answer it, assuming that it was the pizza man. A young man wearing jeans and T-shirt with a pizza advertisement on it was standing there holding a pizza box.

"That's $15.99 for a large pepperoni and mushroom," he said impatiently. Kit figured it would be $20.00 with a tip, as he pulled out his wallet.

"Shit!" was all he could say as he peered into his wallet containing only a five-dollar bill and a couple of Publix Supermarket receipts.

The delivery boy, who bobbed his head up and down to the tunes of "The Cars" and seemed indifferent to the outside world, slid his head phones off his ears and said, "Could you please hurry? I have ten more deliveries sitting in my truck getting cold!"

Kit, unsure what to do, asked, "Do you take credit cards?"

The young man answered sarcastically, "What do I look like a fucking ATM? Now, do you want this pizza or not?"

Kit closed the door slightly and said, "I'll be right back."

Embarrassed beyond belief he entered Carla's bedroom unsure what to say. "Carla, this is kind of embarrassing but I didn't realize that I only had five dollars in my wallet when I left the house."

"Take what you need my wallets in my purse on the chair over there."

Kit opened the Louis Vuitton purse and took out Carla's wallet and sifted through several hundred-dollar bills before finding a ten and a five to add to his five. Shit, she's got more money in her wallet than I have in my checking account, he thought to himself as he put the wallet away.

"I promise I'll pay you back as soon as I get to the ATM," Kit said as he left the room. The delivery boy was again rocking to his tunes when Kit returned and only removed his headphones long enough to hear Kit say, "Keep the change."

"Thanks man!" he said as he turned and ran towards a truck parked in the street with its emergency flashers blaring.

Carla saved what she had already typed before coming into the kitchen area. Kit found some paper plates and served them each a slice.

"Pizza is my only downfall," she said as she carefully bit into the hot mozzarella. "It's so fattening," she added. Kit nodded his head in agreement, his mouth too full of the terrible stuff. Carla, realizing that they had nothing to drink, suggested some wine.

"Sure!" Kit said, and then added, "But what about the paper?"

"You said it's not due for a couple of weeks didn't you?"

"Yeah, but I'll feel much better when it's done."

"I don't have any classes tomorrow so I can work on it all day for you."

"I'll stop by and take you out to lunch and pay you back for the pizza," Kit answered quickly.

"You've got a deal," Carla said and grabbed his hand to shake it sealing the deal.

The first glass of wine went down fast for both of them. The problem was that they were drinking from large Tupperware tumblers, standard issue for wine, coffee or any other beverage a college student drinks. After the second glass, they were both feeling relaxed and slightly uninhibited.

Carla was only going to eat one piece of pizza, but the wine had weakened her willpower. And besides, she thought that eating more would be a good idea in light of the wine drinking. The pizza had cooled down while the couple had heated up. Carla took a big bite and a large piece of mozzarella cheese flopped down on her chin. Quickly, she sucked the cheese into her mouth not realizing that she had left a big smear of tomato sauce extending from her lower lip to her chin. Kit laughed as she looked at him with a puzzled look. He grabbed a napkin and said, "You've made quite a mess young lady." Carla closed her eyes and said, "Well clean me up!" Kit reached forward with the napkin, and then stopped, after having a better idea. He positioned his mouth close to hers and licked the tomato sauce from her chin.

She was both surprised and excited by his actions and reciprocated by placing her mouth on his and passionately kissing him back. It was a short kiss; she didn't want him to think she was a slut. Kit had taken a chance, hoping that she had felt the same feelings that he had, and it had paid off. Carla got up and poured the rest of the wine making sure to divide up equally the remaining spirits into the tumblers.

While taking a second bite of pizza, a piece of pepperoni fell and landed right in the middle of her cleavage. She'd probably had a little too much wine trying to compensate for her nervousness around Kit and was starting to feel a little too good. She smiled and leaned forward as if to say, come and get it big boy. Kit smiled and took the hint. Leaning forward, he placed his face in her bosom and snatched the pepperoni chewing and swallowing it quickly without changing his position. Once his mouth was clear, his tongue began exploring the territory beneath the perimeter of her bra. Carla placed her hands on his shoulders and began to moan.

When his tongue found her nipples, she could take it no longer and began to remove her top and brassiere. Kit backed off far enough to watch the unveiling, his groin area beginning to throb. His breathing quickened as he resumed kissing her highly excited nipples. He took her nipples one at a time in his teeth and held them as his tongue flicked back and forth across their surface.

Carla, wanting to feel his bare body against hers, pulled his shirt up and over his head. For a couple of minutes they held each other kissing passionately, their tongues curling and caressing each other.

They were so caught up in the moment they didn't hear Carla's roommate, Jan, put her key into the door and walk in. Carla opened her eyes briefly only to see Jan standing there with an embarrassed look on her face.

"Oh, hello Jan," she said, reaching back to grab her top. Kit's face was fire engine red from embarrassment.

Quickly, Carla turned her back and pulled her top on saying, "This is my friend Kit."

Then Kit, halfway into his own shirt, managed to say, "Nice to meet you."

"Well, I'll leave you two alone. I've got a lot of studying to do for a biology test tomorrow," Jan said as she walked into her room.

"That's the only problem with having a roommate – no privacy," Carla whispered to Kit.

"But who can afford to live by themselves while in college," Kit said.

Me, Carla thought, and then answered, "You're right about that."

"Well, I hate to leave, but it's getting late and I have to do some studying for some other classes," Kit said awkwardly.

"But how about if I stop by tomorrow around 1:00 p.m. and pick you up for lunch?"

"Sounds good," Carla replied.

She walked him to the door and said, "I wish you didn't have to go."

"Me too," Kit answered, as he placed his arms around her for a goodnight hug.

"Maybe it's better if we take it a little slower and get to know each other first," he whispered in her ear.

"I guess you're right," she said as she pulled his face to hers for one last kiss.

Chapter 6

The Child Support arrived late in Bimini, but fortunately the crew had cleared customs three days earlier in Chub Cay. After Trevor secured dock space and ice for the fish, they headed for the Compleat Angler. Ernest Hemingway started visiting the bar in 1935. Many pictures of Ernest and his fish still adorn the walls. It's always been a place where fishermen gather to tell stories of success and the one that got away. Trevor, Richie and Dave sat down at the bar and ordered a round of Mount Gay and Cokes.

"Here we go again," Dave said.

"We've got to take it easy, that fish is going to rot if we don't get it to the smoke house fairly early in the morning, added Trevor. I still can't believe something cut the tail off a 600 pound marlin in flight."

The man sitting next to Trevor turned and smiled.

"Did I hear you say what I thought I heard you say?" He asked.

"That's right, whatever it was cut his tail off clean while in a full run!"

"I'm sorry, I should have introduced myself. Kit Hanson, and this is my fiancée, Carla Morgan." Trevor reached over and shook Kit's hand. Next, he reached across Kit to shake Carla's hand.

Trevor hadn't even noticed the couple when he sat down. Must be spending a little too much time out on the water not to notice Carla, he thought to himself. She was beautiful; with short blonde hair, captivating blue eyes and that body! Her wife beater T-shirt with no bra left little to the imagination. From this angle Trevor could see the soft flesh on the side of her breasts bulging out. Her Jean shorts were split high enough up the side to reveal that she wasn't wearing any underwear. Trevor had to try hard not to stare, because her boy friend, Kit, was a lot younger and a little taller.

"Oh yeah, I'm Trevor Callaway, and these are my crew and friends, Dave and Richie."

The boys were arguing over who was going to ice down the fish later, but when they heard their names, they turned and nodded in the couples direction.

"Trevor Callaway!   You aren't The, Trevor, Callaway?" Carla asked.

Trevor turned red, being embarrassed, and still shy of his accomplishments.

"Yeah, that's me – famous novelist and fisherman, often compared to Ernest Hemingway," he said in a conciliatory manner.

"I'm a writer too!" Carla said, hoping to strike up a conversation.

"Anything published?"

"Not yet," Carla answered shyly.

"But I'm almost finished with my first novel."

Kit cut in, getting a little jealous at Carla's interest in Trevor, "Do you mind if I take a look at the marlin? I'm a marine biologist and curious about what might have bitten the tail off."

Trevor, also curious replied, "Sure, but you'll have to come before 9:00 a.m. tomorrow. I'm going to have the fish smoked so it won't go to waste. We're docked at the marina. Look for a 45 foot Chris Craft named the Child Support.

Carla jumped in, "I think I saw you pull in – we're in the same marina. Kit and I live on the Black Gold, the 55-foot Hatteras just a little ways from where you're docked."

"Neighbors, huh? That's nice. Are you guys on vacation?"

"No, Kit's doing research on the conch population for the Bahamian Government. They're trying to decide whether some catch quotas should be imposed. As for myself, when I'm not typing his research papers I'm working on my novel."

Trevor, remembering the excitement of his first novel, replied, "I'll be around for a while and if you want, I'll take a look at what you've written to see if I can give you any suggestions."

After saying this, Trevor thought, the rum must be talking, because the last thing I want to do is critique some amateur's work. However, this amateur is beautiful, and I'd do her even though she is young enough to be my daughter.

"Wow! I'd love to have you read my novel," Carla said.

"Kit, do you believe it? Trevor Callaway said he'd read my novel."

Kit not thrilled about this said, "That's great Carla, but remember we're leaving the day after tomorrow for the Westbanks so I can do some more field studies." Carla frowned, then perked up and said,

"Mr. Callaway, if you give me your address in Key West, I'll mail you a copy."

"Sure," Trevor answered, then wrote his address and phone number on a napkin and handed it to Carla. When she stood up to put it in her pocket, Trevor noticed her Jean shorts had crept up, exposing her butt cheeks. Carla caught him staring and corrected her shorts. Kit also saw him staring and decided it was time to leave their newfound friend. Besides, he and Carla had been there since happy hour and they were starting to feel the effects.

"I'll try to get by in the morning, but if I can't, could you cut that tail section off before you smoke it and freeze it so I can study it?"

"Sure," Trevor said. "I'll see you guys some time tomorrow."

The couple made their way back to the Black Gold. Kit tripped on a plank on the dock and almost went for a midnight swim. Carla noticed that he had ordered a double and guzzled it down while she had been talking to Trevor. They both had a little too much to drink celebrating their engagement. As they approached the yacht, Carla thought about Kit's proposal.

Earlier that day, in the morning, after making love, Carla had fallen back to sleep. While she slept Kits eyes devoured her body. He stared at her facial features: high cheekbones, perfectly proportioned nose, and voluptuous lips. Then his eyes roamed down to her breasts, full and firm with nipples pointing high in the air. Her flat stomach ran to a furry blonde mound that was moist and inviting. He couldn't resist reaching out to stroke her firm thighs. Feeling this, she smiled, but pretended to be asleep as to not interrupt his gentle stroking.

Suddenly, Kit jumped up and started digging into the bottom of his underwear drawer. Carla heard the racket he was making and asked Kit what he was doing. Kit knelt, naked on the floor and very solemnly asked, "Carla, will you take me, Kit, to be your lawfully wedded husband?"

"Are you serious, Kit?" She asked.

"I've never been more serious in my life," he replied.

"Of course, I will – I've wanted to ever since I met you!"

Kit took out an anklet and said, "Carla, I don't have a ring, but I bought this for you for your birthday. I would like you to have it now to represent our commitment to each other and as soon as we get to the mainland I'll buy you any ring that you want."

"Gee, I guess you weren't planning on asking me, otherwise you would have already had a ring," Carla said, feeling a little hurt.

"Honey, I've always known that someday I wanted to marry you. And while you were sleeping a little while ago, I came to my senses. I thought about how much I love you, and how beautiful you are, and I asked myself; what am I waiting for?

Carla suddenly snapped back into the here and now, as she kept Kit from falling into the water by grabbing his shirt sleeve, tugging it to help steady him as they made their way onto the yacht. When they entered the master cabin, Kit dove into the bed fully clothed and passed out. "Too bad!" Carla thought, because she was feeling hornier than usual, probably from the alcohol.

As she slipped into sleep, she fantasized what it would be like to make love to a man like Trevor; a man of the world, more experienced – his novels exuded passion. She was suddenly feeling guilty for even thinking these thoughts, after telling Kit earlier that day she would marry him.

"Don't be too hard on yourself girl," she thought.

"If Kit hadn't passed out, you wouldn't be thinking about Trevor."

Carla rid her mind of thoughts about Trevor by planning the next day. I think I'll get up fairly early, write a little, and then start scraping the hull. She had wanted to scrape it before they left West Palm Beach, but couldn't find the time.

Carla enjoyed maintaining the Hatteras, even though she was wealthy enough to pay someone else to do it. The hull had become fouled from sitting idle too long at the Palm Beach Marina. They had used twice as much fuel as they should have on the way over, due to the drag caused by the sea life growing on the hull. Little did she know that her life would take a complicated turn because of her decision to scrape the hull the following day.

Chapter 7

Carla awoke just as the sun was peeking over the horizon, its light bringing life to the sky. She had a hard time sleeping late after years of rising early to jog or swim before starting her daily activities. Today was no different. The drinking last night had given her a slight hangover. Two Advils, a cup of coffee and a banana would cure that.

After breakfast she worked on her novel. Carla liked writing in the morning when nothing or no one would bother her. This was a special time of day, quiet and peaceful. Once writing, she entered a time warp. During this period, she spent hours in a world she created with pencil and paper. A movie took place in her mind and her writing hand had the task of trying to keep up by turning the pictures into words that described what was going on. It was a thrill to think some day maybe millions of other people may enjoy taking the same mental trip through her writing.

An outboard motor sputtering to life brought her world of graphite and paper to an end. Carla glanced up at the clock and saw it was a little after 9:00 a.m.

Time to start scraping the hull, she thought. Quietly she crept into the cabin and grabbed her black string bikini from the drawer and put it on. She then walked over to the vanity and began removing her jewelry. Kit had warned her about the danger of losing it in the water and certain species of fish might think it was food due to the shimmering light caused by the sun reflecting off the gold.

First, she removed her earrings, necklace, bracelet and belly ring. Next, she looked down at the engagement anklet Kit had given her. She didn't want to take it off, but she would die if she lost it. Carla reached down and tried to undo the clasp. She remembered Kit had struggled with the clasp while putting it on her and had promised to have it fixed as soon as they hit the Mainland. I guess if I can't undo the clasp, I don't have to worry about it falling off. Good, a perfect excuse for not taking it off, she thought.

Carla grabbed her mask, snorkel, fins and a paint scraper from a storage chest on the deck and headed for the stern. She was thinking of how proud she was of herself for taking the initiative to scrape the hull. All of the subtle little hints she had dropped on Kit during the last few days hadn't motivated him to do the job.

After the long trip the cuda's relentless search for prey was overcome by his need for rest. Laying mostly dormant overnight, the early morning light was now awakening his senses. He was hungry, very hungry, and wouldn't stop hunting until the hunger was satisfied. His senses began scanning the surrounding waters for the smells, movement, or sound of prey.

After detecting a flash in the distance, he turned and charged at full speed. Seconds later, he had swallowed a finger mullet whole and cut a second one in half. While he was swallowing the second fish, the rest of the school had distanced themselves from him.

Carla climbed onto the dive platform and put on her fins. Next, she spit into her mask and rubbed it around, then rinsed it out with salt water before placing it on her head. Natural mask defogger, a trick Kit had taught her.

The water had a slight chill, due mainly to a difference in temperature from the warmer air. It was crystal clear; one of the characteristics she loved about the Bahamas. The water usually stayed clear because the islands are surrounded by a pristine, ever changing water supply.

The hull was not as bad as she thought; it had mostly vegetative growth, no barnacles or oysters. She started scraping at the bow. It was much like scraping cake batter from the side of a mixing bowl. The green algae and aquatic growth peeled away and fluttered to the bottom, the surrounding area receiving a green tint.

Carla had been scraping for about fifteen minutes when an eerie feeling came over her. She suddenly felt as though she wasn't alone. Anyone that snorkels or dives knows this feeling – thoughts come to your mind that maybe you should stop swimming and take a 360-degree view of the waters around you. Most of the time there is nothing there, but sometimes there is a harmless grouper or snapper, but now and then it's a frightening shark or barracuda.

Carla stopped what she was doing and turned to scan the surrounding waters. Nothing there, she told herself and began scraping the hull once more.

The cuda had chased the school of mullet into the calm waters of the marina. The one and a half fish devoured earlier had been an appetizer. The small meal had only increased his hunger. His keen senses were picking up some other activity in the water.

The cuda followed the noise and movement vibrations, and as he neared, began to see what appeared to be the shimmering body of a fish. He would try to pass far enough away to view his prey without his presence scaring it away.

Still feeling a bit uneasy, Carla kept scraping the hull; however, it was hard to dismiss the feelings of uneasiness she was experiencing. She wished Kit were down here to protect her. Maybe she would wait to do the other side with Kit after he wakes up.

Again, a bad feeling came over her and she turned to study the neighboring waters. This time she saw something! It was large and coming towards her! She knew not to panic. This could cause whatever it was to attack. She watched the fish, which was well over six feet, approach from the distance.

As it came into view, her body began to tremble. It was the largest barracuda she had ever seen. It was both dangerous and beautiful all at the same time. A long, slender, silver body perfectly designed for speed. Two large eyes for seeing his prey and a large pointed mouth filled with sharp teeth for ripping through its quarry. She saw it open and close its mouth several times, usually a sign of excitement or aggression.

Carla had been in the water with many barracudas, but Kit was usually at her side telling her not to worry. He said most cuda attacks are by accident, and usually because the diver is carrying spear fishing trophies or has forgotten to take off jewelry the fish could confuse for baitfish.

Jewelry! My God, my anklet! she thought. Carla looked down to see the sun reflecting off of the anklet. Don't panic – just slowly get out of the water, she told herself. She turned and started swimming backwards so she could keep an eye on the cuda and bring herself closer to the dive platform.

The cuda decided to have a closer look, because its prey seemed to be swimming slowly away. It would not let it get away!

Carla watched in terror as the cuda swam even closer. It was all she could do to keep herself from turning and swimming at full speed to the dive platform.

Then the cuda seemed to stop, ominously watching her from a distance, the large eyes rolling around in their sockets, and its lateral fins beating like a humming bird's wings to maintain its hovering position.

Carla arrived at the dive platform and turned to sit on it, her limbs trembling with fear. It took a couple of seconds to turn so her legs were out of the water entirely.

The cuda, seeing its prey fleeing, decided it was time to attack. It pivoted toward Carla and charged at full attack speed. She moved at the very last moment, and it was left with something hard dangling from his mouth and the taste of blood, different than any other it had ever tasted.

Carla felt something slam into and glance off of her ankle as she turned to bring her legs out of the water. It ripped open the flesh on the side of her leg just above her ankle joint. Blood was beginning to flow from the wound. Quickly, she jumped to the deck, applied pressure to the wound, and began screaming for Kit.

He heard the scream and looked over to see an empty pillow where Carla should have been. Then he heard his name being screamed again from somewhere outside on the deck. Still feeling a little woozy from the night before, he jumped up, grabbed his shorts off the floor, and flew out to the afterdeck.

The scene was gruesome. In an ever-increasing puddle of blood was his fiancé holding her ankle and crying hysterically. Carla was not only crying from fear, but also from anger because the cuda had cut off her anklet.

"Carla, what the hell happened?" Kit asked in shock.

"I was attacked by a barracuda!"

"Can you move your foot?" he said holding her leg.

"Yes, it doesn't hurt that much. Is it bad?"

Kit inspected the wound. It was bad, not life threatening, but would require stitches. It appeared as though no major arteries or tendons had been damaged. Then he ran down to a closet and grabbed an old towel. He returned quickly and wiped the excess blood from Carla's body and then picked her up. By this time Carla's crying had diminished.

Kit carried her across the gangplank and began the journey down King's Highway to the local physician. On the he way began to question Carla as to what happened.

"Darling how did this happen to you?"

"I was scraping the hull and this huge barracuda attacked me!" she said, her voice trembling

"What do you think provoked him to attack you?"

"My anklet, unfortunately," Carla said, and began to cry violently again.

"Don't cry honey, everything's going to be okay. A few stitches in your ankle and you'll be as good as new."

"I tried to take it off!" she said in between sobs, "but the stupid clasp was stuck!"

"Please don't cry – I'll replace it when I buy your ring," Kit said, trying to console her.

He wished he had taken time to put on his sandals because the rustic road punished his bare feet, especially with the added weight of Carla. Kit knew he couldn't think about his own discomfort now, but should focus on getting Carla treatment for her wound.

Many concerned passersby watched as Kit carried Carla, still bleeding, down King's Road. Only one person had the courage to ask, a young teenager, one of the local residents. His eyes grew wide when Kit hurriedly replied a cuda had inflicted the wound.

Finally, they reached the doctor's office. The building acted as his home and office because there wasn't enough income generated on the tiny island to afford both.

Kit turned so Carla could knock on the door. Nobody seemed to respond, so Kit yelled loudly, "We need a doctor out here!" A couple of minutes later they heard a noise coming from inside the house. Slowly the door opened to reveal a middle aged black gentleman in a robe.

"Sorry, sir. It seems I was in the shower when you rang," the man said with an English accent.

"My goodness, what have we here?" the doctor exclaimed as his eyes focused on Carla's wound.

"Take her to the examining room and place her on the table – it's down the hall on the right," he said, pointing down the poorly lit hallway.

The doctor grabbed a vile from a cabinet and filled a hypodermic needle with anesthetic and injected it into the area surrounding the wound.

"Let the anesthetic take effect. I'm going to put some clothes on. Keep pressure on the wound like you have been," the doctor said, then disappeared for a couple of minutes. He returned wearing a T-shirt with "It's Better in the Bahamas" printed on it and a pair of khaki shorts, which he quickly covered up with a doctor's smock and began cleaning the wound with betadyne solution.

"George Symthe," he said smiling, but you can call me Dr. George—everyone else does."

Carla made the introductions, "I'm Carla and this is my fiancé, Kit," she said placing her hand on his shoulder.

The doctor bowed his head and asked, "How did you get this nasty laceration, my dear?"

Carla, trembling from having to think about it, replied, "I was in the water scraping the hull on our boat when a barracuda attacked me."

The doctor, surprised by her answer, said, "I've never heard of barracudas attacking unless the diver had some type of food the fish wanted."

Carla started tearing up and continued, "He was attracted to an anklet I was wearing!"

The doctor, trying to calm Carla down said, "There, there, don't cry my dear. Dr. George will have you sewn up in a jiffy."

She flinched as she watched the doctor push the needle through her skin. It was just a reflex because the anesthetic had done its job – she felt no pain – just the tug on her flesh as the sutures closed the wound.

"Do you remember when you had your last tetanus shot?" the doctor asked closing up the last stitch, and then before Carla could answer added, "If it's been close to ten years you'll need another."

Carla closed her eyes and remembered how much she hated shots, then replied, "I guess you'd better give me one because I can't remember when my last shot was." Big tears rolled down her cheeks as the doctor placed the syringe's needle in her arm.

"You might get a little soreness in this arm," Dr. George advised. He continued, "I've got a pair of crutches I'm going to loan you, and I'll prescribe some Percocet for the pain you might experience after the anesthetic wears off. Also, stay out of the water and do come back and see me immediately if any redness develops – otherwise return next week and I should be able to remove the stitches."

The doctor noticed Carla had calmed down and had to satisfy his curiosity by asking her some more questions about the incident.

"Carla, what was the size of the barracuda that attacked you?"

"Well, I didn't have a tape measure with me, but it was the largest I've ever seen. Its girth was at least two feet at the widest part and I guess its length was around six or seven feet.

"Did he charge at you immediately?"

"No, I backed slowly away from him, but when I turned to sit on the drive platform, the sun must have reflected off my anklet and made him think my ankle was a fish."

"Well, let's hope he was just stopping by on his way out to sea," the doctor said, smiling.

Kit thanked the doctor, and then lifted Carla and the crutches to begin the trip back to the marina. He looked down at his fiancée, forgetting how good she looked in that black bikini.

Carla saw him staring at her and asked, "Is everything okay?"

"Wonderful, but it will be even better when the love of my life is not in pain anymore." Carla smiled, but it soon turned into a frown.

"Kit, how are we going to go on the research trip next week if we have to stay around to have my stitches removed?"

"Don't worry, darling, that's the least of my worries. The trip can wait – you just get better."

By the time they had finished their conversation Kit and Carla had boarded the vessel. He carried Carla into the master bedroom being careful not to bump her head on the narrow passageways. Gently, he placed her onto the unmade bed.

Carla removed her damp bikini and asked Kit for a washcloth, soap and a bowl of warm water. He returned and offered to bathe her. She smiled and winked saying, "Maybe some other time. If you want to do something for me, go to the druggist and have my prescription filled please. My ankle is already starting to throb." Kit left, and Carla bathed herself, remembering that as a Girl Scout they had called this a PTA bath (pussy, tits, and armpits).

Chapter 8

Bobby was a native Bahamian.   Slave traders brought his ancestors to Bimini over one hundred years ago.   In 1845, the sisal plant was brought from Yucatan, Mexico to introduce a new industry to the islands.   Its fibers were used in the production of rope.   Many of Bobby's relatives worked on the sisal plantations until the price paid for the fiber dropped so low that it was no longer attractive to produce. With the demise of the sisal industry, the generations that followed had to find other ways to subsist such as fishing, sponging, and the salvaging of shipwrecks.

Bobby supported his family by fishing.   He sold whatever fish he caught to local restaurants and tourists; the rest he and his family ate. On days when the seas were two-foot or less, Bobby would set out in his 15-foot skiff to fish for yellowtail snapper.   To prepare for his trip he made chum, a mixture of unwanted fish parts, fish, and lobster heads.   Course ground and mixed with fish oil and sand, chum was periodically dropped over the side to attract yellowtail snapper.   The sand and lobster shells helped drag some of the fish particles down to the bottom, luring the yellowtail to the surface in search of the food source.

On this particular day the seas were calm and the visibility was excellent.   Bobby was enjoying the ride to his favorite fishing spot. His 1968 Johnson 25-horse outboard motor was purring like a kitten. It was days like this when he didn't mind being a poor Bahamian fisherman.   No stress man – just had to catch enough fish to at least feed his family for the day.

He arrived at the reef and tossed the anchor over.   First, he made sure the anchor had hooked up, and then he began throwing chum over the side.   This was kind of messy because Bobby had forgotten the scoop on the dock, which meant every time he had to toss some chum in the water he had to wash his hands in the ocean.   No big deal, he thought to himself, it won't be the first time I've smelled like fish.

Within minutes the water was teaming with yellowtails.   Bobby hurried to get his line in the water.   The first two he caught were small. He threw them back, saying, "Go tell Grandpa food's on the table."

Finally, he started catching flag yellowtail, fish over 12 inches. Bobby caught six large fish one after the other. On the seventh fish his luck began to change. While reeling in the fish, the line became slack. When he got it up to the boat all that remained was the head. Off to the port side he recognized two familiar figures. Mutt and Jeff he called them. Two barracudas in the three to four foot range.

"Just leave some for me, guys," he said to the fish. Bobby knew the fish had just as much right to be there as he did – he held no malice. They would eat his fish until they got full, and then leave him alone. In fact, it added more excitement to the fishing because now he would have to try to boat his catch before they could eat it.

Bobby tossed over some more chum to bring back the school, which had temporarily been frightened by the pair of cudas. He tossed his bait over the side and felt a good bite after a couple of minutes. The pole bent toward the water and Bobby started to reel. This is a big one, he thought to himself. A couple of seconds later, the line went slack.

"Damn barracudas!" he screamed out loud. But Mutt and Jeff hadn't moved, they were still watching from a distance. As the end of the line neared the surface, he saw it had been cut. Probably by a large fish, maybe a shark, he reasoned.

The cuda had become frustrated by his feeding attempts earlier that day. He was now hungry and agitated. The large yellowtail had curbed his appetite but a fish his size needed more. His senses were now highly excited by the smell of fish permeating the water.

Bobby tied a new hook on the line and baited it. Noticing that the yellowtail had thinned out again, he scooped some chum out of the bucket with his hand and tossed it over the side. I'll never forget that scoop again – this is a pain in the ass, he thought to himself as he bent over to wash his hands in the water.

When he put his hands in the water, the splashing sound was detected by the cuda's keen senses. The sound was similar to the noise an injured fish makes while flopping on the surface. The large cuda turned and charged at full speed. Whack! He connected, severing a piece of something that tasted familiar. In two gulps the hand was swallowed except for a twitching pinky finger trailing from the corner of his mouth.

Bobby pulled his bleeding stump from the water. He couldn't believe what had just happened. In the clear waters he had seen the huge cuda swimming away with his hand in its mouth. He knew that if he didn't get to shore fast he would die. Grabbing his right wrist with his left hand, he squeezed tightly to stop the profuse bleeding. He used a fillet knife to cut the anchor line, then cut a piece of line off to use as a tourniquet. Unfortunately, to use his left hand he had to let go of his right wrist, which meant significant blood loss. Tying the tourniquet with his left hand was no easy feat. However, he managed to get it tight enough to slow the flow of blood.

Next, Bobby had to pull start the engine although he was already starting to feel lightheaded. Luckily for him it started on the first pull. The engine whined as Bobby headed for the marina at full throttle, feeling more and more dizzy. During the trip, the tourniquet loosened and blood started to ooze out faster and faster. Bobby knew his only chance was to get to the marina and get help. He was a football field away from the marina when he finally passed out. The tourniquet had fallen off during the frenzied trip and within a few short minutes he had bled to death.

The engine returned to an idle when Bobby passed out and released the spring loaded twist grip throttle on the engine. The boat chugged along at an idle, eventually bumping into the 45 foot Chris Craft docked at the marina, and waking its inhabitants.

"What the hell was that?" yelled Trevor, jumping up from a sound sleep.

"Something bumped into the boat," Rich replied while putting on his shorts.

"Better have a look," Trevor said, exiting the cabin. What he saw next brought flashbacks of Vietnam, gruesome scenes of bodies missing limbs and lying in puddles of blood. Trevor jumped into the small skiff and slipped in the blood almost falling down. Next, he shut off the outboard to keep the boat from damaging the Child Support. When he placed his finger on Bobby's neck to check for a pulse; there was none.

The fisherman had died with a look of terror in his eyes, not the peaceful look you see when one dies of natural causes. Blood continued to drip from the stump that formerly supported a strong hand that had helped fish to provide food for his family. Trevor lifted the arm to examine the wound. "What the hell happened?" he said.

"I don't know, man. What should we do?" Richie asked.

"Call the authorities - we have a dead man here!"

Trevor tied off the skiff and returned to his boat to wash the blood off his feet. By this time a small crowd had gathered on the dock.

There was a murmuring in the crowd as to what had happened, or what could have done this? When the local police showed up, they were in shock. They had grown up with Bobby and knew what a fine man and good father he had been to his two children.

After questioning Trevor, they removed the body to take it to Dr. George's to be examined. As they carried away the body, Trevor asked the older of the constables, "What's going to happen to him now?" Trevor asked. "After the Doc's through with him, he'll be laid to rest by his grandma in the only cemetery on the island."

Chapter 9

The incident had awakened the crew of the Child Support much earlier than it probably would have occurred naturally, due to the activities of the previous evening. After the crowd of people and police officials cleared, they realized the ice on the marlin carcass was rapidly disappearing. Even though they didn't feel like dealing with the marlin now, they knew they had to; otherwise the death of the fish would be a waste.

Trevor found a Bahamian with a golf cart willing to haul the fish to the smokehouse for a portion of the prize. Before the fish was hauled away, Trevor remembered the promise he made to Kit and carefully cut a six inch slice from the end of the tail and put it in the freezer for examination at a later time.

Chapter 10

Kit returned with the medication and brought one of the tablets to Carla with a glass of water. She took the tablet, swallowed it, and hoped it wouldn't take long to start working. Carla turned onto her stomach and Kit began to gently rub her back. Within a few minutes her breathing pattern changed and Kit knew she had fallen asleep. Best thing for her, Kit thought.

Unable to do anything more for Carla, Kit decided to see if Trevor had collected the specimen that he had requested. Quickly, he showered and changed. Before leaving, he kissed Carla on the forehead and grabbed a specimen bag from his laboratory supplies. As he approached the Child Support, Richie, in the process of hosing off Trevor's bloody footprints, looked up and said, "You missed all the excitement!"

"What do you mean?" Kit questioned.

Richie filled Kit in on the events of the morning.

"I'm surprised you didn't hear or see the commotion," Richie said.

"I was probably at the pharmacy getting some medication for Carla. You see, we had our own excitement earlier this morning."

"Is Trevor below? He should have something for me."

"He was in the shower, but he should be out by now," Richie said as he rolled up the hose and followed Kit into the cabin.

Trevor's head popped through the neck hole of his T-shirt just as Kit and Richie entered the cabin.

"Ah, if it isn't my marine biologist friend!" Trevor said, as he extended his hand to Kit. Kit squeezed Trevor's hand a little harder than usual to let him know he was no wimpy, nerdy, marine biologist.

"Did Richie tell you what happened a little while ago?"

"Yes and we had our own excitement earlier," Kit exclaimed. "Carla was attacked by a large cuda this morning while scraping the hull. Thank God all she suffered was a laceration on her ankle that required only a few stitches. She's resting now, but should be up and about later."

Trevor thought for a minute and asked, "I wonder if that poor fisherman was attacked by the same fish?"

"Highly unlikely," Kit said. "There are documented cases of barracuda attacks on humans, but they are rare. We're letting our imaginations run wild to think we have a man-eating barracuda in our midst. However, the Great Barracuda species have been known to grow just under six feet and weigh close to 85 pounds. A fish that size could cause some serious damage to a human limb. I wonder where they took the body?"

"They took him to Dr. George's. He's not only a doctor, but also the coroner," Trevor answered.

"Anybody want a beer?" Dave yelled from the galley. Trevor and Richie raised their hands, but Kit replied, "Thanks, but no thanks, I want to go take a look at the corpse before they put him in the ground."

Trevor opened the beer and took a sip, let out a belch and said, "Don't forget your piece of tail!"

Kit became enraged for a minute thinking Trevor was referring to Carla - then smiled, realizing what a fool he was.

"Dave, will you grab that hunk of tail out of the freezer for him?" Trevor asked.

Dave returned seconds later as Kit pulled the specimen bag out of his pocket and opened it allowing Dave to drop the tail section in.

"You guys want to meet at the Compleat Angler for dinner tonight? I should know something by then," Kit said, turning back before exiting.

"Sure -- oh, tell Carla I hope she feels better."

Kit took the specimen and put it in the freezer on the Black Gold. While on board, he checked on Carla and saw she was still in a deep sleep. He left for Dr. George's again, but this time his bruised feet reminded him to put on his sandals.

Kit arrived at Dr. George's door and rang the bell. Dr. George opened the door and upon seeing Kit asked, "Is Carla all right?"

"Yes, she's sleeping like a baby."

"Doctor, I didn't tell you earlier I'm a marine biologist and if it's all right, I'd like to examine the corpse brought in this morning to see if I can determine if he was attacked by a fish."

"Certainly", Dr. George exclaimed, "I'll take all the help I can get."

In the back of the house was a small walk-in cooler, much like restaurants use.

"Nothing like those big city morgues on the mainland, but it serves its purpose" Dr. George stated as he opened the door.

"The cause of death was easy to determine with the volume of blood found in the fisherman's skiff," Dr. George added as he pulled back the cover to expose Bobby's lifeless carcass.

Rigormortis had set in making it hard for Kit to raise the arm and examine the stump more closely.

"Doctor, would you have a magnifying glass, ruler, pencil, and paper?"

"Yes," the doctor said, and went to retrieve the articles requested.

Kit noticed right away that the leading edge cuts were very similar to the ones on the marlin tail. When the doctor returned, Kit asked him to hold the arm up while he measured and sketched the stump.

"Bobby didn't deserve this – he never did anyone wrong," the doctor remarked during the examination.

When they were finished and Bobby's corpse was covered, Kit asked the doctor to join them later at the Compleat Angler for dinner.

"I have a specimen taken from a 600 pound marlin tail with teeth marks very similar to the markings on Bobby's wrist. At this time it is purely speculation the same fish did this. However, after studying the specimen, I will have more conclusive evidence. I've also invited the crew from the boat Child Support to dinner. They caught the marlin and also discovered Bobby's body after his skiff bumped into their boat this morning."

"I'll be there – what time?

"I'll be there at 7 p.m. – after what's happened today I'll need to catch happy hour and have a couple of drinks before dinner.

"Tell Carla not to mix alcohol with her medication, otherwise we'll be picking her up off the floor," added the doctor.

Kit returned to the yacht and removed the specimen from the freezer, carrying it to a small laboratory he had set up in one of the guest cabins. Carefully placing it on a tray, he grabbed a magnifying glass and began scientifically measuring and sketching the severed tail section.

The measurement of the initial tooth impact on the arm and tail matched exactly. He knew these weren't shark bites because they were too clean. A barracuda charges at high speed with its teeth, which are sharp on the front side to slice through its prey. This could explain the surgical precision the wounds displayed.   Kit's heart started pounding when he realized how lucky Carla was to have only a small laceration and a missing anklet.

Kit spent the rest of the afternoon reviewing his notes and researching barracudas. However, he knew quite a bit already about the notorious fish partially from reading and the rest from personal experience. He still had scars from his first encounter with a large barracuda.

Chapter 11

It happened when he was around 19 years old. Kit and his friend, Larry, had anchored his father's 25-foot cabin cruiser off Dania Beach to illegally spear some lobster late in the season, when the water visibility increased the challenge.

In their minds they were able to justify illegally using armlet spear guns with tri-pronged heads because they were free diving and unable to stay submerged any length of time; thus, giving the lobsters a fighting chance. However, they knew if they were ever caught, the Florida Marine Patrol would feel differently.

In the first spot, after swimming for a couple of minutes, they came upon a large reef structure, long, narrow, and rectangular in shape. It had the usual reef inhabitants: small fish, sea fans, and oceanic vegetation. Visibility was about 10 feet, so they had to get fairly close to this monolith before they could actually examine it. Kit got an eerie feeling, or uneasiness, while diving in murky water. It stole from him the early detection of something that might do him harm.

As they drew nearer to the outcropping, they noticed a shape in the distance that became larger and clearer as they swam.

"My God!" Kit exclaimed, "this is the largest cuda I've ever seen. He's acting like this is his territory and we aren't welcome."

Kit was still thinking to himself, I have been known to be a little wimpy, however, often times wimpiness can be confused with intelligence. Somehow I can't see myself spearing a lobster, and this fish letting me get to the boat with it. He suggested to his friend that they find their own reef. After a small amount of protest the Larry agreed. They pulled anchor and proceeded about a half-mile north before anchoring again.

Kit entered the water once more feeling uneasy from what had transpired, but began looking for lobster anyway. He had to put his mask within three feet of the crevices that might hold the quarry, just to see. After a failed attempt to spear a lobster, while traveling to the surface for air, he saw it, a cuda, either the same fish, or one just as large, off in the distance, and silently watching his every move.

Enough is enough, he thought to himself. The water is murky, the lobsters are few, and I don't like swimming with a 6-foot cuda!

"I'm getting out. That cuda is back!" Kit yelled to Larry the next time he surfaced.

Larry took the snorkel's mouthpiece out and replied, "I'm going to try to catch at least a couple for dinner before I get out."

"Well I'm getting out, I don't like the way that cuda is acting, especially if it's the same one we just moved away from."

Kit watched from the boat fearing for his Larry's safety. After his friend dove several times to the sea floor, Kit noticed he was acting oddly. Larry was pointing his spear gun and turning in a circle as if to threaten whatever was causing him to act in this manner. Larry yelled, "He charged me, I'm getting out!" With great speed, he swam to the dive platform.

In all the confusion he handed Kit the spear gun loaded and with the safety off. When Kit set it down, the force triggered the gun. The armlet was not very powerful – in fact, it had just enough power to drive the prongs into prey only at a close distance. Kit looked down in disbelief as one of three prongs entered his forearm just below the elbow joint. It wasn't bleeding; that was a good sign. However, the barbed tip made it impossible to remove.

"They'll probably have to cut it out," his friend remarked.

The trip wasn't pleasant. Kit felt every wave as the shaft bobbed up and down, despite every effort to hold it still, and Kit's car, an M.G. Midget, wasn't designed for an occupant with a two-foot shaft sticking from his arm to sit comfortably.

Next came the humiliation of walking into the emergency room at Broward General Hospital with a spear gun shaft sticking out of his arm and having to explain how it got there.

After being led to an examining room, a doctor arrived resembling Dustin Hoffman in appearance and personality. When Kit explained what happened, he replied, "This spear is going to look good hanging in the doctor's lounge!"

The doctor numbed Kit's arm and made a small incision in an area above the barb's tip. Once the barb had been forced out through the incision, a male nurse resembling Igor came in and cut off the barbed tip with a pair of bolt cutters, allowing the spear head to be removed.

To this day, two small scars remain reminding Kit of his encounter with the large barracuda.

Chapter 12

Kit looked at his watch – it was getting late, almost 5:00 p.m. He was known to lose track of time while doing research. A stirring in the master bedroom pulled him away from his work.

Carla had begun to toss and turn as the pain medication started to wear off. She smiled at Kit when he entered the room.

"Hi honey," she said in raspy, just woke up kind of voice.

"How's my future wife?" Kit asked, hoping the extended nap she took had performed some type of miracle.

"A little groggy and a little pain from my wound, she answered. It doesn't hurt that bad, there must not be many nerve endings in that area."

"I don't want to frighten you, but there has been another attack." Kit said, hoping Carla was able to handle this information in her present state.

"What do you mean – who was attacked?" she inquired, sounding anxious.

"A local fisherman's hand was severed and he bled to death before he could get help," Kit began. "While you were sleeping I was able to examine the tail section from the marlin and the wound on the fisherman and I believe the same fish was involved – a large barracuda, probably the same one that attacked you."

"Something's got to be done!" Carla said raising her voice.

"Calm down," Kit said while rubbing her back.

"I've invited Trevor, his crew, and Dr. George to meet us for dinner at the Compleat Angler to discuss the findings of my research this afternoon.

"I guess I should have waited to see how you felt before I go making plans," Kit said feeling badly about his inconsiderate action.

"Oh it's all right Kit, I'll make a cup of hot tea to clear the cobwebs and start getting ready.

Carla made her way to the galley and put a cup of water in the microwave. Next she grabbed a box of Earl Gray tea from the cabinet, taking a minute to hold the box to her nose and smell the aroma of her favorite tea.

Limping around the boat wasn't too demanding, but she knew the crutches Dr. George had lent her would come in handy for long trips – like the one to the Compleat Angler.

The Earl Gray tea had done the trick; Carla was starting to feel energetic again. She hobbled to the bedroom and began looking for something to wear. Something a little less revealing than the clothes she wore on her last trip to the restaurant. Carla liked the attention, but really wasn't an exhibitionist. She just liked to be comfortable, even if it meant not wearing any bra or panties.

Carla got dressed while Kit gathered some research materials he was planning to bring. I'll wear my denim pedal pushers, a white baby T-shirt and my Nike flip-flops, she thought to herself. She also put on some white cotton socks to cover her ankle and protect her wound.

After dressing, she stood before the vanity mirror, her nipples were about to poke through the white baby tee shirt and her hair looked as though she had gone swimming and slept on it all day.

I guess I'll have to put on a bra and wash my hair in the sink, she thought to herself, as she removed her shirt.

Kit walked into the room as Carla bent over the sink topless to wash her hair. Quietly he walked up behind her and began kissing her back while reaching around and fondling her breasts. Carla moaned, "Honey, that feels really good, but if we're going to meet your friends any time soon, you've got to let me get my hair washed."

"All right," Kit said, like a child that's been punished.

"Why don't you let me help you?"

"Sure, I love having my hair washed!"

Kit lathered and massaged Carla's scalp, then rinsed it being careful not to splash water on the counter. Gently he dried her head with a large fluffy towel. Kit advised Carla to put her shirt on otherwise they might not make it to dinner. When she looked at the large swollen member straining against his tight fitting jeans, she knew he was serious.

The walk to the restaurant took a little longer than usual because Carla hadn't had much practice with crutches. At one point, Kit offered to carry her, but she was too stubborn for that.

Dr. George, Trevor, and crew were already seated at a large table. They all stopped talking and greeted the couple as they approached. After Carla and Kit were seated, Trevor grabbed Carla's hand sandwiching it between his and staring into her eyes said, "I'm very sorry about your unfortunate experience this morning." Carla, not knowing how to react, slowly withdrew her hand and replied, "Yeah, I'm still feeling a little shook up." Kit's jealous reaction was to put his arm around Carla and say, "Don't worry, I'm taking good care of her."

Trevor replied, "I'm sure you are! I know I could, I mean – would."

Richie and Dave chuckled at Trevor's apparent attempt at humor. Carla was blushing, remembering her fantasies of Trevor from the night before.

Dr. George, hoping to end the uneasiness at the table asked, "Carla how's your ankle?"

"It seems to be doing well, I practically slept all day after taking the Percocet.

"Good, just keep it dry and it should heal in a week or two."

Kit opened a small briefcase containing his research data and withdrew two sketches and some notes. Everyone watched as he laid them on the table.

A waitress appeared and handed out menus, and asked, "Can I get anyone something to drink?"

Trevor exclaimed, "Drinks are on me-- I'll have a Mount Gay and Coke with a twist."

"Sounds good," chimed in Richie and Dave.

"Meyers on the rocks," added Dr. George.

Carla ordered a Diet Coke, wanting a beer, but thinking the doctor would disapprove knowing she still had Percocet in her system.

"Anything for you darling?" the waitress said to Kit.

"I'll take a Heiny," he answered.

She winked at Kit and said, "It looks like you already have one!" Then she looked towards Carla and said, "So, I guess I'll bring you a beer.

"Now that we got that out of the way let me share with you some theories about the attacks," Kit said starting his report.

"First, I believe the same fish might be involved in all three instances. The bite marks on the marlin and fisherman had the same measurements" he said, pointing to the sketches. Kit took a long sip of his beer and continued.

"Furthermore, Carla saw a cuda she thought measured at least seven feet. I've researched the Internet and found a web page with a gentleman who has also witnessed a barracuda he thought must have measured at least seven feet. The International Game Fish Association recorded the largest cuda ever caught. A friend of mine, Candice, a marine biologist I went to college with, works for them. She told me the barracuda weighed 84 pounds 14 ounces and measured just less than six feet at 71 inches.

"Wow that's a big fish!" Richie interjected.

"This erases any doubt as to the possibility the cuda Carla saw could have been as large as she describe.

Barracuda hunt their prey by rushing towards them at high speed using their teeth to kill or maim them. A cuda's teeth are sharp on the leading edge to facilitate this, and we've already seen what a seven foot cuda is capable of."

"Poor Bobby, probably didn't know what hit him," Dr. George interjected.

Carla, her voice trembling, added, "I'm still shaking, remembering the cuda off in the distance hovering, fearless, and silently watching me deciding when to charge. Thank God it was just as I pulled my foot out of the water!"

"Do you think we need to post warnings on the island?" the doctor asked.

Kit answered, "My research indicated barracuda attacks on humans are few and far between, mostly accidents, so I don't think we need to panic.

"Yeah," Trevor said, "he's probably already gone to another island. As for us, we'll probably head back to Chub Cay in the next day or so, after we get some of our smoked marlin.

I'll have plenty, if you guys would like some."

"I'd love some!" Carla exclaimed

"I haven't had any smoked marlin in a while – sounds good!" Dr. George added.

"Hey Trevor, you going to make some of your homemade smoked fish dip?" Dave questioned.

"Sure will."

"You ain't never had smoked fish dip until you've had Trevor's," Richie testified to the crowd.

"We'll be around for at least another week, until Carla's wound heals. I'm not going anywhere until I'm sure it's healed with no signs of infection."

"I'm going to be buried here, so I hope this cuda doesn't apply for a visa," Dr. George said jokingly.

The waitress returned with the drinks and everyone ordered dinner except Carla; the trauma of the morning's attack kept her feeling anxious.

After dinner, Carla and Kit excused themselves. "We'd like to stay, but it's been a long day," Carla said.

Dr. George took this as his cue to leave also. "See you gentlemen later. Let me know if you hear or see anything."

"Later Doc," Trevor said, and motioned to the waitress saying, "Hey sweetheart, how about another round of drinks for the boys!"

Trevor and his crew were not ready to call it a night. There would be many more rounds of drinks and flirtations with the waitress before they would stumble back to the boat.

Chapter 13

Jose Rodriguez's family had fled to the U.S. when he was just ten years old. His father, a tailor, had constructed a raft from old sail material he salvaged from a local marina. In April of 1980, when Fidel Castro allowed 124,776 people to leave his country, the Rodriguez family had been included in this mass exodus known as the Mariel Boat Lift.

It wasn't an easy trip. Jose remembered the scorching sun and the relentless waves washing over the side of the raft while his father bailed out the water as fast as he could to keep the family from becoming food for the sharks. In addition, there was a lack of food and drinking water because the small raft could only support a minimum amount of weight.

After several days of drifting at sea, they were rescued by the U.S. Coast Guard and transported to the Khrome Detention Center in Miami for processing by the U.S. Immigration Services. Life in the detention center was also treacherous because they were housed with the many criminals Fidel had released during this time. However, they survived the heat, the mosquitoes, and the fear of deportation, and were eventually released to begin their new life in the United States of America.

Jose's father, with the help of some distant relatives that were already citizens, moved his family to New York. He heard there was a lot of opportunity for someone in his profession in this grand city. His father, Miguel, had come from a long line of Cuban tailors. On the day of his arrival to New York, he was able to find a job working at a sweatshop in the garment district for minimum wage.

The family, consisting of Miguel, his wife Maria, Jose and Pepito, his younger brother, had to share cramped quarters with his father's cousin and family until enough money was made to pay for a place of their own. They had made enough money to move after two weeks of Miguel working double shifts and Maria doing odd cleaning jobs for some affluent Americans. Their first apartment was not too impressive by U.S. standards, but was not as bad as some of the places they had been forced to live in Cuba.

Jose and Pepito were enrolled in school and studied hard to learn their new language, English. It was hard adapting to the U.S. at first, but they soon found out that many Hispanic people from all over the world started their new lives in New York. Puerto Ricans, Dominicans and Guatemalans lived there, just to name a few.

There was often a fierce rivalry between the children of different nationalities, which led to the formation of street gangs. The boys learned at an early age the dangers of hanging out on the street. Their father, fearing for their safety, got them to work sweeping and cleaning for the sweatshop.

Only three years after coming to this country Miguel was able to open up his own tailor shop with the help of some government loans and the money he had managed to save. The boys learned the trade and spent their time after school and on weekends helping out with the business. They often complained, but knew to be quiet once their father gave them a certain look. He constantly reminded them how lucky they were living in a free country, and that someday the business would be theirs.

Miguel's business prospered because of the quality of his work. Many important businessmen and celebrities visited the now famous shop. Work was steady and the boys were getting older. One day when the boys were at high school age, Miguel announced to them that he had saved enough money to send them to college.

"Hijos, I want you to have the education that I never got," he said proudly.

Jose asked, "But father, who will help you run the business?"

"Your brother is two years younger than you. He will help during the time that you are gone, and I will probably hire someone for the remaining time. My boys will go to school and become great businessmen. The Rodriguez family and its descendants will never live in poverty again."

With tears in his eyes, Jose spoke for himself and his brother, saying, "We will make you proud, father."

Jose was in his junior year at New York State University when he and his brother received an urgent message to come home immediately because something terrible had happened. The boys gathered some things and sped home as fast as possible. When they arrived they learned that their father had been murdered.

A friend of the family was already at the house trying to comfort their distraught mother. When she saw her boys she got up and ran to them, hugging them close and crying hysterically. After a couple of minutes she regained her composure and spoke, "Why did this happen to your father? He was such a kind man. I warned him about leaving the shop after dark with his bank deposits."

Jose spoke first. "Mother, who did this?"

"The police don't know. They are talking to businesses in the area to see if anyone saw anything that might help their investigation. The thief hit him over the head with a tire iron and left him in the street to die. The police figure robbery was the motive because I told them that your father didn't have any enemies that I knew of. Who's going to run the business? How will we survive?" she said as she began another round of tears.

Jose rubbed her back and calmly said, "Don't worry mamí. I will take care of you and run the shop.

She stopped crying and replied, "But what about your education?"

Pepito quickly said, "I can run the shop while you finish your last year of school."

"No!" Jose answered. "I am the oldest son. The responsibility is mine and I don't want to hear anything to the contrary."

Pepito looked him in the eyes and said, "Only if you promise to finish school after I graduate. That is what papa would have wanted."

"We'll see," is the only reply he got from Jose.

Miguel was buried in the Catholic cemetery a couple of days later. Pepito returned to school and Jose took over the daily functions of running the tailor shop. Their mother never seemed to be the same after their father's death. In Pepito's senior year their mother passed away. Some say from a broken heart, but more than likely from an artery clogging Cuban diet of foods filled with animal fats.

The business was prosperous and it provided a good income for the brothers. Pepito had become interested in the stock market while in business school, and had decided he didn't want to waste his life as a tailor. The brothers drew up an agreement and Jose eventually bought his brother's share of the shop.

When Jose took over his father's business it became a ritual that he stop every day for a café con leche and Cuban bread with jam at a little Cuban coffee shop near work. The first time he saw the girl behind the counter he told himself that some day he would marry her.

She was beautiful. She had jet-black eyes and hair. Those eyes—he got lost in them every time she looked at him. Her name was Rosita and he found out she was only two years younger than he was. The young woman worked in the family business as he had. Her father kept a close eye on his little girl. At one point, Jose asked her if she could accompany him to the movies. She agreed to go, but only if her older brother went as a chaperone. This rule imposed by her father had scared off many a suitor, but it wasn't going to deter Jose.

After a while, Rosita's father came to know and trust Jose. She was no longer required to have her brother tag along on their dates.

Two years later Jose approached Juan, her father, to ask for her hand in marriage. It was the most nervous he had ever been in his entire life, especially when Juan told him he would have to think about it and left him standing alone while he walked into the next room. Jose heard laughing in the next room and went in to investigate.

Upon entering the room he saw Rosita and her father hugging and laughing together. Juan looked at Jose and said; "I can't believe it took you so long to ask! Of course you can marry my daughter."

Eleven years and two children later, the couple was planning their summer vacation. Jose wished to give his children the same pleasant memories that he had of his childhood, memories like his father and he sitting on the rocks fishing together, enjoying the outdoors and holding intimate conversations. That was it. Jose had to take them to a place similar to his boyhood home, Cuba.

He thought about Miami, where they could also visit some relatives, but decided the waters were nothing like those an island could offer. Jose paid to go out fishing on a previous vacation to Miami and had been disappointed by the over-fished and polluted waters. He thought for a moment and came up with an idea. He jumped up from the table excited, and said, "I've got it! We can go to Bimini. It's in the Bahamas. My cousin, the lobster fisherman, told me about it.

As a matter of fact, his cousin spent a little time in the Nassau jail. The Bahamians took his boat back in the seventies when he ignored their threats to arrest any lobstermen from the U.S. that violated their water boundaries. My cousin – he was mad, but I understood why they were angry; the lobstermen from Miami, mostly Cuban, were catching all of the Bahamian's lobsters and selling them. It's been a while. So, I hope they won't mind a few Cubans coming over for vacation."

"Yippee! Michael, Jose's son, screamed.

His daughter, Mary, said, "Papa, I don't want to go to an island where they don't like Cubans."

Jose replied, "Don't be silly, Maricito. I told you that was a long time ago. We'll have fun. I'm going to take you fishing and swimming, and I'll even teach you how to use a face mask and snorkel."

"Well, okay papa, as long as you say I won't get hurt," Mary said, while hugging her father.

"Then, that's it. I'll call the travel agent in the morning to make the arrangements.

"I can't wait to see you in a bikini," he said to his wife with a wink.

Chapter 14

Two weeks later Jose's family boarded a Chalk's seaplane to begin the journey to Bimini. The planes, some of the safest flying, were first flown to Bimini by Albert Burns "Pappy" Chalk in 1919. Since that time tourists wishing to fly to the tiny islands have used them regularly.

The view of the Miami coastline was fantastic. Mary pointed out the plane's window and said, "Look Papí! The buildings are so small!" Jose leaned over to take in the view and watched as one of the many cruise ships sailed out of Government Cut heading for some Caribbean island.

By the time they lost sight of Miami's skyline, they were able to see the beginnings of Bimini rising up on the horizon. When the plane landed, Michael grabbed the armrests tightly as the plane's pontoons touched down on the ocean's surface, skipping along for a few seconds, and then settling down into the water.

Once the plane climbed up out of the water via the concrete shore ramp, he grabbed his father's arm saying, "Papí, that was cool! When can we do it again?"

"In about two weeks, when we have to fly home."

"Goodie!" the boy said, while clapping his hands.

After gathering their belongings, the family made their way to the customs office to be cleared. Two hours later, the group stood outside the Custom's building in the hot sun waiting at the dock for a ferryboat to shuttle them to South Bimini. Jose had rented a modern condominium apartment on the island with a view of the Atlantic Ocean from their window.

Minutes later a small covered boat pulled up to the dock and the captain, a young Bahamian, helped Jose load his bags. Mary was afraid to get in the boat because she had never been in one. Jose noticed her apprehension and said, "Come on, Maricita. There is nothing to be afraid of."

The little girl had big tears rolling down her cheeks. She pleaded with her father, "Please Papí, hold me on your lap. If the boat sinks, I want you close by."

The captain laughed at the little girl's remark and said, "This boat ain't goin' to sink. Why don't you come up and help me drive? By the way, what are your names?"

Mary hid behind her father and timidly peered around his body at the captain and nervously said, "My name is Mary, and this is my brother Michael."

Jose bent down and looked her in the eyes saying, "You hear that? The captain wants you to help drive the boat. I'll come up and sit in the seat right behind you. Michael, why don't you come up and drive as well?"

Before anyone could say another word, Michael was up sitting in the captain's chair with his younger sister pulling at his arm saying, "Papí said I could drive!"

The captain intervened, "No fighting kids, or no one's going to drive Captain Sebastian's boat. Mary, you get to drive the first half of the trip and Michael, you can drive the second half."

Satisfied with this, Michael relinquished his seat to Mary. The clear waters of the Bahamas mesmerized the children. Each child gazed over the side during their period of time away from the captain's seat and spotted various species of fish scurrying away from the boat's path.

Rosita sat in the only other available seats in the back of the boat with a couple of Bahamian women who looked like they were returning from a trip to the grocery store. While her family sat in the front of the boat, she began daydreaming about what she was going to do for the next few days. I'm going to lie out in the sun and walk down the beach collecting shells, she thought to herself.

She popped back into reality when she overheard one of the women talking about someone dying from a fish attack.

"Poor Bobby, who would have thought he would die from a barracuda bite."

"It wasn't just a bite," the other woman said, "it took his hand clean off at the wrist!"

"How's his wife, Georgina, going to feed the kids now that her husbands gone?"

"I heard the condo owner, Mr. Martin, has offered her a full-time cleaning job."

Rosita wanted to ask the women about the incident, but didn't know how they would react to her eavesdropping. All she knew was that she and her children were not going in any waters with a killer fish around. She realized Jose would be disappointed, but she didn't care when it came to the safety of her family.

The trip took less than fifteen minutes. The captain took the wheel as they approached the rickety dock on South Bimini. Once again, the captain helped Jose with the bags and even offered to call the manager from the condos to come pick the family up. Jose pulled out his wallet and grabbed a ten-dollar bill. He buried it in captain's hand while shaking it in appreciation.

The captain smiled and said, "Thanks ma'an. Have a good time."

Jose noticed that Rosita was upset about something and asked her, "Are you all right honey? Is something bothering you?"

"I'll talk to you about it later. When we're alone," is all she said.

"Sure, whatever you want," he replied, his mind going over what had happened in the last few minutes to have caused her apparent uneasiness.

Shortly thereafter, an oversized golf cart showed up with an employee from the condo. He loaded their bags and they sped off down the bumpy coquina rock road. The foliage on South Bimini was nothing to get excited about, mostly small native trees and bushes, nothing like the trees they had seen on a previous vacation to up-state New York.

The newly built condos were pretty impressive when compared to the architecture on North Bimini. The rooms had all of the modern conveniences AC, dishwasher, and color TV just to name a few. Jose was pleased with his decision to rent there even though it was more expensive than most places on the islands.

The children could hardly wait for their mother to unpack before they were asking to go swimming. Jose said, "I'll take you swimming after we are through unpacking, if your mother says we have enough time before lunch."

"Yippee!" the children screamed as they jumped up and down on the bed.

"Get down off that bed! Rosita said harshly. "Did I raise you to be animals?" she finished swatting them on the butt as they stepped down.

"You children go into the living room and watch TV while I finish unpacking. And I don't want to hear any bickering or you'll be punished. I don't care if it is vacation!"

Rosita closed the bedroom door as the children exited.

"What's up? Jose was quick to ask.

"I heard some women talking on the way over about a man that was attacked by a fish and died."

"What kind of fish?

"I think it was a barraluda"

"You mean bar-ra-cu-da don't you?"

"Yeah, I guess that's what they said.

"Honey, I used to swim with them as a boy in Cuba. Sure, they were scary, but I never heard of them attacking anybody."

"Well, I don't want you or the kids going swimming with a fish that can kill somebody.

"Don't be silly, honey. We would have heard about it in the papers if something like that happened."

"Not necessarily. If they told everyone that a killer fish was swimming around their islands, it would hurt their tourism."

"Listen, I promise that if we go swimming, it will only be close to shore, and I will personally stay with the children and make sure nothing harms them."

"You promise?"

Jose placed his hand over his heart and said, "On my mother's grave."

"Well, okay. But don't stay in the water too long. I don't want to take any chances.

Before Rosita let them go swimming, she made them sit down and eat lunch. The lunch consisted of fresh Cuban bread and jamón (ham) with queso blanco (white cheese) that they had picked up in Miami before taking off. She delayed their swim by telling them they would get cramps if they swam too early after eating.

After lunch, they headed down to the private beach carrying blankets, sunscreen, masks and snorkels. The water was beautiful, emerald green and as clear and warm as freshly drawn bath water. It took a few minor adjustments to get Mary's facemask to fit properly. Each time Jose stretched the mask's strap to pull it down on the back of Mary's head it invariably got caught in some of her hair causing her to scream in pain. He had no problem with Michael's due to his closely cropped hair. Once everyone had successfully donned their gear, Jose began the task of teaching them how to use it.

"Put the snorkel in your mouth and lightly hold the mouth piece with your teeth. Never tilt your head too far back while breathing, otherwise you might inhale some water."

Both children took to snorkeling like they had been doing it for years. Rosita would periodically look up from the book that she was reading to make sure Jose was keeping his promise. One time he caught her and smiled, waving to let her know that everything was okay.

After fifteen minutes or so, Jose decided to take the kids to a small rock he had spotted close to shore. The rock had all sorts of tropical fish swimming around it. There were beau gregories with brilliant blue on the bottom half of their bodies and bright yellow on the top half, sergeant majors with black and yellow vertical stripes, and high hats that have black and white horizontal stripes and long trailing dorsal fins.

At first, Mary was afraid of the small fish, and reacted by tightly tugging at her father's arm and screaming into her snorkel, but once she realized they wouldn't harm her, she began to calm down and enjoy the experience. Michael watched for a couple of minutes, and then dove down and chased some of the fish around the rock.

Jose was constantly looking around remembering the promise that he had made to his wife. Suddenly, out of the corner of his eye, he spotted something a few feet away, hovering just above the sandy bottom. It was a barracuda! Calm down, he told himself it's just a baby, only two feet, like the ones he used to see as a boy.

He thought I must get the kids in before they see it. If they start screaming, and Rosita hears them, she'll never let me take them in the water again. Quickly, before they could see the fish he said, "Come children let's move in closer to shore. Your mother looks like she's starting to worry."

Disappointed, Michael said, "Awe Papí, do we have to?"

The barracuda moved closer, so Jose grabbed their arms and said, "Do you want your mother to tell me you can't snorkel with me anymore?"

Jose pulled them close to shore, far away from the little barracuda. To keep them occupied, he told them a story; "Bimini was once a home to pirates and salvagers. There are many ships that have sunk carrying gold and silver coins to the bottom with them. If you children swim along the shore where the waves break, you just might find some of these coins."

"Were there really pirates living here Papí?" Mary asked nervously.

"Yes, my little Maricita, but they are long gone. Hopefully though, they left some gold for us to find."

Michael asked excitedly, "Do you really think we will find some gold?"

"You can't if you don't start looking!"

The children began snorkeling up and down the shoreline. Waves periodically washed over their snorkels, causing them to come up gagging from the invading seawater. They just shrugged it off like most kids. From time to time, Jose would hear an excited shout from the waterline and the kids would be seen holding up an old beer cap or brightly colored shell.

After several hours the family retreated to the air-conditioned condo for a nap. The salt air and sun had taken its toll on the children and soon they were sleeping. Jose and Rosita took this time to secretly make love in the bathroom.

Rosita undressed and sat on the vanity with her legs spread so Jose could enter her easily. He kissed and licked the salt from her neck, while his hands grasped her butt cheeks firmly, aiding his forward thrusts into her moistness.

Rosita's firm breasts rubbed against Jose's hairy chest as she wrapped her legs around his body pulling him closer. After several minutes of fierce love making, they both came. It had been years since they had done something kinky like this. "We'll have to do this again," Rosita said as the spasms of her intense orgasm subsided. After the furious workout, all Jose could do was nod his head in agreement while trying to catch his breath.

That night the family had dinner at a restaurant located in the marina that was part of the condominium complex. Jose talked to some of the Bahamians to find out what kind of bait would be best for fishing around the rock jetties that ran alongside either side of the condominium's private beach. "Live shrimp would be best," one of the men suggested. "The bait store's out now, but they should have some by tomorrow morning," the second man added. Jose decided that he would get up early and go get some shrimp before breakfast.

While in Miami, Jose purchased a decent rod and reel for himself and two beginner's rods for the children. Mary's was pink with a Minnie Mouse character on the reel. Michael's was blue, with Mickey Mouse on it. He gave them to them the night before the fishing trip and they were so excited they could barely sleep.

Jose woke the next morning without the aid of an alarm clock. It was easy after years of training. Every morning, as part of his daily ritual, he woke up at 6:00 a.m. to help Rosita get the children ready before heading off to the tailor shop.

Sometimes, especially while on vacation, he wished his body would let him sleep in. Not today, he thought to himself as he put on an old pair of shorts. He kissed his wife and she smiled letting him know that she felt his little act of love. On the way out of the condo, he peeked in on the children who were sleeping like little angels.

The walk to the bait store was a short one. It was a good thing because the mosquitoes apparently thought he was breakfast as they swarmed around his exposed legs. "Shit!" he screamed as he slapped one that had already imbedded its feeding tube into his right calf. Got to remember the mosquito repellent for the kids, he thought, as he entered the bait store.

"Good morning!" he said to the clerk behind the counter. "Mornin'," the Bahamian clerk replied.

"How much are the live shrimp a dozen?"

"Only $8.95."

"Are they gold plated?"

"I don't make up the prices ma'an. I just work here."

"Sorry, I guess I'll take three dozen. And try to pick out some big ones for that price."

The clerk took the money and smiled saying, "You sure three dozens going to be enough?"

"At that price it's going to have to be."

In addition to the shrimp, Jose wound up paying another $20.00 for a cheap plastic live-bait bucket to put them in. He was glad he had bought the rest of the supplies for fishing in Miami because he would have gone broke buying them here.

When Jose returned to the condo everyone was up and the smell of freshly brewed Cuban coffee filled the air. "Papí, what do you have in the bucket?" Mary asked.

"Some bait for our fishing today."

"Let me see them," Michael said.

Once the bucket was on the floor, Michael poked his finger into the water causing one of the frightened crustaceans to spring onto the floor.

Alarmed by this strange little creature, Mary screamed at the top of her lungs.

"It's okay," Jose said as scooped the flipping shrimp back into the bucket.

"Hurry and eat your breakfast so we can go fishing before these shrimp die. They'll work better if we can use them while they are still alive."

Rosita peered into the bucket and said, "I don't know if I can ever eat another shrimp again after seeing how ugly they are with their heads on."

"You've never seen a live shrimp before?" Jose asked.

"If I have, I don't remember. I was very young when we left Cuba and moved to New York."

"I guess you've never petted one before either!" Jose said, as he reached into the bucket and grabbed a shrimp.

"Don't even get that thing near me!" Rosita said backing away.

Jose couldn't resist teasing her. "What, you don't want to pet the little shrimp?"

She spoke from her new position on the far side of the room, "Put it back in the bucket you're scaring Maricita."

The little girl was hiding behind her mother with terror in her eyes. Jose realized his wife was right and put the shrimp back in the bucket saying, "Don't worry Maricito, Papí was just playing with Mamí."

"Papí, you scared me. Now I don't know if I want to go fishing."

"Maricita, I'm sorry. I promise not to scare you or Mamí again. And when we go fishing I'll put the shrimp on the hook for you so you don't have to go near it," he said hoping to calm her down.

"All right, I'll go fishing if I don't have to touch the shrimp."

"Good! Then we're all set. Let's eat some breakfast so we can go catch some fish."

Rosita had already spread guava jelly on some toasted Cuban bread and distributed it around the table. Within minutes the children were finished and in the bathroom brushing their teeth after being reminded to do so. Jose gobbled down his share of the food and was gathering up the rest of the fishing supplies. Rosita could tell that she was never going to be ready to leave when they were, so she instructed them to go without her and she would catch up. The children had to line up and get a coating of sunscreen before walking out the door. This didn't occur without the usual protests. Rosita stood back and admired her handsome family as they walked down the beach, then quickly started cleaning up the breakfast dishes so she could join them.

It was a beautiful morning. One like you see in photographs hanging on the walls of travel agents offices, touting you to come to the Bahamas. The water was flat calm and as clear as spring water.

Jose sat in the sand and began rigging the fishing lines with hooks and sinkers. It took a couple of minutes to remember the knots his father had taught him as a boy, but soon he was tying them like a pro. He decided to try rigs without leader wire first because it was easier to rig, and also you don't need leader wire with most small snappers, if you use long shank hooks.

After rigging all of the poles he decided to give Michael a lesson on baiting the hook. Jose reached into the bucket and pulled out a shrimp saying, "There are basically two ways to put a shrimp on a hook. The first way is the easiest. Just poke the hook through halfway down its body below the spinal cord. The second way is a little harder. You have to pinch off the tail and carefully feed the point through the body and out the bottom around the legs. Both ways seem to work, so take your pick."

Mary scrunched her nose and said, "Ewe gross!"

Michael asked with a puzzled look on his face, "Doesn't it kill the shrimp?"

Jose answered confidently, "That's why you have to be careful not hit any vital organs. The shrimp will stay alive for a while. Hopefully long enough to trick a fish into biting your hook."

Jose placed a shrimp on Mary's hook and motioned to Michael to bait his own. It took a couple of tries for him to catch a shrimp and once he finally caught one, he dropped it when it poked him with its barb. "Ouch!" Michael yelped as he dropped the shrimp into the sand.

"They can't hurt you," Jose reassured him.

"Then how come my finger is bleeding?

"That's nothing," Jose said, as he reached down and grabbed the shrimp from the sand.

"You put the first one on," Michael said sucking the blood from his finger."

"All right, but you're on your own after this. No son of mine is going to be afraid of a little shrimp."

Michael knew he wasn't kidding from the time they went lake fishing in New York and his father made him bait his own hook with a live worm.

Before putting their lines in the water, Jose changed the water in the shrimp bucket in an effort to keep them alive. Once that was done he attempted to teach the children how to cast their lines.

"Swing your rod forward and push the button to release the line when you are pointing where you want your bait to go."

It took a couple of times, but soon the children were doing well enough that he was able to bait his own hook and begin fishing.

As soon as Jose got his line in the water, Michael started screaming, "I got one!"

Quickly, Jose had to reel in his line to coach the boy on landing the fish. "Keep your rod tip up!" he screamed at the boy. "Don't horse him in!" he added."

"I think he's a big one!" Michael said, struggling to turn the handle on the reel.

A few seconds later, the proud young fisherman pulled a six-inch grunt onto the beach.

"Look Papí, my first saltwater fish."

"Good job son," Jose said, smiling.

"Papí! Papí! I have one too!" Mary screamed at the top her lungs.

Rosita was on her way down to beach when she heard her daughter scream. She dropped everything and ran down to the shoreline to see what was the matter.

"What's all the screaming about?"

"Mamí, I have a fish on!" Mary exclaimed, while reeling in her line.

"That's good, but please don't scream. Mamí thought you were hurt.

"Sorry Mamí," the little girl said, truly sorry for scaring her.

Soon another small grunt was pulled out of the water and Rosita remarked, "You guys keep this up and we won't have to buy our dinner."

"I'm going to catch a whole bunch, Michael stated proudly."

"Good you do that. Mamí's going to go soak up some sun while you do," she said as headed back to the spot where she had dropped all of her beach supplies. On the way, she told herself you've got to stop freaking out every time you hear one of the children scream or you're going to drive yourself loco.

Soon she had returned to her spot on the beach and had set up her chair, applied her dark tanning oil, and began to read her favorite author, Danielle Steel. After several pages, the quiet beach and warm ocean breeze lulled her into a light sleep.

Jose was kept busy pulling small grunts off the children's lines one after another, until finally he decided it was time for him to do some fishing.

"Children, Papí is going to walk out on the rocks to see if he can catch some bigger fish."

"Can I go?" Michael asked pleadingly.

"Not this time. It is too dangerous for you, besides I need you to stay and help your sister."

Jose ripped a soda can in half and threw a couple of shrimp into it with some seawater and said, "I'll be back shortly. You two stay right here and fish and Michael make sure you help your sister."

"Yes, Papí," he replied obediently.

Jose was halfway out when he looked back and saw that the children had moved into the water with their rods. He looked at his wife and she appeared to be sleeping, so he didn't want to yell at them and take a chance on waking her. Besides, he thought, in water up to their waists, nothing could hurt them.

Finally, he had made it out to the end of the jetties. The water appeared to be quite a bit deeper and he could see larger fish swimming around the rocks on the bottom. He picked a flat rock and sat down to bait his hook.

Jose glanced back at his children once more and saw that they were out of the water probably removing fish from their hooks or rebaiting them. He grabbed a shrimp from the can and pinched off the tail and placed it on the hook. Before tossing it into the water he kissed it and said, "Go bring me a big fish, little one."

Jose cast his line out as far as he could hoping to find even deeper water and larger fish. A school of small jacks had moved into the area and one of them happened to find Jose's shrimp. The little fish hit like a ton of bricks and began struggling to get away.

Jose yelled, "Yahoo!" as the fish peeled of line before he could tighten the drag.   Within seconds, a small cuda two to three feet dashed at the fish cutting it in half right behind the head. He pulled in the head and cursed at the young cuda that was now waiting off of the rocks for his next meal.

The excitement in the water caused the ancient cuda to change course.   He had been heading into the marina's basin   following a school of finger mullet. Slowly he cruised past the end of the jetties his keen senses picking up the scent of blood.

So involved in his fishing, Jose hadn't noticed that his children were back in the water fishing. He pulled the jack's head off the hook and tossed it into the water. When it hit the water it was gobbled up by the same young cuda. Quickly he placed another shrimp on and cast it out into the deeper water. "Catch your own fish!" he cried to the young cuda as his bait hit the water.

Once again a small jack attacked his bait. This time the young cuda seemed to keep his distance. Suddenly, something hit with such force it almost pulled the rod from his hands. "Shit!" Jose yelled regaining his balance.   When his line came up, nothing was left. Everything was cut off clean. Something made him turn and look at the children. Mary was fighting another fish. Her brother was on shore baiting his hook.

The next thing he saw took his breath away. Swimming just off of the jetties towards shore was the biggest barracuda he had ever seen. It was twice as large as any he had seen as a young boy in Cuba. Its speed picked up as it became more excited by Mary's struggling fish. He dropped his rod and started running and jumping over the jetties, screaming, "Mary, get out of the water!"   At one point he twisted his ankle on an odd angled rock, but kept going. He kept screaming the same thing over and over, "Mary, get out of the water!"

When Jose was halfway down the jetties, Mary heard him and said, "Look Papí, I have a big one this time!"

Jose looked at her and said, "Do as I say, drop the rod and run from the water!"

Mary with a puzzled look on her face dropped the rod and ran towards the beach screaming. The large cuda sped up to catch the splashing object unable to discern what it was, but charging anyway thinking it was a fish.

Bam! He hit. The force knocked the little girl down. His teeth had sliced through her right calf removing part of the muscle. He turned and charged again, but only glanced off her leg as her father lifted her up and out of the water. Quickly the cuda turned and headed out to deeper water, confused by all of the commotion.

Mary wasn't screaming now, she had gone into shock. Jose carried her limp body up to his frantic wife. Blood ran down his leg from her deep wound.

"What happened?" Rosita asked.

"She was attacked by a large barracuda," Jose replied, knowing he was in for a rough time.

"Where were you!" she asked harshly.

"This is not the time to discuss this! We must get her to a doctor!" Jose said, concerned for his daughter's safety.

"Where were you?" she said again, crying hysterically.

She began to pound on his back asking again and again, "Where were you!"

Jose took his free hand and slapped her in the face. Rosita snapped out of it and saw the severity of her daughter's injuries. Quickly she grabbed towel and placed pressure on the wound. The family ran up to the condo looking for help. One of the tourists preparing to go fishing saw them and asked if they could help.

"My daughter is hurt badly and she needs a doctor. Could you take us to North Bimini?" Jose asked pleadingly.

"Sure, hop in," the fisherman replied.

The family climbed down into the twenty-five foot open-fisherman boat and braced themselves for the rapid ride to the island. In a few short minutes they were pulling up to the dock. The fisherman helped Rosita and Michael out of the boat, and then held the boat steady while Jose carried his daughter off the vessel. Jose turned and said; "I don't know how I can thank you."

"I just hope the kid's all right. I'm sure you would have done the same thing for me."

"Thanks again," he said, as the fisherman pulled away from the dock.

The Good Samaritan had dropped them off on the dock behind a large yacht named Silicone Valleys. On the yacht's afterdeck were several women in very small bikinis sporting breasts too perky to be natural. Among them was one very fortunate, slightly balding, middle-aged man. He stopped talking to one of the women when he noticed the injured girl being lifted to the dock. As the rescue boat departed, he cupped his hand to his mouth and yelled, "Is there anything I can do? I'm a doctor."

Jose looked up and answered without hesitation, "Yes! Please! My daughter she's been injured! She's bleeding badly!"

The three girls, all wearing string bikinis, were standing side by side talking amongst themselves as they peered over the yacht's railing at the injured girl. The doctor quickly ran into the interior of the yacht and retrieved a first-aid kit he kept for such emergencies. Seconds later he ran down the gangplank and joined the family.

"What happened?" he asked.

"You aren't going to believe this, but she was standing in waist high water fishing and was attacked by a monster sized barracuda. The largest I've ever seen."

The doctor listened while he inspected the little girl's injuries.

"She's got a nasty wound. The good news is that he didn't hit any major blood vessels. We need to get this wound flushed out as soon as possible to ward off any infection. I'm friends with the local doctor. His operating room is kind of primitive, but it will suffice."

After yelling up to his guests that he'd be back shortly, the doctor whisked up the little girl and started down the road to Dr. Smythe's office.

After a few steps, he turned to Jose and said, "You will probably want to make arrangements to have her flown back to Miami after I'm finished. She will need to be observed closely for any signs of infection and be kept on intravenous antibiotics for about a week. Unfortunately, a fish bite of this magnitude exposes her body to some nasty germs." The doctor noticed the concerned look on Jose's face and said, "Don't worry I'll clean the wound well. With today's antibiotics, the chance of infection is almost nil."

He refrained from telling him that she could lose her leg or that she might have a permanent limp. The reassurance worked. Jose looked at the doctor and smiled saying, "Thank you doctor." Before he left he realized he didn't even know the doctor's name and asked, "Doctor, may I ask your name?"

"I'm sorry it's Alazar, Dr. Alazar."

"That sounds Latin."

"Sí, soy de Cuba." (Yes, I am from Cuba)

"Soy de Cuba tambien." (I am from Cuba also)

"Adios amigo," Jose said as he ran towards the Chalk Airlines office to make arrangements for the flight home.

A passing Bahamian in a golf cart noticed the doctor carrying the injured girl and offered to let them borrow it to drive to Dr. Smythe's office. He turned the golf cart over to Rosita and said he would walk down and pick it up, that way she, Michael, Mary, and the doctor could ride together without overburdening the cart. Rosita could only say, "God bless you."

They arrived at the doctor's and she knocked at the door. Dr. Smythe answered the door quickly, wearing a smock with a small amount of blood spattered on it. "Dr. Alazar, mi amigo. ¿Cómo está ?

"I'm fine, but this little girl needs some help Dr. George."

"Please come in. Let's take her to my operating room?"

When they entered the room, a little Bahamian boy was sitting on the examining table with his mother holding his hand. His right ear had a big bandage wrapped around it. Dr. George grabbed the boy under the arms and gently lifted him to the floor saying, "There now, that wasn't so bad, was it? The little boy who had apparently been crying shook his head no.

The doctor turned to his mother and said, "I'm going to have him take some antibiotics just in case. I checked on his tetanus shots and he's okay. I gave him one last year when I stitched up his foot after he stepped on that broken soda bottle. The doctor handed the mother a prescription and patted the boy on the head saying, "Next time catch a fish on the hook, not your ear." The little boy gave him a hug and left.

Dr. Alazar placed the girl on the table and began cleaning the wound. First, he flushed it out with a sterile saline solution, and then soaked it thoroughly with betadyne. He turned to the girl's mother and said, "I guess I should tell you I'm a plastic surgeon. I'm going to place a drain in the wound and stitch her up. I'll need you to sign a release because she's a minor. I'll do this one for free if you promise not to sue me if anything goes wrong."

"Of course not doctor. What could go wrong?"

"I don't expect anything, but you know how sue happy people are these days." He took a couple of minutes to explain her injuries and the possible recovery. "The fish removed a piece from her calf muscle. I should be able to pull the two surfaces back together. Because she is still very young her body should be able to adapt and repair the missing tissue. She will need some therapy after it heals, but should regain full use eventually. It will leave a scar that will dissipate and become only slightly noticeable by the time she reaches adulthood.

The little girl stirred and started to cry. Rosita grabbed her hand and attempted to calm her down. The doctor injected several doses of anesthetic around the wound to deaden it prior to suturing it closed. It was all Dr. George and Rosita could do to hold the girl steady while Dr. Alazar sewed the wound closed. Her brother Michael cringed in the corner while his little sister cried out in fear. It took almost a half an hour to finish the operation due to Mary's constant struggling.

When the doctor finished, Jose walked in and said that Chalk's had been very accommodating by arranging for the family to leave on the next flight out.

"How is she?" Jose asked with concern.

"I think she'll be just fine," the doctor replied confidently.

Rosita looked at Jose with piercing eyes and said harshly, "She'd be much better if this never happened!"

Dr. George stepped in, "Ma'am try not to be so hard on your husband. Things like this don't happen very often around here."

Rosita defended her anger by saying, "I heard some women talking about a man getting killed by a barracuda on the way over, and I told Jose that I didn't want the children in the water, but he didn't listen."

"Oh, I guess you heard about Bobby," the doctor said meekly.

"Yes, you people should have had warnings about a killer fish in the area!"

"Now, now, calm down Rosita. It's very unusual for a barracuda to attack humans. Why, these are the first attacks that I've ever had to deal with as long as I've lived here."

"It's seems to me then that you have a very unusual barracuda swimming around here!"

Jose had heard enough and said, "Rosita, I'm sorry about what happened. This man has been kind to our daughter and us. Please don't be blaming him for what happened. I'm sorry, Dr. George please excuse my wife. I'm afraid she is terribly upset."

"No harm done. I know how mothers can be when it comes to their children."

"Honey, you stay here with Mary while Michael and I go back to the condo and pack our things. The next flight leaves within the hour. Is it okay if she stays here Dr. George?"

"Sure, no problem. Would you like a cup of tea Rosita?"

"I would love one doctor."

Jose rushed back to the condo and threw all their things into suitcases. While checking out, he let the clerk know that there were some fishing poles on the beach if he wanted them. Mary's was probably gone, washed out to sea by now. When questioned by the clerk, he explained what happened. The clerk replied, "I would have warned you, but the attack on Bobby happened quite a ways offshore. If I thought there was any danger to you or your family..."

"Listen, I don't hold you responsible. Barracuda attacks are very rare. And how could you have known that he was swimming so close to the beach. Anyhow, take the fishing poles, I don't think I'll be needing them anymore."

An employee of the condo helped Jose and Michael load the suitcases into the golf cart and then drove them to the dock to await the ferryboat. A few minutes later, the boat pulled up with Captain Sebastian at the helm. He helped them load their suitcases, noticing that they were short a few people he asked, "Where are the women today? And didn't you just arrive the other day?"

"My wife and daughter are at Dr. George's right now. Mary was attacked by a barracuda and needs to return to the states for more medical treatment."

"You've got to be kidding! That's the third attack within a few days."

"What do you mean third attack?"

"Some lady was cleaning her boat with a gold anklet on and was charged by a huge cuda."

"I didn't hear about that one. I heard about the fisherman that died after losing his hand and bleeding to death."

"Bobby, poor Bobby. We grew up together. Sometimes I used to go yellowtailing with him on my days off. How bad was your daughter injured?

"He took a chunk out of her calf, but the doctor said with some time and therapy she should be okay."

Sebastian could see that Michael was upset and tried to cheer him up. "Hey boy, you want to drive the boat?"

"No thanks," Michael said solemnly.

The rest of the trip was silent, except for the humming engines and water slapping against the hull. They pulled up to the dock and Sebastian helped them off with their bags, this time refusing the tip Jose offered him. "I hope your little girl is going to be all right," he said, before leaving.

Jose went to customs to let them check the bags and notify them of their change in travel plans. The custom officials said it wouldn't be necessary for Mary and Rosita to come in before leaving due to the fact that this was a medical emergency.

He checked the bags in at the Chalk's office, then left for Dr. George's to pick up the women. Mary was sleeping as he crept into the operating room to check on her. Rosita came up and gave him a hug saying, "I'm sorry for the way I acted today. I know you would never do anything to intentionally injure our children. Though, next time, please listen to my mother's intuition."

Jose looked over his wife's shoulder at his daughter while he hugged her and with tears in his eyes said, "I love you guys so much."

Within the hour, the family was on its way back to Miami. The trip home was dismal. At one point Mary woke up and started screaming and crying. Both parents took turns holding her to calm her down and eventually she fell back to sleep.

Back in Bimini, Dr. George was making his way to Commissioner Newbold's office. After three attacks, he felt like something should be done, either post some type of warnings for swimmers and divers, or try to capture the fish.

His knock on the door was answered by a housekeeper. She smiled and said, "Dr. George what a pleasant surprise."

He returned her smile and said, "Marva is the commissioner around? I need to speak to him."

"Sure, he's in his office. I'll let him know you're here."

The commissioner was just hanging up the telephone as the housekeeper knocked on the office door. "Commissioner, Dr. George would like to have a word with you."

The Commissioner, always happy to talk to his good friend said, "Show him in please." He stood as the doctor entered the room and extended his hand saying, "George it's so nice to see you do come in my friend, I haven't seen you for a while."

Dr. George shook his hand and replied, "This isn't a social call I'm afraid. There's been three barracuda attacks in the last week or so and I've come to discuss how we can prevent anymore."

"The only one I heard about was Bobby's. And who's to say it wasn't a shark that inflicted the wound. You say there's been more? I saw you at the funeral the other day and you didn't say anything."

"The first attack was on a young woman cleaning the bottom of her yacht. I didn't think much of it at the time. I thought it was a rare incident. Now I'm not really sure because there have been two more: Bobby's, and an attack that occurred today over on South Bimini. A little girl was surf fishing with her brother and was bitten on the leg by what the father describes as a huge cuda."

"Is she all right?"

"She sustained a good sized laceration on her calf, but myself, and an American, a plastic surgeon who happened to see the girl arrive at the docks, think that she'll heal up fine."

"That's good. So, what do you think we should do?

"I think we should post some type of warning signs for swimmers and divers at the immigration office."

Sure, I can see it now. Welcome to Bimini; don't go in the water because a giant barracuda will attack you! Don't do the one thing that you came to these tiny piles of sand to do. Come now George; let's be sensible. We can't be scaring off tourists when we don't exactly know what's going on."

I think we do. The boyfriend of the first victim is a marine biologist. Kit, I think is his name."

"I know him. I was contacted by the Nassau authorities to inform me that he would be in the area doing some conch research for them."

Dr. George continued, "His fiancée, Carla, was the first victim. She got a good look at the fish before the attack and said it was a large barracuda. Also, Kit checked out Bobby's wound and compared the teeth marks with the ones on the tail section of a marlin carcass that was brought to Bimini. He said both the teeth patterns were consistent with barracuda bites."

"Well, nobody but Bobby knows what took his hand off. I think you're jumping the gun."

Dr. George stood up and pounded his fist on the commissioner's desk saying, "Damn it! I'll hold you personally responsible if anyone else is injured."

"Calm down George!"

"I'll not calm down until something's done," Dr. George said, as he left the office slamming the door on his way out.

Chapter 15

long A few days later during the early evening hours, a 35-foot Dakota open fisherman named Dear John pulled into the marina. Its passengers: John, his son Johnny, and his son's wife, Nicole, were planning to spend a fun filled weekend in Bimini. After clearing customs, they grabbed their gear from the boat and checked in at the hotel.

It was 9:26 a.m.; twenty-six minutes after the hotel's wakeup call had invaded the vacationers' deep sleep. John wished he had gone to bed after checking in, but his son Johnny and his wife weren't ready to retire and had talked him into going to The Compleat Angler for drinks.

He had to admit he had a good time, and even met Trevor Callaway, the famous author. But while in the bar, he heard some cockamamie story about a large man-eating barracuda. John had wished Nicole wasn't around when they had talked about the barracuda, she was already nervous about the dangers of diving.

After lying in bed for a couple of minutes, John realized the headboard banging against the wall in the next room is what had awakened him. Just like his old man, John snickered, knowing the noise was Johnny making love to Nicole.

He figured he'd wait a couple of minutes after the banging stopped to knock on the door and tell them to get ready to shove off. In the mean time he would get dressed and find the local that had promised to show them a secret lobster spot. They had planned to pig out on the lobster they'd catch that weekend and hopefully get enough to bring some home.

John got dressed and began the short walk down to the marina. He spotted Willy, (short for William), sitting on a homemade stool weaving hats from palm fronds. When he wasn't working as a cash-only tour guide, he sat around weaving various objects to sell to tourists.

The day before, Willy had seen him struggling with their baggage and offered to help (another one of his side jobs). During the walk to the hotel he asked them, "What's up for the weekend, a little fishing, a little diving?

John replied, "We're here for bugs."

"You've come to the right place ma'an," Willy was quick to say.

"And Willy has a secret spot. It's like a hotel for lobsters, just waiting for you to help them check out. And for a very minimal fee, Willy will take you there."

"What do you consider a minimal fee?" John inquired.

"Only 50 American dollars."

"I'll give you $30," countered John, knowing things like this were negotiable in the islands.

"You want a man to starve? I'll be gone at least half a day with you. I need a minimum of $40. I got bills to pay too, ma'an!"

"Done!" John said, not wanting to squeeze Willy too hard.

"See you around 9:00 to 10:00 a.m. tomorrow at the marina."

"I'll be there," Willy said smiling, knowing he would be making at least $40 the following day.

Willy looked up and smiled when he noticed John was standing before him.

"Good mornin' Mr. John. Ready to catch some lobster?" Willy asked enthusiastically.

"Yeah, as soon as I can get my son off his wife," John stated with a wink.

"Let him be, the man's got better things to do than looking in holes for crustaceans," Willy added, thinking about how long it's been since he'd gotten lucky.

"We'll be back in a few minutes. I just wanted to let you know we're running a little late," John said and turned to walk back to the hotel.

"Take your time ma'an – no need to hurry in the Bahamas," Willy yelled to John as he walked off.

In a matter of minutes John was knocking on his son's hotel room door. Johnny opened the door and invited his dad in.

"Nicole's almost ready. She's still doing her hair," Johnny informed his dad while motioning for him to sit down.

"Hey Nicole! Don't spend too much time on your hair. It's going to be soaked in salt water in about 30 minutes," John yelled to his daughter-in-law.

Nicole appeared minutes later wearing a butt flosser bikini highlighted by a fluorescent green diaphanous beach cover-up. John wished she wouldn't dress in this manner. He didn't feel right lusting over his daughter-in-law.

"You kids ready?" John asked, purging his mind of impure thoughts.

"We're ready, captain," Nicole said with a salute.

"Let's go Willy's waiting for us," John said, walking over to the door and opening it.

As the three vacationers approached, Willy's eyes focused on Nicole and he thought to himself; he gave that up to go lobstering?

When the group got to the dock John introduced his son and daughter-in-law to Willy. Willy grabbed Nicole's hand, and looked into her eyes saying, "The pleasure is surely all mine!"

The adventurers boarded the vessel, Willy jumping in first to help the lady on board saying, "Watch your step, missy."

John fired up the twin 250 horsepower Yamaha outboards and they growled like two tigers awakened from a nap. Willy untied the bow and stern line, and pushed on the piling to start the boat on its journey.

Once out of the marina, Willy asked if John would mind if he took over the controls. Willy proudly stated, "I know these waters like the back of my hand."

It was mid morning and the sun was climbing higher and higher into the cloudless blue sky. There was a slight breeze – just enough to battle the staggering heat. The ocean was calm and Willy was able to cruise at ¾ throttle, approximately 40 miles per hour. At this speed Nicole's eyes had to fight to stay open, until she turned to face the stern. John stood next to Willy at the console while Johnny and Nicole faced the rear watching the outboards eat their way through the Atlantic Ocean.

Ten minutes later, Willy slowed the vessel down to an idle. "We're almost to my secret spot," Willy yelled, his voice competing with the chugging engines.

"It's that large dark area over there," Willy shouted, while pointing to an area off the bow.

"Johnny, how about getting the anchor out?" his father asked.

Johnny gave him the thumbs up sign, and headed to the bow to grab the anchor from the forward compartment. Willy put the boat in neutral and asked Johnny to drop the anchor. Johnny said, "Wow, this looks like a really cool spot—what is that down there?"

Willy jumped up on the bow like an actor on a stage and began his story. "This is Willy's secret spot and you all will have to be hypnotized and brainwashed before we leave here. Nicole got a concerned look on her face and Willy, seeing this, started laughing.

"You mainlanders need to loosen up maan! But seriously folks – the large object you see lying on the bottom of this big beautiful sea is a barge. Its unfortunate owners lost it when it drifted over this reef in the 60's and sank. The barge's rusting hull has many exposed areas for one of our favorite food sources, the lobster, to hide.

Johnny, anxious to get in the water, had already begun to put on his scuba gear.

The school of cero mackerel had run from the predator and were now searching for food on the man-made reef. The ancient barracuda had made several unsuccessful charges during the journey to the barge. Tired now, the aging cuda was resting several feet off the ocean floor, ever watchful for its next meal. The cero mackerel's oily flesh made it one of the cuda's favorite foods. However, hunting them tired the cuda, for the mackerel's speed and maneuverability closely matched the cuda's.

Its senses had picked up the sounds of a boat traveling in the vicinity. Experience had taught it an easy meal might be close by. After resting for several minutes it started swimming slowly towards the area where the sound had originated.

Johnny was perched on the dive platform ready to fall backwards into the water when he asked, "Anyone else going in?"

John was in the process of adjusting his weight belt when he replied, "I'll be right behind you. Don't take off too far!"

Willy was on the bow talking to Nicole who was preparing herself for sunbathing by rubbing baby oil all over her body. He stopped talking and shouted back, "I'll stay on the boat, just in case the anchor comes loose. You don't need me, the lobster will be jumping in your nets!"

Nicole blew them a kiss saying, "Be careful honey!" Willy and Nicole had already invaded the cooler full of ice cold Kaliks and were ready to kick back, drink a few brews, and soak up some sun.

As Johnny neared the barge he saw antennas protruding from dark crevices everywhere. "Yahoo!" he screamed, his regulator bubbles exiting like a small underwater explosion. One of the rusty lairs had least 20 legal-sized lobsters peering out at him, waiving their antennas like whips. He figured he would go for the large holes first, while he was fresh and full of energy.

Johnny was armed with a net, lobster gloves (designed with a sandpaper texture for gripping), and a tickle stick (a rod with a slightly bent end used to coax lobsters from their hiding places). He had become quite proficient at persuading the lobsters into range by carefully sliding the tickle stick under their bodies, making them believe something was behind them.

The lobsters maintained their guard in the front by moving their barbed antennas in a threatening manner hoping to escape their unknown assailant in the rear. They would come out from their place of hiding after the fear of not knowing what was behind them overrode the fear of facing the enemy at hand.

Johnny knew once the lobster left his home, there must be no hesitation to slap the net over it because its next move was to flee from both attackers, the real and imagined. The technique of inserting the tickle stick slowly, deliberately, and never hesitating once his catch was in range, had been quite productive.

Fifteen minutes later Johnny was swimming to the surface with a catch bag full of lobster tied to his waist. Nicole was lying on her stomach while Willy rubbed oil on her shoulder blades and back. All the time he was thinking to himself, "I'm getting paid for this, what a life!"

He was working his way down to her buns, but quickly set down the oil when he heard Johnny shouting for someone to empty his catch bag. Rapidly he ran to the stern and took the catch bag from Johnny and said, "I told you there would be plenty of lobster." Willy emptied the bag and handed it back to him. Johnny gave him the thumbs up and sank underwater to return to the barge.

John had been in the water several minutes when he surfaced, holding a single lobster too big to fit in his catch bag. He cautioned Willy to step aside as he tossed the monster into the boat.

"Dinner for four," he said as it flew through the air. Willy jumped up on the console seat and was now trying to figure out how he was going to get this crustacean that was acting like an enraged bull in a bull-fighting arena, into the live bait well. Finally, he spotted a large beach towel and threw it over the lobster. Carefully he picked it up and placed it in its new home, the live bait well.

Having delivered his catch, John returned to the Lobster Hotel to help a few more guests check out.

The barracuda had watched the two large figures swim to the surface and unload their catch. While their heads were above water it had positioned itself several feet below the rocking vessel.

From this position it was hidden from view and able to watch and assess the danger level of dealing with two large predators instead of one. However, it had one advantage. They were in its domain. From what it could see they moved very slowly through the water, no match for its speed. The creatures were very skilled hunters, able to capture prey from the rocks.

John swam to the edge of the barge and decided to explore the other side, figuring it would be a good idea to see if the lobster were as plentiful on the far side as they were on this side. Johnny went back to the same spot and began netting the lobsters that had begun to walk from the crevice, frightened by the earlier invasion of their home. In his excitement, Johnny didn't realize his every move was being watched.

Having scooped up all the walking lobsters, Johnny was swimming back to the boat when an eerie feeling came over him. His subconscious sent a warning to his conscious mind reporting something had been seen from the corner of his eye. Johnny stopped swimming to scan the underwater environment. About ten yards to the right was a chilling sight – the largest barracuda he had ever seen.

Common sense would tell him to untie the catch bag and swim slowly back to the boat. But, Johnny, like his dad, had always liked to ride the edge. Both were pilots, scuba divers and hang gliders, and they had learned to laugh in the face of danger.

His first idea was to let out a loud underwater scream to frighten the fish away. "Ahhhhhhhh!" He screamed into his regulator. Bubbles went flying out the vents. It didn't work. The fish stayed motionless, staring him down with its oversized eyes. The boat isn't that far away, he told himself. And cuda attacks are rare, he thought, hoping to alleviate the fear building inside. Johnny decided to start swimming with the catch bag still tied to his waist and flopping between his legs.

His father heard the scream as a lobster he had missed swam off into the distance. John saw his son swimming towards the boat with something very large not too far away.

The cuda, deciding it was time to eat, bolted for the swaying bag. Upon impact the bag bounced off its upper jaw slicing the net and allowing the lobsters their freedom. Its lower jaw sliced through Johnny's inner thigh as his leg came forward during the swimming motion. The fish removed flesh the size of a baseball containing a section of Johnny's femoral artery. The cuda swallowed the flesh, and then charged one of the escaping lobsters, swallowing it whole. John watched in horror as his son disappeared in a cloud of crimson water.

In shock and injured, Johnny plunged motionless to the bottom. John swam at full speed to his son's aid, heedless of any danger. He unclasped Johnny's weight belt and tanks. The regulator had already fallen from his son's mouth. He knew he must act fast if he was to save his son's life. Grabbing Johnny around his chest, he swam to the surface.

Upon reaching the surface he spat out his regulator, shouting, "I need help! Johnny's hurt real bad!" Nicole and Willy jumped up, a little buzzed from the beer. The pair ran to the dive platform and each person grabbed one of Johnny's arms and pulled his lifeless body into the boat.

"Oh my God, there's a chunk missing from his leg," Nicole screamed, as blood poured onto the deck. Willy wasn't a doctor, but he knew something must be done to stop the bleeding. The islander took his right hand and pushed hard on the upper area of the wound causing the flow of blood to slow. By this time John was in the boat and partially out of his scuba gear.

"He's not breathing – we must get the water out of his lungs," he said as he turned Johnny on his side. John pushed on his son's side as Willy did his best to keep pressure on the severed artery. Water flowed from Johnny's mouth as they rolled him on his back to begin CPR.

Nicole was frozen with horror when Willy shouted to her, "Nicole! Go find something to use for a tourniquet! Nicole!" Willy shouted once more. She was as white as a cloud.

"Find something for a tourniquet!" She repeated his words, and then started to look in various compartments, throwing gear about the deck. On her way to the bow she tripped over a Hawaiian sling (a long pole with a spear head and rubber tube attached) and almost fell. "Dammit!' she cried, and realized she had found the perfect tourniquet. Nicole removed a fillet knife from the knife rack and cut the length of rubber tubing from the sling.

The sight of blood made her woozy, but she knew Johnny's life depended on how fast the bleeding could be controlled. Carefully, she slid the band under his thigh and tied a knot. Willy released the pressure and grabbed the ends of the band, pulling with all his might to stop the bleeding.

John gave his son CPR for several minutes, frantically trying to revive him. Then suddenly, after a few violent coughs, Johnny started breathing on his own. He regained consciousness for several seconds, just long enough to murmur something about a barracuda, and then passed out again. His pulse was very weak, but he was alive. Seeing his son breathing again, John bolted for the radio and tuned it to the emergency channel, number 16. Frantically, he called the Coast Guard.

"Coast Guard, this is the Dear John requesting medical evacuation. Over." He waited several seconds for a reply, and then tried again.

"Coast Guard, this is the Dear John requesting medical evacuation. Over." The radio came to life.

"Roger Dear John. What's your emergency? Over." John quickly replied, "My son was attacked by a cuda about eight miles west of Bimini and I think his femoral artery has been cut. Over."

"Roger Dear John. Can you meet us in Bimini? Over."

John answered, "Roger. We'll be waiting for you at the marina. Over."

John asked Willy to pull up the anchor as he fired up the engines and crept forward to loosen the anchor from the reef. Nicole placed a towel under Johnny's head and used another towel to soak up some of the blood puddled around his limp body. John warned everyone to hold on as he pushed the throttle levers as far as they would go. The boat seemed to jump forward instantly, planing at breakneck speed. They were at the marina in eight minutes and someone was trying to contact them on the radio.

"Dear John, do you copy? Over."

John grabbed the mike. "You've got the Dear John."

The voice came back, "This is Dr. Blumberg. Is the patient conscious? Over."

John looked down at his son and replied, "He regained consciousness after I performed CPR to clear the water from his lungs, but he's been unconscious ever since. Over."

The doctor asked, "Can someone check his pulse and tell me how many heart beats there are in a ten second interval? Over."

Nicole heard the instructions and placed her index and middle fingers on Johnny's neck and began to count out loud while staring at her watch. She looked at her father-in-law and said in a concerned tone, "His pulse is really weak, but I think I counted ten beats."

John relayed the information to the doctor and the physician said, "His condition sounds bad, but not critical." Dr. Blumberg instructed them to cover Johnny with towels or a blanket and surround the blood-starved leg with ice to prevent deterioration from lack of oxygen.

Nicole placed all the extra beach towels over Johnny's limp body while Willy tied off the boat to the dock and ran to get Dr. George.

A few minutes later Willy and the doctor returned with a stretcher and an I.V. Carefully, the three men lifted the blood-soaked victim to the stretcher.   Dr. George checked Johnny's vital signs and immediately started an I.V. to replace fluids lost from the bleeding. Once the I.V. was flowing, Willy and John carried the stretcher to an area large enough for the Medivac chopper to land.

Nicole ran to the hotel to change because she planned to fly to Miami with her injured husband. Wap, wap, wap, wap, they heard as the Medivac chopper approached, stirring dust and leaves up on the landing area. The blades slowed and two figures jumped from the aircraft and ran toward the group.

"Thank you for responding so fast!" John said to the men, reaching out to shake their hands. Dr. George filled them in on Johnny's status and one of the men yelled, "Let's get this young man to the hospital! We have room for one family member." From the far side of the landing area a panicked Nicole came running. She had a large suitcase in one hand, and her other arm was flailing in the air.

She was screaming, "Wait! I'm coming!"

John turned to the medic, "That's my daughter-in-law. She'll be going to Miami with you and my son."

The medic nodded his head and signaled his partner to start walking to the waiting chopper. The medics loaded the stretcher into the helicopter, making sure Johnny was secure and ready for the flight to Mt. Sinai Medical Center. As Nicole approached the door to the helicopter, one of the medics moved to help her into the aircraft and noticed the suitcase.

"Sorry ma'am, but the suitcase will have to stay. We're pushing our weight limitations taking you."

"Sorry," Nicole said as she dropped the suitcase to the ground and climbed into the helicopter.

John watched Nicole drop the suitcase as he neared the helicopter. He wanted to see his son alive one more time just in case he didn't survive. Entering the helicopter, he kissed Nicole and assured her everything would be okay. At that point he realized he hadn't found out which hospital they were taking his son to. John leaned over and kissed his unconscious son on the forehead thinking of how not long ago they were together enjoying one of their favorite pastimes.

A firm hand on his shoulder and a deep voice interrupted his pleasant thoughts, "Sir, sir, we really need to get your boy to the hospital!"

"Sure, I'm sorry," John said, feeling guilty for delaying the flight.

He turned to Nicole and said, "I'll see you in an few hours." John turned to exit the helicopter again, but remembered he didn't know which hospital they were flying to.

"What hospital are you taking my son to?"

The medic replied, "Mt. Sinai Medical Center sir, it's one of the best in Miami."

John nodded his head and climbed down. He picked up Nicole's suitcase and began the walk back to the hotel. The wap, wap, wap of the rotor blades got faster and faster as the Coast Guard helicopter became airborne and turned toward Miami.

Dr. George put his arm around John to comfort him. He knew it must be hard on him not knowing his son's fate. On the way back to the hotel the doctor asked if John would meet him at the marina along with a couple of other fellows to describe what had happened to Johnny. He explained there had been other attacks recently and he was becoming concerned for the safety of people in the area. "Certainly I will," John said as he left for the hotel to gather the groups' belongings and check out.

While in the room, he called his wife to inform her of the situation. She cried in disbelief, "John, why must you two always be living so dangerously?"

John knew it was just her emotions speaking and the last thing he needed right now was to feel guilty and take blame for what had happened. Very calmly he replied, "Darling, if we were hang gliding and Johnny crashed I would have to agree; however, diving for lobster is one of the tamest things we do." He continued, "I love you and we don't need to fight right now. All of our thoughts and prayers need to be focused on helping Johnny get better." Realizing her husband was right, she calmed down and listened as he told her Johnny was being transported to Mt. Sinai Medical Center. After telling his wife how much he loved her, he advised her to drive carefully, and then prepared for his journey home.

The crew from Child Support had been eating lunch at the Compleat Angler when the terrorized crew from the Dear John pulled into the marina. Kit had been away in their dinghy on a local shallow water drive measuring conch and recording data.

Now everyone returned and had gathered on the docks to look at the blood-spattered vessel and wonder what had happened.

"Someone must have been run over by a propeller or attacked by a shark," speculated one of the locals. Dr. George approached the crowd and noticed his newfound friends were among the onlookers. "Trevor! Kit! Carla!" he shouted.

"May I have a word with you?" He called them aside not wanting to cause panic among the locals.

"Do you mind if we go someplace quiet to talk?" he asked the group in a whisper.

"We can go to the Black Gold," Carla quickly suggested with no dissension from the group. They walked to where the vessel was moored and seated themselves in her spacious stateroom.

Dr. George began the narration. "Several hours ago our worst fears came true – another person was attacked by a large barracuda. A young man named Johnny was returning to the family's boat with a catch bag full of lobsters tied to his waist when a large barracuda charged at him slightly missing the catch bag, removing a portion of his thigh, and severing his femoral artery." Carla's hands flew up to her mouth.

Feeling sickened from the description, her face became pale and her body began to tremble. Even though her wound had healed and the stitches removed, it would be a long time before she could forget the terror of the attack.

"I'm sorry my dear," Dr. George said, when he realized Carla was not yet over the trauma of her attack.

"Are you okay Carla?" he asked, feeling foolish about his insensitivity.

"I'm okay Dr. George. I guess I just have a vivid imagination and I was thinking about how that could have been me."

Suddenly, Dr. George stood up and made his way to the main dock. "John!" He shouted.

Willy and John's arms were loaded down with suitcases. They turned to see who was shouting as Dr. George came running up. "I know you want to be at your son's side as soon as possible, but could you please take a minute to describe to my friends exactly what happened?"

The three of them carried the suitcases to Carla's boat and placed them on the deck outside while they joined the group. After saying hello they recounted the day's events.

"This has gone on long enough God Dammit!" Trevor said with fire in his eyes. "I'm going to catch that bastard if it's the last thing I do!

"I'm offering a $10,000.00 reward to the first person to bring him in," John added.

"Gentlemen," Kit said, hoping to stop a lynching. "This fish did not attack these people intentionally. It was more a case of mistaken identity."

Trevor became enraged hearing Kit defend the barracuda.

"That fish earned his death certificate when he attacked Carla as far as I'm concerned," Trevor said, looking at Carla.

"Don't' you care about what he did to her?" Trevor asked, turning to stare Kit in the eyes.

"Of course I do!" Kit shouted back. "Its just a fish this large is a rare find, and it's a shame to kill it when it was simply acting on instinct."

Kit was trying to make a point, although he knew everyone in the room disagreed with him – even his fiancé. It didn't help having Trevor make it appear as though he didn't care about Carla's safety.

John was eager to be at his son's side and so he bid farewell to the group.   Before exiting the parlor, he reaffirmed his offer, "Don't forget. If anyone delivers that fish to me I'll give him or her a $10,000 reward – I'd love to have that cuda hanging over my fireplace!" Trevor stood up and looked at Kit saying, "I've got to go get ready – the Child Support is going hunting tomorrow."

"Good luck," Carla said smiling at Trevor as he left. Kit became angry with this and yelled to Trevor as he walked down the dock, "Go ahead if it makes you feel like more of a man to pick on a defenseless fish!" Trevor didn't even turn around, he just waved him off, thinking his first chore was to get a chart and pin point the fish attacks to identify the fishes territory.

Doctor George was feeling guilty as he walked back home. He couldn't find the nerve to tell the visitors about the attack on the little Cuban girl, Mary. If the Commissioner had listened to him and posted warnings Johnny may have not been injured. He hoped that the reward money that John had offered would increase the chances of this fish being caught and destroyed.

Back on the Black Gold trouble was brewing. Kit returned to the parlor and began questioning Carla about her lack of support.

"So you think it's right to kill an innocent fish?" Kit asked Carla hoping to make her understand his position. She had always loved the creatures of the sea, so he was unable to comprehend why she was behaving this way.

"Kit, that fucking fish almost ate my leg for breakfast!" Carla said, using language Kit was unaccustomed to. She continued her tirade.

"He's killed one man, and possibly another! He's a menace to society, can't you accept that?"

Kit thought for a minute, and then replied, "I'm terribly sorry about what has happened, but in each instance the victim had possibly been mistaken for prey.

Carla, still angry about Kit's indifference to her feelings, said, "I think you'd feel different if you were the one that got attacked or I had been the one flown to Miami in a helicopter."

Kit knew arguing was useless, Carla would never understand his feelings and he doubted whether he could truly ever understand hers. He walked over to Carla and hugged her saying, "You know how much I love you, and I would never want anything bad to happen to you."

Carla remained cold and stiff, unwilling to look into Kit's eyes. She broke free from his arms and said, "I'd like a little time by myself, I don't know if I should be mad – I need some time to think."

Carla slipped on her sandals and grabbed her waist bag containing her wallet from the counter. "I'll be back in a little while," she said as she exited the parlor.

Kit watched in silence not knowing what to say and wondering where Carla was going.

"See you in a little while," he said, hoping her time away would crumble the wall that had come between them.

Kit wasn't a big drinker, but right now it sounded like a damn good idea! He reached into the bar cabinet pulled out a bottle and began reading the label out loud, "Barbencourt Rum aged in oak barrels eight years, 43% ALCOHOL BY VOLUME (86 PROOF)."

That should do the trick, he thought to himself. Next he looked for a glass, but changed his mind saying, "Fuck it!" Quickly he removed the lid and took a big swig. "Whew!" he said as the first sip exploded in his lungs and stomach. He hadn't done that since his college days, but it felt good knowing soon the alcohol would start taking effect, numbing the emotional pain he was feeling right now.

Carla wasn't sure where to go during her being alone time, but she brought her wallet just in case she wanted a drink.

I'll go to the Compleat Angler and have a couple of drinks to calm down and make him worry a little bit, Carla thought to herself. Maybe we've got cabin fever from living on the boat so long.

Chapter 16

When Carla walked through the doorway, the sound of people having a good time flooded her ears. Most of it was coming from a group sitting in the back. As her eyes adjusted to the combination of smoke and low lighting, she realized who the culprits were.

Trevor and his crew were seated at a table, surveying a nautical map of Bimini and the adjacent waters. She wasn't sure she wanted to be around anyone right now, but it was too late, Trevor had noticed her walk in, and was motioning her over to the table.

Carla wished she had put on a bra, because all the men were staring at her chest as she neared the group. Trevor stood up and pulled out a chair for her saying, "Have a seat, we're making plans to catch that bastard of a barracuda." Carla sat down and studied the map, noticing several areas had been circled with a red marker and then connected to surround the area between them.

Trevor noticed her staring at the map and began explaining it to her, "Those circles are where the barracuda attacks have occurred: one here at the docks, the second off the Mosell Banks, and the third one south of here." We figure he's in this area, and we're going to fish there until he's caught."

Carla felt a tap on her shoulder—she hadn't noticed the waitress standing behind her. "Can I get you somethin' darlin'?" the waitress asked smiling.

"I'll have what they're having," she replied. The waitress looked at Trevor and asked, "Should I bring another round?"

"Yeah, and this lady's money is no good here!" he replied.

Carla smiled and said, "That isn't necessary, I brought money."

Trevor winked and said, "I've got to pay for those guys' drinks," pointing to Dave and Richie. "And you're a helluva lot better looking than they are!" Dave and Richie raised their glasses and clinked them together in a toast, saying, "I'll drink to that."

After a couple of more rounds of drinks, Dave and Richie had started to nod out. They had been sanding and refinishing some woodwork on the Chris-Craft earlier that day and the combination of fatigue and alcohol was taking its toll. Trevor and Carla were busy talking when Dave's head came crashing to the table. The clanking glasses woke Richie up and prevented everyone at the table from experiencing deja` vu.

Dave looked up, a little embarrassed and said, "Wow man, what a rush!"

Trevor, annoyed at the interruption, suggested Dave and Richie return to the vessel before he had to carry them back.

"Later man," Dave and Richie said as they headed back to the boat.

"Later," Trevor answered, and then turned his attention back to Carla.

"So, where's Kit?" He asked.

Carla, surprised by the question, took a couple of minutes to formulate her answer.

"Oh, he's doing some research. So I told him I was getting cabin fever and I was going out for a beer."

After what happened earlier that day and the uneasy way Carla answered the question, Trevor figured she was lying.

"Well, I'm glad he let you out. I've really enjoyed talking with you. Would you like another drink?"

Carla thought about it and realized how wonderful the rum was making her feel, then answered, "Sure, why not?"

They continued their discussion of literary subjects, such as editors, agents and publishers. Trevor promised to help her get published, if her writing was as good as her discussions of it.

Before they knew it, they had consumed two more rounds of drinks. At this point they were in their own world, oblivious to the other patrons of the bar, their worries and troubles, and unfortunately their morals.

Carla noticed throughout the evening how handsome Trevor actually was. A little gray hair in a man was attractive, she thought. Combine this with his literary brilliance and you have a natural aphrodisiac.

No woman had turned Trevor on this much in years. Why, just sitting next to her, made him feel a tingling or throbbing in his groin. His mind began to imagine what it would be like to make love to her young supple body.

Carla's speech had begun to slur and she knew it was time to stop drinking. Her next idea came from the blue.

"You wanna go swim-zing?"

"What?" Trevor asked.

"I said, do you wanna go swim-zing?"

Trevor finally figured out what she was trying to say "swimming" and replied, "I don't have a suit with me."

Carla laughed and said, "Who needs a bathing suit, silly?"

Trevor couldn't believe Carla was asking him to go skinny-dipping, but he wasn't going to waste any time taking her up on her offer. Quickly, he took out his wallet and slapped a hundred-dollar bill on the table without a thought about the overpayment. Carla had already started staggering toward the door, he was quick to catch up and take her by the hand.

The night was beautiful, a full moon with a light ocean breeze caressing the beach. The only noise was the couple's giggles as they attempted to remove their clothes.

At one point Trevor's foot got caught on his underwear and he fell backward into the sand, which was still warm from the intense daytime sun's heat. Carla's clothes came off easily because she wore no undergarments. After seeing Trevor fall in the sand, she pounced on him like a wrestler, giggling as she pinned his arms back.

"You're pinned," she said, laughing hysterically. Her breasts were hanging perilously close to Trevor's mouth and he couldn't resist leaning forward to take one of her nipples into his mouth. Carla, horny from the alcohol, moaned with pleasure and sat down on his groin area. Trevor's mouth and tongue moved from breast to breast, not wanting to make either feel cheated. He could feel her vulva heat up and moisten, causing his manhood to stiffen and throb under her weight.

Carla, consumed in passion, reached down and guided him into her moistness. Wildly, she began moving her pelvis with no thoughts or guilt about what she was doing – that would come later. Even though they were both intoxicated, within minutes both of them were coming. Carla collapsed on top of Trevor while her body convulsed with pleasure.

Suddenly, she jumped up and ran into the warm surf. The water took over where Trevor left off, gently caressing her body. She yelled to Trevor, but he didn't respond. Probably passed out, she guessed.

The physical activity and the water had started, unfortunately, to make her come back to reality and realize what had just happened.

Don't panic! she told herself.

You'll have to pretend like this never happened and hope that Trevor understood he had only experienced her passion in a weak moment and in a drunken stupor. Carla laid back into the water and floated, to give herself time to sober up.

Chapter 17

Barracudas are considered diurnal by nature, except on nights when the moon is full. Normally it would be hovering several feet from the ocean's floor in a sleep mode, waiting for daylight to continue its incessant search for food. However, the moonlight tonight was bright enough to permit navigation in the shallows off the beach.

A splashing in the water had attracted it to an area not far from where Carla was enjoying her moonlight swim, and now the shimmering of finger mullet brought it even closer. In a flash, it charged and the frightened school of fish spread out jumping in all directions. Several fish inadvertently rammed into Carla, startling her. Adrenaline pumping, she flew out of the water, realizing some type of predator had caused the mullet to scramble. Remembering the cuda was still at large made her think, "That's two stupid mistakes I made tonight."

She tried once more, unsuccessfully, to wake Trevor. It was no use; he was so relaxed he began to snore. Carla had to go, but realized she at least had to try to cover his naked body. Looking down, she spied his boxer shorts still hanging on his left ankle. Unbunching them, she fed his right foot through the boxers and inched them up his legs. When she got them up to his torso she had to roll him to either side in order to get them pulled up to his waist. Carefully, she covered him up with his shirt and shorts, not wanting to attempt dressing him completely. This should keep him from getting arrested for indecent exposure, she thought.

Carla turned to walk up the beach. Halfway up to the road she realized that in all of the excitement she had forgotten to get dressed. "Oops," she murmured, "Lady Godiva, you'd better put your own clothes on." Quickly she ran to her pile of clothes, shook out the sand, and put them on.

She jogged back to the boat because she knew it had to be getting late. The whole way back she worried about what she was going to tell Kit once she got there.

The lights in the parlor were still on. Bad sign, she thought. Once inside, she breathed a sigh of relief. Kit was passed out on the couch, still clutching an almost empty bottle of Barbencourt Rum.

Quickly, she went into the head and turned on the shower. She grabbed her douche bag from the cabinet and began to fill it with warm water. Cleansing herself would clear the evidence of Trevor from her body, but not from her mind. She washed herself thoroughly, hoping to wipe any trace of the evening away.

After showering, she put on a robe and went into the parlor. She grabbed the bottle from Kit's hands and placed a sheet over him. Next, she shut off the lights and went to bed. However, before falling asleep, she thought about the events of the evening. Carla loved Kit dearly and felt bad about what had happened. Although it had been very exciting to screw someone else, she knew it was wrong.

She began thinking about Trevor being inside her, and her clit began to throb. Unable to stop herself, she reached down and began to caress it. In seconds her body was convulsing, and her mind was in a dreamy state, where nothing mattered. Her body spent, she fell into a deep sleep.

Chapter 18

The sun had risen a quarter of the way into a intense, powder blue, sky, when a moist tongue gently licking the salt crystals from Trevor's neck woke him up.

His eyes refused to work initially, because the bright light had the intensity and effect of a camera's flash on them. Once his eyes were open and functioning, he saw his lover, a scraggly old dog, standing over him with his tail wagging.

"Stop it boy," he said calmly, knowing this dog wouldn't hurt a flea. He then sat up, his shirt falling into his lap. When he picked it up, he noticed his shorts were also lying there. Dazed and confused he asked himself, "Why am I sleeping on the beach with my clothes off?" Slowly, from his subconscious, flashbacks of Carla's supple breasts hanging in his face came to mind.

Boy, you must have been drunk not to remember those puppies right away, he thought.

A little ways off, two local kids were pointing at him and laughing.

What a sight I must be, he thought.

Slowly Trevor put his clothes on and brushed the sand from his face and hair. When he stood up his head started pounding and he almost passed out.

After regaining his composure, he started back to the boat, hoping no one would see him on the way. Trevor wondered whether Carla had made it home safely. He felt bad about sleeping with another man's woman, but he was only human and unable to say no to a woman like Carla. Besides, he thought, it was only the booze. She never would have cheated on Kit while sober.

He knew however, he would never be able to look at her the same, knowing she had given herself to him, no matter what the circumstances.

When he reached the boat, Richie and Dave were still sleeping. They were both snoring, but despite their annoying duet, he knew he wouldn't have any trouble joining them. He went to sleep knowing it would probably only be for a few hours, until activity in the marina created enough noise to bring him back to consciousness.

Chapter 19

It had been four hours since the Coast Guard helicopter carrying Johnny's unconscious body touched down at Mt. Sanai's helipad. Immediately a crack trauma crew met them and transported Johnny to an operating room.

His vital signs were weak, but stable. The blood-starved leg had grown pale and lifeless. A vascular surgeon had been called in to try to restore blood flow to the limb. The surgery went well, but Johnny's leg was given a 50/50 chance of survival. Nervously, Nicole and Johnny's mom, Karen, waited in the recovery room.

Karen was terribly upset, wondering how something so terrifying had happened to her only child. She turned to Nicole, her voice trembling and said, "Those two have given me gray hair worrying about them. Why do they have to live so dangerously?"

Nicole, trying to calm Karen down, said, "Karen, Johnny's going to be fine, we got him here as fast as we could, and the doctor is optimistic about his leg."

Karen replied, "You were the only smart one, you didn't go in the water."

Quickly Nicole said without thinking, "I wasn't going in the water after I heard there was a barracuda in the area that big!"

"What?" Karen exclaimed. "You mean they knew about the cuda and still went diving? If anything happens to Johnny, I'll never forgive his father."

The seas were only 1 to 2 feet when John left Bimini bound for Ft. Lauderdale. He was on a mission – get home as soon as possible. The throttles were pushed forward almost all the way, causing the twin 250 HP Yamaha outboards to scream through the water. Normally he would use the autopilot to navigate, but at this speed he had to be alert and in full control. As vast as the sea is, there were always objects appearing in your path, such as the old discarded refrigerator, floating just below the surface that he had grazed on a previous trip.

Speeding along at almost 50 mph, he estimated the trip should take a little over an hour and a half. John still couldn't believe a barracuda had attacked his son. It was a nightmare, and it kept playing over and over in his mind during the trip home.

His first duty was to make sure his son was safe and given medical attention. His second duty was to get revenge. No fish was going to cause this much pain and trouble in his life without paying for it. John almost hoped no one would catch the fish until he came back to try himself. He knew once the word got out about the $10,000 reward there would be many fishermen out after the fish.

Suddenly the 35-ft. boat became airborne, then slammed back down on the ocean's surface with a crash. Quickly John pulled back on the throttles to prevent a second occurrence. Unfortunately, the Gulfstream was producing slightly larger waves such that traveling at top speed was no longer possible without damaging the boat's hull. John cursed out loud knowing it was only for his own benefit—there was no one else around to hear it. His trip would now take slightly longer than expected, but still faster than any previous trip.

Once in Port Everglades he telephoned customs and explained what had happened, knowing full well if they chose to search his boat, he could do nothing to stop it. So far, customs had never inspected his vessel and he was hoping today would be no different. He didn't feel like sitting at the dock for hours waiting for them to arrive.

A half an hour later, John was at the hospital with Karen and Nicole. Johnny was now in ICU and could be visited by family members only.

The doctor came into the waiting room to inform the family of Johnny's status. Karen, upon seeing the doctor, stood up and took her husband's arm, tugged him over to the doctor and said, "Doctor this is my husband John."

The doctor reached his hand out and said, "Dr. Kielly, nice to meet you, but I'm sure not under these circumstances."

John quickly grabbed the doctor's hand, asking, "How's my boy?"

"He's stable and we've got him on antibiotics. The blood supply to his limb was cut off a little longer than I'd like, but there's a chance he won't lose it. I had to take a small piece of artery from the other leg and some tissue from his buttocks to try to repair the damage. At this time all we can do is wait and see how the limb reacts. However, the first sign of gangrene and his leg has to come off."

With this news John turned and hugged his wife, burying his head in her neck so the doctor wouldn't see him bawling like a baby.

The doctor patted him on the back, and said, "Don't give up yet. We've got hours before we make that decision. He's in ICU resting if you guys want to go see him."

John dried his eyes on his shirtsleeve and replied, "Thanks doc."

The three walked into Johnny's room and saw him lying there, IV's in both hands, a drain tube running down from his leg, and all sorts of monitors arranged behind his bed.

His color was much improved and when Nicole grabbed his hand, he lightly squeezed hers back.

In a low groggy voice Johnny asked, "Where am I?"

His mom replied, "You're at Mount Sinai Hospital in Miami. You've had an operation on your leg to repair damage from the cuda attack."

Johnny's eyes opened wide, and all that came from his mouth was, "Shit!"

He began to sit up, but was held down by his father gently pushing on his shoulders and saying, "Just take it easy son. You've got to rest, you're not out of the woods yet-- and don't worry about that fish, he's as good as dead."

Nicole started stroking Johnny's head and within minutes he was resting comfortably.

The family discussed their plans, and it was decided that someone should stay at the hospital at all times. Karen would be the first to stay, so Nicole and John could go home and shower.

Several hours later, John and Nicole returned to the hospital. The three of them spent the next two hours patiently standing vigil over Johnny, and pondering over the events of the day. Finally, Nicole suggested John and Karen go home and get some sleep, promising to call them if anything new developed.

Nicole, lulled to sleep by the gentle beeping of the heart monitor, awoke at 7:00 a.m. and opened her eyes to see a doctor examining Johnny's leg. The doctor noticed Nicole was awake and said, "I'm sorry did I wake you?"

"No, don't be silly."

"How's he doing?" She asked as she stood to take a look.

Before the doctor could reply, Nicole stood up and studied the injury. The sight of it made her cringe. The skin had been pulled tightly and stapled and a drain tube was protruding from the end of the wound. The tissue from where the tourniquet had been applied and on down was an odd color, rather yellowish, and a faint red line was starting to form above the wound running upward toward Johnny's groin.

The doctor quickly covered up the leg and answered Nicole's question.

"He's still stable, although his leg doesn't seem to be responding favorably to the surgery."

With this news, Nicole started sobbing uncontrollably. Johnny woke up with all the noise and asked why Nicole was crying. She went over and hugged him and said, "I'm just upset at seeing you lying here with all these tubes in you." The doctor timidly said, "I'll leave you two alone for a little while, but I'll be back to check on you shortly."

Johnny looked at his beautiful wife and said, "Don't worry honey. We'll be jogging down the beach together in a couple of weeks." This statement made Nicole want to cry even harder, but she knew she must be strong for Johnny's sake. She dried her eyes and laid her head on his chest saying, "You're right darling. I love you so much."

A half an hour or so later, John and Karen walked in. Johnny greeted them, "Good morning."

Glad to see his son so alert and talking John asked, "How do you feel son?"

Johnny thought about it, then answered, "I feel like I've been run over by a Mack truck."

His mom not satisfied with this answer, asked, "Johnny, how does your leg feel?"

He strained for a minute causing some movement under the sheet and said, "I guess I'm a little worried because I don't feel anything as far as my leg is concerned. However, the other leg and my butt hurt."

John explained to Johnny why he was feeling pain in the other areas, so he wouldn't move around too much.

After a while three doctors entered the room. They politely asked the family to wait outside. The team included the vascular surgeon that operated on Johnny, his partner, and a blood specialist. Carefully they examined and performed several tests on him. The blood specialist withdrew a specimen while Johnny joked about not taking too much, because he couldn't spare any after almost bleeding to death the day before.

When the doctors left the room Johnny's father confronted them, "What's going on with my son?"

The vascular surgeon replied Mr.... I'm sorry I don't recall your name.

"Hartwig, John Hartwig," John replied.

The doctor continued, "Mr. Hartwig, we've got to run a few tests, and then I'll meet with you in an hour or so.

"Can you at least tell me how my son is progressing?" John asked in a pleading manner.

The doctor answered uneasily, "I'd rather not say until we have the test results."

John looked the doctor in the eye and said, "If you know any specialists that may be able to help, call them—money is no object."

"I'll remember that.   However, myself and my colleagues are considered some of the best in the field," replied the doctor confidently.

The family returned to Johnny's room. Nicole turned on the TV, trying to lessen the anxiety brought on by the wait for Johnny's test results. America's Funniest Videos was on and it usually caused them to chuckle, but right now nobody felt like laughing. After a while, Johnny dozed off, and John excused himself to the rest room.

On the way back, the vascular surgeon saw him in the hallway and asked him to go where they could talk in private. John sat down, preparing himself for the news, good or bad.

The doctor started out; "I was quite pleased with the surgery; however, I was concerned about the length of time Johnny's leg had gone without proper blood flow. I'm sorry to tell you, but we— the other doctors and myself, feel it would be in Johnny's best interest to amputate the leg."

"What? You've got to be kidding!" John shouted angrily.

The doctor quickly tried to calm the irate father.

"I know you're upset, but the blood tests show his injured leg could be poisoning the rest of his body."

"No, no, no!" John said pounding his fists on his knees.

"This can't be happening—my boy, an amputee!"

"Mr. Hartwig!" The doctor said sternly. "Your strength and support is what Johnny needs now. The operation needs to take place as soon as possible, so we don't endanger the young man's life."

The doctor quieted his tone, saying, "He needs to be told. Would you like to tell him or should I?"

"I'll tell him," John said, fighting back tears.

John rose slowly and the doctor placed his arm around his shoulders in a conciliatory act. John dreaded having to tell his son about the doctor's decision because he knew Johnny's life would never be the same and this weighed heavy on his soul.

The look on his face when he entered the room must have alerted his wife something was wrong.

"What's the matter dear?"

"Nothing," he replied, and then asked quietly, "Can I please talk to Johnny alone?"

"Why, what's wrong?" Karen asked nervously.

"I'll talk to you later, but right now I need to talk to Johnny alone. "Okay?"

The women left the room, both stopping to kiss Johnny on the forehead before leaving. John sat on the bed and took his son's hand. Johnny looked at his dad – he'd been preparing for this moment since regaining consciousness. He had overheard the doctors discussing the condition of his blood-starved limb, and recently there had been a strange odor seeping from under the sheet. It was like the odor from an empty bloody chicken package that's been left in the kitchen trash a bit too long.

"They're going to take my leg aren't they dad?" Johnny said, while staring at the ceiling.

"Yes, son."

Johnny sat silently for a moment then blurted out, "I can't believe that fucking barracuda attacked me!"

John put his hand on Johnny's shoulder saying, "Don't worry as soon as you're on your way to wellness, I'm going to catch that son of a bitch and hang him on a wall. But that's if someone else doesn't kill him first. I offered a $10,000 reward before I left Bimini."

Upon hearing this, Johnny shouted, "Dad, neither killing that fish nor all the money in the world can replace my leg!"

John knew what his son said was true; however, he had worked with many shark-like people in the business world and had learned how to deal with them—this fish was no different. Nothing was going to fuck with his world without paying the price.

"Son, I'm going to tell your mother. Would you like me to send Nicole in so you can tell her?"

Johnny started crying. In-between the tears and the heaving chest movements, he managed to say, "I just want to be alone right now. Would you all just go—and could you please tell Nicole about this – I can't tell her that her husband is about to become an amputee."

"Sure son. Whatever you want."

Then he thought for a short while and said, "Johnny you're going to make it through this. You've always been good at whatever you do. We'll get you the best prosthetic money can buy and you'll still be able to accomplish whatever you put your mind to."

Johnny stopped crying and smiled, then said "Dad it's been a while since I told you this, but I love you."

"I love you too, son," John replied, then left the room.

John took Karen and Nicole to the hospital's cafeteria for coffee. After they got their drinks, he told them about Johnny's situation. They were both upset, but not surprised, because the appearance of Johnny's leg had deteriorated over the last twelve hours.

The nurses entered the room and began unhooking the various wires and tubes from Johnny's body. He was then rolled into the operating room and prepared for surgery.

As the anesthesia began to work, Johnny started to dream he was in the ocean. From his peripheral vision he saw the barracuda coming – however, this time in slow motion. It seemed to take forever. The cuda's mouth was wide open, exposing its rapacious teeth. When it hit Johnny's leg, he jumped, feeling the terror and pain being played out all over again.

The surgeon had placed the scalpel on the amputation site and had begun to cut though the tissue when Johnny's body jerked high into the air. He looked at the anesthesiologist and said, "Is he under, Bob?" The anesthesiologist checked all the monitors and I V s and replied, "You should be able to do whatever you want to do to him right now. Maybe that was an unconscious reflex, poor guy."

Chapter 20

The morning light found its way into Trevor's cabin and focused its light as if through a magnifying glass to the center of his face. His first reaction was to cover his face with the thin cotton sheet. No use, he thought. If it's that high in the sky, it must be time to get up.

His mouth and throat felt like they had been put through the same process that produces beef jerky, but he knew it was from the slow and steady evaporation of alcohol from his system. Trevor tried repeatedly to force fluid from beneath his tongue to satisfy the thirsty tissue inside his mouth. Whatever fluid he did produce, was quickly soaked up like a drop of water on a dry sponge. If nothing else, he had to get some water – lots of water. As he raised his body up two more things became apparent. First, his head was pounding like a big bass drum and each blow of the mallet made his eyes feel as though they would pop from their sockets. Second, all the fluid he drank the night before was impatiently waiting in his bladder to exit his body. The pain in his groin told him the boat's head was the first stop on his agenda.

Trevor slowly made his way to the head, and while passing through the doorway, he forgot to duck and banged his head. "Ouch – shit!" He cursed, rubbing the top of his head and thinking, you'd think I'd know to duck by now.

Once inside, he had to wait for an erection to subside, one of the side effects of having an overly full bladder. Unfortunately, his first spurt of urine missed and splashed all over the commode. "Son of a bitch!" Trevor said, as he concentrated on aiming so the rest would go where it belonged.

Afterwards, he turned on the shower and rinsed away the mess. At least the cleanup is easy in a boat, he thought.

As he exited the head, Dave woke up from all the noise and asked, "Trevor, you okay?"

Trevor replied, "Yeah – I just banged my friggin' head and pissed all over the commode. I'm going for some Tylenol – you want some?"

"Yeah – sounds good."

Next, Richie, barely audible because his head was buried under his pillow, said, "I'll take some too man."

Trevor opened the Tylenol bottle and emptied six capsules onto the table. He grabbed Evian water from the refrigerator and popped two of the pills into his mouth. It seemed no matter how much he drank nothing could eliminate the dryness in his mouth. However, hangovers were nothing new to him, so he knew this would soon pass.

Trevor scooped up the rest of the capsules and grabbed three more waters, one more for himself, and one each for Dave and Richie.

"I guess we won't be going fishing today, but I'd like to take a look at the condition of the line on the Penn reels and make up some extra heavy rigs before tomorrow," Trevor said, as he threw out his second water bottle.

"Sure boss," Richie answered.

Dave added, "Trevor, I saw some finger mullets hanging around the end of the dock yesterday. Maybe I'll try to cast net some at dusk if they're still there tonight."

"Great, that'll make some good bait," Trevor replied.

Chapter 21

Kit woke up feeling a bit disoriented after finding himself sleeping in his clothes on the couch in the yacht's parlor. When the pounding in his head stopped, he remembered the events of the previous evening.

Suddenly his heart started racing when he realized he didn't know if Carla had returned home safely or if she had even returned home at all. Quickly, he ran to the master cabin only to find Carla sleeping like a baby.

Kit removed his clothes and slid in beside her. She was on her side facing away from him. Slowly, he slid into a spooning position next to her naked body, afraid to wake her, but unable to control his desire to be near her. Within seconds he was hard and his penis was throbbing against her butt cheeks.

"Not now, honey I need to sleep," she said in an aggravated voice and rolled onto her stomach.

Kit's erection dissipated, realizing that he might piss her off more than she already was if he persisted. So he laid back and thought about their fight from the previous evening. It was stupid to fight over a fish, and he knew no one, not even Carla, was going to accept the way he felt about the situation.

The movie Jaws and the fear it created just about put sharks on the endangered species list. Man has no idea what indiscriminately killing predatory fish could mean to the ocean's fragile ecosystem, he thought.

His thoughts changed to the previous evening and he contemplated about Carla getting angry and leaving him alone with his rum bottle. Kit then began to wonder where she went and what she did. Why, he didn't even know what time she got home! But he knew the way Carla was – he could never ask her, because she would accuse him of not trusting her. He would have to wait for her to tell him.

She probably went to the Compleat Angler, got drunk, came home and went to sleep. Yeah, that's what she did. She left, blew off a little steam, and now she's going to make up with me when she wakes up. His scenario of what happened brought a feeling of relief.

Unable to fall asleep, Kit decided to get some research done. Quietly he grabbed a pair of blue speedos and a T-shirt from the dresser.   Next, he went to the galley and grabbed a half-gallon container of milk, opened the lid and drank half of the contents. Carla would kick his butt if she saw him do this, but it was a bad habit he picked up in college and sometimes he regressed.

He only had a slight hangover, probably because he took a break during his rum chugging to eat a whole bag of Lay's potato chips and a ham and swiss on rye. In addition, he had passed out relatively early feeling the effects of the rum

Kit assembled the equipment he needed for the excursion: a mask, snorkel, fins, underwater writing tablet for taking notes, tape measure, and specimen vials. He put the equipment in the 13-foot Boston Whaler, released the tie downs, swung the dinghy over the water and then slowly lowered it into the water with the electric wench.

Next, he climbed into the boat and pumped the primer bulb on the gas line, engaged the choke, and turned the key for the starter. The 25 horsepower Mercury outboard spit out a couple of clouds of blue smoke and then started, running roughly at first, but smoothing out as it warmed up.

Kit felt like he was forgetting something, but he couldn't remember what it was. He idled from the marina and after reaching open waters, pushed the throttle lever forward bringing the boat up on a plane.

The Bahamian waters are beautiful. The outer lying waters are a royal blue due to the great depths that occur, and the shallow waters along the shoreline are a bright emerald green. Most of the time the waters are crystal clear, unless stirred up by a passing storm.

Today, Kit was heading to Bimini Bay; shallow waters cradled by North and South Bimini. This area was harvested for conch during the 1950s and 60s. After the conch was gone, the harvesters moved elsewhere. Kit was going to see if the discontinuation of commercial harvesting in the bay had lead to an increase in the size and number of the conch inhabitants. The trip didn't take long because the marina was actually located on the perimeter of Bimini Bay.

Kit pulled back the throttle bringing the boat back to an idle. He hoped to spot conch from the surface before anchoring. Within minutes, he observed some small humps on the ocean floor, only identifiable by their slight difference in color and three-dimensional shapes.

Quickly, he turned off the engine and tossed a small sand anchor over the side. Kit removed his T-shirt and jewelry and carefully rolled them up and placed them in a safe, dry spot under the center console. Next, he grabbed his mask, spat in it, rinsed it with salt water, and placed it on his head. Finally he grabbed the rest of the gear, jumped into the water, and put on his flippers after placing the tape measure inside his speedos for safe keeping.

The first conch was fairly small, probably less than a year old. When he picked it up and turned it over to inspect it, the conch's long brown toenail was flailing back and forth trying desperately to escape while Kit measured its shell.

"Don't worry little conch, I'm just going to measure you."

After writing down the data, Kit moved on to the next conch. This one was slightly larger and reacted the same way to Kit's examination.

As he placed the second conch back to the ocean floor, a large shadow passed overhead. Somewhat startled, Kit looked up to see an exceptionally huge barracuda. He immediately had to start calming himself down. I don't have anything shiny on, and I don't have any food odors – so I should be okay. Kit slowly swam to the surface, keeping the fish in sight at all times. He swam with as little motion as possible, hoping this would keep the large fish from becoming excited.

The barracuda had just charged through a school of snapper feeding under the mangrove trees. The sound of the outboard motor had aroused its curiosity. Its first pass had not picked up any reflections or scents indicative of prey. However, it did see a large, blurry, object, probably another predator, but it would cruise by one more time just to make sure.

Kit watched as the massive cuda got almost out of sight; then turned and slowly swam back towards him. His heart started pounding while he wondered what would happen if this fish decided to attack. The cuda maintained his slow steady pace, his lower jaw opening and closing with each swish of his tail.

Kit remained perfectly still hoping the cuda wouldn't notice him and swim right by. The cuda cruised by so close that Kit could have reached out and touched him.

What a magnificent fish he thought to himself. He had to be over 12 years old. His body was scarred, probably from other cudas and Kit noticed that its eyes had been damaged. They were clouded over, much like the eyes of someone with severe cataracts. He watched the barracuda swim off into the bay and used this opportunity to return to the safety of the boat.

The cuda hadn't sensed any indications of food, so it continued its patrol of the bay. The damage to its eyes several years ago had made the task of feeding itself more difficult. Had it not been for the years of hunting experience, it probably would have died.

Some vengeful marlin fishermen had impaired its vision. The cuda had made the mistake of swallowing one of their hooks. It lodged itself perfectly in the corner of its mouth, making it impossible to bite through line. It put up quite a fight, but was eventually hauled in through the tuna door. Once on board, the hook, having no pressure on it, fell from its mouth.

Not willing to give up his freedom, the cuda flipped around on the deck trying to escape. One of the men grabbed a bat and began pounding on the cuda's head screaming, "You'll think twice about eating our bait you bastard!" After beating the fish unconscious, he gaffed it and slid it out of the opening in the stern, thinking it was dead. The cuda fell into the water and sank twenty feet until it regained consciousness. One eye had taken the full blow of the bat causing complete blindness, and the other eye, the one facing the deck, had been damaged but was still able to make out shapes and reflected light.

Kit sat thinking about what had transpired while he waited for the adrenaline to wear off. Suddenly he thought that's it, that's why Carla and the other people were attacked! The barracuda can't see well. In every instance there was either a food source or a shiny object.

Carla woke up shortly after Kit left. She didn't remember him trying to wake her earlier or the noise from the Whaler starting up. She grabbed a T-shirt and panties, putting them on before going into the parlor. The couch was empty. Where was Kit, she thought? She looked for a note, but there was none. Panic started seeping into her mind – what if Kit found out what happened last night? Don't be silly. How could he find out? Trevor! She must talk to Trevor and explain last night was just a mistake and it must never happen again.

Quickly, she threw on some shorts and went to the head to brush her teeth. She had to wet her hair and brush it to smooth out the kinks from going to bed with it wet last night. Carla grabbed her Foster Grants, hoping to cover her bloodshot eyes and protect them from the bright sunlight.

The crew of the Child Support was hard at work preparing for the next day's fishing excursion. Trevor was sitting in a fighting chair reeling new line onto a deep-sea reel while Dave held the spool on a pencil, keeping tension with his thumb. Trevor looked up when something cast a shadow on his face. He smiled when he saw it was Carla.

"Hey Carla, what time did you guys leave last night?" Dave yelled

"Not long after you," Carla added quickly so Trevor understood no one was to know what happened last night.

"Trevor, could I talk to you for a minute?" Carla asked.

"Sure," Trevor said, placing the rod in a rod holder.

"I'll get a beer while you two chat," Dave said realizing Carla and Trevor wanted some privacy.

Trevor jumped up on the dock where Carla was standing; noting that even hung over she was beautiful.

Carla began by grabbing his hands and saying, "Trevor, you know last night was a mistake."

"No I didn't, but I guess I do now."

Carla continued, choosing not to look into Trevor's eyes, "You're a handsome, intelligent man, but I love Kit and I've promised to marry him. I apologize for misleading you, but sometimes I do stupid things when I drink too much. I hope we can remain friends, and I ask you to never tell anyone about what happened."

Trevor swallowed his pride, winked at Carla and said, "Sure thing, kid."

Carla hugged Trevor and asked if he'd seen Kit. He nodded toward the Black Gold. Carla saw Kit tying off the dinghy to a cleat. Trevor had seen Kit pulling up to the vessel and had even let Carla hug him knowing Kit was watching her every move.

Kit came running up to the couple and yelled, "Carla, what the hell's going on here?" Before Trevor could defend himself, Kit punched him in the mouth, knocking him to the ground. Carla jumped on Kit's back screaming, "Stop it Kit! What are you, fucking crazy?"

Kit, still wild with jealousy, yelled, "Why are you hugging my fiancée you asshole?"

Carla, thinking fast said, "He hugged me to comfort me. I was scared because I didn't know where you were!"

Trevor rubbed his jaw and began tasting blood flowing from a laceration on his lip. He thought about what Kit would do if he knew about what happened the previous evening.

"Kit, I want you to go back to the boat right now!" Carla said sternly.

"If you would have left me a note like I've asked you repeated times, this wouldn't have happened."

"I'm sorry," Kit said, halfhearted.

"But you better keep your fucking hands off my girlfriend, if you know what's good for you!" Kit said, getting the last word in before walking back to the boat.

Carla helped Trevor to his feet saying, "Thanks for not fighting back. Kit can be such an asshole sometimes."

"Yeah, yeah," Trevor said wiping his bloody lip on the bottom of his T-shirt. Carla kissed him on the cheek and said, "Thanks again." She left Trevor standing on the dock bleeding from both his lip and broken heart

Dave came out to see what the commotion was about and upon seeing blood on Trevor's shirt, and swollen lip, asked, "What the hell happened to you?"

"Ah, that punk kid thought I was trying to put the move on his girlfriend."

"Imagine that! You two looked pretty cozy last night," Dave said turning his back towards Trevor and reaching his arms around to give the illusion someone was hugging him. Dave couldn't resist one more jab; "By the way what time did you get home last night?"

Trevor replied, "It's none of your business!"

"I was just testing you. I woke up when I heard you stumble into your bunk. I hope his old lady didn't get home that late."

Trevor changed the subject immediately, "Are you going to play around all day? We'll never get this line changed at this rate, but let me grab a beer first, maybe it will stop this bleeding."

Trevor held the ice-cold bottle against his lip before opening it. His first sip was a combination of beer and blood. "Oh well, a fat lip was a small price to pay for one last hug," he thought.

Unfortunately, at his age almost every woman he met was attached to somebody or carried far too much baggage to deal with. Sometimes he had to take risks to satisfy his body's need for sex. All of the intimate encounters during the last few years had only been for sex, and not love. It was easier that way, no emotional attachment, no fear of being rejected or hurt. But Carla was different – somehow he had let himself feel things he hadn't let himself feel for a long time. For what, he asked himself? Only to be hurt, he told himself. He took another sip of beer and went out to help Dave change the line on the reels.

Back on the Black Gold, Kit nervously awaited Carla's return. He knew he was going to catch hell for what just happened and was planning to plead for forgiveness.

Minutes later Carla entered the boat's parlor. Quickly, Kit tried to apologize by saying, "Honey I'm sorry for the scene, but I love you so much, I just get crazy thinking about you with someone else!"

Carla thought I'm glad he doesn't know everything; he probably would have killed Trevor. She knew she had to do something to restore Kit's confidence in the relationship. She looked at Kit and was reminded of how handsome he was. He was wearing a T-shirt and Speedos. Kit was one of the few men she had seen that looked good in Speedos. He had round and muscular butt cheeks, and his package made most women sneak a peek whenever he wore his Speedos in public.

"I forgive you," Carla said walking up to Kit and reaching down to caress the bulge in his swimsuit. "Let's go to bed," she said in a guttural tone.

Standing before the bed the couple embraced. Kit reached down and grabbed the bottom edges of her shirt and slowly raised it over her head, exposing her full, round, breasts with nipples drawn tight and erect.

Kit lowered his head to rest his cheek on her right breast while his tongue and lips caressed the nipple of her left breast. Carla moaned with pleasure and after several minutes, began to remove Kit's shirt.

After their upper torsos were bare, they hugged and kissed, enjoying the warm sensations of bare flesh against bare flesh. Carla laid her head against the soft brownish blonde hair on Kit's chest, and then began trailing kisses lower and lower down his body.

She began to tease him once she reached his stomach, poking her tongue down inside the waistband of his Speedos and licking up to his belly button. Kit was fondling her breasts and moaning with his eyes closed, and his head tilted back.

The Speedos were no match for his highly excited penis because it appeared as though the package was about to unwrap itself. Carla, passion taking over her actions, was ready to stop teasing and get down to business. She grabbed the bulging Speedos and pulled them down, exposing a rock hard penis. Carla kissed it on the head and pushed Kit back onto the bed.

Once he was on his back, she positioned her head over his groin, her breasts hanging down, the nipples tickling his thighs and causing him to become even more aroused.

This act was more than oral sex to Carla. In her mind it was total submission to her partner. Although she enjoyed the activity, she was giving and he was receiving. However, this giving helped to eliminate some of the guilt she was experiencing from the previous night. It also kept Kit from entering her vagina, a place where Trevor had been only a few hours before. She was afraid, in a strange way that traces of Trevor still loomed inside her and somehow Kit would know.

She caressed Kit's penis with her tongue and lips, as she never had before. His body writhed with pleasure until she felt spasms occurring that signaled an orgasm. His penis ejaculated loads of hot cum into her mouth. Quickly, she swallowed it, taking only seconds to taste its unique flavor, and then laid her head to rest on his stomach.

After several minutes Carla noticed Kit's breathing had slowed, signaling sleep. Quietly she crawled up and took a position next to him, thinking a nap was not such a bad idea.

Chapter 22

Trevor and the rest of the crew spent the remainder of the day preparing for the next day's fishing adventure. After all the tasks were completed, Trevor suggested they get cleaned up and he'd treat them to dinner at the Compleat Angler. Dave showered first, and while the other two men took turns showering, he grabbed a cast net and bucket and headed to the east end of the dock where he had spotted finger mullets feeding the night before.

Dusk was rapidly approaching as the sun sank below the horizon. Sunsets were always more spectacular on the water, because the view was not hindered by buildings and trees.

By the time Dave got to the end of the dock, only the top edge of the sun was visible. Its fading shape seemed to submit to the darkening skies. Dave unwrapped the net and began positioning it to throw. He had already heard evidence of finger mullet around the docks, a small plopping sound caused by the frightened fish jumping.

He stood up, cast net ready to throw, and watched the school, waiting for them to come close. It seemed every time they got within range and he was ready to throw, they changed direction, delaying the cast. After several minutes the school finally swam close to the dock and Dave turned, skillfully tossing the net. When released, the spinning action caused the net to open wide and once in the water, it rapidly sank capturing the prey below. Quickly, Dave pulled in the net, causing the weights to draw up and catch several finger mullet.

He cursed once he had them on the dock, realizing he had forgotten to put some saltwater in the bucket. Rapidly, he dunked the bucket into the water filling it only halfway so the mullets wouldn't be able to jump out. He then dumped the mullet into the bucket counting eight fish as they plunked from the net. Not bad for my first cast, he thought to himself. Carefully he laid out the net and prepared for another throw. He was in no hurry, because he knew it would be several minutes before the frightened mullet would approach the dock again.

Once more Dave stood ready, watching the school, waiting for his next opportunity. One more good throw and his job would be finished.

Sometimes it seemed as though the fish knew he was there, teasing him with their movements in and out of range. But he knew fishing always required patience.

He stood for at least 10 minutes before an opportunity presented itself again. Rearing back, he tossed the net, but unfortunately some of the weights snagged together, keeping the net from opening fully. "Shit!" Dave yelled as he pulled in the net. Oh well, at least I got a couple, he thought as he dumped four mullet into the bucket.

It was now starting to get dark as Dave readied the net for a third try. The increasing darkness triggered the photosensitive switch turning on the marina lights, which extended his visibility on the dock and adjacent waters.

I've got a dozen and it's getting late – I'll take one more toss to see if I can get a couple more, he thought. His eyes strained to watch the school in the darkness; his view only slightly aided by the marina's lights. Slowly, the school meandered about until finally they swam into range.

Dave forcefully tossed the net – a perfect throw, but before the net hit the water a large fish blasted through the school scattering them in all directions. Dave, frustrated, pulled the net in cursing, "God damn it!"

He was amazed at the size and speed of the fish, thinking to himself, it was big enough to be a tarpon, but was much faster. Then he said out loud, "I'll bet it's that friggin' cuda!" Dave knew it was useless to try to net any more mullet so he rolled up the net and walked back to the boat.

Trevor and Richie were outside drinking a beer when Dave came walking up.

"How'd you do?" Trevor asked.

"Got a dozen, but I could have had more if it wasn't for that cuda."

"What do you mean?" Trevor said with a puzzled look on his face.

"On my last cast – it was perfect by the way – a large fish charged the school and spooked them. It had to be the cuda – too big and fast to be anything else."

Trevor's eyes lit up as he said, "Enjoy your last night of freedom my friend, because tomorrow your ass is mine!"

Richie raised his beer bottle and clanked it against Trevor's saying, "Damn straight!"

"You guys ready to get some grub?" Trevor asked.

"Been ready, I'm starved," replied Richie, while rubbing his stomach.

The hostess at the Compleat Angler seated the crew in one of the small dining areas. The walls were made from weathered, but beautiful wood salvaged from an old barge that was used to store liquor waiting to be smuggled to the U.S. during prohibition. The hotel and bar were built in 1933 to accommodate the growing number of sports fishermen frequenting Bimini.

Among the most famous was Ernest Hemingway. Trevor couldn't visit the restaurant without studying the large collections of photographs adorning the walls.   Picture after picture of anglers proudly standing next to their catches caused him to dream of what it must have been like to live during that period.

While his eyes were scanning from this wall to that wall something caught his attention. On the far side of the room he saw Carla intermittently staring in his direction. Fortunately, Kit had his back to Trevor and hadn't noticed his arrival. Once, while Carla was looking at Trevor, he winked to let her know he had seen her glancing in his direction, but she pretended not to notice.

Dave and Richie were talking about what rigging to start with the next day when Richie asked, "Trevor do you think we should start with artificial or live baits?" Trevor didn't answer, causing Richie to say, "Hello – earth to Trevor!" Just then Richie figured out what was distracting his boss and said, "Didn't you learn your lesson this morning, boss?"

"What are you talking about?" Trevor replied somewhat agitated.

"You know, the broad," Richie replied nodding his head in Carla's direction.

"There isn't anything going on between us, and if there was it wouldn't be any of your business."

Richie, afraid Trevor was angry, said, "Take it easy. Boss, I'm on your side. Why if you want, Dave and I will go kick that over-educated punk's ass right now."

"No, that won't be necessary. Let's just eat and get the hell out of here."

Trevor joined the conversation, but couldn't help but notice Kit and Carla were having somewhat of a heated discussion. He wondered if Kit had seen Carla looking across the room at him. Trevor decided not to let his imagination run rampant and took a long sip of beer.

***

"Kit, I think you should go apologize to Trevor!" Carla said.

"Why?" Kit asked, and then finished, "I don't care if I ever talk to him again!"

Carla grabbed his hand trying to calm him down and said, "He's our neighbor at the marina and I'll feel uncomfortable if you guys hate each other. Besides, he's promised to look at my novel when it's finished and that's what unpublished authors dream of. Do it for me...please!" With this, she reached her foot up and began massaging his crotch.

"All right," Kit said. "But only because you asked me to, not because I want to."

Trevor saw Kit scoot his chair back and stand up. He looked towards the wall, not wanting to make eye contact with Kit. When he turned back Kit was standing before the table. Kit spoke without feeling, "I'm sorry for acting like a jerk today"

"Don't worry about it kid," Trevor replied.

Kit reached his hand out to Trevor, who grabbed it, shaking it firmly. With nothing else to say, Kit turned and went back to his table.

Minutes later, a waitress showed up at Trevor's table with a round of beers saying, "This is from the gentleman and lady across the way." Once the beers were distributed, Kit and Carla turned and raised their beers in a toast. Trevor and the boys raised their beers and nodded their heads in a symbol of gratitude.

The tension in the room had subsided and the crew enjoyed the special of the day, whole pan-fried yellowtail snapper with pigeon peas and rice.

After two more rounds of beer, Trevor and crew were ready for some shuteye, five o'clock was going to come awfully fast, and they wanted to be well-rested for the fishing trip. They politely waved goodbye to Kit and Carla before leaving.

The mid-day nap had refreshed the couple and Kit and Carla were ready to party. After dinner they went into the bar area. Like the rest of the building, it had a certain ambiance. People from all over the world visited the bar and exchanged tales of their experiences and travels.

There were no pool tables or pinball machines, only a simple ring game, which was comprised of a brass ring hung from the ceiling by a length of string, and a hook on the wall, the string's length away. The object of the game was to aim the ring and swing it with the right force to catch on the wall-mounted hook.   Although crude, the game provided entertainment to the bar's patrons, and became more challenging after several drinks. All of the bar's customers seemed to take turns in an orderly manner, playing the ring game until they either became proficient or frustrated.

After an hour or so, Kit and Carla returned to their boat and made love until the wee hours. Only a stone's throw away, in a dark, musty cabin, Trevor laid in his bunk unable to sleep. He was unsure whether his thoughts of Carla or the anticipation of the next day's trip was the cause of insomnia

Chapter 23

It seemed he had finally fallen asleep, when the alarm clock rattled on the dresser. "Shit!" Trevor said as he slapped the snooze button down to quiet the contraption. Although his physical body was tired, the noise had caused his brain to jump-start and think about what to do first. He lay in bed for several minutes, then eased himself up and pushed the alarm's off button before it sounded for the second time.

After putting on his shorts and Jimmy Buffet T-shirt, he went to wake his snoring crewmembers. Next, he headed for the galley to brew a strong pot of coffee.

It was still dark outside and the no-see-ums were ravenous. Unlike mosquitoes, these bugs are, as the name implies, unable to be seen. Their bite, though trivial in nature, is magnified by the shear number. When Trevor walked outside the air was heavy due to the high humidity. In a matter of seconds his arms and legs were covered with no-see-ums. He spent a minimal amount of time checking everything to make sure it was in order, slapping and scratching the whole time.

Once inside, he wondered how the early settlers survived without air conditioning and bug repellent.

"Mornin' boss," Richie and Dave said as Trevor entered the galley.

"Mornin' guys – the no-see-ums were eating me alive out there," Trevor said, still scratching his arms and legs.

"Let's grab some doughnuts and shove off," he said once the itching subsided.

"Sounds like a game plan," Dave answered.

The crew drank a couple of cups of coffee and ate a package of Velvet Cream powdered doughnuts. Being typical males, they chose to use their clothes instead of napkins to wipe their hands and wound up covered with powdered sugar.

"Yah ready?" Trevor asked as he walked to the controls on the bridge.

Dave yelled, "I'll grab the lines. Richie, how about you pulling the shore power?"

"You got it," Richie said springing to his feet, doughnut crumbs and powdered sugar falling to the deck.

Trevor turned on the blower to clear the engine compartment of any combustible fumes and after a couple of minutes he turned the key to start the starboard engine. It came to life with the low undulating rumble of a high-powered diesel.

When he was sure the starboard engine was running he fired up the port engine. The boat seemed to come alive. The powerful diesels vibrated the whole boat, and their breath, the faint aroma of burning diesel, was now permeating the air. Trevor watched as his crew completed the various tasks associated with getting under way. Finally they gave him the thumbs up and he engaged the engines and pulled away from the dock.

Trevor, Dave and Richie discussed their game plan the day before. They decided that since the barracuda had been spotted around the marina, they would try to get some lines out as soon as they left the dock. Dave and Richie were already scrambling to get some lines in the water. They had to use surface lures for now, because the waters were shallow inside Bimini Bay. Once outside the Bay they could use whatever baits they wanted because the water became deep not far from shore.

An orange hue on the eastern horizon indicated the approach of sunrise. The men were excited knowing off the coast of Bimini anything could happen once they had their lines in the water. They hoped the preparation yesterday would bring the ancient cuda in through the tuna door before the day's end.

After reaching the deep waters, they would troll to the west of Bimini, and then head south to the area of Bobby's attack. Trevor had suggested trolling a little faster than usual, eliminating some of the other types of fish that might feed on the baits.

Within fifteen minutes they were in deeper water. Richie swung the outrigger out and into position while Dave attached a pre-rigged ballyhoo and squid to the two Penn International rod and reels. They each grabbed a rod and began feeding line out until it was the proper distance then snapped them into the outriggers.

"Here fishy, fishy," Dave said jokingly.

Within a short time a knockdown occurred on the port outrigger. Unfortunately, something had eaten half the bait without getting hooked. Dave put on a new bait and put the line back out.

A couple hours had passed since the Child Support had left the dock. The sun was up and already beginning to warm the air. The seas were calm except for a gentle swell that occasionally caused the boat to rise and fall. The diesels hummed, churning the ocean in their path.

It was days like this when Trevor was truly grateful for the life he was living. It wasn't perfect – there were some things missing – like a woman to keep him warm at night and grow old with. Once that was a priority, but now as he got older he had learned he could survive and be happy by himself – if he had to. It was women like Carla that made him remember as a man he still had needs. But how many people could say they got to do what they really loved in life. Writing and fishing were two things he loved, and after being published and writing several successful novels, he could now choose when he wanted to write.

Snap! The starboard outrigger signaled a fish, bringing Trevor out of his introspective thoughts. Whatever hit the line was already hooked and running wildly. Dave ran to the rod, grabbed it, and reared back hoping to drive the hook deeper into the fish. Slowly, he walked over to the fighting chair and sat down. If he didn't attempt to tighten the drag, the fish would run out all of the line. Trevor quickly threw the boat into reverse and tried to back down on the fish to reclaim the line.

"It's big, whatever it is!" Dave yelled as he carefully tightened down the drag.

Richie hurriedly pulled in all the other lines so the fish wouldn't foul them up. Trevor strained his eyes, watching for the fish to jump so he could identify it. The fish had turned several times allowing Dave to take up some line. Suddenly, off in the distance, the large fish jumped several feet into the air.

"Did you see that?" Trevor screamed.

"Yeah!" Richie said, "but I didn't get a good look at him."

Trevor added, "It's definitely not a sail or marlin – it might be our fish."

The excitement level was high as the crew envisioned pulling up to the dock with their trophy fish proudly displayed.

Dave was determined to land this fish. Several times he had gotten half the line in, only to have the fish run it back out again.

Finally, it seemed as though the fish was tiring. His runs were becoming shorter and much slower. Dave kept turning the crank on the reel, bringing the fish closer to death.

As the fish drew near the boat his long silver body was visible, even though he was still forty feet below the surface.

After a couple of last minute escape attempts, Dave was finally able to bring him to the surface.

"Shit! – It's a wahoo!" Trevor said, disappointed.

"Nice fish, Dave!" Richie said, trying to make Dave feel better.

Richie gaffed the Wahoo and threw him in the cooler. He figured the fish weighed around 40-50 pounds.

"Who wants a beer?" Trevor asked, knowing this was a stupid question.

After grabbing the beers, Trevor asked Dave to take the helm so he could help Richie get the lines back in the water with fresh baits.

The sun was past its midpoint, but still shining brightly in the clear blue sky. There was a slight ocean breeze – just enough to keep the heat from being stifling. Trevor wondered how ancient mariners survived without sunglasses, as he scanned the waters looking for signs of feeding birds.

The crew experienced several more knockdowns during the afternoon, but no hookups. One of the artificial lures, a bright orange fish, had been savagely attacked several times by a large fish with teeth. After inspecting it, Trevor remarked it was an effective lure, but the hook configuration needed to be changed because the fish were able to attack it without getting hooked.

They trolled all afternoon up and down the western shore until finally, Trevor suggested they head in.

"I'm getting hungry – let's go steak up that Wahoo and marinate it in some Mo Jo. We can break out the hibachi and have a nice little barbecue."

"Sounds good to me!" Dave said as he pointed the boat towards the marina.

The crew decided to troll on the way in, hoping to get one last chance at catching the cuda. In a half an hour they were cruising into Bimini Bay. The outrigger had been pulled in and Trevor was reeling in the artificials. He had just about reeled in the last one when something caught his eye.

The large cuda spotted something brightly colored speeding through the water and decided to follow it. The vibrations from the diesel engines told it humans were around, which meant caution should be exercised. However, if it didn't act fast this morsel of food was going to escape.

"Holy shit!" Trevor yelled as the massive cuda charged at the lure.

It hit with tremendous power, almost pulling the rod from Trevor's grip. In a flash it was over. Trevor reeled in the line and stood in disbelief after seeing the lure had been bitten in half.

"No more wooden artificials for that fish," he said, displaying the lure for Dave and Richie to see.

"Looks like he must have been hanging out in the bay today," Richie said to the dumbfounded Trevor.

As they pulled up to the marina, they couldn't help but notice a large crowd composed of Bahamians and visitors gathered on the dock next to one of the local charter boats. When they got nearer, they could see a large fish lying on the dock in the middle of the crowd.

Seconds later they were tying up to the dock as an excited Dr. George scurried down to meet them.

"Trevor! Trevor! They've caught the fish! They've caught the fish!

"Hold on, Dr. George. What fish are you talking about?"

"You know. The killer barracuda – the one John put the $10,000 reward on."

Trevor, not wanting to burst his bubble without first checking out the evidence said, "Let's go see this fish."

When they got to the crowd, Pappy, the local credited with catching the fish, was already talking about how he was going to use the money to fix up his ailing vessel and home. He reached out and grabbed Trevor's hand and shook it furiously saying, "Trevor my man, long time no see!"

Trevor knew many of the locals, and had become close to a few after spending many years visiting the island.

"Where's this prize catch of yours?" Trevor asked, knowing it had to be in the middle of the small crowd.

"You mean my $10,000 fish? Follow me," Pappy said as he walked over to the group of spectators.

The crowd spread as Trevor and Pappy neared the fish. When the fish was in plain view, Trevor took a minute to study the carcass and decided it must be around 5 feet long and probably weighed close to 70 pounds.

"That's a big cuda!" Trevor remarked.

"He's 5 feet 2inches and 68¾ pounds," Pappy said proudly.

"He's a nice catch Pappy. You should be pleased, but he's not the one that's been wreaking havoc around here," Trevor said, not really enjoying being the messenger of bad news.

"What do you mean ma'an? You're just jealous you didn't catch the $10,000 fish."

"Pappy, I wish that was the $10,000 fish for your sake, but it's not."

He looked over and saw Dave had joined them and asked, "Dave go grab the lure that got hit on the way in."

Dave ran off to the boat while Trevor explained what happened just a short while ago on their trip in. He started by telling Pappy about fishing all day and the fight they had with the large Wahoo. Just as he got to the part about the cuda hitting the lure, Dave came up out of breath and holding the damaged lure in his hand.

Pappy looked at it and said, "That t'ing doesn't prove not'in'."

"It wouldn't, except the fish hit right behind the boat and I got a good look at him. I'm sorry to say he was much bigger than this one," Trevor said, pointing to the fish on the dock.

***

Carla and Kit were finishing dinner when they noticed an unusual number of people parading down the dock. This type of activity usually occurred when some lucky angler brought in a large fish such as a marlin or tuna. They decided after clearing away the dinner dishes to take a walk and see what all the commotion was about.

As they wandered up to the crowd, the couple noticed Trevor standing there talking to Pappy. Kit wasn't over his jealousy, but had decided to treat Trevor humanely for Carla's sake. Carla began to flush at the sight of Trevor and hoped the hand Kit was holding didn't heat up to the point he'd notice.

"Hi Trevor, how's it going?" Kit said, trying to hide his disgust for the man. Carla smiled and raised her other hand in a little waiving motion.

"Great," Trevor replied, then added, "Pappy thinks he's caught the cuda that attacked Carla."

Carla heard this and started having trauma-induced flashbacks of the cuda. She was visualizing it off in the distance watching her every move. She snapped out of it when Kit released her hand to examine the fish.

He immediately knew although this was a big cuda, this was not the one he had seen during his conch research. Besides its lack of size, its eyes were clear and in perfect condition. Even though Kit knew this, he decided to agree with Pappy, so the hunt for the real fish would be called off.

Kit walked back to Carla and asked, "Carla, did you see the cuda?"

"No, and I don't want to either," she replied, her hands trembling at the thought.

"Looks like you've got a winner," Kit lied to Pappy.

Trevor held up the half-eaten lure and said, "Look at this!" Kit took the lure from him and examined it. Trevor explained its condition. "We were trolling this lure on the way in. I was reeling it in and had almost gotten it up to the stern, when a huge cuda hit it and chopped it in half. I slowed him down just long enough to get a good look at him."

"Well, I didn't tell anybody, but I saw the cuda while collecting conch and I think this the same one," Kit lied, getting satisfaction from making Trevor look like a fool.

"You see Trevor!" Pappy said, glad Kit was supporting his right to the prize.

Trevor just said, "Whatever," and turned to walk back to the Child Support, only stopping just long enough to say, "Later people, I've got to get some rest. I'm going back out tomorrow to catch the cuda I saw."

With this statement he politely let Pappy and Kit know he didn't agree with them. His eyes met Carla's and he fantasized briefly of their interlude.

Trevor thought of the strong rum drink he'd mix back on his boat. He'd need it to forget the memory of Carla's body against his.

Chapter 24

Later that night John and his passenger, Skeeter, motored into the marina. John had talked to some friends in Miami about hiring a fishing guide for the trip and they had recommended Skeeter. The man was a native Floridian and had grown up on a charter boats. Skeeter's father was a charter boat captain, and ever since Skeeter was old enough to hold a fishing pole, he had been his mate. He had caught hundreds of barracudas in his lifetime, but most of them by mistake. This constant exposure to the fish had taught him a lot about the cuda's feeding habits.

He warned John he had never in his life tried to go fishing for one fish in particular.

"The ocean is a big place to hide, and trying to catch a single fish in it is like playing the lottery," he explained.

"However, if you pay me enough, I will try anything," he told John with a big smile on his face.

They had gotten a little wet on the way over to Bimini. A squall had popped up out of nowhere while they were passing through the Gulfstream. For a short while the wind and seas had pummeled the 35-foot Contender.

Now, as they walked towards the hotel with their gear, all they could think about was taking a hot shower and drinking a few cold beers.

After checking in and getting cleaned up, they headed to the Compleat Angler for food and drinks. When they sat down at the bar, Skeeter couldn't help but notice a pretty blonde down at the other end. As a matter of fact, she had been looking in their direction for several minutes.

"Hey John, do you know that woman down there? She seems to be staring at us."

John turned his head and saw Carla smiling and waving to let him know she recognized him. He also noticed her turn toward Kit, say something, and point towards them.

"Look, that guy John is back," she said to Kit.

"Do you want to go say hello?" he asked.

"Sure, why not?"

John watched the couple approach. His eyes feasted on Carla's beauty; her unharnessed breasts jiggled as she walked. John fantasized he was lifting her shirt and burying his head between them. He was only on his second beer, but was already starting to feel a little horny.

He had to catch his breath before he introduced his friend.

"Carla, Kit, this is a friend of mine, Skeeter."

Carla stuck her hand out and shook Skeeter's hand. She felt uncomfortable because he looked as though he was undressing her with his eyes.

"Nice to meet you," she lied.

"The pleasure is all mine," Skeeter replied, his eyes scanning her up and down.

Next, Skeeter shook Kit's hand. Kit went through the motions, but had already decided he did not like the man.

"How's your son?" Carla asked.

"Not so good. The doctor's had to take his leg because of that damn fish!"

Carla brought her hands up to her cheeks and exclaimed, "How terrible I'm so sorry."

Kit felt bad hearing about Johnny, but he still felt he had to ask John to cancel the reward before a number of barracuda were slaughtered in an attempt to capture the prize fish.

He began, "John, now that you're here, I presume to try to catch the cuda, would you consider canceling the reward?"

John replied sternly, "No chance!"

Kit continued, "One cuda has been killed unnecessarily already and God only knows how many more will die.

John came back, "Do you think I care about a bunch of stupid fish, after what's happened to my son?"

Kit knew this was going nowhere, but he still had to plead his case. "Killing barracudas isn't going to change what's happened. During the 70's, after the movie Jaws came out, the shark population was almost fished to extinction because fishermen were killing them just for sport. Not to mention the thousands that were slaughtered so their fins could be sold to the Japanese.

These fish, just like barracudas, served a special purpose in the ocean's ecosystem. They helped to eliminate weak or injured fish.

It's a delicate balance, we haven't even begun to understand the ramifications of mans interference."

John replied, "Sorry, Kit. You're not going to change my mind. I'm going to catch that fish, and then you won't ever see me again.

"Why don't you help me with your expertise?" John pleaded. "The sooner I catch him, the sooner everyone else will stop fishing for the reward money."

Kit listened and thought about what John had said, and then replied, "I couldn't do that. Nice meeting you Skeeter," Kit said as he grabbed Carla's hand to indicate he was done talking to the men.

Suddenly Kit said, "Carla, do you mind if we go now? I've got some paper work to do."

"No problem," she said, deciding she would use the time to write.

On the way back, Carla had a few choice words for Kit.

"Kit, I can't believe you were trying to talk John out of catching that barracuda."

"Carla, I don't want to talk about it. You know how I feel about this."

"You know how I feel too!" she said in a huff as she let go of his hand and picked up her pace, leaving him behind.

When she got to the boat she grabbed her writing pad and headed up to the bow so she could be alone.

When John asked Kit to help him, it gave Kit a crazy idea. He considered the idea of somehow catching the cuda, and relocating him to an isolated area to live out the rest of his days in peace.

After Carla took off, he decided to call a friend in Miami, a fellow marine biologist, for help. His friend had invented a device that used sound to attract fish. With the advent of small, inexpensive and battery-powered microprocessors, his friend, through his research, had produced an attraction device that could be placed inside bait. The inventor claimed no fish could resist the sound it emitted.

He went to the marina's office and telephoned his friend to explain the situation, and his friend agreed to mail him several devices immediately. After the call, Kit went back to the boat to look at his charts and select an area suitable for relocating the cuda.

John had hoped to see Trevor at the bar that evening to find out if anyone had sighted the cuda recently. He didn't bother asking Kit, because he knew Kit would not tell him anything to aid in his hunt for the cuda. John finished the last sip of his beer and said to Skeeter, "I'd like to go by Trevor's before it gets too late."

Skeeter asked, "You mean the Ernest Hemmingway wanna-be you told me about on the way over?"

"Yeah, that's him. He should know if there's been any encounters with the cuda lately."

John said, "Let's go," and stood up, but waited while Skeeter took the last swig of his beer.

Trevor was sitting in a fighting chair nursing a large Meyers and Coke when John and Skeeter came strolling up to the boat.

"John--how's it going?" Trevor yelled.

"Okay, I guess. This is my friend Skeeter."

Skeeter stuck out his hand.

Trevor stood up and tripped on the footrest of the fighting chair. "Shit!" he said, as half of his drink spilled on the deck. He wiped his hand on his pants, and then extended it to shake hands with the two men. John began his questioning even though he could tell Trevor was close to being drunk.

"Trevor, has anyone seen the cuda lately?"

"I saw him today, as a matter of fact. He hit an artificial on the way in—cut it in half. When we got in, Pappy, a local, has this puny cuda on the dock claiming it was the one you were looking for, and that asshole Kit agreed with him so no one else would fish for the real cuda. But I know better. I saw the cuda we're looking for. He's a big son of a bitch and strong—cut this wooden lure in half like nothin'." Trevor reached down into a nearby tackle box and tossed the lure to John.

"Wow!" John said as he inspected the mutilated lure.

John then asked, "Where were you when he hit the lure?"

"He grabbed it inside Bimini Bay after we wasted gas fishing all friggin' day outside."

Trevor tried to be as vague as possible, because he still wanted to be the one that lands the cuda.

"Thanks for the info," John said, and then asked, "you goin out tomorrow Trevor?"

"Sure am—gonna fish til' I catch that bastard."

"I guess I'll see you out there," John said, as he turned to walk away.

"Have your checkbook out when I pull up to the dock tomorrow!" Trevor yelled at the two men as they strolled down the dock toward the hotel.

Trevor stumbled into his bunk and passed out, fully clothed. Dave and Richie were sitting inside playing poker. They watched Trevor walk by knowing something was bothering him.

Richie turned to Dave and said, "Looks like you're in charge of the wake up call."

Dave replied, "I don't look forward to waking the boss up tomorrow. I don't think he's going to be feeling too good."

Chapter 25

It was morning and the marina was alive with activity. John and Skeeter were already trolling in Bimini Bay while on their way to the West Banks. Skeeter thought the cuda hitting inside the Bay was a fluke because no fish that large spent all his time in the shallows. Besides, from the information John had shared with him, the attacks had occurred in several locations, and he planned on visiting all of them.

Dave shook Trevor several times to wake him, then handed him a glass of water and two Tylenol. He told him to take it easy; he and Richie would get things done so they could shove off. Within a short while they were motoring out to sea trolling lines in search of the elusive cuda.

Pappy watched the two vessels set out to sea in his binoculars, and planned on following them now that he was convinced he hadn't caught the prize cuda. He felt it only makes sense he should catch the prize cuda. After all, he had grown up on these islands, and had probably spent more time in the water fishing than he had spent on land. Besides, he thought, his vessel was in need of repairs, and this would be a perfect opportunity to get the money to pay for them.

Black clouds puffed from the stern exhaust ports as Pappy started the ancient diesels. The bilge pump came on and pumped a toxic looking fluid from the bilge in the boat's leaking hull into the clear ocean water as he pulled away from the dock. His first mate and nephew, Tommy, was already swinging the outriggers out starting to prepare for a day of fishing.

"Uncle, I caught some fresh baits while you were at the bar last night," Tommy yelled, loud enough to overcome the noisy diesels.

"Good boy, now get them in the water before it's time to come in," Pappy replied smiling.

Pappy and his wife had never been able to have children, so he treated Tommy as if he was his son. They had fished together since the boy had wandered down to the docks as a toddler and asked to go fishing with Pappy. They earned a meager living taking tourists fishing and commercial fishing when times were slow.

Pappy wasn't quite sure whether to believe that a cuda as big as Trevor had described actually existed. Living in the islands, he had seen many large cudas in his days. In fact, he had caught more than he would have liked.

Usually the cudas were hooked while fishing for other fish, or caught in a desperate attempt to keep his customers happy. The fact is, not many people set out to actually fish for barracuda because the large fish of the species can't be eaten due to the fact they may contain ciguatera, a toxin that builds up in their system from eating reef fish.

The barracuda he caught the other day was one of the largest he'd ever seen. They had gone to a spot he knew was occupied by schools of barracuda. They caught a small yellowtail snapper for live-bait, back-hooked it, and then floated it out with a balloon bobber.

After catching several small cudas, a granddaddy showed up. The barracuda's age and experience made him leery and he swam by several times before attacking the bait. Once the cuda realized he was hooked, he swam away in a panicked frenzy peeling expensive line off the reel. Tommy ran over to the rod and jerked it into the air, setting the hook. The cuda jumped into the air several times trying to free itself.

It was several hours before Tommy was able to pull the exhausted fish alongside the boat. Pappy drove the gaff hook into its flesh just behind the gills. It took both of them to hoist the fish into the boat.

Once on the deck, Tommy beat the fish unconscious with a Billy club. He wasn't going to take any chances with a cuda that size.

On the way in they discussed what they were going to do with the prize money. Everything was going great until that American, Trevor, showed up at the docks and told everyone their barracuda wasn't the prize fish.

Pappy had gotten depressed and started drinking after admitting Trevor was probably right about the fish. Tommy didn't worry though, he knew his uncle was only temporarily drowning his sorrows.

After his uncle slept it off, Tommy was the one who suggested they not give up.

"Uncle, are we going to let some mainlanders come in here and catch that fish?" he asked, knowing he could get his uncle motivated.

"Hell no!" Pappy replied, his face lighting up.

That was how the day started, and they both hoped it would end with them catching the prize fish. By noon the sky had begun to cloud up and the seas were becoming restless. Nature was always changing the atmospheric conditions and a good sailor takes notice, but sometimes these signs are ignored on purpose. Pappy knew many a man had paid the price for this foolishness, but decided they weren't going in until they had caught the prize fish.

Tommy watched the dark clouds forming on the horizon and felt the wind temperature drop, signaling rain. He mentioned this to Pappy, and Pappy asked if he was afraid to get a little wet. Pappy was determined to fish no matter what. He thought the storm would blow over and the fishing would be great. After all, almost everyone knows fishing is always better right after it rains. Pappy figured they weren't that far offshore and if things got too bad they could make it in rather quickly.

The seas had gone from a 2 to 3 foot chop to 8 to 10 foot swells, and the two sailors knew they had made a serious mistake by not heading in sooner. Within a short time, a dense rain being driven sideways by an intense wind reduced visibility to just a few feet. Just before they lost visibility, Pappy nervously watched as a funnel cloud formed and dropped down from the dark clouds and hovered low over the turbulent seas. He didn't say anything to Tommy about it, because he knew the boy was already frightened and that his knowing about the funnel cloud wouldn't change anything.

The waterspout was huge and had positioned itself right off the bow of the charter boat, but without any visibility, neither Pappy nor Tommy knew what was about to happen. They both heard a sound that was unfamiliar to them. If they had lived on the mainland, they would have equated it to a speeding freight train.

All of a sudden they were surrounded by water. The old wooden boat was no match for millions of gallons of water traveling at hundreds of miles per hour; it disintegrated and joined the swirling water and debris in the bowels of the huge waterspout. Pappy's neck was broken and his body was tossed around like a china doll by the massive storm. Tommy was knocked unconscious, and his body slipped into the depths of the ocean. Soon, the reef sharks would arrive and clean up after the storm.

When the seas first began to signal an impending storm, Trevor had expressed a desire to return to the marina. He was feeling a bit under the weather from his excessive drinking the previous evening. Richie and Dave harassed him a little bit, but knew Trevor was not normally prone to seasickness. Besides, they didn't like fishing in a monsoon any more than Trevor did.

John and Skeeter also took notice of the approaching storm and decided to call it quits for the day. The size of their vessel and limited cover was enough reason to make the decision easy.

Neither Trevor nor John witnessed what had happened to Pappy and his nephew. They were drinking in the safety of the Compleat Angler when the tragedy occurred.

Later that night, Pappy's wife alerted the Bahamian Coast Guard that he had not returned to port. It was not unusual for Pappy to stay out at night, but it was unusual for him to do it without telling her. They had a radio in their home and she was unable to contact him. The Coast Guard official tried to calm her by telling her Pappy was probably catching so many fish he didn't have time to answer her call.

"I hope you're right," Pappy's wife said, with a forced smile.

Unfortunately, the official knew the weather had been rather severe that day and had now just calmed down enough to begin a search. All attempts to contact the vessel by radio had produced no results, and it was now dark, limiting the usefulness of a search. However, they would try — it was their job.

The patrol boat spent the whole night traveling up and down the coast, spotlight cutting through the darkness in search of the vessel and crew. It wasn't until daylight that one of the officers spotted wreckage from Pappy's boat. A section of the transom was floating with part of the boat's name exposed. Only the word Mama was left of the boat's full name Bahama Mama.

"It doesn't look good," the captain said to his officer.

"What do you think happened?" the officer asked.

"Well from the looks of it, they must have gotten a piece of that water spout reported offshore yesterday. We'll keep searching for survivors, but I don't think we'll find any."

About halfway through the day, the captain called off the search. He didn't want to, but with the island's limited resources he couldn't see wasting any more fuel on what he considered a hopeless mission.

His next duty was to inform Pappy's wife their search efforts had only located part of the boat's transom. He knew she wasn't going to take the news well. After all, she and Pappy had been married over 40 years. He knew this because he had grown up with both of them and had been present when they exchanged marriage vows.

The patrol boat glided up to the docks while Pappy's wife stood there impatiently waiting to hear the news of her husband's fate. When the captain stepped onto the dock holding a piece of their boat's transom, she fell to her knees and started weeping uncontrollably.

"Why, why, why, dear Jesus? Why my Pappy? He was such a good man."

"There was no finer," the captain said as he held her.

"Do you think he might still be alive," she asked?

"No I think not, otherwise I'd still be out there searching. This was all we found of the vessel," he said pointing to the splintered piece of transom.

"It's all because of that damn barracuda. He was determined to catch him for the reward. Otherwise, he probably would have had enough sense to come in when the weather got bad. First, the pretty American woman was attacked, then poor Bobby, next the little Cuban girl, and now my Pappy and Tommy have disappeared. That fish is a curse from hell, sent by the devil himself."

Chapter 26

The next day a boy from the marina stood on the dock screaming at the top of his lungs, "Mr. Callaway! Mr. Callaway!" Trevor heard the commotion and stuck his head out of the parlor door to find out who was yelling his name.

"Mr. Callaway, there's a call for you at the office."

"Thanks, I'll be right there," he said, wondering who it could be.

On the way to the office he figured out who it was. It had to be his agent. He was supposed to have been home several days ago and had forgotten to call her to let her know.

"Hello," Trevor said, knowing he was going to get an ear full.

"Trevor, where the hell have you been?" she asked.

"Listen Maggie, I'm really sorry I haven't called you. I got sidetracked."

"Do you know how hard it was to find you? I was worried sick that you were floating around somewhere in the Gulf Stream or had drowned!"

"Again, I'm sorry. I promise I'll call you next time."

"The publisher's on my ass wanting to know when you're going to be finished with the book they've already paid you for."

"Screw them. I've always met my deadlines. They can kiss my ass!"

"Trevor, just remember, without them you wouldn't be able to go on these little fishing trips," Maggie reminded him.

"Yeah, well just tell them I had a little engine trouble and I'll be back in plenty of time to get the manuscript done."

"Okay love, I'm glad you're all right, and give me a call when you get back to Key West. There's a new restaurant on Duval Street I want to take you to."

"Maggie, you know if you weren't my agent I'd probably try to get in your pants."

"Well, I guess some day you'll have to get a new agent," she said with a chuckle.

"See you in a few days," she finished.

"Good bye," Trevor said, and then hung up.

Trevor had already known it was about time to park the Child Support and return to work, but he didn't like anyone else telling him he had to.

He decided to go back and inform his crew that they were heading back to Key West in the next couple of days. They all partied a little too much the night before and overslept. Otherwise, they'd be out fishing for the cuda.

When he returned to the boat, Jimmy Buffet was belting out Margaritaville from the boat's CD player. Richie and Dave were lying about half-asleep, mouthing the words to the song.

"Hey guys, what's up? Trevor yelled, over the Buffet tune.

Richie reached over and turned down the volume and asked, "Is everything okay boss?"

"Yeah – believe it or not, my agent tracked me down to tell me the publisher is on her ass. I guess I'm going to have to start writing soon to pay the bills."

"We have been out a little longer than planned, haven't we?" Dave asked.

"Yes, tomorrow we'll take one more shot at the cuda, and then we better gas up before heading home."

"I'll run up to the store and pick up some provisions for the trip home," Dave suggested.

"Let's see if we can buy some fish on the docks to grill for dinner. I'd like to retire early tonight so we can get a full day of fishing in," Trevor recommended.

Chapter 27

Kit walked up to the marina's office to ask if any mail had shown up for him. The clerk smiled and produced a small package from under the counter.

"Here you go, sugar," the clerk said as she winked, flirting with Kit.

"Thanks," he said smiling as he grabbed the package.

"Is there anything else you need?" she asked, holding the package tightly so as not to let go, forcing Kit to look into her eyes.

"No, that will be all –I'm engaged," Kit said, smiling.

"Oh, I couldn't tell by the way your woman acts," she replied.

"What do you mean by that?" Kit asked, becoming upset.

"Oh nothing, but we are open 24 hours and sometimes we get to see a lot," she hinted.

"Is there something I should know?"

"Forget I said anything. Just keep your eyes and ears open," she finished.

"Thanks again," Kit said as he stormed out the door.

Carla was laying face down on the bow catching some rays with her top's straps untied when Kit stormed onto the boat. Startled, Carla almost forgot to hold her top on when she sat up.

"Carla, the clerk practically accused you of having an affair when I went to pick up my mail. What the hell's going on?"

"She's always minding everyone else's business; she's a trouble maker. I wouldn't believe anything she says," Carla replied.

"Where did you go the other night after our fight?" Kit asked.

"I just went up to the bar and had a couple of drinks, and came home to find you passed out on the couch," she lied.

"Maybe she saw our little scene on the dock the other day and was trying to draw some conclusions from that," Carla said, trying to defend herself.

"Yeah, well, I'm still not too sure what was going on there either," Kit added.

"Kit listen, I love you and I hope you're not going to let some floozy troublemaker cause problems between us."

"I guess you're right," Kit said, "I'm sorry."

"I agreed to marry you didn't I?" Carla asked, grabbing him by the shoulders.

"Yeah, I'll just feel a lot better once we've left Bimini and I can have you all to myself again," Kit finished.

"Silly boy," she said as she dropped her top and flashed him. Kit let the package fall to the deck as he scooped Carla into his arms and carried her to the cabin.

Chapter 28

News of Pappy and Tommy's demise spread quickly throughout the island. Johnny and Skeeter were sitting in the End of the World bar having a beer when they overheard one of the locals talking about it.

"Pappy was such a fine man. He didn't deserve to die like that," they heard the man say.

"His wife said the fish is a curse from hell. He's here to punish us for our evil ways," he finished.

"Excuse me," John interrupted. May I ask what you are talking about?"

"Pappy and Tommy, local fishermen, were killed yesterday while trying to catch the barracuda that's been terrorizing the island. The fish is evil. He's already attacked three people and his wife thinks her husband and nephew would still be alive if it wasn't for the reward money offered for him. Pappy wanted it so bad he must have risked his life to try to catch him."

"I'm sorry," John said.

"What for?" the man asked.

"I'm the man who offered the reward, but it's because my son was one of the people attacked by the cuda," John finished.

"Well it wasn't really your fault. Pappy has been a captain for many, many years and if not for greed, he might still be alive," the man said trying to alleviate John's guilt.

"Thanks," John said, and ordered a round of beers for everyone at the bar.

After finishing their beers, John and Skeeter went to Captain Bob's restaurant in Alice Town for dinner. While eating, they discussed the death of Pappy and Tommy, summarizing they must have been killed by the waterspout Skeeter spotted off the coast yesterday. Next, they talked about how and where they would pursue the cuda on the following day.

Chapter 29

Trevor, feeling a little nervous about the deadline on his manuscript, decided to get out his lap top computer and try to write a little. While writing, an evil little thought came to mind. Since Carla said she had read every single one of his books, he decided that somehow he was going to write about their interlude, using fictitious characters, of course. He hoped that someday if she read it, she would think about him, if only for a minute.

Writing sometimes made Trevor tired, and he started to doze off. He dreamt he was fishing and Carla was with him. It was a beautiful day and he was staring off the stern watching some lines he had in the water. When he looked over at Carla, she was totally naked and he started becoming aroused. The scene shifted and he was standing behind her; the soft flesh of her buttocks was against his groin. Trevor wanted to make love to her, but was unable to control the events of the dream. However, it was even more exciting to stand next to her aroused, and not be able to do anything about it.

Finally, when he thought he might penetrate her, something hit one of the lines, ruining the moment. Trevor ran to the pole and began reeling it in.

As he reeled in the line, the fish jumped into the air and Trevor could see it was the barracuda. He looked at Carla and she was trembling with fear. He said, "Don't worry I won't let him hurt you!"

Seconds later the fish was at the stern of the boat and Trevor gave the rod a tug, pulling him onboard. As the fish flew through the air it transformed into Kit and landed on Trevor; then both of them fell to the deck. Kit was on top with a strangle hold on Trevor. Carla was in the background, now fully clothed, screaming, "No, Kit!" Trevor was fighting frantically, trying to remove Kit's hands from his throat.

Suddenly, Trevor opened his eyes to find Dave shaking him and asking, "Trevor, are you all right?" It took Trevor a minute to figure out he was only dreaming, because everything seemed real to him at that moment.

"Yeah, I'm all right. I guess I was dreaming," he said feeling embarrassed.

"Man, that must have been one hell of a dream. I came down here and you were mumbling and thrashing all over the couch."

Trevor lied, "I dreamt we caught the cuda. I pulled him on board a little green and he was flipping around on the deck. I was trying to knock him out when you woke me up."

"Maybe that's a sign we're going to catch him tomorrow," Dave interjected.

"I hope so," Trevor added.

"I heard the marine forecast for tomorrow and the weather is supposed to be nice," Dave said.

"Good, we'll try to get an early start. How's the fuel situation?"

"We've got a little less than half a tank in the port and starboard tanks. I figure we have enough to troll as long as we want to tomorrow. We can burn that fuel up and fill up with fresh fuel before the trip home."

Chapter 30

Kit returned to the bow and retrieved the package he had dropped earlier. Carla saw him walk into the lab with it and asked what it was. Kit lied, "Oh, it's just some research materials I ordered from Miami." Carla, satisfied with his answer, returned to her spot on the bow to continue her sun bathing.

Once Kit knew he was alone, he opened the small box. Inside the Styrofoam packing material he found four devices, each one the size of a peanut in a shell. The exterior was capsule shaped and composed of clear plastic. Inside you could see a small microprocessor powered by what appeared to be a watch battery. At one end of the capsule there was a miniature speaker, similar to those used in transducers. The device was activated by slightly twisting the capsule halves.

Kit turned on one of the capsules and held it up to his ear. He heard a clicking noise and could feel the vibration being produced by the sound. "Unbelievable," he muttered to himself. Next, he tested the other devices to make sure they worked.

Once placed inside a finger mullet, it should be irresistible to the cuda, he thought.

After putting the devices back in the box, he laid out a chart of the Bahamas to plot a relocation site for the barracuda. The area had to be far enough away to prevent the cuda from wandering back to Bimini. Several minutes later, Kit had decided on a small patch of reef north of Bimini called East Brother.

There were still many details to be worked out concerning the capture. He knew from what he'd seen so far that the tackle must be able to resist the sharp teeth and power of the cuda's jaws. The hook he selected was a squid hook; the shaft was extremely long to prevent him from possibly biting through the leader. However, if he did swallow the bait deep enough, the leader, a multi-strand thin steel cable, should be able to resist the cuda's attempts to bite though it.

Kit's original plan was to tow the cuda with the dinghy to the release site, but he decided that was too risky. Towing the cuda would make it vulnerable to other predators and injury.

The final plan was to catch the fish, sedate him, surround him in a special net, and eventually place him in a live bait well on the Hatteras. The hard part was the capture and release had to be done without Carla or anyone else finding out. Kit wondered how she would react to his plan. She'll probably be pissed, he surmised. But he wouldn't worry about it now. He knew she'd get over it.

There were many people out there that would like to see that fish dead, and Kit knew it was his responsibility to make sure this didn't happen. He walked over to the cabinet in the lab and pulled out an old canvas tarp. Carefully, he measured and marked a piece long enough and wide enough to envelop the cuda's torso. Next, he cut the pattern out and laid it on the table.

Now it was time to find some netting for the ends. In the same cabinet where he found the canvas were several nets he had used in the past to catch various specimens for study. After rummaging through them, he decided an old cast net was the one he would miss the least and began measuring two pieces to be used for ends of the canvas enclosure.

The net would allow water to flow through and bring life giving oxygen to the cuda's respiratory system. The canvas would hide the precious cargo from anything that would harm him. Kit grabbed a heavy-duty needle and thread he used to do repair work on damaged nets and began sewing the enclosure. After a little cursing, and a few pokes to his finger, the job was completed.

Maybe I should have been a tailor, he thought to himself as he inspected the finished product. He rolled it up and placed it in the cabinet so he wouldn't have to answer any questions from Carla about what he was going to do with it.

Last but not least, Kit had to check on his supply of the drug Finquel that would be used to anesthetize the barracuda while he was being transported. The last thing Kit wanted to do was deal with a fully-rested 7-foot barracuda that was pissed off from being captured and placed in a small holding tank.

Chapter 31

Trevor and the boys were once again busy readying the Child Support for another day of trying to catch the elusive cuda. Trevor had talked to some anglers from Miami he had met on a previous trip – serious big game fisherman. They offered him a special lure they said; "No fish could resist." It was two-tone orange, made from fiberglass, with a hook configuration that looked perfect.

He bought a bottle of Mount Gay and dropped it off to them to show his appreciation. While he was at the liquor store, he purchased a second bottle to celebrate with the following night after they caught the cuda. Regardless of what happened the next day, the fishing episode was about over. He could only waste so much of his time on one fish.

The last few weeks had added material for future novels to his mental database. First, the marlin, then the cuda attacks, and Carla – he would never forget about Carla.

Trevor had seen her sunning herself on the bow of her yacht earlier that day and almost fell, tripping on a nail sticking up from the aged planks of the dock. She happened to look up just in time to find him juggling his legs to keep them underneath his body. Carla giggled and gave a little wave to let him know she had seen the whole thing. Trevor waved back, cursing at the nail. He reassured himself by thinking that in just a few weeks, Carla would be nothing more to him than a character in one of his books.

Chapter 32

John hung up the phone in the marina's office and joined Skeeter outside in a conversation with one of the locals. The two men could see by the tears in his eyes that something had upset him. Skeeter asked, "Is everything okay?"

"Yeah, they just let my son out of the hospital. He was telling me about his new prosthetic leg."

The Bahamian, Cocoa, said, "I can't believe that fish has caused so many problems. It is the devil incarnate."

"Has anyone seen him lately?" John asked.

"A couple of conch fishermen thought they spotted him the other day, but they said it could have been a tarpon. Needless to say, they didn't stay in the water to find out."

"I don't blame them after what I've heard," Skeeter said.

"I listened to the marine forecast and that storm system is gone. The weather's supposed to be nice tomorrow."

"Good, I want to catch that motherfucker and get back to my boy."

Kit knew he must act fast if he was to save the fish. He suspected Trevor, John, and Skeeter would be going out again the following day, not to mention several locals, who were greedy for the reward money. Kit was aware of one thing that they weren't; the cuda's territory was now inside the bay, not outside. This was something they would eventually figure out, so he needed to capture it and relocate it as soon as possible.

One of Kit's concerns was how to carry out his plan without Carla's knowledge of it. He'd have to deceive her by telling her they were going to East Brother Reef because some locals had told him there is a big conch population around there and he needed to check it out. If he could catch the cuda and get it in the live bait well without her finding out, the rest would be easy.

He made up the rigs while she was sun bathing on the bow. Quietly, he snuck into the cabinet and grabbed the canvas net enclosure and placed it in the Whaler. When he turned around she was standing there. "Hi hon, what are you doing?"

"I'm putting some equipment in the boat for some research I'm doing tomorrow."

"What's that canvas thing?"

Kit lied, saying, "That's something I made to keep conchs in, so I can collect a bunch, then measure them on the surface instead of one at a time on the bottom."

Kit continued. "Listen, I'm going to run into Alice Town and grab a few things for the trip."

"What trip?"

"Shoot! I guess I forgot to tell you. Some friends of mine told me about a reef that's supposed to have conch all over the place and I want to go check it out."

"Good! I wouldn't mind taking a little cruise and doing some diving."

"Do you want me to go to town with you?

"Nah – why don't you take a shower and whip up something to eat? I'd like to go to bed early tonight," Kit said with a wink.

"Besides, I have to take a run out with the Whaler early in the morning to do some last minute research before we cast off."

"We'll leave around lunch time, so we can get there before dark and anchor."

The grocery store in Alice Town was reminiscent of ones that occupied early western American towns. The interior had wooden shelves, low lighting, and a musty smell. Yes, you could buy some modern conveniences, such as Nacho cheese flavored Doritos and Velveeta cheese, but at two to three times what they cost on the mainland.

The produce consisted of a few lonely potatoes, peppers, and onions scattered about a dusty wooden shelf. Not much meat, because most people on the island lived off fish, conch, lobster or chickens they raised in their backyards.

After paying close to a hundred dollars for one bag of provisions, Kit thanked the clerk and headed to his next destination – Bonefish Bill's Bait Store. It was a short walk down the Queen's Highway, a narrow street occupied by locals driving golf carts, the major form of transportation second only to bicycles. Several Bahamians smiled and waved to Kit as he strolled down the street. During the past few weeks he had come to know several of them and they had even shared a few beers.

Kit purchased half a dozen live finger mullets and had the clerk put them on ice to kill them because they had to be dead when he placed the devices inside their body cavities. He used live finger mullets instead of frozen finger mullets to make sure the flesh was firm so it wouldn't disintegrate if he decided to troll them.

On the way back to the marina he went over the plan step by step trying not to forget any of the details. He was still worried about Carla's reaction to his plan as he approached the Black Gold.

It was getting dark now, and the sun was sinking into the horizon, overshadowed by a few purple clouds. The interior lights of the yachts docked in the marina were coming to life and the heavenly smell of fried seafood aroused his empty stomach. Kit was now close enough to see Carla in her bathrobe wearing a towel turban on her head and cooking something on the stove. He had hopes the intoxicating smell was coming from their boat.

"Something smells good!" Kit said as he entered the cabin.

"Fried Cajun breaded conch," Carla replied looking up.

"Here, let me help you," Carla said taking the bag from Kit.

"What's the bait for?" She asked.

Kit stuttered a little bit, and then replied, "I thought we might do a little grouper fishing while we're at the reef."

"That sounds like fun. I'm really looking forward to this trip," Carla said, making Kit feel even worse about his lies.

In addition to the fried conch, the meal included seasoned rice, canned asparagus, and a bottle of good Chardonnay. Kit lit some candles while Carla served the food. A Kenny G compact disc played softly in the background as the two devoured the food on their plates. The wine went down like water, giving them a slight buzz in spite of their full stomachs.

Kit stared at Carla, watching the candlelight cast shadows on her cleavage, now visible from the increasingly open neckline of her bathrobe. She noticed his stare, and untied the sash, letting it fall to the floor.

They moved to the couch in the parlor so they could have more room. Slowly, Kit began by kissing her behind the ears, inhaling the pleasing aroma of her freshly washed hair. He nibbled and kissed her neck while she moaned and squirmed. A trail of kisses positioned his lips on her nipples, first caressing one and then the other, while he gently cupped her breasts in his hands. She moaned, "Kit, you're getting me so hot."

"Not yet," he said moving down to her feet. Not many people can claim to have sexy feet, but Carla's were, and Kit knew a little secret – she loved to have her toes sucked. Kit grabbed her by the ankles and began sucking and licking her toes.

"That's not fair!" Carla said, squirming and becoming moister by the minute. Knowing she was close to coming, Kit spread her legs and began kissing and licking his way up her inner thighs to her crotch.

Once there, his tongue darted in every nook and cranny until he concentrated on her swollen clit. He used his tongue to slap it back and forth until she exploded into a gut-wrenching orgasm. After her spasms subsided, he entered her, and made love to her like a mad man until they both had an orgasm and passed out.

Kit woke up early at 6:00 a.m. badly in need of a glass of water. When he saw what time it was he cursed at himself, because he had planned on waking up much earlier. He took Carla's robe and covered her up, hoping to sneak off without waking her.

He tried to put on his bathing suit quietly, but missed a leg hole, stumbled and almost fell over. Carla stirred slightly but remained asleep. Next, Kit walked to the galley and opened the refrigerator to get the bait and to take it to the lab to begin making the rigs.

He sat down and began the process. The eye of the squid hook was shoved in the mullet's anus and through the body cavity until it protruded from its mouth. The stainless steel leader was then attached, coiled, and pushed back into the mouth, leaving only a couple of inches visible.

Once out on the water he would turn on one of the devices and place it in the fish's mouth, sewing it shut with a copper wire.

Kit tiptoed with the bait and deep-sea rod to the ladder leading to the dinghy and climbed down into the Whaler. He untied the bowline and rowed out into the bay before starting the outboard. Kit couldn't help but notice the other boats had already left the marina and had probably already started fishing.

Chapter 33

John and Skeeter got up before sunrise and headed to the spot where the yellowtail fisherman had been attacked. The seas were calm and the sun had started peeking over the horizon as they approached their destination. Skeeter figured trolling ballyhoo with heavier rigging would be sufficient to catch the cuda—no matter how big it was. They put out two outriggers and a couple of artificial lures to increase the menu.

The sky began glowing on the eastern horizon. Small patches of clouds appeared, but for the most part the sky was clear. The bow of the craft plowed through gently rolling seas. John remembered when fishing was a pleasure, a way to relax, not an obsession. Maybe some day the joy would return because it was something he and his boy enjoyed doing together. He wondered if Johnny would ever return to the water, and if he did, would he be able to stand in a pitching boat with his prosthetic leg?

Suddenly, the line snapped from the outrigger and one of the deep-sea rods bent over as line peeled from its screaming reel.

"Grab the wheel Skeeter!" John said, as he lunged for the rod. Quickly, he picked it up and maneuvered himself over to the fighting chair.

"Can you see what it is?" Skeeter yelled.

"Not yet, but it's a pretty good sized fish!"

"Don't horse him!"

"I've done this before!" John replied egotistically.

"Tighten the drag a little!"

"Who's catching this fish, you or me?"

"All right, I'll shut up," Skeeter said, knowing John didn't want his advice.

Several minutes later, the line went slack and John began reeling at high speed.

"He's either off the line or charging the boat. Use the boat to take up some slack!"

Skeeter eased the boat into gear and began moving forward. The line passed the boat up and John could feel the fish was still on the line.

"Put it in neutral!" John screamed. "He's trying to wrap the line around the outboards."

No sooner had he said this, and the fish was again out behind the boat. Only this time, the line was caught on the front side of the twin outboards lower units.

"Raise the engines quick, the lines are caught on them!"

Skeeter turned off the engines and hit the toggle switch to raise the massive outboards. Halfway up the line slid off the units unscathed.

"Nice try you bastard!" John screamed at the fish while taking in some line.

Back and forth the fish swam in a frenzy; however, his frantic attempt to free himself was wearing him out. John kept reeling even though his arm needed a rest. Skeeter stood ready with a gaff hook at the stern. Slowly the fish zigzagged, expelling whatever energy he had left.

"Nice cuda," Skeeter said as the fish came into view. When the fish swam close to the boat, Skeeter slammed the gaff hook into its head right behind the gills and flung him into the boat. Out of the water, the cuda realized he was about to die and started flopping on the deck, hoping to flip back into the water.

John dropped the rod and grabbed a billyclub he used to stun large fish, and started beating the cuda mercilessly over the head. After two full swings to the cuda's head, the fish had stopped moving, but John kept battering him like a maniac.

When the fish's head was nothing more than a bloody mass, Skeeter decided he had seen enough and said, "You can stop now. I think he's dead." John stopped hitting the fish, dropped the club, and began to cry. Skeeter knew this fish wasn't big enough to be the one they were looking for so he cut the leader and threw what was left of the cuda into the water.

The area where the fish had been pummeled looked like a grizzly murder scene; blood was spattered on the floor, center console, and side of the boat. Skeeter flipped on the switch to the wash down pump, grabbed the hose and began washing the fish blood to the back of the boat before it started to dry. A foamy red stream swirled down the drain by the transom.

When he went back to the console to shut off the pump he noticed John had his eyes closed and was breathing erratic. Upon closer inspection Skeeter also noticed his face was pale and he was sweating profusely. When he tapped John on the shoulder, he slumped to the deck and began vomiting.

Skeeter had seen many heart attacks in Miami, the retirement capital of the world, and realized John was probably having one right now.

"John can you hear me?" he yelled. John gave no response. He turned him on his side so he wouldn't drown in his own vomit. Skeeter took his index finger and probed John's mouth for chunks of food, because he didn't appear to be breathing. Next, he felt for a pulse on his neck – no pulse. Skeeter had taken CPR when he became a fishing guide – he figured he might have to use it someday with all of the retirees he took out.

Quickly, Skeeter retrieved a bottled water from the cooler and cleaned the vomit from John's face. He hesitated for a minute because the thought of placing his mouth on another man's mouth disgusted him. After thinking about it, he reminded himself how stupid it was to let something so trivial come in the way of a life or death situation. He realized he could be the one lying on the deck. He placed his mouth over John's and rhythmically breathed air into the dying man's lungs.

Next, Skeeter rolled John on his back and straddled him, placing his hands just below the sternum. He started CPR on John, taking time every few minutes to check for a pulse.   After that, he began alternating between CPR and mouth-to-mouth. At one point, Skeeter himself had to vomit from the act of placing his mouth over John's vomit crusted lips. After administering CPR several times, he started feeling a pulse and John began breathing on his own.

Skeeter ran to the forward compartment and withdrew a seat cushion to put under John's head. Next, he wet a towel with water and folded it before placing it on the patient's forehead.

The race was on. Skeeter started the outboards and pushed the throttles wide open. The boat was cruising at top speed in a matter of seconds. John was bouncing around a little bit, but that couldn't be helped because time was of the essence. Skeeter radioed the marina and asked them to have a Medivac helicopter dispatched from Miami.

A couple of hours later, John was in stable condition in the ICU at Mt. Sinai Medical Center, and Skeeter was on his way to Miami with the boat.

Chapter 34

It was close to noon when Richie spotted the dorsal fin zigzagging through the water, making its way to the skipping bait. During the first pass the fish batted the bait with its bill and knocked the line from the outrigger. The second time it took the bait and the fight was on.

"Holy shit!" Trevor yelled as the large marlin started fleeing for his life. "Figures! You go fishing for marlin; you catch cuda – you go fishing for cuda; you catch marlin.   But trust me, I'm not complaining!"

The fish started sounding, so Trevor tightened the drag slightly to prevent him from going too deep. Minutes later the marlin turned and headed for the surface. Richie saw Trevor cranking like a mad man and reacted by using the boat to take up some line. Trevor's shirt was already soaked with perspiration and the fight had only just begun! A hundred and fifty yards off the stern, the large marlin rocketed out of the water tossing his head violently from side to side. He raced along the surface and away from the boat, exiting the water once more trying to shake the hook.

For the next half-hour, the fish darted back and forth, but Trevor kept the tension on and took in line every chance he got. After hours of running and sounding, the massive fish was giving up, allowing itself to be brought closer and closer to the stern. Finally, the fish was alongside the boat exhausted, but still very much alive.

Dave ran to the cabin and grabbed the 35mm Minolta camera and the tagging kit.

"Look, it's been tagged once already," Trevor said, as he peered down at the fish

Richie put on some leather work gloves, leaned over the side and carefully grabbed the marlin by the bill. Trevor took the camera and snapped several pictures. Next he removed the old tag, held it up close so he could read it, and saw the tag was from the South Carolina Department of Marine Conservation.

Richie, his hand starting to cramp up, said, "Hey boss, I can't stay like this much longer!"

Trevor and Dave quickly stretched the tape measure down the length of the fish. The marlin was just under 10 feet, total length; the bill measured a little over 2 feet.

Trevor recorded the data on a card that would be sent to an address in South Carolina to help scientists there study the fish's migratory routes. Then he placed a new tag in the end of the tagging pole and drove it into the fish where it would cause no damage.

"Well boys, I think I'm about ready to go back to work – screw that cuda!"

The final step was to revive the fish and make sure he swam away. Dave went to the helm and put the boat into gear, keeping the forward speed at an idle. Richie held the fish's head down in the water and after several minutes, he started moving his tail. He let go of the bill and they watched as the magnificent fish swam slowly into the shimmering deep.

"Who wants a beer?" Trevor asked, heading to the ice chest.

"Here's to you boss!" Richie said, as they clanked their bottles together in a salute.

"Let's head in, clean up the boat, and party. We'll sleep in, and take off tomorrow when we wake up," Trevor suggested.

Chapter 35

Once away from the marina, Kit pushed the throttles forward and began speeding across the small chop of the bay. The sun had begun to rise and he could tell it was going to be a hot one. In a short time, he was over the conch bed where he had spotted the cuda on a previous trip.

The cuda was patrolling the waters of the bay searching for its next meal. So far, its efforts had produced only one small finger mullet. Its senses began to pick up a familiar noise echoing from the distance, so it turned to intercept it.

Kit cut the engine and glided to a stop. He decided not to anchor, because the wind wasn't blowing and it was slack tide. Besides, an anchor line would be one more obstacle he would have to worry about if he hooked the cuda. Next, he opened the Playmate cooler and took out one of the baits and activated one of the devices before placing it inside of the mullet. From the top drawer of his tackle box he removed a length of bare copper wire to tie the mullet's mouth shut to ensure the device would remain inside the bait. After preparing the bait, he snapped it to the swivel on the rod and dropped it overboard.

The cuda heard the sound of a fish nearby, but was unable to locate it. Its eyes scanned for whatever movement they were able to detect, but didn't see anything. Its olfactory organs were picking up the smell of finger mullet, which caused its jaw to move up and down in a chewing motion in anticipation of a meal.

A half an hour had passed, and Kit's miracle bait hadn't worked. A slight breeze had started and the Whaler was being blown towards the shallows. Kit decided to start the engine and try trolling the bait. He placed the rod in the rod holder and started the engine.

The noise startled the cuda and it darted off to maintain his vigil from a safe distance. It was at full attention now, its subconscious equating the noises to a previous source of food.

The bait rose up off the bottom as the boat traveled forward. Kit, confidant his plan would be easy to execute, was beginning to wonder now. He intended to zigzag across the area staying in the deeper water.

As the boat pulled away, the cuda sensed the movement and with a few strokes of its tail, was rapidly in pursuit. Now traveling at the same speed as the boat, its partially disabled vision spotted what appeared to be a finger mullet swimming through the water. Its instincts told it to be careful. This could take it to the creatures that had beaten it so savagely in the past. However, it thought, this object was swimming and also making fish noises, so surely this was just another lost mullet.

The cuda charged the mullet swallowing it whole. As it turned to swim away the leader uncoiled and the tension drove the hook into the corner of its mouth. Panicking, it tried to bite through the hook's shaft and broke off a tooth. With all of its might it ran the opposite direction, and away from the boat.

Kit, convinced he was going to fail, wasn't prepared when the rod bowed down towards the water with line quickly leaving the reel. He put the boat in neutral and grabbed a leather fighting belt from inside the console and strapped it on. The line was still running out and the reel was making a high pitched buzzing sound as he placed the rod's butt in the waist belt's leather cup.

The line on reel was getting low, and he was beginning to worry. He had set the drag pretty tight to begin with, and was afraid if he tightened it any more it would break. However, he had no choice. He had to take a chance and tighten the brake on the spool. Otherwise the fish was going to pull out all of the line. When Kit grabbed the spindle to tighten the drag, he burnt his fingers and said, "Shit!"

I'd better cool this thing down before it burns it up, he murmured to himself. He reached over and grabbed a piece of ice from the cooler and placed it on the spool of line, which melted it instantly. Kit tightened down the drag and the fish's forward momentum was halted. The cuda now swam sideways, dragging hundreds of yards of line through the water. Frustrated, the fish jumped into the air, thrashing about, trying to throw the hook.

Kit saw the cuda jump and was sure the fish on the other end of the line was the one he had come for. "Take it easy old timer," he said to the fish.

The cuda, beginning to tire, turned and headed towards the boat. Kit felt the line slacken and quickly turned the crank hoping the fish hadn't gotten off. When he felt the fish tug again it was straight off the port side. Again, the line went slack.

The cuda darted about at times, feeling it had freed himself from the line. However, the throbbing pain in its jaw reminded it this wasn't the case. Once more, it turned and headed towards the boat. Suddenly, with the boat in its path it decided to jump. The massive fish flew through the air surprising Kit, and then splashed into the water on the opposite side. Kit ducked, just barely avoiding a collision with the snapping jaws of the cuda.

The line was trailing across the boat in danger of tangling on one of the many obstacles poking up from the gunnels. Kit quickly guided the line off the stern, praying it didn't become entangled on anything. Within seconds the line was again taught and off the starboard side moving towards the bow.

The unanchored boat was actually towed a short distance by the fish. Next, the cuda circled the boat seeming to purposely wrap the line around the outboard's lower unit in an effort to cut it. Kit tried to stop him, but the fish succeeded in tangling the line up.

He tried to unwrap it with the rod tip, but was unsuccessful. Without hesitating, Kit placed the rod in the rod holder and jumped over the transom into the water. Adrenaline pumping, he grabbed the line and unwrapped it from the outboard. While doing this, the fish ran, causing the line to slice through the skin on his forefinger. The cut wasn't deep, but a red tint appeared in the water around his finger.

The cuda heard the splash and circled around to investigate. He passed several feet from Kit, confused by the smell of blood and the large creature in the water.

Kit saw the cuda and decided he didn't want to be in the water anymore. As he reached for the stern to pull himself up, the cuda circled causing the line to wrap around his ankle pulling him under. Quickly he reached down and freed his ankle. Then, Kit practically jumped into the boat, gagging on saltwater he inadvertently swallowed during the struggle. The first thing he did was raise the outboard to prevent the line from becoming fouled once more.

When Kit picked up the rod again he could tell the fish was beginning to tire. The cuda was no longer running from the boat and was allowing Kit to pull him closer. Halfway in, the cuda used two more bursts of energy in an unsuccessful attempt to free itself.

Kit placed the rod in the rod holder so he could tie one side of the canvas enclosure to the gunnel in preparation for the cuda. After readying the enclosure, he took the syringe with the tranquilizer from his tackle box.

His goal was to get the fish in as quickly as possible, but he must make sure the cuda was exhausted before trying to surround him in the enclosure. Kit picked up the rod and let the fish swim around for several minutes before he maneuvered him alongside the boat. He decided it was time to attempt the capture. Once in position he pulled the ropes attached to the far side of the enclosure. The fish thrashed and splashed for a short while, then calmed down.

Now the tricky part – anesthetize the fish without being injured. Kit took the cap off the premixed Finquel solution and filled the bulb syringe. He made a sign of the cross and took a deep breath before placing the bulb syringe's nose close to the barracuda's gills to start dispensing the anesthesia. Kit heard the cuda gnashing his teeth against the shaft of the hook as he squeezed the bulb.

The tranquilizer acted within a couple of minutes, immobilizing the large fish while not affecting the essential bodily functions. Kit double-checked the knots securing the enclosure to the side of the Whaler and removed the hook from the cuda's jaw. The fish seemed to watch his every move with those large round eyes.

Kit idled the boat back to the marina, hoping Carla was still sleeping. He had to act fast, because the drug would only work for forty-five minutes to an hour. He gunned the engine a couple of hundred yards away, then shut it off, to coast up to the yacht in silence. Quietly, he crept up to the lab to retrieve a camera, tape measure, and a scale. Kit had decided earlier that this fish was too magnificent to go unrecorded.

The fish measured seven feet two inches from head to tail – definitely a record. Next, Kit hooked the hanging scale onto the enclosure and lifted the fish, straining to read the dial. It read ninety-five pounds, but he would have to weigh the enclosure later to find out how much weight to subtract. Nevertheless, he estimated it weighed approximately three pounds. "Smile," Kit said as he snapped several photos of the cuda.

It was a real strain carrying the fish to the live bait well, and as the time approached 10:00 a.m., Kit worried Carla would wake up and see what was going on. After placing the fish in the tank, Kit went to the lab for some more tranquilizing drug. The fish must be kept sedated until it was released, so it wouldn't harm him or itself. He noticed the fish was already starting to show signs of the drug wearing off.

When Kit returned, the fish was moving his head from side to side, his pectoral fins becoming animated.

"Oh shit!" Kit said, realizing he underestimated the cuda's size, thus miscalculating the desired dosage of drug to keep him incapacitated.

He didn't give himself time to think about what might happen as he placed a second dose near the fish's gills with the bulb syringe. With a big splash, the cuda moved his tail with almost enough force to exit the tank. Surprised, Kit fell backwards onto the deck, landing on the lid, and making a terrible racket. Carla, bewildered, dressed in only a T-shirt and panties came out to investigate the noise.

"Kit, are you all right?"

"Yeah, I just slipped," he said, as he quickly placed the cover on the tank.

"Kit, what's in the tank?"

"Just some conchs I brought back this morning."

Carla still suspicious spotted a bulb syringe on the deck, and asked, "What's that syringe doing on the deck?"

"I used it earlier, I must have dropped it."

Carla knew something was up and whatever Kit was trying to hide was in the tank. Without hesitating she walked over to the tank and opened the lid. The cuda's large eye rolled around trying to focus on her. Startled, she dropped the lid.

Now physically shaken, she screamed, "You bastard!"

Kit was afraid she was going to react like this – which is why he tried so hard to keep her from finding out.

"You lied to me – we weren't going to the reef for research, we were going to release that fish! When were you going to tell me?"

"I'm sorry, but I knew you wouldn't understand," Kit said in his defense.

"You're right, I don't understand. Just take your little fish on the cruise, because I'm not going! I'll stay at the Compleat Angler while you're gone." Carla turned and stomped back into the cabin with Kit at her heels.

"Carla, please don't do this," he pleaded. She ignored him as she began packing her things. When she tried to leave, he blocked the doorway. She ducked under his arm and pushed him aside.

"Maybe I'll feel like talking by the time you return," she said as she headed for the hotel. Kit stood in silence, mad at himself for risking his relationship over the cuda. Her spunky personality was one of the many reasons he loved her, but also made her difficult to deal with at times. His plans now were to relocate the fish as fast as possible and return to salvage his relationship. Making up could be fun he thought to himself and smiled.

Carla, half-carrying, half-dragging her things, walked into the hotel and said, "I need a room for two nights."

"Where's your man?" asked the clerk.

"He's going on one of his boring research trips and I don't want to go," she lied.

After checking in, Carla entered the room, flopped down on the bed, and began to cry. One part of her agreed with Kit's notion that the cuda was an innocent creature doing nothing more than what God had designed him to do; the other part of her felt like an enraged rape victim trying to identify her attacker in a line up when she saw the cuda staring up at her from the tank.

She laid back trying to calm herself down. The mattress was kind of lumpy, but after a short while her breathing slowed, as she drifted off to sleep.

Chapter 36

The crew of the Child Support had finished off a twelve pack by the time they had arrived at the marina. Excited, they couldn't wait to brag about the big one that didn't get away. While talking to some locals on the docks, they learned about John's heart attack and Skeeter's swift departure.

"I guess it's up to you guys to catch the fish, I'm heading back to Key West tomorrow," Trevor said to the Bahamians.

"That's okay, you don't need $10,000 as much as I do," one of the Bahamian fishermen replied. When are those pictures of the marlin going to be developed? Nobody's caught one like that for a while around here."

"You'll have to take my word for now, I don't have time to get them developed on the island. I'll make sure I bring them back with me next time."

"Make sure you do," the Bahamian said with a big-toothed smile.

The rest of the day was spent cleaning the boat, drinking beer, and listening to Jimmy Buffet, reggae, and 60's music way too loud.

The captain and crew worked on cleaning themselves up next. One at a time they showered, shaved, and applied excessive amounts of cologne. Now that all of the work was completed, they headed to the Compleat Angler for a night of partying.

Carla woke up around 3:00 p.m. feeling a bit groggy. She went into the bathroom and took a shower to wake herself up. After combing out her hair and plucking out a few eyebrows, she pulled out her legal pad and pencil and began writing. This wasn't the time she usually liked to write. However, TV reception on the island was poor and she told herself she wasn't going to drink the whole time Kit was away. However, nothing was to stop her from having a good time tonight, she thought to herself, a half-baked smile coming to her face.

Time flew as she wrote in the tablet. It had been a good afternoon. Twenty-one newly filled pages were added to her legal pad over the last three hours. After counting them twice, she thought to herself, not bad – now go enjoy yourself!

From her things she selected a pair of leopard print spandex pedal pushers and a sleeveless black top. She always felt sexy when she wore this outfit, kind of like Cat Woman in the old Batman shows. She even took time to put on makeup, something she rarely did, or needed to, for that matter.

Carla headed for the bar feeling good about herself because she knew she looked good and had spent the afternoon being productive.

When she entered the bar, one by one every man's eyes found and studied this new arrival. She pretended not to notice as she sat down in the only vacant chair. To her right was an extremely fat man with an English accent and a dark tan. He had been drinking way too much and was trying to pick up one of the local women. No one sat to the left of Carla because her chair was at the end of the bar next the door. It took a few minutes for her eyes to adjust, but once they did, she spotted Trevor, Richie, and Dave sitting at the opposite end of the bar.

The fat Englishman had been so intent on picking up the Bahamian woman he hadn't noticed Carla sit down next to him. However, when he slid his stool back to go empty his bladder he looked at Carla, and, while staring at her leopard skin pants said, "Hello pussycat."

"I just love pussies, can I pet yours?"

"I don't think my fiancé would like that," Carla said quickly.

"I don't see him around right now – bartender, give this woman a drink. We'll talk about it when I get back," he said as he waddled to the restroom.

"The man is a pig!" the Bahamian woman said to Carla after he left.

Carla told the bartender, "I don't want a drink from that man!"

But he smiled and gave it to her anyway saying, "It's paid for – I don't care if you drink it or not."

Carla ordered another rum and Coke and paid the bartender. Next, she grabbed the drink that she paid for, left the full one sitting at the bar, and walked to the other end where Trevor and his crew were sitting.

Trevor had seen her come in, but wasn't sure where Kit was, so he pretended to ignore her. When he turned around she was standing behind him – his heart almost stopped beating.

"Hi," he said unable to say anything else.

"Hi Trevor."

"Kit's not going to jump me if he sees you talking to me is he?"

"No, he's on his way to East Brother Reef to do some conch research."

"I've never been there," Trevor replied.

Feeling a little more relaxed knowing Kit wasn't around, he said, "Wow, you look great!"

"Thanks," she said, blushing slightly.

"Do you mind if I join you? There's an obnoxious man at the other end of the bar trying to pick me up."

"Of course not," Trevor said, and stood to give her his chair.

Richie quickly stood up and said, "Keep your seat boss Dave and I were going to play the ring game, weren't we Dave?" he said nudging his friend on the shoulder.

"Oh, yeah, yeah, we were just leaving."

The two stood up and checked out Carla's backside. As they passed behind her, they were discreetly shaking their hands as if they'd touched something hot, thinking only Trevor could see what they were doing. Carla caught them out of the corner of her eye and smiled as they acted as if they had done nothing wrong.

"I guess the guys liked your outfit," Trevor said laughing.

Carla smiled, and then asked, "Hey, if that guy comes down here, would you pretend you're my fiancé so he leaves me alone?"

"Sure, whatever. Have a seat," Trevor said, motioning to the stool.

"I wrote twenty-one pages this afternoon," Carla said, proudly.

"That's great!"

"How much more do you think it will take to get your first draft done?"

"About four more chapters – I hope to be done in about two months."

"Great, don't forget to send me a copy."

"Don't be silly, you'll be the first person I send one to," she said, unknowingly placing her hand on his knee – something she did while in an intimate conversation with Kit. Awkwardly, she removed it when she realized what she'd done.

"Hey, if you're not doing anything tonight, why don't you have dinner with the boys and me? We're celebrating out catching and releasing a 500 plus pound blue marlin today."

"Wow!" she said. "I hope you took pictures."

"Yeah, I just don't have them developed yet."

"Besides, I won't see you for a while. We're leaving tomorrow. I've got to get back to work," Trevor said, hoping to get an answer to his dinner invitation.

"I'm going to miss you!" she said.

"So, what about dinner?" he asked, hoping to get a response this time.

"Sure, I'd love to have dinner with you guys on your last night here."

Meanwhile, Richie and Dave were having fun with a couple of girls playing the ring game. The two women had strolled over and bet the men drinks they could hook the ring first. "You're on!" Dave said, enjoying the challenge. The girls were rather plain looking, but had Scandinavian accents and brilliant blue eyes. One was a chef, and the other was a hostess. Both were employed on a 150-foot yacht from Europe that had docked earlier that day. This was the only free time the girls had enjoyed in several weeks and they planned on having fun.

Richie and Dave wound up buying the ladies' drinks, whether they won or lost, and in a short time the girls were feeling no pain.

An hour after meeting the girls, Dave and Richie brought them over and introduced them to Trevor and Carla.

"Gerd and Wilma, this is our boss and captain, Trevor, and this is our friend, Carla.

"Pleased to meet you," Trevor said, shaking hands with the women.

"Nice to meet you," Carla said as she also extended her hand.

"Hey boss, if it's all right with you, we're going to head over to the boat?" Dave asked.

"What about dinner?" Trevor inquired, thinking that he may have a chance to be alone with Carla.

"Tube steak," Richie said with a wink.

"Oh, I see. Well, have a good time."

The group said goodbye, then walked away, but suddenly Richie stopped and turned shouting back to Trevor, "By the way, do you mind if we crack the seal on the Meyers you bought?"

"No, just remember we are leaving tomorrow and I don't want to have to drive the whole way."

"Bye, bye," the girls said smiling and looking back as their dates helped them walk.

"Those girls were trashed," Carla said.

"Yeah, I guess it happens to the best of us," Trevor said, remembering the night Carla and he were in worse shape. Carla slapped him on the shoulder, realizing what he was referring to. "Be quiet!" She said laughing.

"Are you getting hungry?" Trevor asked.

"I could eat"

The fat man made meowing noises at Carla as the couple left. Trevor wanted to say something but Carla tugged his arm and said, "Forget it, that asshole's just drunk."

Chapter 37

The hostess seated them in a dark corner of the restaurant. Trevor still couldn't believe he was sitting across from Carla. He was close enough to smell her perfume and essence. He became excited by the female pheromones scientists say they're there, but Trevor didn't understand how they worked. Her beauty caused a tightness in his chest. He felt like he was back in high school on his first date, stumbling over his words, afraid to make eye contact for any length of time.

A specials sign featuring lobster had been prominently displayed as they walked into the dining room. They both remarked how wonderful lobster sounded. Trevor ordered a bottle of Liebfermilch and two of the specials, lobster with garlic potatoes and salad.

They had finished half the bottle waiting for their food and Carla was starting to feel a bit tipsy. She hadn't planned on telling anyone about the real reason Kit had gone to the reef, but right now, between the wine and her urge to tell someone, she was weakening.

"Trevor, you know how I said Kit went to the reef for conch research?"

"Yes," he replied.

"Well I lied – he caught the cuda and is heading there to release it."

"You've got to be shitting me!" Trevor said in disbelief.

Carla continued, "He lied to me about what he was doing, but I saw it with my own eyes this morning. He fell, probably after almost getting bitten while anesthetizing it and the noise woke me up. I looked in the tank and there it was – staring back at me. At first, I was scared, then I got mad and told him I wouldn't go with him."

Trevor listened then added, "I hope he knows what he's doing. If that fish attacks anyone else he'll be responsible!"

The food showed up, and suddenly they were both ravenous. Carla had trouble removing her lobster from the shell, so Trevor came around and helped her. Before he returned to his seat, she kissed him on the cheek and said, "You're so sweet."

The last drop of wine splashed into Carla's glass. The remnants of the bottle filled it only a quarter full, so Trevor asked if he should order another bottle. "No, I think I've had quite enough," Carla said with a glazed look in her eyes.

"You know, I'm not so sure I want to marry Kit after what happened today," Carla said out of the blue. "It seems he values his work more than he values our relationship."

Trevor took a big chance and said, "Come to Key West with me."

"What?" Carla said with a startled look on her face.

"You heard me. Get away from him for a little while to see if you really love him."

"Do you have enough room for me?"

"Sure. You can have my room and I'll sleep in my office where I spend most of my time writing. I'll be right there if you need any help with your manuscript. I can take you around and introduce you to some agents and writer friends of mine."

Carla thought of what it would be like to live in Key West with a famous author and socialize with people that loved to write as much as she did.

"Purely platonic?" she asked uneasily.

"Whatever you want."

She reached across the table and shook his hand.

"Let's get some more wine. I'll buy – I want to celebrate," Carla said, thinking about her new life.

The waiter returned and Carla ordered another bottle of wine.

"What about the rest of your things?" Trevor asked.

"I have everything that's important to me, except the boat, but I can always buy another one."

"That's your boat? I thought it was his."

"Actually, I inherited it when my mother and father died in a plane crash."

"I'm sorry. How old were you?"

"Just turned eighteen."

"Is your last name Morgan?"

"Yes"

"I read about your parents in the newspaper. Your father was in the oil business."

"Yeah, where do you think the boat's name, Black Gold, came from?"

"Well, I guess I won't have to support you," Trevor said, laughing.

"No, as a matter of fact, I'll be happy to pay rent."

"Don't be silly!" Trevor said.

Halfway through the bottle they replaced the cork and paid the check.

Trevor walked Carla to her hotel room. At the door she hugged him, planning to kiss him on the cheek. However, the wine took over and she placed her lips on his. After several minutes of passionate kissing they decided to go inside.

Carla lay on the bed as Trevor started to take off his clothes. Once fully naked, he laid next to her only to discover she had fallen asleep. He thought about making love to her anyway, but decided that wasn't part of his character. Trevor removed her sandals and stretch pants and started to remove her top until he remembered she wasn't wearing a bra. He took his time pulling her top back down, reminding himself of his earlier decision to be good.

Trevor put his underwear back on, set the alarm clock for 8:00 a.m. and crawled in beside her. She turned on her side and he moved into a spooning position, his member throbbing against her backside. Heaven must be like this, he thought to himself as he drifted off to sleep.

Chapter 38

Kit reached the reef before sunset. He dropped the anchor far enough away to give it room to catch again should it become dislodged during the night.

The cuda was still sedated, but was expected to start waking up sometime within the next hour. Kit placed the canvas enclosure in the bait well and slid one side under the fish. He felt uncomfortable being watched by the cuda, but accomplished the job with no surprises. Carefully, he lifted the fish and carried it to the dive platform on the boat's stern. He tied the enclosure to the dive platform and went to grab a beer to make the wait a little more pleasurable.

While he was in the galley, he turned on the stereo. The Kenny G CD was still in the CD player, which made Kit think about Carla and the previous evening.

After returning to the stern he said to the fish, "You've caused quite a few problems, make sure you stay out of trouble now."

Kit wished he were with Carla so he could tell her he was sorry and how much he loved her. I'll leave at sun up and get back around 10:00 a.m., he thought to himself.

Slowly, the cloud lifted from the cuda's brain. One by one, body parts began functioning. Kit looked down and noticed the fish's pectoral fin had started fanning the water. The cuda's large eyes became reanimated as it calculated its escape. Kit quickly untied the weighted side causing the enclosure to drop away from the fish. The cuda darted ten feet, then stopped and hovered, while its large eye stared at Kit. Maybe this was its way of saying thanks and goodbye. Minutes later the large fish disappeared in a tremendous burst of speed. Kit returned to the cabin and drank himself to sleep.

Chapter 39

The alarm went off, startling Trevor and Carla because alarm clocks were simply not a part of either of their lives. However, Trevor reached over and hit the snooze button just like an old pro. Carla's eyes remained open as she tried to recall why Trevor was laying next to her. Finally, she said, "Trevor, why are you in my room?"

"You mean you don't remember?" he said teasing her.

"No, actually I don't."

"Don't worry, nothing happened. You passed out and I took your shoes and pants off to make you comfortable. I hope you don't mind me sleeping here. I figured the boys could use some privacy and I was pretty messed up."

"No, of course not – what time is it?"

"It's 8:05 a.m., still early. Do you think you can be ready shortly?"

Carla, recalling what had been discussed the previous evening, replied, "I'll take a quick shower, gather my things, check out, and meet you at the boat."

"Sounds good," Trevor said as he stood to begin dressing.

As Trevor approached the boat, he could hear two or more people snoring. The galley was littered with an empty rum bottle, several empty Coke cans, two full ashtrays, and four dirty glasses. He walked to the forward cabins and saw naked bodies occupying two of the bunks. Trevor tried calling Richie and Dave's names, but got no reaction, except for a change in the snoring pattern. Trevor moved down into the cabins and shook them into consciousness.

They both looked severely hung-over and had to roll their guests aside to get up. The girls woke up as the men moved them aside, but made no attempt to cover their naked bodies. They were healthy European stock, muscular, with hairy armpits and legs. They smiled at Trevor as he innocently watched them dress.

"Maybe your captain wants some, too," Dave's friend kidded him.

Trevor realized he was staring and excused himself to the galley and began cleaning up.

It was several minutes before the couples emerged from the cabins. Dave asked, "Hey boss, do you have a pen? The girls said their yacht docks in Key West once in a while, and I want to give them our address and phone number."

"Sure, the top drawer in my cabin," Trevor answered.

Dave went to the cabin and came back with a piece of paper with the address and phone number on it. He handed it to Wilma and she tucked it in her bra.

Dave and Richie escorted the women back to their yacht and returned a little hungover, but in a good mood. Trevor tried to get things in order while they were gone.

Richie noticed he had begun to clean up and protested, "Boss, you don't have to do that."

"I just wanted the boat to look nice, we're taking someone back with us."

Richie and Dave looked at each other and started to giggle.

"You dog!" Dave said.

"What about her old man?" Richie asked.

"She asked me to take her to Key West," Trevor lied.

"She's pissed at Kit because he caught the cuda and took it to East Brother Reef to release it."

"He caught the cuda?" Dave asked.

"That's what she said – saw it with her own eyes."

Richie added, "He's giving up $10,000 and his woman for a fish – all that book learn'n done warped his brain!"

Trevor shook his head and reached into the cabinet for the Tylenol, held up the bottle, and asked, "hangover medicine anyone?" After passing out the tablets, Trevor went to the marina's office to settle up. Before leaving he instructed the crew to begin preparing for the trip.

Richie disconnected the shore power and water supply. Dave turned on the blowers and checked the navigational equipment.

Trevor walked out of the office just as Carla walked by. He hurried to catch up, taking the heaviest bag from her.

Carla stepped on board the boat with trepidation mainly because she wasn't sure if she was doing the right thing. She left an envelope at the hotel's office, knowing Kit would be looking for her there. In the note she explained to Kit she needed a little time away to make sure he was the man she wanted to spend the rest of her life with and that she would be contacting him in the near future to let him know where she was.

Dave started the large diesels one at a time and let them idle for a few minutes before pulling away from the dock. The sky was clear and blue, the ocean like glass. It was a good thing too, because none of the boat's occupants could handle rough seas right now. The vessel motored out of Bimini Bay, with the GPS, radar, and autopilot running with a course set for Key West.

Chapter 40

Kit woke up with a pounding headache and very thirsty. It took a couple of minutes to remember where he was. He went into the galley and took something for his headache, drinking a whole bottle of water in a couple of gulps. Next he went to the head, splashed some water on his face and hair. He dried his face and used a comb to slick back his hair. As he gazed into the vanity mirror, he had to admit he looked a little scary

Getting back to Carla was the most important thing to him right now. Quickly, he readied the vessel for the trip back to Bimini. He turned on the blowers while he attempted to pull up the anchor. No use – it was stuck. He'd have to use the boat's forward motion to break it free. Kit tied the anchor rope off to a cleat, started the engines, and then eased the boat forward dislodging the anchor from the reef. Putting the boat in neutral, he ran to the bow, pulled up the anchor, and quickly stowed it away.

He returned to the controls and pushed the throttles forward causing two big puffs of black smoke to exit the exhaust ports at the stern's water line. The yacht was built for cruising, not for speed, but Kit was going to push her to her limits as she sped back to Bimini.

Several hours later he pulled into the marina and docked. He secured the boat and then went to look for Carla. As Kit walked down the dock he noticed Trevor and the Child Support had departed.

"Good riddance," he mumbled to himself as he walked into the office at the hotel and inquired about Carla. The clerk handed him the note she left.

As soon as he was outside, he tore open the envelope almost ripping the letter in half. Tears came to his eyes as he read her words.

Kit,

By the time you read this, I will be on my way to Key West. I am going there to have a little space to figure out what's going on with our relationship. Please take care of the boat until I return. Trevor has offered me a place to stay and I will call you to let you know I have arrived safely.

Carla

Panic overtook him as he re-entered the marina's office.   He pushed open the door with a little more force than was needed and caused it to slam against the adjacent wall.

"Take it easy!" the woman behind the desk said with a startled look on her face.   It happened to be the same woman that accused Carla of cheating.

"How long ago did the Child Support leave?" Kit asked.

"About two hours ago.   I saw him helping your lady get on board with some suitcases," she said knowing his real motive for asking.

"Thanks.   Just total me up," he said throwing down his Visa card.

Kit forgot to leave his exit papers with the marina, but didn't worry; the Bahamians rarely ever made an issue of them.   He took a couple of minutes to chart a course to Key West, then started the engines and let them idle while he untied the lines.   Kit wouldn't be able to cruise at full speed, because he would burn up too much fuel, and besides, he didn't think the boat's aging diesels could take that kind of punishment.   Alone, he had to be careful about using the boat's autopilot.   If he fell asleep, the boat could plow into almost anything on the high seas.

Chapter 41

The Child Support chugged along the route to Key West. Her occupants, with the exception of Dave and Richie, were lying about enjoying the sun and mild ocean breeze. Trevor was writing on his lap top computer and Carla was scratching text onto a yellow legal pad still wondering if she made the right decision. Richie was passed out on the couch in the parlor recuperating from the previous evening's activities, and resting for when it was his turn at the controls.

Dave didn't have to steer with the autopilot on, but he kept a constant vigil on the radar screen searching for storms and other obstacles. At one point he noticed a small blip on the bottom of the screen that seemed to stay with them. It was at least 20 miles away and invisible to the naked eye. Must be somebody heading the same course we are he thought and decided to pick up a little more speed just in case they were being followed.

Chapter 42

The Landers were successful business owners from Fort Lauderdale. They enjoyed the islands and had purchased a condo in a newly built resort on South Bimini. After several months of visits, they had explored all of the areas immediately adjacent to North and South Bimini. Being adventuresome, Bill Landers suggested to his son, Chip, they check the charts and select an area they hadn't explored. Chip, eager to comply, ran to where their boat was docked and grabbed the charts.

They cleared off the table and spread out one of the charts, using beer bottles to keep it from rolling up. After studying the chart for several minutes, Chip asked, "What about here?" Bill shifted his eyes to where his son's finger was positioned and said, "East Brother Reef, hmm, I've never been there or heard of it – looks good!"

"Let's head there tomorrow. Are the scuba tanks full? I might want to get some lobsters."

"What about the barracuda the clerk warned us about?"

"This reef is a long way from here, we have nothing to worry about."

Chapter 43

It was around noon when the Child Support cruised into the Key West Marina. Many of the boat slips were empty. The charter boat fishermen were out trying to keep their paying customers happy. If they had no luck trolling, they'd drift over a wreck to let the customers reel in a huge amberjack. Or, they'd take a troll by the reef to hook a couple of high-spirited barracudas. The fisherman's reputation as a producer is what keeps fuel in the tanks and food on the table.

Other than a spring break trip during her college days, Carla had never spent much time in Key West. It was hard to think of this town as an island off the coast of Florida, but it was. The road leading there was nothing more than small patches of land connected by a series of bridges. The longest was seven miles, so of course it was called the Seven Mile Bridge.

There was a slight bump as the bow of the boat bounced off the piling. Richie jumped onto the dock with the bow rope in his hand and secured the vessel to the forward cleat. Trevor threw him the stern line to tie off on the rear cleat. Once the boat was docked, the thundering diesels were shut down creating a strange new silence.

It was then that Carla realized that she actually had left Kit and was about to go to a man's house that she really didn't know a whole lot about. Her knees started shaking as she handed her bags to Richie. Trevor noticed, and asked, "Are you all right?"

"Yeah, I think I just need to get something to eat—blood sugar feels a little off."

"I'll take you for a burger at Sloppy Joe's."

"Sounds good," she said trying to hide the real reason for her discomfort.

"How about getting the boat squared away while I run Carla to the house and to get something to eat?"

"Sure thing boss," Richie replied.

"No problemo," Dave added.

"I'll be back in a couple of hours. There's still plenty of sandwich stuff and beer in the galley," Trevor said before walking away.

The pickup truck was parked right where he had left it. It had rained. The tires had stains left on them by the chalky standing water that had once been. He hoped that the battery would have enough power to crank the aging engine and prayed as he turned the key. After a couple of tries, the engine coughed to life spewing black smoke from the tailpipe. "Nice truck," Carla said sarcastically.

"It gets me where I need to go."

It was a far cry from the Mercedes and Bentleys Carla had grown up riding in. "That's all that counts," Carla replied, trying to recover from her snooty remark.

The interior of the truck smelled like a combination of sun-baked vinyl, rust and body sweat. Carla hoped Trevor's house was in much better shape. The truck's AC didn't work, so the smell of ocean air replaced the previous odors when she rolled down her window. Jimmy Buffet blared on the tinny speakers as they headed for Trevor's house to drop off their bags. "Changes in attitude, changes in latitude," were the words to the song. How appropriate Carla thought.

Within minutes they were pulling into Trevor's drive, which was lined with colorful bougainvilleas on either side. "Watch your arms on the bougainvilleas," Trevor warned. "I need to trim them when I get a chance. They grow like crazy down here. Unfortunately, just like the rose, their beauty comes at a price; they have very nasty thorns."

Other than the beautiful variety of bougainvilleas, the rest of the yard didn't impress Carla. The house was pretty but some of the paint was faded and peeling. Trevor struggled with the lock to the front door and cursed, "I meant to oil this before I left!" Finally, the key turned and Trevor was able to open the door. When Carla entered the house, she stood there like a little kid in a museum, eyes darting about the room, mouth wide open in awe. "Wow! This place is really cool. I have to admit I wasn't too impressed with the outside, but this is really incredible."

Carla's eyes locked on the woman's torso figurine that had impressed Richie and Dave the first time they entered the house. "Where'd she come from?"

"I picked her up in San Francisco. Do you like her?"

"She's beautiful!"

"I guess you can tell I'm a breast man," Trevor said, causing Carla to blush.

"Your room's back here," he said, pointing towards a short hallway.

Trevor followed Carla and placed her bags near the wall and out of the way. "Nice bed." Carla walked over and ran her hands over one of the large mahogany posts of the ornate four-poster bed. Next, she bounced on the mattress testing it for firmness. Trevor watched as her breasts bounced up and down causing him to flash back to their interlude on the beach in Bimini.

"Trevor?"

"Yeah, what?"

"It's just you had this blank look on your face. Is everything all right?"

"Yeah, I was just thinking I need to change the sheets. I wasn't expecting company."

"I'll do it. Where's the washer?"

"On the back porch, but you don't have to…"

"Don't be silly!" Carla said as she began stripping the sheets.

Trevor followed her to the back porch and showed her how the machines operated.

Once the sheets were safely inside Trevor asked, "You ready to get something to eat?"

"Yes, I'm famished."

"Let's go then."

Carla headed out the front door and walked over to the truck. Trevor strolled over to a mass covered by a tarpaulin and began pulling it off. "Oh, we're not going in the truck. Locals use bikes to get around. With all of the tourists invading our town, there isn't much parking. Besides, we're only a few blocks away from Sloppy Joe's".

"I don't care. I love riding bikes. I think I'm going to like it here."

Chapter 44

Kit was just ten miles from Key West when the engines alarms started sounding.

"Shit they're overheating! I knew I should have had those fucking impellers replaced!"

He knew it was useless to run them anymore and take the chance of ruining the engines. Smoke was rising from the engine hatch probably from oil residue and rubber components sizzling from the intense heat generated by the water-starved engine blocks.

"This is just great! I wonder what the fuck else is going to go wrong!"

Kit pulled out his wallet to make sure he had his credit card before radioing a local company, Sea Tow, to tow him into Key West. After making the call, he had time to think about the events that had taken place over the last few days. He became more determined to find Carla and make things right.

A squall line crept up from the horizon. The black clouds were split by fierce lightening. The rain fell from the heavens like a liquid wall. The seas began to buck like frightened horses fearing the oncoming storm. Kit went down below to put on his foul weather gear. The boat began to toss him to and fro as it bobbed like a cork powerless in the raging seas.

Kit's thoughts became frantic. This is all I need. Sea Tow was going to have a hard enough time finding me in good weather. They'll never find me in this crap. Kit turned on the navigation lights hoping to aid in their search. During the next few hours, he had to quickly start the engines and use them just long enough to keep the vessel pointed into the huge rolling waves that came with the storm. The storm passed and the weather cleared just in time for a beautiful sunset.

Kit worried whether the towboat would make it before dark. He was startled from his thoughts by a voice booming from the radio's speaker. "Black Gold this is Sea Tow Key West. Over"

"You've got the Black Gold. Come on."

"Black Gold we've got you on radar. We're still five miles off. Are you okay? Over."

"Roger. There was a hell of a storm came through earlier. Over"

"Roger that. Sit tight we'll be there shortly. Over"

"Don't have a choice. Over"

After Kit placed the microphone in its spot on the VHF radio, he looked up to see a fairly large vessel just off the starboard bow. Wow! I thought they were five miles away. He quickly realized who it actually was when he saw the familiar orange and white paint job flanking the U.S. Coast Guard vessel.

A voice came over a loudspeaker! "Permission to board your vessel captain!"

Kit quickly replied, "Glad to see you. Come on board."

The vessel glided alongside and two sailors jumped on board to secure ropes forward and aft. An important looking man wearing stripes boarded the vessel.

"Captain I'll need to see your registration and immigration documents."

"Sure. I have them right here."

"What was your point of departure?" The officer asked already aware that Trevor had left Bimini a few hours earlier.

"I came from Bimini and I'm heading to Key West. My engines started overheating, so I had to shut down. Sea Tow's on their way."

"Mind if we look around?"

"No problem. Look, I'm a marine biologist. I was doing some work for the Bahamian government. I'm on my way to Key West to meet my fiancé. You haven't seen the vessel she's on have you? The Child Support," Kit said hoping to get some information on her whereabouts.

"If we did, it was just a blip on our radar screen. Everything seems to be in order captain. Sea Tow is off your port side, so we are going to shove off. Good luck!"

"Thanks. Luck is what I need right now."

The Sea Tow vessel pulled up alongside the stranded boat and tied off.

"Howdy captain. Name's captain Mike. Is your vessel taking on any water?"

Kit grabbed his hand. "Kit Hansen.   No the engines just overheated, but I shut them down before any damage could occur."

"Where do you want to be towed to?"

"Key West."

"Anywhere in particular?"

"I guess to a marina with a good mechanic."

"I have a friend of mine who does good work and can be trusted."

"Sounds good to me."

Chapter 45

Trevor and Carla zigzagged through the neighborhood and eventually made it out to the main drag of Key West, Duval Street. Carla noticed most of the businesses catered to tourists; they either sold food, T-shirts or knick-knacks. The street was narrow, and people, usually slightly inebriated, liked to wander into it whether on purpose or by accident. The smell of food and the rush of cold air from open doors bombarded her senses as she peddled harder to keep up with Trevor.

After a few near misses with the drunken tourists, Carla and Trevor pulled up to the sidewalk in front of Sloppy Joe's and locked their bikes to a No Parking sign. The restaurant was slightly crowded but they were able to find a table for two towards the back. Carla noticed the place smelled of deep fried food and old beer, probably like most of the restaurants in Key West. Within minutes, a waitress approached the couple with her breasts practically falling out of a bikini top and a jean skirt barely covering her bottom.

"Hi Trevor. Long time no see."

"Hey Crystal. How's it going?"

"Ahh you know—S.O.S different day. Canadian tourists are in town. I just got stiffed"

"Sorry to hear that, I'll see if I can make up for them."

"Where have you been?"

"I spent some time in the Bahamas fishing."

"Must be nice to be you!"

"Sometimes it's not all it's cracked up to be."

"Who's the lady? I'm jealous."

"I'm sorry. This is a friend of mine, Carla."

Carla shook hands with the woman and said, "Nice to meet you."

"What will you guys have to drink?"

Carla said, "I'll have a Bud Light draft."

"Sounds good, make that two," Trevor added.

"I'll be back in a flash to take your food order."

Carla sat silent for a minute then said, "Seems like she knows you pretty good."

"Everybody knows everybody in Key West."

"But she seemed to know you on a deeper level."

"All right, I had a few too many one night and she took advantage of me. I guess there's something about me and alcohol that women can't resist," Trevor said winking at Carla.

Carla turned bright red and whispered, "That's just wrong."

Trevor smiled and said, "I'm sorry, but I couldn't resist."

The cold beers arrived just in time to break up the silence that had just invaded the table. A musician began to play a medley of Jimmy Buffet tunes with an electronic sound machine and a wide variety of musical instruments attached to his body. Their lunch consisted of cracked conch sandwiches and piles of hot salty french fries drowned in ketchup. Three beers later, Trevor was beginning to notice how sexy Carla looked. He sat there staring at her, his thoughts returning to that beach in Bimini. Finally, Carla broke the silence.

"Trevor, are you okay?"

"Yeah, I'm sorry, I was just daydreaming."

"You about ready to go?"

"Sure, just let me finish my beer," Trevor said, not wanting to stand at that moment due to a half woody.

The trip home was even more treacherous now that they were just as inebriated as the tourists they were dodging. Carla swerved to miss a homeless man and took a tumble. She was okay except for damage to her ego and a scraped elbow. Her only words were, "Do you think we could walk next time?"

When they arrived home, Trevor offered to bandage Carla's elbow.

"Come with me to the bathroom. I have some peroxide and some Band-Aids to patch you up. Tears poured out of Carla's eyes as the peroxide bubbled the road debris from her scrape. Trevor tenderly held her wrist in his left arm and smeared her tears away with his right hand. The closeness of her body and sweet smell of her breath was too much for him. He tried to kiss her tender lips. She turned her head and said, "Trevor this is not going to happen!"

"I'm sorry. You bring out the animal in me."

"Just let me know if you can't handle this—you know our arrangement. If not, I'll go get a hotel room."

"I'll be good. I promise."

Trevor finished bandaging her arm in silence.   When he was through, Carla gave him a peck on the cheek and thanked him. "I'm going to go unpack and take a shower," Carla said as she left the bathroom.

"Just let me know if you need any help washing your hair because it's kind of hard with one hand."

"Trevor!!"

"Lighten up. I was only kidding."

The phone rang. It was Trevor's agent, Ilsa.

"It's pretty bad that I have to find out that you're back in town from a waitress at Sloppy Joe's instead of a phone call from you."

"Would you quit it Ilsa, I just got in and needed to eat."

"Who is the young lady you were with?"

"Are there no secrets in this town? Why? Are you jealous?"

"No.   I just hope she's not going to be a distraction to the manuscript you've promised to complete by next month."

"Are you sure that's it?"

"Well, okay. Maybe I'm a little jealous."

"You needn't be.   She's just a friend that I've taken in temporarily."

"Since when do you take in strays?"

"Put away the claws. She got into a fight with her fiancé in Bimini and needed to get off the island to have some time to think. Her last name's Morgan—ring a bell?"

"Not 'the Morgan', only heir to the oil tycoon's fortune?"

"None other than. She's a nice girl I befriended while I was in Bimini. She's also trying to break into the writing scene. I offered to take a look at her manuscript."

"I've asked you to do that before. You said you didn't like to critique novice writing."

"Well, she seemed so passionate about her writing that I figured what the heck. Besides maybe you might be able to pick up a new client. It can't hurt having a Morgan as a client."

"Maybe you're right. I'd like to meet this girl. How about having dinner tonight at that restaurant I told you about?"

"What time?"

"I'll come by and pick you up at eight."

"Sounds good."

Chapter 46

After hanging up with Trevor, Ilsa immediately called her hairdresser to make an appointment for that afternoon. She decided it was time to let him know exactly how she felt about him. It may not happen tonight, but she wanted to look her best to improve her chances.

It didn't matter to her that he was ten years older. She was tired of the lowlife men she'd met in Key West that had nothing intelligent to say, and if they did say anything, it was just to try to maneuver her into bed.

Her crush developed over the tumultuous years she had managed Trevor's literary career. She had observed him drinking and leaving bars just before sunrise with local barflies. She understood why—men had needs, but it didn't hurt any less. She often thought about telling him about her feelings, but she didn't want to hurt her business relationship with him in case he didn't feel the same way.

Ilsa's parents had been gypsies, which is probably the reason she took so keenly to managing writers. She could talk her way into any office and probably convince whoever was listening that the world was square.

In addition, she inherited exotic looks, long black hair and mysterious large brown eyes. She was small in stature, but large and curvy in all the right places.

There was a time when she was talking to Trevor that her feminine instincts told her that he was aware of her bumps and curves. She could have sworn she caught him looking at her bumps when she had worn a low-cut silk blouse during a meeting with him.

The problem was this was the only time that she'd ever evidenced any interest from him, even if it was an act that any red-blooded male would have been guilty of. It may have been his lack of interest that had created this sustained lust she had for him. All of the other men in Key West followed her around like drooling dogs in heat. She could have had her pick of any number of them, but she wanted what she couldn't have—Trevor.

Chapter 47

The mechanic at Al's Marine came out of the engine room with good news, "You shut her down just in time. Nothing seems to have any extensive heat damage. I can have her fixed in a few hours. I've just got to locate some new impellers for these ancient engines."

Kit breathed a sigh of relief and said, "Sounds good to me. Hey, I'm looking for a friend of mine, a man by the name of Trevor Callaway. Do you know him?

"No, I don't know the name"

"Are you sure? He's supposed to be a famous writer."

"Tell you what. I'll call my girl friend in a couple of minutes when she goes on break. If he's famous, she'll know him. She conducts tours down in the city and she knows about everyone famous and where they live.

Kit hung out for a couple of minutes sitting on the dock staring down into the water. Several dock snapper were patrolling the water looking for handouts. From the size of them, he could tell that someone was feeding them.

The bottom and rocks had an unnatural algae growth probably caused by fertilizer run off or sewerage discharge from the various boats in the marina. Kit often wondered what things must have been like a hundred years ago, before man brought his machines and pollution to the seas.

Kit jumped when the mechanic walked up behind him and said, "She knew just who you were asking about. Trevor's quite well known in the city. He's always hanging out at the bars partying with the other locals.

I guess I forgot that I met him once at Fantasy Fest. I wouldn't recognize him if I saw him today on the street though; he was dressed as a drag queen that day. Anyway, he lives in the third house on the left side on White Street. The house has green trim and huge bougainvilleas lining the drive. Tell him Annie says hello when you see him."

"Thanks for the info. Do you know where I can rent a car?"

"Unfortunately, all of the car rental places are in the city. I have an old bike you can use. It's not that far."

"Sounds good. I can use the exercise."

Kit thought about the stealthiness of using a bike. He could ride to White Street, hide the bike, and sneak up to the house to find out what's really going on.

The trip to Key West by bike was thoroughly enjoyable even though it felt like it was a hundred degrees outside. Water was constantly in view. It appeared either on the right or left or on both sides while crossing one of the many bridges spanning the channels that allowed the Atlantic Ocean to kiss the Gulf of Mexico.

At one point a sign reading Key West Marina caught Kit's eye. He remembered Trevor saying that he kept his boat there. Kit scanned the boat slips looking for the Child Support. It didn't take long to find her because she was one of the few boats left in the marina on a day that looked perfect for fishing. Richie and Dave were busy scrubbing her down in an effort to keep her in good shape for their boss. Kit turned his head so they wouldn't recognize him and blow his plan to sneak into Key West.

When Kit pulled onto White Street, there was no one in sight. Quickly, he stashed his bike in the bushes of the house next door to Trevor's. Next, he crawled behind the house so he could look in the window to see if anyone was home. It appeared that no one was. He noticed the back door had a skeleton key lock that could easily be picked.

Once inside, Kit was amazed at how the condition of the outside of the house in no way reflected the inside of the house. The outside was nothing special, in fact it was kind of run down looking, but the inside was a world of nautical treasures all meticulously displayed.

He found what appeared to be Trevor's bedroom and immediately recognized Carla's luggage in the corner with a pile of her dirty laundry sitting on top. The aroma of her favorite shampoo was still drifting from the bathroom. She must have just left after taking a shower he thought. The comforter on the bed was all in disarray as though someone had quickly made the bed—he didn't know that it was from Carla jumping on it. Kit pictured Carla and Trevor making love on the bed and almost became ill.

He walked over to the pile of dirty clothes and pressed them to his nose to inhale Carla's scent. His right hand held something silky and smooth on the bottom of the pile; it turned out to be one of her thongs. He quickly shoved the underwear into his pocket. For now, this is all that he had to remind him of the love they once shared.

Kit had seen all he needed to see. It was evident that Carla and Trevor had become lovers. Distraught, he rushed from the house forgetting to lock the back door. Catching himself, he dropped to the ground and inched his way next door, where he'd hidden his bike. He peddled away like a madman, running the stop sign on the corner and narrowly missing the Conch Train. Surprised tourists in their flowered shirts and Bermuda shorts shouted at him from the tram as he sped off.

Chapter 48

Carla and Trevor returned from their walking tour of the area. After taking a shower, Carla had asked if any other famous people lived in the area. Trevor offered to take her on short tour to the homes of some of the better-known celebrities in the area, Calvin Klein, Ernest Hemingway, and several others.

During the walk, he stopped to introduce Carla to an editor from a major publishing house, Bill Simmons. Bill was always after Trevor to jump ship and let his company handle Trevor's books, but Trevor had signed a water-tight contract with his current publishers so that would never be possible. In an effort to help Carla get published, he invited Bill to have dinner with them to discuss her manuscript.

Chapter 49

The trip home from Trevor's to the marina took half the time it took going. Adrenaline must have been a major factor. Kit was afraid that someone had seen him break into Trevor's house or that he was being pursued by a mob of angry tourists after the near miss with the Conch Train. He pulled off the main drag and almost lost it by trying to turn too sharply in the white sugar sand.

Kit parked the bike where he had gotten it and walked down to the docks to check on the mechanic's progress. The mechanic bumped his head on the top of the engine room when Kit startled him by calling his name.

"Hey Jim, how's it going?"

"Shit! Not so good!"

"Sorry. I didn't mean to sneak up on you."

"It's okay. You'd think after working on these things all these years I'd remember not to raise my head in such tight spots. I had to come back down and recheck the numbers on the engines because they didn't match the supplier's specs. It may take a couple of days to get the parts; these babies are dinosaurs."

"Do you know of a good hotel in the area?

"Yeah, there's one around the corner. Doesn't look like much from the street, but the price is reasonable and the rooms are clean."

"Sounds good."

"Did you ever find that writer fella?"

"I found his house, but he wasn't home."

"I'll need a credit card before you go to cover the parts and dockage."

"Sure no problem."

Kit took care of business, and then grabbed some clothes before heading to the hotel. The hotel clerk told him about a car rental agency just down the road where he could rent a car. Once in the room, Kit decided to take a shower before heading to the agency. While undressing, he remembered the prize he had taken from Trevor's house.

He pulled Carla's red thongs from his pocket and pressed it to his nose. Memories of her sexy body and scent filled his mind as he pleasured himself in the shower. All he could think about was finding his true love and winning her back. He wasn't going to let some over-the-hill romance novelist steal her.

Chapter 50

Trevor and Carla returned from their walk and plopped down into the antique leather chairs in the living room. The room had a smell of oldness. It was like the scent of an antique store or museum. One could sit and take in all of the visuals for hours. Carla was doing so when Trevor broke the silence.

"So what do you think of Bill?"

"He seems like a very nice man."

"He is. Maybe we can get him to consider publishing your book."

Carla jumped up from her seat and hugged Trevor saying, "That would be wonderful!"

"Now hold on, I didn't say publish, I said consider."

"Oh, I know. It's exciting just having somebody in the business take a look at my book!"

Once again, Trevor was in close quarters with Carla, her perfume invaded his body with every breath. Carla felt the hunger he had for her and moved back to her chair to continue the conversation.

"In addition to Bill, there's someone else I like you to meet tonight my agent, Ilsa."

"Your agent's a woman?"

"Yeah, are you surprised?"

"No, just curious. Is she pretty?"

"No, she's a real dog," Trevor answered, trying to keep a poker face.

"Come on, tell the truth."

"I am. She looks like an old librarian that's spent her entire life at home eating Little Debbie cakes and chocolates; she's huge!"

"Well she's got to be a good woman to put up with you."

"What's that supposed to mean?"

Carla realized she may have hit a nerve.

"What's the matter? Can't you take a little teasing?"

"No, because just being around you is a tease."

The conversation suddenly turned serious as Carla replied, "I can leave if it's too much for you."

"Don't be silly.   Now you're the one who can't take a little teasing!"

They both sat for a couple of minutes digesting what had just transgressed. Suddenly, Trevor broke the silence.

"We better start getting ready if we want to make our dinner date. I'm going to wash some clothes if you have anything that needs washing."

"I have a few things. I'll go grab them."

As Trevor opened the back door, something clicked in his head. It was unlocked.

He yelled from the back porch, "Carla, did we lock the door before we went out?"

"Yeah, I'm pretty sure you did," Carla said, joining him on the porch with her pile of dirty clothes

"That's weird it was unlocked."

Carla suddenly blurted out, "Wait a minute, my red thong is missing!"

Trevor looked puzzled. "Red thong?"

Carla stared at him. "You didn't take it did you?"

"Listen, I may be a little kinky", he said indignantly, "but I haven't resorted to stealing woman's panties yet. Maybe whoever broke in took them. There are plenty of freaks in Key West. Next time we leave, I'll use the dead bolt."

"Yeah, please do. I only have so many pairs of panties. And, it gives me the creeps."

They finished putting the clothes in the washer and returned inside. Trevor carefully inspected the entire house and decided that nothing else was missing.   Carla also checked the rest of her belongings and came up with the same results. She returned to the living room and asked, "Why did they only take my thong when there are so many other desirable things lying around like my diamond tennis bracelet?"

"I told you Key West is full of weirdoes. Every day you can read about something odd occurring here. I know I've read of at least one instance of someone getting caught stealing panties from their neighbor's clothesline in broad daylight. Down here someone might not have taken them because the man was sexually attracted to you. He might have been a cross-dressing transsexual kleptomaniac."

With that, Carla began laughing uncontrollably and shouting, "A cross-dressing transsexual kleptomaniac? Boy, what an imagination you have!"

"Well, as I said before, we had better start getting ready. We don't want Bill and Ilsa waiting on us too long."

Chapter 51

The car rental agency was right where the hotel clerk had said. Kit barely broke a sweat during the short walk. He decided to wear black slacks with a black shirt to make him less visible at night. The car rental agent had a slight lisp and he winked at Kit when he commented on how well Kit's pants fit. Disgusted, Kit picked up the keys and practically ran from the agency to his 1997 two-door Kia in the parking lot. It wasn't much, but the price was right.

During the drive to Key West, Kit thought about how he might salvage his relationship with Carla. First, I have to find out just how serious this thing with Trevor is. If she's just staying with him, I may be able to persuade her to come home with me. And if she's fucking him, I may just kick his ass and steal her away! Tears welled up in his eyes as he thought about what he had seen that afternoon. "Shit!" he yelled while pounding on the Kia's steering wheel.

Chapter 52

Trevor, Carla, Bill and Ilsa agreed to meet at the Pink Dolphin, a new restaurant on Duval Street. Ilsa had been dying to take Trevor there for dinner. The restaurant was owned by two former drag queens and was already the rage of locals and tourists alike.

The inside was decorated like an underwater reef with small grottos, which acted as booths to give diners privacy. Of course, seafood was the specialty of the house, but the beef and lamb were gourmet as well. Ilsa wanted to take Trevor there alone, but she would have to wait. At least she would get to check out this girl he was supposedly helping out.

Ilsa showed up first and tipped the maitre d' to get the best table in the house, an extra large grotto in the back of the restaurant. Of course, Bill was the next to show up; Trevor would be late for his own funeral.

"Hi Bill. Long time no see."

"Yes, you'd think in a city as small as Key West we'd run into each other more often."

"Well, I guess it doesn't help if I rarely go out because I'm so busy."

"I know what you mean. This business can dominate your life if you let it."

"Yeah, but I wouldn't want to be doing anything else."

"Have you heard from Trevor? It's 7:15 and we agreed to meet at 7:00."

"I'd swear he's Cuban if I didn't know any better. He's always late, but don't worry he's never stood me up."

"And I never will," Trevor chimed in appearing in the opening of the grotto.

"Sorry I'm late. I must still be on Bahamian time."

"But the Bahamas are in the same time zone as us," Bill said matter-of-factly.

"Yes but the Bahamians aren't. They have no need for clocks or watches. We should learn from them and maybe we wouldn't need tranquilizers or suffer from heart attacks."

Bill smiled and said, "Well, my friend you may just have a point there."

Trevor noticed Ilsa staring at Carla and decided it may be a good time to introduce them to each other. "I'm such a fool. Ilsa, this is my friend Carla." Ilsa studied her imagined competition and replied, "Trevor, you didn't tell me your friend was so beautiful." Carla smiled and responded, "And you didn't tell me you had such a gorgeous agent."

"I guess I'm just one lucky guy to have so many beautiful women in my life!"

The women smiled uneasily as they sized each other up. A waitress appeared and took their drink orders. After the first drink, everyone started to relax and they slipped into friendly conversation. The women were talking about Carla's family history, and the men were swapping fish stories.

Chapter 53

Kit arrived on White Street just before Trevor and Carla left for the restaurant. He had to duck to avoid being seen by them as they drove down the street. Trevor was concentrating on the road and Carla was laughing and talking to him as they drove, so he knew they hadn't noticed him. He kept his lights off and pulled a u-turn to follow them keeping enough distance so as not to arouse suspicion.

The drive was a short distance to the Pink Dolphin. Kit watched them pull into the parking lot as he cruised past to find a place to park out of sight. As luck would have it, he found a spot on a side street with a view of the interior of the restaurant.

The lighting was low, but Kit was able to see them join another couple at the table inside some type of area modeled to look like an underwater cave. If it wasn't for the circumstances, it looked like a place he'd enjoy dining at. The sight of Carla with another man made his blood boil with jealousy. He sat there motionless not sure what his next move would be. The tears in his eyes made it hard to see what was happening in the restaurant.

Chapter 54

Trevor finished telling Bill about the marlin and barracuda, and then Bill's attention turned to Carla.

"That was quite a close call you had with the barracuda young lady," he suddenly blurted out to Carla.

Carla, engrossed in a conversation with Ilsa about her book stopped and replied, "Yes, I still have nightmares about it."

"I've seen some pretty big cudas in my days of fishing, but not as big as the one Trevor described."

"My boyfriend, he's a marine biologist, said the fish is probably a world's record."

"I don't doubt that for one minute. Where is your boyfriend? I'd like to meet him. I have a few questions I'd like to ask about a fish I caught the other day."

"He's in the Bahamas right now. We needed a little time away from each other. That's why I'm staying with Trevor."

"Sorry, I hope it's nothing serious. Watch Trevor. You know he has a reputation with the ladies," Bill cautioned as he winked at Trevor. Embarrassed by Bill's statement, Trevor gently kicked him from under the table to let him know to cool it with the attack on his character. Ilsa grabbed Trevor's hand and said, "Oh don't worry Carla, he's nothing but a big Teddy Bear.

Trevor had never had any physical contact with Ilsa other than a peck on the cheek. The feel of her warm, soft, slender hands felt good wrapped around his. Ilsa realized she had left her hands around his just a little too long and withdrew them slowly.

Trevor glanced into her eyes and noticed something had changed about the way she was looking at him. She had been nothing but a snot-nosed kid fresh out of college ten years ago when she knocked on his door and demanded he speak to her about her taking over as his literary agent. Up until that point his books had drawn little attention to his literary prowess. They sat in bookstores around the country gathering dust. It wasn't until she had gotten him with a publisher that was willing to spend the money to promote them that his popularity had grown to such heights. She was fifteen years younger than him at the time, and he was still married.

Maybe it was the weeks he had spent away fishing in the Bahamas that had given him a new perspective. Ilsa had aged wonderfully like a well-made violin.   All the curves were the same, but the little imperfections that occurred only contributed her character and beauty. He sat back and listened to the resonance of her voice while she spoke and laughed with Carla.

"Trevor's a perfect gentleman and a good friend. I can't tell you how much I appreciate him offering me a room at his house while I try to work things out with my fiancé," Carla reassured everyone as she patted Trevor's thigh. Ilsa noticed her actions and wrapped her arm around his back pulling him towards her saying, "Yeah, he's such a nice guy."

"Stop it. I'm not always nice," Trevor interjected as he flashed a look at Carla.

The waitress arrived with a fresh round of drinks and a spiced shrimp appetizer. It was just in time to dissipate any uneasiness that may have occurred between Carla and Trevor. A glass was raised and Trevor broke the silence, "To Carla. May this mark the beginning of a long and prosperous literary career!"

Turning red, Carla brought her glass to the center of the table and clinked it against the others saying, "Trevor don't be silly. They haven't even read my manuscript."

"If Trevor says it has merit, I'd be willing to take a look at it," Bill reassured her.

"And if Bill is interested, you'll need a good agent," Ilsa was quick to add.

"See there. You're practically published," Trevor said before he downed his drink and ordered another.

Chapter 55

Kit couldn't stand it any longer. He decided it was time to make his move to try to regain Carla. The entrance to the restaurant was crowded with patrons waiting to be seated. Kit pushed his way roughly through the crowd until he faced the maitre d', a large man with a bald head and an oversized diamond earring in his right ear. "Say fella, where do you think you're going," he said blocking Kit's way into the restaurant.

"Some friends of mine are waiting for me inside. I'm late for a dinner engagement. Please let me in," Kit implored him.

"I here that line all the time buster. Listen, nobody mentioned anything about you joining their party, and there's already too many people standing knee-deep around the bar. Do you want the fire marshal to shut us down? Just go wait your turn like a good boy like everyone else. Give me your name and I should have you seated in the next couple of hours."

Kit reached in his wallet and pulled out a one hundred dollar bill and said, "My name is Ben, Benjamin Franklin." The maitre d' quickly grabbed the bill and stuffed it into his pocket saying, "I think I just saw someone leave the bar if you want their stool," he said with a wink. "And if you need someone to push your stool in, I get off at four," he mumbled under his breath while checking out Kit's bottom as he entered the door.

Kit hesitated for a minute not sure what to do or say, but adrenaline was controlling his actions right now. He walked into the grotto and stood across from where Carla and Trevor were seated. The couple looked as though they'd seen a ghost. Carla was the first to speak.

"Kit, what are you doing here?"

"I might ask you the same thing."

"Did you get the note I left you?"

"Yes. That's why I'm here."

"Well this isn't the time or place to discuss our relationship. Just tell me where you're staying and I'll call you later."

"No! I want you to leave with me now!"

"Kit. Don't be silly. Just tell me where you're staying and I'll come by later."

"Carla what I have to say won't wait."

Trevor had endured Kit's interruption of their dinner long enough.

"Didn't you hear what the lady said?" he asked standing up to make his point.

"You need to sit down and stay out of my business!" Kit answered pointing his finger in Trevor's face. "And besides, if it wasn't for you, we wouldn't be having this conversation, so butt out if you know what's good for you!"

Their voices rose above the chatter and clatter of the restaurant, and the maitre d' was already making his way to the table immediately recognizing Kit as the man he had just let in. Trevor replied to Kit's last comment angrily, "Why don't you just leave like the lady asked, asshole!" That was all Kit could stand, so he dove over the table at Trevor, drink glasses flying onto the floor with the sound of breaking glass overpowering the already noisy background sounds of the packed restaurant. His hands were around Trevor's throat with Trevor struggling to keep from being choked.

The maitre d' was not a man to be reckoned with because he outweighed Kit by fifty pounds. He quickly grabbed Kit by the shoulders in an effort to break up the struggling men. Seconds later, the three men were rolling around on the floor while Bill and the ladies stood back and watched helplessly. Carla screamed, "Kit let go of Trevor right now or I'll never speak to you again!"

Even in his fit of rage Kit acknowledged her words and let go of Trevor's throat. It was too late however, the waitress had dialed 911 on her cell phone and two officers from the Key West police department were rapidly making their way to the fight scene.

When the officers arrived, Trevor was lying on the floor rubbing his throat and trying to catch his breath. The maitre d' and Kit were now standing with the maitre d' positioned behind him attempting to restrain Kit's arms. One of the officers knelt down and spoke to Trevor, "Are you okay sir? Do I need to call a paramedic?" Trevor shook his head no. The other officer recognized the maitre d' and asked, "Bobby is this the troublemaker?"

"Yes. Geeze, I thought he was going to kill this poor man."

The officer moved behind Kit and said, "I'll take over Bobby. Sir, keep your hands behind your back and don't move. I'm going to place you in handcuffs. Just stay calm and nobody's going to get hurt."

Kit reached around to wipe his eye because some type of liquid was beginning to cloud his vision. The officer pushed him to the ground and put his knee in Kit's back saying, "I told you to keep your hands behind your back!" In seconds the officer had Kit in cuffs and was attempting to help him stand. Kit responded to the officer's excessive force, "Shit, I was just trying to wipe my eye so I could see. You didn't have to do that!"

The officer responded, "I told you to keep your arms behind your back. You could have been reaching for a weapon. Now just listen to what I tell you from now on and there won't be any more trouble. It looks like you have a small scratch above your eye from some of the broken glass, but it appears to have stopped bleeding."

The other officer started questioning Bobby, the maitre d', "Bobby, why don't you tell me what happened?"

"All I know is this man pushed his way into the restaurant... "

Kit interrupted shouting, "I didn't push my way in. I paid you a hundred dollars to let me in!" Bobby turned red and changed his story, "All right I let him in, but I didn't know he was going to do this!"

"Just tell us what happened next," the officer instructed him.

"I'm standing at the door taking care of customers when I hear all this shouting in the back of the restaurant, and before I can make it here, this man (pointing at Kit) is diving over the table and trying to choke this other gentleman."

"Is that true sir?" the officer asked Kit.

Kit nodded his head yes and added, "I'm sorry, but I was mad because this man is trying to steal my fiancé."

Carla jumped in, "Kit, that isn't what Trevor is trying to do. He just offered me a place to stay while I figure out what's going on between us. Your acting this way isn't helping matters."

"But, why were you sleeping in his bed?"

"He gave me his room to sleep in and he's sleeping in his office."

Trevor's voice returned just in time to join the conversation, "Wait a minute. How do you know where she's sleeping?"

"Just a guess."

Trevor didn't accept this answer and asked, "How long have you been in Key West and were you in my neighborhood this afternoon?"

Kit looked fiercely at Trevor and shouted, "I don't have to answer any questions from you asshole!"

The officer tightened his grip on the handcuffs and raised Kit's hands slightly in the air to let him know who was in control. He was tired of listening to this bantering back and forth and was ready to do his job. The officer raised his voice and said, "This gentleman clearly attacked you without any provocation. I'm placing him under arrest. Do you want to press charges," he asked Trevor.

Trevor replied with a smile, "You bet your ass I do."

Carla pleaded for Kit, "Trevor, you don't want to do this. Officer this is all a misunderstanding."

The officer responded, "Miss, this man physically attacked this gentleman."

Trevor added with a smirk, "He's got to learn one can't do this in a civilized society."

The officer began to search Kit for weapons or drugs. "Do you have any weapons on you?" he said, as he patted him down

Kit answered, "No, come on do you have to do this? I promise I won't be any more trouble."

The officer ignored him saying, "Do you have anything sharp in your pockets that might poke me? He reached in Kit's back pocket and pulled out his wallet and extracted his driver's license and asked him, "Have you ever been arrested before?"

"Just once for trespassing when I was eighteen."

The officer gave him a stern look and said, "Make sure you are telling the truth because I'll find out if you're lying."

Next, he reached into Kit's right front pocket and pulled out his car keys. He then patted the left pocket and felt something and pulled it out. He held it up for everyone to see.

Carla placed her hand over her mouth amazed by what he'd found. Trevor smiled and shouted, "Explain those jerk off!" The officer was holding a women's red thong. Kit quickly said, "I don't know where those came from! They must have got there in the wash!" Carla pulled her hand away from her mouth and said, "Kit how could you?"

Trevor spoke up, "Officer, in addition to the battery charge, I want this man charged with breaking and entering."

"What do you mean?" the officer asked.

"Someone broke into my house this afternoon and stole some lingerie from this lady."

"Is this the lingerie?" he asked holding up the red thong.

Carla attempted to take them saying, "Those are mine. I'll take them,"

The officer tightened his grip on the panties and said, "I'm sorry mam. I'll have to keep them for evidence until after the trial."

Bill, in a stupor over what had transpired said, "Carla, I hope your manuscript is as exciting as this evenings been."

Embarrassed by everything that's happened Carla responded, "I hope your opinion of me hasn't changed. This is all one big misunderstanding. I'm sorry my boyfriend ruined the evening."

"Don't be silly young lady. Shit like this happens all the time in Key West, especially when Trevor's around."

Kit decided to put his two cents in and says, "Yeah, I'm sure you're not the first woman Trevor's had an affair with!"

The officer decided it was time to take Kit to the station and said, "Come on troublemaker. You're going to jail. He'll probably be allowed to post bail after a judge hears the case in the morning if anyone's interested. He smiled at Carla knowing she'd probably be there first thing in the morning if she had any feelings for the man. He started Kit towards the front door quoting the Miranda as he went, "You have the right to remain silent…"

The maitre d' righted the table and an army of waiters and busboys quickly cleaned up the glass and spilled drinks. Ilsa walked over to Trevor and checked him for injuries. Her hands gently caressed his neck and head. She felt a bump on the back of Trevor's head and said, "There's a nasty bump on the back of your head where it hit the floor. You should have it checked out." Trevor rubbed it and said, "Aw, it's not that bad. Maybe he knocked some sense into me." Bill, unable to resist another jab said, "I doubt it."

Once again Trevor was intrigued by the gentle touch of Ilsa and the way she looked at him. Why hadn't he noticed her exceptional beauty before? He casually reached for her hand and tenderly squeezed it saying, "I could get used to all of this attention."

Carla, slightly jealous asks, "Are you sure you're all right Trevor?"

Yeah, like I said, it's just a little goose egg," he reassured her.

"Once again, I apologize for my boyfriend's outlandish behavior. And, thank you for not hurting him again Trevor."

"Yeah, it's a good thing that maitre d' came. I was trying to hold back," Trevor said, trying to keep his masculinity intact.

Bill laughed and said, "I could see that any minute you were going to be on top of him with your hands around his throat. And, what is this about not hurting him again?"

"Oh, Trevor and Kit," Carla started to speak, but Trevor gave her a look and shook his head nonchalantly.

"Listen Bill, let's just say this isn't the first time we've butted heads. This kid's insanely jealous when it comes to anyone talking to this woman. And, can you blame him?" Trevor asked, glancing at Carla.

"No, I'd strangle anyone that tried to talk to her if she were my girlfriend," Bill replied.

Carla, embarrassed by the men's comments said, "Stop it you guys."

Ilsa changed the subject, "Carla, when do you think you'll have the first draft of your manuscript ready so that I can take a look at it?"

"I hope to have it done by the end of this month, depending on how things go."

"That would be great. I look forward to reading it."

Bill jumped in, "I'd like a copy of it when it's ready."

Ilsa looked at him and said, "Bill, as her agent, I must tell you that we haven't decided which publisher we're going to use, so it wouldn't be proper for you to read it until that's been discussed."

Feeling slighted Bill responds, "I was asking as a friend and not an editor, but you do what you need to do."

Carla, feeling an opportunity slipping away asks, "It wouldn't hurt if he wanted to read it, would it Ilsa?"

"It's a little unorthodox, but I guess it would be okay."

"Don't do me any favors," Bill replied snidely.

Trevor relieves the mounting tension at the table by recommending that they order some food. Carla only orders a salad. She has no appetite. She's worried about Kit, and wondering how she'll post bail for him in the morning.

Chapter 56

Kit had been processed and put in a holding cell with a couple of drunken street people that had been arrested for becoming violent when tourists had denied them a handout. One was snoring and had peed himself while he slept. The other was barely awake when Kit entered the enclosure but came to and asked, "What the fuck are you looking at!" when Kit glanced his way.

Kit decided it was best to ignore him and avoid trouble; he had been in enough for the night. The place was dimly lit and stunk of urine and beer/cigarette breath. Kit wandered to the far side of the cell and staked his claim. He found a fairly clean spot and lay on the cold concrete floor. He had to urinate, but decided to wait because the only commode stood on the far wall near the vagrants and afforded no privacy. He theorized that they would probably both be sleeping soundly within fifteen minutes—he could wait. After ten minutes, he questioned his theory. The man who had been sleeping woke up and was holding a conversation with a nonexistent person. He probably suffered from untreated schizophrenia, the plight of many homeless people.

Kit was feeling like his bladder was going to burst when the cell door swung open and a parade of scantily clad gay men paraded in. What now, he thought. Many of them paired off and sat together along the same wall as Kit. None of them sat near the homeless men.

One of the men dropped his pants and began to urinate in the commode. He turned and faced the crowd before pulling up his shorts. Catcalls erupted from the crowd. He had the biggest, longest penis Kit had ever seen and was proud to show it off.

The cries got louder as he began to swing it in circles. A guard came to see what the commotion was about and cautioned the man to put his thing away or he would be spending the night in solitary confinement. Kit jumped up and ran to the bars saying, "Can you put me somewhere else. I don't belong here."

The guard responded with little or no emotion, "That's for the judge to decide in the morning."

"Please, I have to take a piss," Kit begged.

"The commode is over there," the guard said with a laugh.

"Fuck You!" Kit said angrily.

"Sorry you're not my type. I prefer women. Unlike your other playmates," the guard added as he turned to walk away. "Try to keep it down ladies," he said over his shoulder as he exited down the corridor.

Kit fearing his bladder might burst had to make a decision. Should he pee his pants or risk the commode? It probably would have been better to pee his pants, but he didn't feel like having urine soaked clothing clinging to his torso all night. The smell he would have been able to deal with because it would have blended in with the urine smell that already filled the air.

The jeers started as he approached the toilet and pulled down his zipper. A couple of men stood and positioned themselves for a better view. Kit saw them and cried, "Sit your asses down before I beat you to a pulp!"

One of them replied, "Geeze, testy are we?"

"I just want to piss in peace. Do you have a problem with that?"

Another one whispered to his friend, "Say, I didn't see him in the paddy wagon did you?"

His friend answered, "Heavens no. I would have remembered him. He's a fox!"

Someone from the far side of the room shouted, "Don't be shy honey! We all have one!"

With that, a large part of the population started giggling.

Kit pushed the last of the urine from his bladder and breathed a sigh of relief. It seemed like it took forever for it to empty. When he turned to walk away someone shouted, "Party Pooper!" and someone else started singing in an effeminate voice, "everybody likes a pooper that's why we invited you. Party pooperrrr!"

Kit raised both his middle fingers and displayed them to the crowd saying, "Fuck you faggots!" Once again, Kit had let his emotions control his actions. He really didn't have any problem with gay men. One of his best friends in college had been gay. "Live and let live," was his motto. All the trouble he was in right now related back to the fact that he stood up for a fish that only wanted to live its life in the ocean free from man's interference.

Chuck, the pimp, already pissed off about being arrested was in no mood to be called a faggot, stood and said, "I think we have a hostile heterosexual fellas!" Kit faced the man and said, "Back off Jack!"

"The name's Chuck asshole! What right do you have calling us faggots?"

"Yeah!" came from a chorus of men now standing.

Kit decided he better start backpedaling, "Listen everyone. I'm sorry. I've just had a bad night and I want to be left alone."

Chuck bitch slapped him in the face and said, "It's too late for that cum wad!"

Kit decided to take out the leader. He threw a right hook and connected with the man's jaw; some of his rotten teeth fell from his bleeding mouth. The man hit the floor and didn't get up. A crowd of angry men pounced on Kit and began beating, clawing and slapping him about the body. He wound up on the floor with a man wearing spiked leather boots kicking him in the ribs before the guard heard the commotion and came charging into the cell. "All right girls! Everyone backup against the walls and sit down! Now!"

All that was left was Kit and Chuck too injured to comply. Kit was moaning, so the guard knew he was alive, but he had to take a pulse on Chuck's neck to verify that he was. The officer radioed for help.

Within seconds two more officers entered the cell. By that time Chuck had come to and was belligerent. He shouted a threat at Kit with his new speech impediment caused by having no front teeth, "I'm going to pucking kill you when I see you on the street!" Kit ignored the man whose formally white silk shirt was now crimson. Paramedics took Chuck away, but Kit refused treatment and was put in a separate holding cell. His last words to the guard were, "If you had done this in the first place, none of this would have happened!"

Chapter 57

The rest of the dinner went well. Carla and Bill talked about their college days and the various writers they had studied. Trevor and Ilsa discussed things they had never spoken of before: failed relationships-- their childhoods.

"Trevor, how come a handsome man like you isn't married?" Ilsa asked suddenly.

"I haven't found the right woman. Besides, I'm kind of moody when I'm writing and when I'm not writing, I'm fishing," Trevor replied truthfully.

"I love to fish," Ilsa said.

"I never knew."

"I have a little Boston Whaler I take around the out islands to fish for mangrove snapper, grouper, or whatever else is biting," Ilsa said proudly. "Why live in the Keys if you don't fish?"

"My sentiments exactly," Trevor said, and then asked, "how come you never mentioned this before?"

"Most of our contact in the past has been over the phone. When we met in person it was to discuss business or sign papers, and you treated me like I was an annoyance in your life."

Trevor swallowed and said, "I didn't even realize I acted that way, but it's probably true. I hate the business aspect of writing, and I damn sure don't like anyone that makes me work instead of fish."

Ilsa chuckled and said, "Well you must hate me then!"

"With a passion", Trevor said grabbing her hand.

Their cold, business relationship disappeared somewhere into the night. Suddenly, they were staring into each other's eyes and understanding that things would never be the same. They both started to speak, but Trevor let Ilsa speak first. "Are you ready to get out of here?"

Trevor replied, "I thought you'd never ask. Would you like to stop by my house for a nightcap?"

Ilsa smiled and said, "I thought you'd never ask."

Within minutes, Ilsa's car pulled into the driveway behind Trevor and Carla.

Carla sat in the love seat, which forced Ilsa to sit in overstuffed chair by herself. Trevor went to the small, but well stocked wine cellar he had added to the house after he purchased it. He brought up a bottle of some fine Napa Valley wine he had bought last year while on a visit to California during one of his book signings. While he was in the kitchen opening the wine and getting some glasses, the girls struck up a conversation.

"Don't you just love Trevor's house?" Carla asked.

"Yes. He has quite a collection of antiques" Ilsa remarked.

"His bed is really cool isn't it"?

"I don't know I've never been in it," Ilsa replied coldly.

"Neither have I, at least in that way. He's letting me use his room while I'm staying here," Carla said, hoping to clear the air.

"I'm sorry. I don't know why I said that," Ilsa said, and then asked quickly while Trevor was out of the room, "do you have any feelings for Trevor?"

"He's a handsome, talented man, and any woman would be lucky to have him, but I'm still in love with my fiancé. I have to admit, I've thought about what it would be like, but he's old enough to be my father," Carla answered, knowing that if she wasn't involved with Kit, she wouldn't have any problem dating Trevor.

Just then, Trevor strolled back in the room with a bottle of wine and three wine glasses on an antique tray from China. The two women stopped talking immediately, which made matters worse because the room became strangely silent. Carla was the first to speak, "I don't know how much more wine I can drink. It's been a long day and I'm feeling sleepy."

Ilsa replied, "You don't have to stay up for me. If you start feeling too tired, feel free to go to bed."

"Why thank you Ilsa. You're so considerate," Carla retuned sarcastically.

"Did I miss something while I was out of the room?" Trevor asked.

"Whatever do you mean Trevor darling? We became great friends while you were in the kitchen. Didn't we Carla?"

"Best of," Carla said.

They finished the first bottle and Carla started to nod out while sitting up straight. She was startled when Trevor touched her shoulder and said, "Carla, why don't you go to bed? You're falling asleep."

Groggily she replied, "Good night. Nice to meet you Ilsa. Hope to see you soon."

As an afterthought, as she was entering the hallway to the room, she turned and asked, "Trevor will you take me to the police station in the morning?"

"Yeah, I guess so," Trevor grumbled, his heart not in it.

Ilsa smiled, stood up and walked over the love seat to take a seat next to Trevor. He picked up the wine bottle and emptied a drop of wine into her glass. "Oops! I forgot we finished this bottle. I have another chilling in the kitchen", he said, as he stood to go fetch it.

Trevor walked into the room with the new bottle saying, "This is one of my favorites a Cabernet from Cakebread, a small winery in Napa."

Ilsa took a sip. "I don't know how much more wine I can drink. I might get crazy and take off all of my clothes and rape you!" Trevor smiled and said, "Then you must have another glass!" They both giggled and put down their wine glasses at the same time.

Nothing more was said, but they knew from the look in each others eyes that there was an attraction that neither of them could deny. Their arms, as if being controlled by some strange puppeteer from above, moved to embrace one another. They took a moment to drink of the desire they felt for each other. Slowly, Trevor inched his mouth closer to hers searching for any sign of resistance—there was none. After what seemed like an eternity his lips contacted with hers. Fluids from their bodies were being exchanged as his tongue gently probed her mouth. A slight moan seemed to inch its way up from her bowels.

Trevor gently slid his hand into the neckline of her dress and gently cupped her full breast noticing that her nipple was fully erect. She moaned again. Ilsa's hand slid down to Trevor's waist and stopped at his throbbing member to gently caress its length through his pants. In a guttural tone she managed to get out, "I need you." Trevor didn't need to be told twice. Instantly he rose and led her by the hand into his office. The bed hadn't been made, so it was easy to strip it of its top sheet and comforter so they wouldn't be in the way.

Ilsa began to unbutton Trevor's shirt revealing his manly chest of salt and pepper hair. Next, she undid his belt, pant clasp and zipper— his pants slid down his legs to the floor. She bent over and kissed his stomach following the patch of hair leading down to the tent in his boxers.

Like a child opening a Christmas present, she pulled down his boxers and took him into her mouth. Trevor was the one doing the moaning now. Her warm soft mouth was gently caressing his manhood making it stiffer than before. He reached down and undid the zipper to her dress and the clasp to her bra. As she stood up her bra and dress fell to the floor to reveal a sexy of black thong with a diamond kitty on the front. "Here kitty, kitty," Trevor said, as he took in the beautiful form before his eyes.

Her breasts were full and natural. Gravity made them hang with her light brown nipples pointing slightly into the air. They glowed in the dimly lit room when contrasted by the tan skin that surrounded them. Trevor didn't like it when women got an allover tan. He liked the moistness that skin seems to maintain when it's locked away from the harmful rays of the sun.

Trevor felt her body shiver as he pulled her close and embraced it. His member pressed against the soft tissue above her bellybutton, and her breasts flattened amongst the hairs on his chest. He reached down and cuddled her firm round buttocks with his slightly calloused hands as she gently squeezed his phallus. They passionately kissed until they could stand it no longer. Finally, Trevor hoisted her into the air and roughly threw her onto the bed. He started to go down on her, but she grabbed his head and said, "I want you to fuck me!" a little bit louder than she had intended. Trevor responded, "I thought you'd never ask," as he parted her moist tissue with his fingers and guided himself in.

Carla was awakened by a knocking noise. Groggy from the wine, she strained her ears to listen for any danger. The sound was rhythmic and included what she believed to be the creaking of bedsprings.

When she faintly heard Ilsa saying, "Yeah, baby! Right there baby!" she knew what was happening and became a little jealous. It had been almost a week since she had gotten laid. She unconsciously reached down and began to caress herself. Aided by the knowledge that two people were in the next room making wild love, she quickly had an orgasm and fell back to sleep.

Chapter 58

Kit rolled over on the lumpy cot and was awakened by a pain in his ribs. Quickly he turned to the previous position, lying on his back, and let out a small moan. Prisons weren't known for their sleeping accommodations and this one wasn't any different. He had managed to get a couple of hours sleep in between the discomforts and noises of his temporary home, but knew it would be impossible to sleep now because he had started thinking about Carla and whether she would come bail him out.

Being in jail gave Kit time to think about his approach to solving his problem—making Carla love him again. I guess the macho man thing isn't the right way to go, he thought, but smiled when he relived the previous evenings actions, particularly his hands clenching Trevor's throat. His smile faded when he realized he could actually do some jail time if Trevor wanted to press charges for the assault and B&E. Kit figured he could kill two birds with one stone by apologizing to Trevor; he might drop the charges and Carla would see that he could be a rational human being for a change.

Chapter 59

Carla awoke the next morning with a dry mouth and a pounding headache. The room was slightly warm even though a small window air conditioner ran at full throttle to compensate for the hot humid air outside. She had kicked off her covers during the night and was laying butt naked in a strange bed.

It took a couple of seconds for her to recall where she was and why she was there. "Oh shit!" she voiced out loud after remembering that Kit was stuck in jail. She looked at a digital alarm clock on the nightstand and saw that it was 10:45 am. I need to get my ass in gear, she thought as she grabbed a housecoat from her open suitcase.

Carla charged into Trevor's office forgetting that he had a guest in there. On the bed she saw Trevor and Ilsa in a spooning position with their naked bodies fully exposed. Ilsa, a light sleeper, turned when Carla entered the room and said, "Do you mind!" Carla backed out of the room and stood to the side of the doorway out of sight and lied saying, "I'm sorry, I didn't know Trevor had a guest."

"Do you always come into a man's room without knocking?" Ilsa queried.

"No. I wasn't thinking because it's late and I'm worried about Kit."

Trevor woke up when the women started talking and said, "You woke me up because you're worried about Kit? He can rot there as far as I'm concerned."

"Come on Trevor you promised," Carla pleaded.

"Okay. I'll do it under protest," Trevor conceded.

"Hurry. I don't want him in there any longer than he has to be. I'm going to take a quick shower."

"Yeah, yeah, I'll be ready in a little while," Trevor replied.

Once Carla left for the shower, Trevor got up and shut the door to the office and locked it. Ilsa raised her arms and said, "Come here, I want some more of what I had last night!"

"My pleasure!" Trevor said as he started kissing her breasts.

Fifteen minutes later, Carla was banging on the door asking, "Are you guys ready yet?"

Trevor never thought it would happen, but Carla was rapidly becoming an inconvenience.

"Cool your jets! We still have to get in the shower," he said in an aggravated tone.

"Trevor, I know I'm being a pain, but please hurry!"

"Alright we'll be ready in about twenty minutes," he said, and then asked Ilsa, "I'm sorry, you are coming aren't you?"

She picked up an imaginary schedule book and thumbed through its pages and answered, "Nothing scheduled for today, so I guess I'm available."

Trevor grabbed her by the face and kissed her saying, "You're so cute. I could just gobble you up!"

Ilsa giggled and replied, "I'll take a rain check for later."

A half an hour later, the three companions were backing out of Trevor's driveway in Ilsa's black BMW. They decided to take her car because it had A/C, unlike Trevor's old pickup. The streets were crowded with pedestrians because a gigantic cruise ship had just spilled its cargo of tourists onto the streets of Key West.

Ilsa masterfully weaved her way the short distance to the Key West Police station. Once inside, the trio was informed that Kit and the other prisoners that had been arrested last night were taken to the courthouse on Whitehead Street for their bond hearings, and if they hurry, they would have plenty of time to sit in.

Carla chewed on her newly painted nails as Ilsa sped over to the courthouse. Parking seemed to be a problem today for some reason, but they drove around the block until someone left a metered parallel spot on Whitehead Street.

Ilsa and Trevor had to nearly jog to keep up with Carla as she sped up to the courthouse. Once inside, they got directions to the appropriate courtroom, and then Trevor was sent back to the car in a huff with their cell phones since they weren't permitted inside the courtroom. The girls found a spot fairly close to where Kit was being detained. He noticed them enter the courtroom and smiled uneasily in their direction.

He was relieved to see that Trevor was nowhere in sight, but soon realized his misjudgment when he turned again and saw him seating himself between the women. Carla grabbed his arm and nonchalantly pointed to where Kit was and whispered, "Look there he is. He looks a little beat up doesn't he?"

Trevor smiled, and replied, "Yes, he does look like someone got the best of him."

Kit had small scratches and bruises about his neck and face from the punching, slapping and scratching that had occurred the previous night. None of them were severe enough to last more than a few days; however, the bruises on his ribs were another story, because they would take several weeks to heal. He definitely came out better than Chuck, the man he had punched in the mouth.

One by one each of the prisoners was called before the judge. They were a strange lot; some of them were scantily clad in leather and others had been given some prison clothes to make them decent for court. As luck would have it, Kit was one of the last ones called up before the judge. Most of the other prisoners were residents of Key West and had been given bail set at a thousand dollars due to their charges and low flight risk. However, this wasn't the case with Kit.

He approached the bench and the judge spoke, "Mr. Hansen, you have been charged with assault and breaking and entering. These are serious charges. In addition, you haven't been able to provide the court with a local address. Can you explain this?"

Kit spoke up for himself, "Your honor I don't maintain a regular address on land. Currently I'm living on my fiancé's yacht. However, it's being repaired at the moment, so I'm staying in a local hotel."

They judge wrinkled his nose and said, "In light of this information I consider you a flight risk. Bond is set at ten thousand dollars. Next!" Kit tried to complain, "But your honor. I can't afford ten thousand dollars!"

The judge snapped back, "Move on Mr. Hansen or I'll add contempt of court to your list of charges."

Kit bowed his head and ambled back to the bench. Carla mouthed, "Don't worry," and held up her checkbook when he looked her way. He smiled and shook his head knowing what she meant. He was happy that he was to be free again, but his ego made him unhappy that it was at his girlfriend's expense. Kit had a hard time dealing with Carla's wealth and her role as the provider in their relationship, but right now it was a blessing.

An hour later, Carla was finishing her signature on the check that would buy Kit's freedom. Within minutes the correction officer would be reuniting them. Carla turned to Trevor and said, "Trevor, I know

Kit behaved like an asshole last night, but I hope you guys can learn to get along. Try not to say anything inflammatory to him."

Trevor laughed and said, "You mean like—I hope the other guy looks worse than you."

She playfully slapped his arm and said, "Yeah, that's what I'm talking about."

Suddenly the door buzzed and Kit walked into the room. Carla ran up and embraced him saying, "Thank God you're out of that place." He looked at Trevor over her shoulder and started practicing self-control. Ilsa broke the silence, "I've heard from a couple of friends of mine that wound up there during Fantasy Fest last year that it's not a nice place." Kit shook his head and said, "It's not a nice place to visit and I wouldn't want to live there."

Kit noticed Ilsa and Trevor were holding hands and decided it was time to make amends, "Listen Trevor. I'm really sorry about last night and I hope you'll forgive me." He looked at Carla and continued, "This girl makes me crazy. I love her so much that I can't think about losing her."

Kit noticed some bruising on Trevor's neck and pointed towards it asking, "Is that from me?" Trevor responded, "I don't think anyone else choked me last night." His response evoked a look from Carla that told him she wasn't happy. Trevor thought a minute and said, "I'm sorry. Yes, it's from you, and I forgive you if you promise to never do it again." Kit extended his hand to Trevor, smiled and said, "No problem buddy." Trevor released Ilsa's hand and gripped Kits in a handshake.

"Let's get out of here!" Carla said suddenly.

"I second that motion!" Kit followed.

After everyone was in Ilsa's car, Kit asked, "Would you mind taking me to my car?"

"Sure where is it?" Ilsa queried.

"Still at the restaurant."

"Alright, it's not that far from here."

Nobody spoke much on the way to the car. When they arrived, Carla said, "I'm going to go with Kit so we can talk. Are you going to be at home later Trevor in case I need to get in your house?"

Trevor, delighted at the prospect of being alone with Ilsa again, replied, "Yeah I should be around later. Just knock before you come in."

"Don't worry. I learned my lesson this morning. Thanks again for taking me to bail Kit out. I really appreciate it."

"What are friends for?" Trevor said, as she closed the door.

"Yeah, thank you.   And once again, I'm really sorry about what happened," Kit added trying to act sincere. "Nice to meet you Ilsa," he said as he extended his hand to shake hers.

"Those two make a nice couple," Ilsa said, as she drove off with Trevor.

"Yes they do," Trevor replied, thinking that a couple of days ago, he would have been bothered by that comment.

Chapter 60

The trip to Kit's hotel started in silence. Finally, Carla spoke, "Kit, you know if we are going to be a couple, you need to go to anger management or something."

"I know. I act sometimes without thinking. However, I never acted this way before I met you. And, I never did anything stupid until you became friends with Trevor. I just kept getting this strange vibe that there was more than a friendship going on."

Carla started to blush and said, "Don't be silly. We're just friends. Nothing more. Now that you see the relationship he has with Ilsa, you should know that I wasn't lying."

"Yes, I have to admit I was very relieved when I saw him kiss her for the first time."

"Yeah, and they're doing more than kissing. They woke me up last night because their headboard was banging against the wall."

Kit laughed and said, "You're kidding me. I didn't think the old guy had it in him."

"Kit, he's not that old. And, I hope you can perform like that when you get to be his age."

Kit grabbed his crotch and said, "If we're together, there won't be any problems. And if there are, I'll take some Viagra and fuck your brains out all night long until you beg me to stop."

Carla laughed and said, "You promise! All this talk about sex is making me horny!"

The crunching gravel under the car's tires signaled the exit from the paved highway to the parking lot of the single story motel that Kit was staying in. Kit and Carla jumped from the car and frantically tried to get the rusting tumblers of the lock to the door to respond to the key. Finally, they applied enough pressure in the right place and the lock opened. Once inside, Carla passionately open-mouth kissed Kit. Suddenly, she remembered where he had been the night before and said, "Kit, you need to take a shower. I don't want to catch any diseases." Kit looked hurt, but understood and said, "You're right. That jail was really scummy."

The warm water of the shower felt good, but the small nicks and scratches on his face and body began to sting as he washed with the cheap motel soap. The white towel he dried with felt like a scouring pad against his body. He assumed the motel didn't spend the money for fabric softener.

When he emerged from the bathroom, Carla was already naked and lying on the bed. With water still dripping from his hair, Kit pounced on her like a lion on a gazelle. He passionately kissed her on the mouth, but quickly moved to her excited nipples. She moaned with pleasure having missed the feel of her man's mouth on her body. Normally Carla relished foreplay, but right now it didn't matter. She whispered in Kit's ear, "I want to feel you in me right now."

Kit moved his mouth to hers and caressed her mouth's flesh with his tongue as she took her right hand and guided his rigid shaft into the warm, soft area between her thighs. It was amazing how the short time they had been apart made their love making seem as though it was their first time.

Their bodies buzzed with excitement as each of Kit's thrusts brought both of them closer to climax. It wasn't long before both of them exploded into warm fuzzy spasms of bliss. Kit rolled onto his back pulling Carla on top of him to lie for a few minutes of silence and feel the warmth of each other's bodies.

"Whew! I needed that!" Carla said, breaking the silence.

"Me too!" Kit concurred.

Carla stared at the ceiling for a short time and then asked, "Kit what did you do with the barracuda?"

"I took him to East Brother Reef and released him. What a magnificent fish. I swear he thanked me before he swam away. Over there, he should be able to live out the rest of his days without hurting anyone."

"I hope you're right. If anyone else gets hurt, you'll be responsible."

"Now wait a minute. I moved the fish away from Bimini. Trevor is responsible for bringing the fish into Bimini."

"You don't know that!"

"Don't you remember the bite study I did on the marlin tail and man's arm? It's highly unusual, but I think the fish followed Trevor's boat to Bimini; it may have been attracted to the blood seeping from the marlin's carcass."

"Still, he wanted to kill it and you didn't."

"Is it wrong to want to protect a helpless creature?"

"Helpless! Kit that fish could have killed me!"

"Listen. I am upset about what happened to you and all of the other people that were injured, but I don't blame the barracuda. It was just doing what nature intended. We are the ones invading its environment. If you go into the jungle and are attacked by a tiger, is it the tiger's fault? Besides, I noticed that this fish might have had some type of eye injury that may affect its decisions about what is prey and what isn't."

"What do you mean?"

"I didn't tell you about this, but one time while I was collecting conch for my research in Bimini Bay, the cuda swam by extremely close. One of his eyes had a glazed over it like it had been traumatized at some point.

That might explain why a fish that usually will flee when confronted by a human in the water has been attacking instead. They are inquisitive creatures, but not aggressive towards humans intentionally. Most attacks are a case of misjudgment or mistaken identity. Losing the full use of one of its sensory inputs could decrease immensely the cuda's ability to discern humans from its natural prey."

"I guess when you explain it like that, I don't feel as angry towards the cuda, but I'm glad you moved it to where it can't make any more mistakes. I mean, I only got a little scar on my ankle, but the Bahamian fisherman wasn't so lucky."

"Listen Carla, I studied marine biology because I love the sea and wanted to protect its treasures for future generations. I am very passionate about what I do. That's just the way I am. Doctors don't kill criminals because they make mistakes. In fact they are asked to treat criminals if they are injured."

"Yeah, but they don't help them escape from prison either."

"Good point, but you know what I mean don't you?"

"Yes, I guess so. I just want to forget about that fish and put this all behind us."

"Honey, there is nothing more I'd rather do."

"Oh Kit, I love you so much!"

Kit cradled Carla's face in his hands and began to smother her with kisses. Within seconds Carla felt his stiff manhood knocking at the door of love again. She rolled onto her back and offered herself once more.   This time their lovemaking was slower and more methodical. They savored each other like wine connoisseurs sampling the first batch of a fine wine.

Chapter 61

The weather in Bimini was for the most part some of the best in the world. However, being in the tropics also meant that periodically large storms that originate somewhere off the coast of Africa would pass over on their way to the east coast of the United States.

For two days a tropical storm's downpour had practically ruined all outdoor activities for the Landers. They had to delay their diving excursion to East Brother's Reef. During this time Bill Landers and his son Chip spent their time imbibing various imported beers in several of Bimini's finest drinking establishments.

Bill took a sip of his Kalik beer, swallowed and said, "I hear the weather is supposed to clear tomorrow. Is all of the gear still ready?"

Chip was staring at a hot little island girl and took a moment to respond, "Oh, yeah. It's just a little soaked from all of the rain we've had.

"Well, I want to get an early start, so how about running down and checking everything after you finish your beer."

"Sure dad. No problem."

A Bahamian fisherman that they had been chatting with spoke up, "You guys be careful if you're going in the water. There's been a crazy cuda in the area. We think he even had something to do with the death of one of my best friends, Bobby, a fisherman by trade."

Bill bragged, "Don't worry we'll both have our Magnum spear guns with us when we go in the water. He'll be chum if he tries anything. Besides, what are the chances of him being on East Brother Reef?"

"I don't know ma'an, but many people are saying there's something evil about this fish. Another friend of mine died trying to catch him. He and his nephew got blown away in a waterspout and drowned."

Chip looked at his dad and asked, "Hey dad are you sure you want to go diving with this fish in the water?"

After his son's question, Bill addressed the Bahamian, "No disrespect sir, but this evil barracuda is nothing but some island superstition. It is just a rogue barracuda, and someone's got to take care of him. And, if he gets in my way, it's going to be me.

I had a friend in high school that used to spear cuda's just for the sport. Yeah, Alphonso was his name, a crazy Cuban, the son of a doctor. He had nothing to do but swim off the Dania pier and spear cuda's while disgruntled fishermen threw sinkers at him. He said the trick was to spear the cuda close to a piling so that when it went berserk, it would wrap itself up around the structure. I never did agree with killing anything just for the fun of it, but I wouldn't hesitate killing this fish."

Chip took the last sip of his beer and said, "Dad I'm going to check on the gear like you asked. Are you going to be here when I'm done?"

"No, I think I'll mosey back to the motel and get some shuteye. I want to be well rested when we go spear fishing tomorrow."

Chapter 62

The after affects of the day's beers helped the Landers sleep well even though the window A/C unit of the motel room struggled to lower the temperature of the air inside of their room just a few degrees. They awoke early cursing at the small travel alarm clock.

"Ahh, is it time to get up already?" Chip bitched as he rolled over to turn off the nagging device. "I feel like I just fell asleep. The fucking mosquitoes were eating me alive and whatever was left the sand gnats finished. I thought we stayed in a hotel to avoid this."

Bill replied groggily, "Quit your bitching this room cost me two hundred a night. This is one of the best hotels on the island. We're not in Nassau you know. At least the beds are comfortable."

"Maybe yours is, but mine has a spring that poked me in the ribs all night."

"When we're sleeping on the boat tomorrow night, you'll appreciate this room a little more."

"I don't care. I love sleeping out on the water with the gentle rocking of the sea and the shooting stars in the pitch black sky."

"Geeze. Stop it. You're starting to sound like some light-in-the-shoes poet. Now get your ass down to the boat and make me some coffee. These fucking Bahamians couldn't make a good cup of coffee if their lives depended on it."

The sun was just beginning to make its grand entrance on the horizon when Chip made his way down to the boat. The bugs were horrendous and the thick humid air was like breathing split pea soup.

He cursed and swatted at the small, unseen pests as he attempted to make coffee for his father. Thick dew had covered everything out it the open and he almost lost his footing as his deck shoe slipped in the moisture. After making coffee, he double checked the equipment warmed up the engines.

When Bill arrived, he smiled because he could hear rumble of the powerful diesel engines on his forty-seven foot Riviera sport fishing boat and see Chip standing at the rear holding a steaming cup of his favorite blend of coffee.

He had worked hard to get to this point in his life. Being an agent for a major insurance company in Florida wasn't always an easy job. In recent years the number of hurricanes rolling through the state had kept him away from home for months trying to settle claims. Now it was just he and his son alone together and about to do something they both loved, spear fishing.

As Bill took the coffee from his son he said, "Thanks son. Did you punch the coordinates into the GPS that I gave you?"

"Yeah, and I checked the radar for any storms in the area. It looks like smooth sailing. I'll disconnect the water and power and cast us off if you want to grab the helm."

"Sounds like a plan."

By the time the Landers pulled away from the dock, the morning had begun to blossom. The sunlight spread like syrup on a plate of pancakes. The ocean's bottom suddenly became visible through the pristine waters of the Atlantic Ocean. They were now able to visually see the channel instead of relying on the myriad of electronic gadgets purchased to guide them through in darkness or foul weather.

Once in open waters, Bill pushed the throttles forward and the large vessel began rapidly spreading the water with its sleek bow. It would only be an hour or so before they reached their destination and both men were psyched about diving in a spot they had never been.

The anticipation brought on excitement and fear. Excitement for doing something they truly enjoyed and fear for challenging the unknown. Once in the ocean environment, one never knew what would show up, especially in the Bahamas, islands that were nothing more than small patches of land that had sprung up in the middle of a vast ocean.

Chapter 63

Trevor and Ilsa spent another sex filled night together. They awoke the second day to the reality of the situation. A strange transformation had taken place in their relationship; the two were no longer an agent and her client but two people in love. The reality struck when they realized that they both had to work to pay their bills. Trevor was way behind on his promise to complete his latest work by the following month, and Ilsa had a meeting with another client at 1 pm. that day.

Earlier, the couple had rolled over in unison and locked eyes, drinking in the vision of each other without saying a word. After a while, Ilsa began to speak, "Where do you think we should go from here?

Trevor, not sure what she was asking replied, "I don't know about you, but I'm heading to the bathroom first."

She giggled and continued, "No silly. Is this just another one night stand because it could be if you want it that way?"

Somewhat hurt at the implication he replied, "Is that what you think? I thought it was something more."

"It is. I mean that's what I want. I just don't want to get hurt. I know you have had a lot of one night stands in the past and I need to know that I'm not being added to your list of conquests."

"Maybe I never felt this way about any of those other conquests. Yes, you are on my list but right now you're at the top and not going anywhere if I have anything to say about it. Life has taught me that I really don't have any control over anyone.

I can be loving and faithful and that won't keep you from walking out the door. Just don't start something you aren't planning to finish because I've been that route before. I know things won't be perfect, they never are. I just need to know that you'll be there. My life is great right now. I get to do the two things I love: write and fish. However, there is a void that I feel in not having someone to share this with."

Ilsa took in all that Trevor had to say and answered him, "I know it's crazy to talk about forever this early in a relationship. Intimacy often blinds people when it occurs too early but I feel like I've known you as a man for quite some time. I've seen you give street people money and food. I've witnessed you take in stray dogs and cats and nurse them back to health until you could find new homes for them. I've witnessed your work ethic when deadlines are put before you. And I've secretly yearned for your touch for years.

I can't promise anything right now, but I think I've fallen hopelessly in love with you. And one more thing, I hope I didn't ruin things by telling you this."

Trevor took a long hard breath and digested what he had just heard. He couldn't believe it. He had found a woman who felt for him like he felt for her, and she been under his nose the whole time. He reached for her face and cradled it in his hands and said, "You're one beautiful woman and I think I will come to treasure your love." At that, he placed his lips gently on hers and proceeded to sensuously kiss her until she responded by rolling on top of him and plunging his manhood inside of her already wet mound.

Chapter 64

The trip to East Brother's Reef was uneventful. The seas were a mild chop which permitted the vessel to travel at three quarter speed bouncing only slightly as the bow sliced through wave after wave. The GPS told the Lander's that they had almost reached their destination, and the reef with its visible shades of light and dark verified it.

Bill throttled back the boat and it settled down to an idle. Chip went to release the lock on the auto anchor so that his father could lower it when the time was right. Bill watched the depth finder with its graphic images of the ocean floor to spot an area with varying depths indicating rocky structures that attract fish. It took several minutes of motoring around until he found an area that suited their needs. "This looks like a good spot!" he yelled to Chip.

"Yeah, it looks good to me!" Chip replied with a smile on his face.

Bill flipped the toggle switch and the heavy anchor made its way down to the reef. The anchor smashed through some fine coral branches that had taken years to grow as it plummeted to the bottom. Once on the bottom, it cleared out several more coral formations as its teeth searched for a place to take a bite. Finally it clung to a small brain coral almost toppling it over and destroying hundreds of years of growth. The anchor line became taut and the boat swung around into the current signaling to the men that it was time to start preparing for their dive.

"Last one in the water is a rotten egg!" Bill shouted at his son as he grabbed his gear from the storage box and began putting it on.

"It doesn't matter if you beat me in the water. I'm still going to spear the first fish," Chip responded.

"Screw you boy. I was spear fishing when you were still shitting yellar."

"We'll see!" Chip said as he finished putting on his mask and jumped into the water seconds before his dad.

Chapter 65

Splashing on the reef usually meant food. Splashing meant schools of fish jumping to avoid being eaten by birds or some other predator. Splashing always drew the barracuda to where it had occurred. Splashing was to the barracuda what alcohol was to the alcoholic.

When the fish arrived, it perceived two large blurry shapes with a familiar scent moving about on the reef. It sensed no smell of food, but knew that would come. It always happened when humans were around.

The fishing hook from its last experience with humans hung from the corner of his mouth like a war medal. The oceans corrosive properties had not yet begun to take its toll on the device. The hook would either be expelled from the fishes mouth by its own bodies defense mechanisms, or slowly corrode until it fell out on its own. This wasn't the first medal of escape it had ever owned, and it was it sure wouldn't be the last.

The barracuda slowly maneuvered to a spot near the surface on the far side of the boat in the shadows to wait for the food to arrive. It watched as the humans clumsily searched for prey having to return to the surface every few minutes for a breath of life giving oxygen. Every now and then a gleam of light would reflect from the stainless steel shafts of their Magnum spear guns temporarily arousing the interest of the fish.

Chip, being younger and more athletic and with his eyesight more intact, naturally spotted the first quarry. It was a Nassau grouper taking refuge under a large rock ledge that lie twenty some odd feet below the surface. The trip to the bottom used up most of Chip's oxygen giving him only a few minutes to try and line up a shot. His father had moved into the area to observe and assist if he needed to. He knew that groupers are known for wedging themselves between rocks to prevent their capture and many a fisherman has blamed the bottom for the loss of a hook not knowing that it was in fact attached to a stubborn grouper. For this reason it was important for Chip to either shoot the grouper through the head, thus disabling him, or shoot him far enough away from the rocks to prevent it from cramming itself into the safety of a cave.

The grouper kept moving in and out of a large cave-like formation of the reef poking his nose out only long enough to see if any prey had moved within reach. Chip watched patiently, but was becoming exhausted traveling up and down from the surface to observe. Finally he came up with a plan; he would shoot a small reef fish and bait the grouper to draw him out far enough for a good shot. He didn't feel like having the grouper run into the cave after being shot and having to wait while he died so he could pull him out. If he could get a head shot, he could avoid all of this.

The barracuda sat almost motionless only moving the small fins near the front of his body to maintain its position. The sun's rays warmed his body from the short distance to the surface, and it almost fell into a fish-style sleep state. Down below Chip had speared a small grunt and tucked it into the waistband of his swim trunks and was reloading his Magnum spear gun for a shot at the grouper. Neither Chip nor his father had spotted the barracuda basking in the sun just a few yards away. If they had, they would have reconsidered being where they are, and doing what they were about to do.

Chip rose to the surface and began to hyperventilate hoping to increase his down time. The molecules of blood from the injured grunt began to float along the surface towards the anchored boat. Sensors in the barracuda's finely tuned nose began to pick up their presence. The smell reminded the fish that it hadn't eaten for a while. Its eyes began to roll about searching for the source of the smell.

Chip's last breath was huge, but would be expelled halfway out to reduce buoyancy on the way to the bottom. He pulled the dead grunt from his waistband and dropped it into a sandy area several feet from the entrance to the grouper's lair. The large fish spotted it and moved cautiously out of its lair. It saw Chip, but figured it could snap up the fish and be back to its cave before anything could happen. As it gulped down the small fish in one bite, Chip took aim and fired the spear.

The spear pierced the fish just behind the head, a good shot but one that wouldn't immediately disable the fish. As the grouper sought the safety of the cave, Chip swam backwards hoping to stop its retreat. Bill watched with excitement as his son struggled with the fish. He readied his gun to take another head shot if the fish began to win the battle.

Bill wasn't the only entity watching the struggle; the barracuda was now on full alert and beginning to move from his position on the surface. With several thrusts of its powerful tail the cuda was on its way towards the injured grouper.

With the first pass it took off the fish's tail causing it to drop to the bottom. Both men were in shock. They didn't know whether to flee or face the predator. Bill screamed into the water, bubbles flying out of his mouth hoping to scare the huge fish away. Chip had dropped his gun still stunned at what he was seeing and seconds away from fleeing to the safety of the boat. Bill raised his gun and took aim as the cuda came back for another swipe at the grouper. Without thinking about the danger of only injuring a large fish like this, he pulled the trigger.

The spear connected just as the cuda turned to swim away with a large chunk of grouper in its mouth. The tip tore through the upper lateral part of fish's back halfway between the last dorsal fin and tail. It hit no vital organs, which left the fish highly agitated and fleeing for its life.

Within seconds the nylon cord attached to the spear became taught and Bill thought, "I got you now you bastard." When the fish felt the tug of the cord, it turned and headed in the opposite direction, which was unfortunately towards the spear fishermen. As it approached Bill he used his empty gun to fend it off. It passed between the men and headed off and away from them. Bill watched in terror as the nylon cord hit his son's shoulder and moved towards his neck. He flashed back to his youth and the stories of Alberto and the pier pilings. He dropped his gun hoping to keep the inevitable from happening, but it was too late.

The taut chord began to strangle Chip. Eventually the gun became lodged between some rocks and the line tightened and piano-stringed Chip like a Mafia hit man. After several minutes of tugging the spear ripped through the upper surface of the cuda's back freeing it. The injured fish swam away now in fear of becoming prey itself trailing blood off into the expanse of the reef.

Chip's body fell to the ocean floor lifeless; his eyes wide open revealing the terror of being strangled in this watery grave. Bill returned to the surface to take a breath and swam furiously to the aid of his son. He drew his dive knife from its sheath and cut the cord from Chip's neck.

As soon as he got him to the surface, he began CPR. He tried over and over to revive Chip, and probably longer than he should have. Eventually, sobbing like a baby, he had to give up or drown himself.

"You motherfucker!" Bill cried as he hauled his son's body out of the water and into the boat. He stared in disbelief into his son's horror filled eyes that had now lost their brilliance either from the salt water or lack of life energy. Slowly he reached down and tried to close them, but they stubbornly remained open only adding to the surreal feeling of seeing a person alive one moment and dead the next.

Bill started the engines and moved the boat forward. When the anchor prevented any more forward movement, he gunned the engines and tore it from the reef toppling the brain coral it had been lodged beneath. He hit the switch on the electric winch to pull it up from the bottom. Normally he would have been more careful, but right now he didn't care about anything that lives in the water. His only mission was to bring his son's body home to be buried, and come back to kill the fish that had caused his death.

Chapter 66

On the way back to Bimini, Bill recounted what had happened in his mind and came to the sad realization that it was his actions that caused his son's death. If he only hadn't shot at the barracuda, his son would be alive right now. He broke into tears and screamed to God or anyone that may be listening, "Why? Why? Why did I have to pull that trigger?" He pounded his fist on the consol until it began to bleed.

After what seemed like an eternity, Bill idled the boat up to the dock at the marina. Not sure what to do, he ran in a panic up to the marina's office and mumbled something about his dead son's body being in his boat. The clerk gasped and called her boss who was in the middle of giving directions to a vessel approaching from Great Britain. He in turn quickly finished and followed Bill back to the boat and shouted, "Call the authorities!" before exiting out the door.

Down on the dock, the harbormaster confirmed that Chip was indeed dead. "What happened man?" was all he could say to the distraught father.

"I shouldn't have done it," Bill replied.

"Shouldn't have done what?" the apprehensive harbormaster asked.

"I shouldn't have pulled the trigger and shot the barracuda."

"I don't understand. What did that have to do with the death of your son?"

"The line strangled him. Can't you see?"

The harbormaster studied the body and noticed some bruising around the neck. The frightful look on the boys face kept him from looking too long. While the men stood talking, the constable appeared and began to assess the situation. A golf cart was brought in to take the body to Dr. Smythe's house. Bill was reluctant to be separated from Chip's body but the constable assured him that it would be well taken care of. "You'll have to come with me and answer some questions. I'll have to complete an investigation before you'll be allowed to leave the island," he said, helping Bill into his golf cart.

The constable recorded Bill's narrative on his son's demise. Afterward he released him with the stipulation that he mustn't leave the island until he was cleared to go. With a little doubt in his mind, the constable went to see Dr. Smythe to corroborate the story with the physiological damage to Chip's body.

Dr. Smythe was in the examination room when the constable arrived. He looked up from the corpse and said, "Ay constable. I wish we could meet under more desirable circumstances like two cold beers."

"Yes I agree George," the constable said casually. He was the only person on the island that called the doctor by his first name. He meant no disrespect. They had been childhood friends and he just couldn't get used to calling him anything else. "George, I thought all of these people dying was over. It's been a week or so since I've heard of any barracuda related stories."

"I guess you didn't hear about the father and son that had the wits scared out of them yesterday while fishing at East Brother's Reef?"

"No. What happened?"

"The boy hooked a yellowtail which was in turn swallowed by our barracuda, or one just as large as our fish. Well, the father said the fish jumped over the boat and almost hit him. The boy's fishing pole was lost to the sea after the boy got scared, dropped it and the fish pulled it overboard. I had to treat the boy for a mild case of shock. White as a ghost he was."

"It sounds like the barracuda has moved away from our island to East Brother's Reef. Hopefully it'll leave there shortly and head further out to sea. We don't need this kind of thing to dampen our tourist trade. What about this poor boy? Does it look like a spear gun's cord strangled him like his father described?"

"The injuries definitely suggest that he was straggled by a fine instrument around the neck. See the bruises in this area under the neck that proceed to the anterior. His lungs didn't have any water in them, which means his airway was blocked while he was still alive."

"What a horrible way to die," the constable commented. "The look on his face tells it all. And, the father feels responsible because he shot at the fish without realizing that he was putting his son in danger. I'll go back and tell him he's free to go. If you could pack his son up for travel I'd appreciate it."

"Do you think we should post some sort of warning for East Brother's Reef?" the doctor asked his friend.

"George, do you want to cause some sort of panic?"

"Constable, if we had done what I suggested in the first place, there would be a few more people walking around on this earth instead of sitting with the almighty!"

"Now George don't get yourself in an uproar. I'll tell you what I'll do. I'll tell the dive boats and fishing charters to stay away from East Brother's Reef."

"That's not enough!"

"Well that's the best I can do. Our people have to eat. Who's going to come to our islands if they hear about a giant fish that's causing all sorts of deaths? Now good day George!"

"You haven't heard the end of this!" Dr. Smythe called to his friend as he walked out the door.

The doctor returned to the corpse and placed him in a body bag to be shipped home. He washed up and walked to his office to decide what to do next. Something had to be done he told himself, only he wasn't sure what it was. Suddenly, an idea popped into his head.

A while back, when a shark had injured a senator's son, a reporter from the Miami Herald had contacted him for the details. After their conversation, the shrewd reporter, always looking for a story, offered to pay him for any tip that turned into a good story. He knew Floridians were always interested in things that happened anywhere in or near their state, especially when it involved some type of terror from the sea. A good shark story always made it on the evening news.

Dr. Smythe wasn't looking to be paid for the information he was about to provide. He just wanted people to be warned about what was going on. The belief that people would stop coming to the islands was ludicrous. The adventurous types that come here would still come; however, they would know to be careful and keep a watchful eye for the fish. He dug through his rolodex and found the number for the reporter and dialed it.

Chapter 67

Ilsa and Trevor became inseparable. She wound up spending more time at his house than her own. Every evening they wandered down to Mallory Square to watch the sunset. Besides the sunset, Mallory Square was a great place to people watch. It had a carnival-like atmosphere. There were all sorts of entertainers putting on shows for the passengers of the cruise ships that docked in close proximity. There were sword swallowers, musicians, mimes, acrobats and any number of acts that tried to bleed money from the tourists.

After their trek to Mallory Square they would stop and buy that night's ingredients for their meal at one of the mom and pop grocery stores. Ilsa was an excellent cook and Trevor loved having home-cooked meals for a change. Their evenings were spent reading. Trevor didn't own a television except for a small black and white portable that he used only when a hurricane was approaching to keep up to date on its progress. This didn't bother Ilsa because she was constantly reading manuscripts to determine their worth in the literary market. Trevor enjoyed reading some of the local author's, whose stories involved fishing or detective-like heroes.

In the morning, Trevor would wake up as early as 4 a.m. to begin his writing for the day. He found that this was the only time he could possess his own thoughts. Later in the day, there were too many distractions to pull him away from his work.

One of them was now a welcome distraction. Around 10 to 11 a.m. Ilsa would wander naked into his study and drape her voluptuous breasts over his shoulders and nibble on his ear. This put an end to the day's writing, but not before Trevor had completed five to ten pages. Ilsa had actually increased Trevor's productivity by supplying material for the romance novelist's creative thought process by helping him feel again what it is like to love and be loved.

On this particular day, after the daily routine of writing and lovemaking, Trevor and Ilsa decided to step out for breakfast at one of the many small restaurants lining Duval Street. Before entering the restaurant, Trevor grabbed a Miami Herald newspaper from a dispensing machine by the door. After they placed their order and received their first cup of coffee, Trevor dissected the paper and handed the business section to Ilsa while he opened to the headline page. "Holy shit!" was all he could say.

"What's the matter?" Ilsa questioned.

"You're not going to believe this!" Trevor said as he turned the paper so she could see it.

"GIANT BARRACUDA RESPONSIBLE FOR NUMEROUS DEATHS IN THE BAHAMAS"

"What does it say?" was all Ilsa could get out before Trevor started reading it aloud.

By the end of the article they had learned that there had been a recent attack that resulted in the death of a Fort Lauderdale man, the son of a local businessman. The writer had theorized that the barracuda moved from the waters around North and South Bimini to East Brother's Reef, the site of the most recent attack.

"This is my fault! I should have stayed until that fish was captured and killed!" Trevor said loud enough to capture the attention of some of the other patrons.

"Don't be silly. How can you blame yourself for the actions of a fish?"

"Kit, that whacko, said he thought the fish followed me to Bimini from Chub Cay."

"Consider the source," Ilsa said trying to make her case.

"Speaking of Kit," Trevor continued, "the reason Carla became so enraged at him was because she discovered he had captured the fish and was planning to move it to East Brother's Reef."

"There you go! He's the one who's really at fault!" Ilsa reasoned.

"Yeah, I know, but I should have never left knowing what his plans were. We've got to find him and tell him what's happened. He's got to do something about it! Do you remember the name of that marina he said he was having work done on the Black Gold?"

"I don't remember the name but he said it's on the left hand side before the light where US 1 heads into Key West. It's on one of those little side canals."

"I think I know where it is. Let's go."

"What about breakfast? I'm hungry?"

"I've suddenly lost my appetite, but we could grab a couple of bagels to go."

"Alright, but next time I want a western omelet."

Chapter 68

When Trevor and Ilsa arrived at the marina, they were told that the boat had been repaired and moved to the Key West Marina. "Imagine that," Trevor said, as he drove the familiar route to his second home. The boat was easy to find being one of the larger vessels docked in the marina. Ironically, it was only several moorings down from the Child Support.

"Trevor, just try to remain calm because you two have a history. Remember what happened in the restaurant," Ilsa cautioned as they strolled down the dock on their way to the vessel.

"Yeah, I still owe him one. I'm not afraid of him," Trevor said defiantly.

Trevor forgot all about his anger when he noticed Carla in a pink dayglow thong and on her hands and knees sanding some woodwork on the vessel.

"Permission to come aboard!" he shouted, startling her at first. She wiped her brow, stood up slowly and grabbed a sarong to wrap around her waist, saying, "Hey guys, welcome aboard." Kit's head popped up from an area further aft where he was also sanding. He didn't look exceptionally happy to see Trevor, but warmed up at the sight of Ilsa. "What brings you to our neck of the woods?" he asked.

"This!" Trevor said, as he held the newspaper out stretched in his two hands so that Kit could see the headlines. Kit snatched the newspaper from his hands saying, "Let me see that!" He read the newspaper article in its entirety, taking time to flip back to the continuation towards the center of the paper. The afternoon breeze made it difficult to read outside so he suggested everyone have a seat in the air-conditioned parlor. The air was thick with emotion as Kit finished the article shaking his head and exclaiming, "Damn it!"

"What are you going to do?" was all Trevor could say.

"What do you mean, what am I going to do? Kit asked.

"If you had killed the fish like everyone else wanted, this young man would still be alive!"

"His father is the one responsible for his death. The cuda was just doing what cudas do, eating an injured fish. If they had just gotten out of the water, they would both be alive today," Kit argued in defense.

Trevor paused a minute and asked, "You really don't believe that do you?"

Trevor knew it was senseless to try and change marine biologist's mind. In fact, on the way over, he had thought about what to do if it wasn't possible. He would pretend to agree with Kit so that he could use him to capture the fish, and then do what should be done—slay it. For now, he had to act as if Kit was able to change his position.

"Yes I do! Whenever a man invades a predator's environment, he is the one taking a chance. Bears, alligators and many other of nature's creatures attack people each year. Is it their fault? They are simply doing what nature designed them to do, eat or protect their territory? Did the barracuda knock on these people's doors and perform a home invasion? No, it was they who were guilty of home invasion. I tried to move it to a place that seemed relatively safe from human interference, but I failed. Maybe we should take it back to where you originally caught the marlin. It lived there for years without any human interaction."

Trevor thought about how to sound convincing, "You might have a point. The barracuda was never a problem until he wound up in Bimini; however, the marlin I had on the line may have a different opinion. I would be willing to help you move him back to where I caught the marlin if it means keeping it away from people in the water. In the Chub Cay waters, the worst thing that may happen would that it's caught and the problem would be solved once and for all.

Kit got excited and said, "Great! I'm leaving tomorrow for East Brother's Reef. Do you want to help?"

Trevor played it up, "I don't know, I'm awfully busy right now."

"Come on, I need your help. With the two of us working together, we can have it relocated in no time. You don't want anybody else to get hurt do you?"

"No I guess not. What time do we leave?"

"Great! We'll leave at 4 a.m. I'll get what we need this afternoon."

Ilsa, who had been silent until now, spoke up, "I want to go."

Trevor, not sure if he wanted her to be around when he slayed the fish said, "What we are about to do could be dangerous. Besides, don't you have a full calendar the next couple of days?"

She stood her ground, "Trevor, I want to go. I'm not letting you do something this dangerous without being there. I work for myself, so if I want to cancel all of my appointments for the next couple of days to be with the one I love, I can."

Trevor knew trying to change her mind was senseless. After all, she had been his agent for several years and he had attempted to do so repeatedly. She was the most stubborn person he had ever met, but he loved her now. He reluctantly caved in, "Alright, but you better stand clear when we are working with the fish."

She squeezed his hand and kissed him on the cheek saying, "Aye, aye captain."

Carla spoke next, "I'm so happy there's going to be another woman around. We can give each other a pedicure while they're playing with that stupid fish."

Ilsa smiled and said, "That sounds great. I could use one."

Kit interrupted, "I hate to break up this little party, but we had better get packing if we're going to leave in the morning."

Chapter 69

Ilsa began to have second thoughts on the way back to Trevor's and vented her feelings, "I hope this doesn't take too long. You have a manuscript due in a couple of weeks."

"I'm hoping we'll be back in a couple of days," Trevor assured her.

"I need to take care of this fish one way or another."

"What do you mean by that?" she asked.

"Oh nothing, it's just that this fish has caused me a lot of headaches and wasted time recently and I need some closure," Trevor answered without revealing his real plan.

"This will be our first trip together as a couple. I hope the weather's nice," Ilsa said snuggling up to Trevor as he pulled onto White Street.

Meanwhile, back on the Black Gold, preparations were being made for the trip. Carla had to slap a quick coat of varnish on the areas she and Kit had sanded to protect them from the salt water. They had planned to take several days to refinish the woodwork before returning to Bimini, but had to put their plans on hold due the urgency of this trip. Kit went about checking the electronics, fuel and other necessities on the vessel.

After finishing her varnishing and clean up, Carla walked into the galley where Kit was checking food provisions and said, "I think it's great that Trevor has agreed to help you relocate the barracuda."

"Yeah it's great alright, but I don't trust him any further than I could throw him."

"What do you mean?"

"I don't know. It just seemed a little too easy to change his mind that's all."

"You are always so suspicious of people. Here a man offers to help you and you think he has ulterior motives."

"Well, you have to admit trust has been an issue with us since I met him."

"Don't remind me Kit. I was just thinking how wonderful it would be if you two became friends."

"I don't know if that will ever happen. I think that someday I will be able to tolerate him on a higher level."

"Well, please try for me. He's trying to help me get my book published. The gentleman with us at dinner the night you created a scene is an editor for a major publishing house. Fortunately, he had a sense of humor and is still interested in my manuscript. He said if he had a girlfriend that looked like me, he would probably steal her thongs too."

Kit grunted, "There's another scumbag I have to keep an eye on."

"Oh Kit, don't be such an asshole."

"I'm sorry. I just don't like other men drooling over you."

"Get over it. Men are dogs. It's a simple fact of life. You're the same way. I saw you checking out some of those tourist girls with their boobs hanging out in Key West."

"They looked like they were lost."

"Yeah right! Kit don't try to bullshit me. Just admit that you have the same tendencies as other men and this discussion is over."

"Woof! Woof! Guilty as charged, but I would never cheat on you."

"Hopefully we'll have a life time for you to prove that to me."

Kit changed the subject. "I need to take a run to Key West for some provisions. Do you want to come along?"

"I've got a lot of cleaning to do if we are having guests on board. Would you mind if I stayed here?"

"No problem. With both of us doing things that need to be done, maybe we will have time to go to Key West for a relaxing dinner."

"Yeah, I could call Trevor and Ilsa to see if they want to go."

"I meant just you and me."

"Come on Kit. This will give you a chance to start working on your relationship with Trevor before we are stuck on a boat together for a couple of days."

"Whatever, I guess it will be okay as long as we don't go to the Pink Dolphin. I think the maitre d' has it in for me."

"Don't worry I don't think I'll ever show my face there again. Maybe we can go someplace fun like Sloppy Joe's."

"I didn't know you've been to Sloppy Joe's."

"Yeah Tre... I mean I went there on spring break during my college days."

"That isn't what you started to say."

"Alright, the truth is that Trevor took me there when we first got to Key West, but I did go there during my college days too. Does that mean we can't go there either?"

"No, don't be silly, but I'm glad you told me the truth. There aren't any secrets in a good relationship. Is there anything else you want to tell me?"

Carla's mind raced back to the moon-drenched beach in the Bahamas, but she decided that was one secret Kit could never know about. "You know everything now, so let's get going so we can make it an early evening."

The couple kissed and started their separate tasks. Carla grabbed the sheets from the guest quarters and the rest of the dirty laundry and headed to the marina's Laundromat for an afternoon of fun. Kit slid into the driver's seat of the same rental car he had driven to the Pink Dolphin only days earlier and was reminded of his night in the Key West jail. His thoughts turned to the man who had put him there—Trevor. He hoped he could overcome the disgust he had for the man so that they could work together to capture the barracuda.

The first stop on Kit's agenda was a bait store to pick up some live cigar minnows to be used as bait for the barracuda. Fortunately, he still had four of the peanut-sized fish attraction devices left over from the first capture. He hoped the barracuda would not be spooked this time by the devices. The baits were put in a portable live bait bucket to keep them alive until he got back to the boat and could put them in the bait well there. Kit would have to hurry shopping for the food provisions at the supermarket so the water wouldn't become deadly hot in the noonday even though placed in a shady spot in the back of the rental car.

Chapter 70

Carla called Trevor and Ilsa after things were in order to invite them to dinner. She suggested they bring their clothes and sleep on the boat since they would be leaving so early in the morning. Trevor wasn't real happy about the suggestion, but realized it was the logical thing to do. They agreed to meet at Sloppy Joe's around 6 p.m. to have a few beers and enjoy the local musicians.

Trevor and Ilsa arrived first and secured a table towards the back of the restaurant away from the stage where they could at least make an attempt to hold a conversation. During a break from a performer who sang mostly Jimmy Buffet tunes, Trevor relayed every story he had heard about the barracuda while he was in Bimini. "Some of the islanders even thought the fish was a demon sent up from the depths of hell to punish them," he concluded.

Ilsa grabbed his hand and said in a meek voice, "You'll protect me won't you?"

Trevor kissed her on the forehead saying, "I won't let that fish get near you."

Suddenly, the couple felt a presence and looked up to see Kit and Carla standing there accompanied by the hostess. The women did the usual thing women do and checked each other out from head to toe. Ilsa was wearing a backless silk wraparound top with no bra, which showed off her more than ample breasts. Her jeans were low-cut to reveal a thong strap with a small tattoo of a dolphin swimming just above.

The fish tattoo was something she had been peer pressured into doing on a drunken night out with her girlfriends. Carla wore a diaphanous light blue blouse tied at the bottom with a spandex bra that left her light pink nipples just discernable through the pockets. She covered her bottom with a pair of white Daisy Dukes frayed at the hem and too short for a modest person. Both men, though loyal to their mates, were enjoying the eye candy seated at their own table.

Trevor stood up, gave Carla a brief hug and shook hands with Kit. Ilsa also stood up and gave Carla a peck on the cheek and extended her hand to Kit. It was awkward as Kit ignored her hand and stepped closer to hug her too. Kit glanced at Carla as if to say two can play this game. A waitress showed up just in time to take a drink order and help the uncomfortable situation.   After the first round of beers, everyone mellowed out.

"I listened to the weather station before we left the boat and they said the seas are supposed to be three to five tomorrow," Kit said, trying to make conversation.

"I hope you packed your seasick pills Ilsa," Trevor said.

"Don't you worry about me. I've been out in rougher seas than that."

"Well, I'm not bashful. I'll do whatever it takes to keep from getting seasick. No matter how many times I've been in rough seas, I still get sick," Carla admitted.

"The Black Gold takes the seas pretty good. She's got a good hull design and plenty of length," Kit said to reassure his passengers.

Their conversation ended when the musician returned from his break and began to fill the pub with music. This time he began with a run of Bob Marley tunes, which eventually brought people to the dance floor. Ilsa stood up and begged Trevor to dance, but like a lot of men, Trevor refused. Carla turned to Kit and said, "Kit, why don't you dance with Ilsa?"

He looked at Trevor, shrugged his shoulders and said, "Why not?"

By the time they got on the floor the song was almost over. It had been the type of song conducive to individual freestyle dance, but the second song was for slow dancing. Ilsa didn't really want to slow dance with Kit but it seemed silly to leave the floor after such a short time. Kit wasn't sure what to do, so she grabbed his hand and said, "We might as well stay for this one." He smiled uneasily and said, "Sure, I'd love to."

They started out dancing as though each other had the plague, but as the song progressed their bodies naturally began to rub up against each other. Kit's hand felt good on her bare back and she swore she felt something poking her at her waistline. In addition, he was feeling her unintended excitement evidenced by the two points prodding him through the thin silk material of her top. They were both in a world of their own until they looked up only to see Trevor and Carla out on the floor and looking very comfortable dancing cheek to cheek.

Kit forgot all about his partner and danced them near the couple. Once there, he released Ilsa and asked, "Mind if I cut in?" Startled and unaware of his presence, Trevor replied, "Uh, yeah, sure."

As soon as Ilsa and Trevor moved away she asked him, "How come you wouldn't dance with me when I asked, but you danced with her?"

"You didn't ask me to slow dance. I don't mind slow dancing."

"Are you sure that's why?

"Don't be silly. You're my girl--nobody else. Besides, you started dancing with Kit first."

"That's not fair. The only reason I wound up with him is because you wouldn't dance with me."

"Alright, you're right. I promise never to turn you down again, no matter how ridiculous I look out on the dance floor."

When the music was over they all sat down at the table. Someone mentioned it was getting late, so they paid the tab and headed back to the Black Gold for a good night's sleep.

Chapter 71

Carla awoke when the big diesels were started to warm up for the early morning departure. She thought she remembered the alarm clock going off earlier and feeling Kit slip from beneath the sheets of the bed in the master cabin. It wasn't long before the gentle vibrations of the engines lulled her back to sleep.

Several hours later, after the jolting feeling of the vessel's bow plummeting off of one wave to the next, she was awake again and reaching for the seasickness tablets in the night stand. The ride was beginning to feel like a roller coaster in slow motion. Her stomach being empty is probably why she hadn't already started feeling the effects of the rough seas.

The young heiress laid back down for a couple of minutes, but decided that it would be best if she got dressed and headed topside. The sun was up but overshadowed by the thick grey clouds of a tropical storm. Kit reassured her that everything was all right, "We should be through the Gulf Stream in about a half hour, and then the seas should lay down a bit."

"I hope so. I don't like it when it's like this," Carla answered weakly, her arms wrapped around her torso. She watched as the bow of the boat dipped above and below the horizon with each large oceanic swell. Several times waves came crashing over the bow sending water running down the deck and off the sides.

The sight of the waves only worsened her already fragile stomach, so she decided to return below to the comfort of her bed. She probably would have gotten sick already if it weren't for the medication; however, they hadn't come up with one that was a hundred percent effective, so she was still miserable.

Two hours later, Carla realized she had experienced one of the wonderful side effects of seasickness pills and had fallen asleep. The boat seemed to be moving along at cruising speed with little or no interference from the sea. When she returned topside, the warm penetrating rays of the noonday sun welcomed her. "Where are we?" she asked, still feeling slightly disoriented.

"We're just past South Bimini en route to East Brother's Reef," Kit answered as he let go of the wheel with one hand and wrapped it around her shoulder.

"What happened to the storm?"

"It's heading for South Beach to give the sunbathers there a run for the money. Things should be clear over here now for a couple of days."

"Good, I don't know if I'll be lucky enough to sleep through the next one. Is anyone else hungry besides me?"

"I am, but you'll have to check with the others when they come back. They went below to change into their bathing suites, but they've been gone a little too long for a simple change of clothes."

Trevor watched as Ilsa removed the T-shirt she had thrown on earlier in a rush to help with the departure. She hadn't even taken time to put on a bra, but that seemed normal with women who spent time on the water. He was overcome with her beauty as she stood there topless smiling at him. Slowly he stood up and crept behind her. He slid his hands under her arms and cupped her full breasts. His warm lips began to gently caress the soft skin of her neck and behind her ears. Each warm exhale brought shivers down her spine.

She moaned as his manliness began to signal arousal. Trevor moved his hands down and began to tug at the waistband of the spandex shorts she was wearing. She in turn reached behind and undid the button to his shorts letting them drop to the floor. Her excitement increased when she realized he wasn't wearing any underwear.

Unable to wait any longer, Trevor didn't take time to remove her thong, but pulled it aside and pushed his way into her wetness. Immediately, she spread her legs and bent over placing her hands on the bunk to brace herself. His thrusts were fast and hard causing her breasts to sway to and fro adding to the passion of the moment. Trevor, feeling ready to explode, reached around to stimulate her so that they could both orgasm at the same time. It worked, and they both moaned in ecstasy falling forward onto the bed with Trevor lying on top of her supporting his weight with his arms. They both started giggling like a couple of high school kids, and turned to face each other in a frontal embrace. "Wow that was hot!" Ilsa moaned.

"Short but sweet," Trevor added.

"We better get cleaned up and head topside before we're missed," he continued.

"Do we have to?" Ilsa purred.

"No, but it would be the right thing to do."

"I don't like doing the right thing all of the time."

"Are you being a bad girl?" Trevor joked.

"Yes, I'm a very bad girl."

"Do you know what happens to bad girls?"

"No, why don't you show me?"

With that Trevor positioned Ilsa's bare-thonged rump over his knees and began to spank her white cheeks until they turned bright pink. Ilsa played along saying, "I've been a very bad girl. Ouch! Ouch! That hurts sooo good!"

Their fun over, the couple finished what they had gone below to accomplish and returned to the wheel room.

"I thought I was going to have to send out a search and rescue team for you two," Kit said, when they entered.

"Kit leave them alone. Are you guys hungry? I have some guava pastries I bought in this wonderful little bakery in Key West," Carla said, changing the subject.

"I could eat a horse," Trevor answered.

"Is it that bakery just off of Duval?" Ilsa asked. "I love their pastries."

"That's the one. I have apple and blueberry too, but the guava is my favorite."

Kit checked the screen on the GPS and noticed that they were almost to the area where he had released the barracuda. "I'll have mine in a couple of minutes after we're anchored."

"Do you mean we're almost there?" Carla inquired.

"Yep. We're about a quarter mile away according to the GPS."

Chapter 72

Kit noticed a smaller craft earlier approaching from the rear but paid no attention to its path because of its distance away; however, now it seemed to be on a collision course with the Black Gold. After the anchor had taken hold, the boat pulled alongside the yacht surprising the other passengers. Trevor recognized the captain and called out, "Hey John long time no see!"

"How's it going Trevor?" John asked.

Carla, trying not to stare, noticed that the other passenger was wearing a prosthesis that replaced his right leg. Quickly, her mind put two and two together and she surmised that this must be Johnny, the captain's son, and the one who was attacked by the barracuda. She was glad to see that he had lived, but sad to see he had lost his leg.

"I'm glad to see Johnny's up and about," Trevor said, nodding toward the young man.

"Don't expect a reply from him. He hasn't spoken a word since he lost his leg and his wife left him. The bitch promised to stay by his side, but ran off with the pool boy while he was in therapy."

"Where are you guys headed?"

"Right here, East Brother's Reef. Say, what are you doing here?"

Trevor, not sure he wanted to divulge their real purpose replied, "Just here for a little R&R."

"Good! I thought you might have read the same article in the newspaper that I did and were here to try and catch the barracuda. I brought the boy over here to catch and kill that bastard. I thought it might be therapeutic for him. You know, take all of his anger and frustration out on that fish. I even had to bribe the officials an extra thousand dollars to bring this in. Go grab the AK son."

Johnny obediently left his father's side grabbed something from the forward storage compartment. "Ain't she a beauty?" John asked, as his son brandished a shiny black AK-47.

Surprised by the gun Kit blurted out, "What the hell are you going to do with that thing?"

"Well, if it isn't the old fish lover himself. Not that it's any of your business, but if we can't catch the cuda, Johnny here is going to blow it to kingdom come!"

Kit, unable told his tongue said, "That's crazy! And illegal!"

Johnny slowly raised the AK and pointed it in Kit's direction. John noticed his son's gesture and reacted quickly, "Put the gun away son." Johnny didn't seem to hear him so he repeated himself, "Put the damn gun away son!" Slowly Johnny obeyed his father and put the gun back in the storage compartment. John stepped behind the wheel and shouted before speeding away, "I don't know what you're doing out here, but you had better stay out of our way. I don't know if he'll listen to me next time."

Kit shook his head as the two sped off and said, "What a couple of whackos. I hope they don't get to the fish before we do."

Trevor mumbled under his breath, "Yeah, that would be a real shame."

Ilsa, not sure about what just happened, questioned him, "Trevor, how do you know that man? He looks like a dangerous individual."

"We met in Bimini. The barracuda attacked his son there while he was diving for lobster. We knew he had almost died from a wound to his leg, but never found out what happened to him. I guess we can assume he lost his leg, and now it appears also his mind."

"How terrible. And we're here to save this fish?"

Trevor has to bite his tongue and say what Kit wants to hear, "Yes, but it's not the fish's fault. Like Kit said, it was only doing what nature designed it to do."

"I'm glad you finally understand my point," Kit said, with a smile.

"When are we going to get started?" Trevor said, wanting to put all of this behind him.

"Let's grab a bite to eat first, and then you can help me get the Whaler in the water and make up some rigs."

A half hour later, the boat was in the water and Trevor and Kit were in the makeshift lab rigging the baitfish and inspecting the fish attraction devices.

"Can you get me some of these?" Trevor asked, intrigued by the devices.

"Sure, I'll call my friend

"You say this is how you managed to catch the barracuda the first time?"

"Yeah, it worked like a charm; although, once I got him on the line, it wasn't that easy. In fact, at one point, I wound up in the water with the line wrapped around my ankle after jumping in to remove the fouled line from the outboard. I'll warn you right now he's old, but he's a fighter."

"So am I," Trevor returned and both men chuckled.

"I'll let you pull him in once we get him hooked," Kit offered.

"I'd love to."

"Let's get going. We still have a few good hours of sunshine."

The men packed up their gear and said goodbye to the women. The anglers were warned to be careful several times between farewell kisses. The outboard on the Whaler took several tries before it started. Upon inspection Kit noticed that water separator canister on the fuel line was long overdue to be changed. For this reason, Kit decided to drift fish not far from where the Black Gold was anchored just in case the engine started acting up.

The reef was amazing. Yellowtail snappers could be seen boiling below the surface even before the use of chum to bring them up. Trevor was impressed by the amount of fish even though he was mainly a sports fisherman and only bottom fished when he needed a quick meal. "Let's get started," he said, as he grabbed the rigged bait from the cooler.

The attraction device was activated by a twist of its outer two-piece cover and rammed down the throat of the baitfish. A hook was placed through the front lips of the fish with another trailing on a secondary leader that was imbedded in the anterior region. This was an insurance policy in case the barracuda hit the back of the fish instead of swallowing it whole. As before, a small piece of copper wire was threaded and tied around mouth of the fish to prevent the attraction device from falling out.

The rig was then attached to a Penn International reel with heavy monofilament line. Trevor put on fishing harness so he wouldn't be stumbling around trying to find it when the barracuda strikes. "Ready?" Kit asked as he lowered the bait into the water. Trevor nodded his head and watched as the bait floated downward.

The yellowtail seemed to flock around it not sure whether to strike or not. Its sheer size kept them at bay. "It may be a little trickier here," Kit mentioned, "there's a lot more competition on the reef than there was on the sandy bottom of Bimini Bay where I hooked him the first time."

As Kit finished the sentence, something hit the bait with so much force it almost pulled the rod from Trevor's grip. "Yee ha!" he screamed, as he sat back in the small bucket seat of the Whaler to prevent his being pulled over. The line peeled out fast but stopped suddenly. It felt like he was hooked on the bottom. "It can't be the barracuda unless it was able to wrap me around something on the reef."

"Let's cut the line. We don't want to waste any time trying to get it loose."

"I'll let it sit for a minute while you prepare another bait. Maybe it will come free."

A couple of seconds later, Trevor felt some movement on the line so he began to crank furiously. There was heavy resistance, but whatever it was began to move towards the surface. "I think it's coming up!"

"What do you think it is?" Kit asked.

"Well, it's definitely not our barracuda. It feels more like a nurse shark or grouper. I felt a little head shake and it didn't make much of a run for it."

With each crank on the reel, the form began to take shape. "It's a black grouper, a mycteroperca bonaci," Kit said as it neared the surface.

"Nice fish! It must weigh twenty pounds or more," Trevor commented as he gaffed the fish behind the head and hauled it into the boat.

Suddenly, a burst of gunshots could be heard. The men surmised it was the AK-47 they had seen earlier. About a quarter mile east of them they spotted the boat. Within several minutes hundreds of rounds of ammunition tore through the ocean's surface, and then there was silence.

What a wacko!" Kit reiterated.

"I hope they stay over there. I don't what to get shot by an errant round," Trevor added.

The grouper, realizing its life was in peril, began to thrash about on the boat's deck. Next, the sound of twin outboards being started could be heard in the direction of the other vessel. As the two men had feared, the boat was heading in their direction. They watched as the high-speed boat sped towards them not sure what was going to happen.

When the boat got near, Johnny could be seen standing on the bow wielding the AK-47 with a glazed look in his eyes. Smoke was still swirling out of the overheated barrel.

"My boy almost got him! We had a live yellowtail in the water for bait and the bastard came by and cut him in half. He kind of hung around for a few minutes, just long enough for Johnny to break out the AK. The boy shot up all the ammo I brought. Good therapy! He looks better already doesn't he?"

Trevor and Kit looked at each other in disbelief. Their fears were calmed by the knowledge that Johnny was out of ammo.

"Do you boys know where I might be able to buy some AK ammo on Bimini?" John asked.

Sarcastically, Kit answered, "Maybe a Russian spy, or a subversive group trying to take over the Bahamian government."

"Real funny! You wouldn't be talking like that if Johnny had some ammo for the gun. Maybe I'll pick up some dynamite while I'm at it, so we can blow it up if we can't get a clean shot. We'll get that fish even if I have to fly home and smuggle some AK ammo back in. Come on boy. Let's go. If you see that cuda, tell him his days are numbered!"

With that he turned the vessel and buried the throttles almost causing Johnny to tumble from his stance on the bow.

"I think you might want to be a little more careful about what you say to those two next time," Trevor said, as the boat roared away. Then he added, "Next time he might not be out of ammo."

"Yeah, I guess you're right," Kit conceded.

"Well, at least we know the barracuda's still in this vicinity," Trevor said, changing the subject.

"But where is he now after being practically blasted out of the water?

"He probably didn't go too far. You know how barracudas are. They generally don't let people or things scare them much."

"Let's move the boat in the direction of the gunfire and try again," Kit suggested, "but I don't want to go too far until I change the fuel filter.

"Sounds like a plan," Trevor said as he readied the fishing equipment for the move.

The men estimated the direction to be southwest of their current position. With everything stowed, Kit started the engine and motored off to the new position. They had barely gotten the rigged bait in the water when a squall line moved in and drenched the pair.

Because it was getting late in the day and the men were somewhat fatigued from the early morning departure for the Bahamas, they decided to call it a day. Besides, they didn't bring much ice along because they didn't expect to catch any fish for eating; that wasn't what they came out for.

The little ice they brought started to melt away from the dead grouper. Kit peered into the cooler and said, "We had better get this fish back to the boat if we're going to eat it for dinner."

"Sounds good to me," Trevor said, as he took his shirt off and wrung the water out of it.

"Tomorrow's another day," he added as he put his shirt back on.

Chapter 73

The women's sunbathing was interrupted by the same storm that drenched the men. They both peered over the side as the men approached the yacht and clapped when Trevor hoisted the large grouper from the ice chest.

"That doesn't look like a barracuda!" Carla yelled down at the men.

"It looks more like dinner," Ilsa commented.

After the Whaler was hauled out of the water and secured to the aft deck, Ilsa asked Trevor, "What was all of that noise we heard out there, and what did those weirdoes want?"

"The kid got close enough to the cuda to take pot shots at it. In fact, he shot up all of the ammo they had. He's got some serious problems. Hopefully we can finish what we came for and be back in Key West drinking margaritas before they return with more ammo."

The storm had long passed and the seas returned to a lake-like quietness. The setting sun painted the sky in brilliant reds and pinks and grey clouds flowered along the horizon. Trevor stood on the stern over a hot fry pan blackening the grouper. The burning spices charged the air with a pungent smell that would make even the most finicky eater hungry.

Inside, the women prepared yellow rice and black beans Cuban style and a delectable salad of greens painted with balsamic vinaigrette. A warm ocean breeze caressed the diners as they sat about the aft deck consuming the delicious meal.

Kit broke the silence, "Well, I guess the day wasn't a total loss."

"I'll second that," Ilsa said, raising her wine glass.

The others raised their wine glasses and brought them together in a toast.

Trevor took a sip of wine and asked, "Kit, what time do you want to hit the water tomorrow?"

He thought for a minute and responded, "I think we should try to be out there as the sun rises. That's the time the cuda's most likely to start feeding. It was early in the morning the last time I caught him."

"Sounds good do you have an alarm clock?"

"Yeah, I'll set it for 5:00 a.m."

Carla rolled her eyes and said, "Try to catch it on the first ring. I need my beauty sleep."

Kit set down his wine glass and gently placed his hands under Carla's jaw line and planted a kiss on her lips. When he drew away he said, "Waking up a little early won't hurt you because if you get any more beautiful, I won't be able to take it."

Carla a little embarrassed returned, "Thank you baby."

Ilsa asked Trevor "Wasn't that sweet?"

"Yes, but not as sweet as you are."

Carla remarked, "They must really love us, or they are trying to get laid,"

Ilsa added, "Probably a little of both."

Trevor's glass was empty so he went below to open another bottle of wine. After everyone's glasses were refilled, the men started telling each other fish stories while the women discussed Carla's manuscript. Kit bragged about the summer he worked as a mate on a boat that landed one of the largest marlins and won the most prestigious tournament in the Bahamas. Trevor bragged about being in the record books for catching a large marlin on extremely light gear.

When the second bottle of wine started to kick in, the group became strangely silent. The long day on the water and full bellies began to take their toll. After Trevor started to snore, Ilsa suggested that they all retire for the evening. "Remember, let's get up at five," Kit said to Trevor as he entered the parlor, "that way we will have enough time to rig the baits, get the rest of the gear and be out on the reef before sunrise when the cuda starts feeding." Trevor gave him the thumbs up as he entered his cabin.

Within minutes Trevor was in his birthday suit and happily snoring away. Ilsa, used to sleeping by herself with nothing to distract her, was having trouble dealing with her new love's annoying sleep condition. She bought some cute pink earplugs before they left Key West at the pharmacy on Duval Street. They took a little getting used to, but before long, she too was in a light slumber.

After an hour or so, Ilsa was awakened when Trevor rolled over in his sleep and kneed her in the buttocks. "Shit!" she whispered to herself, "I hate these little beds." She settled back down and tried to make herself sleep, but Trevor's snoring was even louder now.

Suddenly she realized that the noise she heard wasn't him at all but the sound of a small, rough running outboard engine. She wondered what someone would be doing out on the reef at this time of night in a small boat. Her mind thought of all sorts of excuses but none of them really made sense.

As the noise seemed to get closer, she removed the earplugs to hear better. The small boat was definitely heading in their direction. She thought about waking Trevor, but decided to wait.

Ilsa wondered if she was the only one awake and aware of the boat. She listened intently but didn't hear any other stirrings inside.

Her fear escalated when she heard a thump on the side of the yacht and the muffled voices of uninvited guests. Quickly she reached around and placed her hand on Trevor's mouth and whispered quietly in his ear, "Trevor wake up. I think someone is boarding the vessel." Trevor, a heavy sleeper before he reached his forties and began to snore, awoke and nodded his head when Ilsa repeated her original message.

Without hesitation he reached for his shorts and the 357 magnum he kept close by just in case a situation like this should arise. Seconds later the cabin door opened slowly and a black figure much shorter than Kit peered inside. Trevor aimed for the head and shot.

The high caliber bullet entered the middle of the forehead and exited the back of the skull taking half of it with it. The body slumped to the floor and quivered in a death rattle. Kit yelled, "What the fuck is going on!" as he raced from his cabin.

The second intruder was already in the skiff pulling away at full throttle as Trevor emptied the clip of his gun trying to take him out. Carla came into the small hall and slipped in the blood that had already started to puddle on the floor. Brain matter was running down the wall across from the cabin door. Ilsa vomited when Kit turned on the lights to investigate the area. "What the hell happened?" is all Kit could say as Trevor returned inside.

"We had some unwelcome guests on board and this one wasn't so lucky, Trevor said, pointing to the corpse on the floor still clutching an old 38 special. "Shoot first and ask questions later, is my policy when someone boards your boat without permission in the middle of the night," Trevor said, feeling no remorse for shooting the invader.

"It looks like a good thing you did," Kit said, as he removed the gun from the dead man's hand finding it fully loaded.

"I wouldn't touch too much Kit," Ilsa said, "this is a crime scene."

Trevor, suddenly aware of his actions said, "Well, we have two options: call the Bahamian authorities or feed this guy to the reef sharks. I'm for option two; however, I'll understand if you guys want to call the authorities, but this scum bag doesn't deserve a decent burial."

"I think we had better call the authorities, Carla said nervously knowing that you never know what's going to happen in a foreign country. Kit and Ilsa nodded their heads in agreement.

"Do you want to call or should I?" Trevor questioned Kit.

"I'm the captain on this vessel so I guess I should."

Kit stepped over the body and made his way to the boat's radio. A couple of minutes later he returned and said, "They want us to come to the custom's dock in Bimini and the authorities will meet us there. They cautioned us to try and leave the crime scene intact. In addition, they are going to send out a patrol boat to see if they can catch the guy in the skiff."

"I'll take a look around and make sure everything is secure on deck," Trevor offered.

The trip to Bimini was uneventful; however, the seas had picked up from a passing squall, which made the corpse slide to and fro in the hall where it laid in a huge puddle of blood. Periodically, the sound of the head hitting the wooden wall could be heard creeping out all of the passengers. Upon arrival at the dock, a local constable, two fellow officers and Dr.Smythe met them.

"Permission to board captain?" the head constable said, as he jumped on to the vessel without waiting for an answer.

"Yes sir," Kit replied as an afterthought.

"Show me where the body is, and then I would like you and the rest of the passengers to go to the customs building so we can take your statements."

Dr. Smythe immediately recognized most of them and said, "Kit, Trevor and Carla, I didn't know you were on the island."

"Well, actually we weren't on the island. We were anchored over on East Brother's Reef doing a little diving and fishing," Kit volunteered.

"Carla, you're even prettier than I remember. How's the ankle?" Dr. Smythe said with a wink.

"You can barely see the scar. You did a great job sewing it up," she said, giving him a hug.

"And might I ask, who is this beautiful young lady?" he said, extending his large round hand.

"Hi I'm Ilsa, Trevor's agent and friend," she replied, extending her hand.

"Last night she was my girlfriend," Trevor interjected, feeling a little hurt by her description of their relationship.

"I'm sorry darling. Dr. Smythe, I am Trevor Callaway's girlfriend, and proud of it.

"How's the book coming Trevor?"

"I'm almost finished, and I haven't forgotten about my promise to send you a signed copy when it's done."

"Tell me what happened out there, and don't worry I'll make sure the local authorities know what good people you are."

Trevor spoke up, "Ilsa was awakened by the sound of someone boarding our vessel, so she woke me up to let me know. I grabbed my 45, and before I could go see who it was, he was already forcing our cabin door open. I didn't ask any questions—I just blew him away. And it was a good thing I did, he was packing a fully-loaded 38 special."

"Sounds like self defense to me. I'm sure the authorities will clear you of any wrongdoing. In the mean time why don't you folks go inside the customs building and have a seat while we sort things out."

The group was led into an air-conditioned room to await their fate. On board the Black Gold crime scene investigators stormed over the body and surrounding areas. It was quickly determined that things had happened just as they had been described. The blood splatter pattern and subsequent hole in the teak wall of the hallway provided the evidence to back up the story. Official statements were taken from the group while the evidence was collected and the body removed.

A teary-eyed constable spoke with Dr. Smythe, and then quickly left the scene. Dr. Smythe approached the group and spoke, "I've got some good news and some bad news. The good news is the constable is not going to file any charges against Trevor. The bad news is the perpetrator is a cousin of the constable. His name is Harry. He got involved with crack cocaine. He was such a nice boy before his involvement with the drug; however, once he became addicted, he spent time in and out of jail for felony theft and aggravated assault.

A while back, he disappeared. We thought one of his dealers might have killed him or he went to the mainland for more victims and a more easily obtainable supply of crack. The truth is that he must have been hiding on an out island and robbing and murdering foreigners on their yachts.

We've had the U.S. Coastguard alert us that a couple of American vessels are missing within the last six months. He probably would have killed all of you, taken any valuables and either scuttled your vessel in deep water, or sold it to Cuban smugglers. I don't blame you for what you did; however, blood is blood. I suggest you leave the area as soon as possible before the constable changes his mind. By the way, isn't East Brother's Reef where a man's son was killed in a diving accident?"

Kit played dumb and answered, "I didn't hear anything about it."

"Thanks doc," Trevor said, patting him on the back. "We best be going Kit," he said, motioning towards the door.

"You don't have to tell me twice."

The couples swiftly moved to their boat under the watchful eyes of the immigration officers and a few of the regular police that had gathered. There weren't many killings on the island, so they were curious about the perpetrators. Their presence made the group uneasy and even more motivated to leave as quickly as possible. As soon as they were away from the dock, Carla began pleading with Kit to head back to Key West, "We're going home now right?"

"I thought about it back at the immigration building, but I think we have a bigger responsibility to keep anymore innocent people from being injured or killed by the barracuda. We have to move the fish to where Trevor originally came into contact with it so that it can live out the rest of its life in peace. After all, you never heard of it causing any problems before it came to Bimini did you?"

"I guess you're right, but I didn't like the way those Bahamians were looking at us. Usually they are very friendly and hospitable, but I didn't see that in the faces of the men that watched us leave."

"I know what you mean, so we will take care of our business as fast as possible and be on our way. Does everyone agree?"

Trevor felt uncomfortable about staying, but was on a mission to make sure the fish died for all of the trouble he's caused. With a poker face he smiled and answered, "Sure thing Captain."

Ilsa voiced her opinion, "I hate to be a party pooper, but I think we should get while the getting's good. Trevor, I think they were real close to throwing your butt in the clinker back there. Kit can tell you what that's like," she said with a smirk.

Trevor grabbed her hand and said, "Honey, you heard what they said, that man was a criminal and what I did was self defense. It's a law of the sea that no one boards a man's boat in open waters without asking permission. Christ, even the US Coast Guard asks before boarding a vessel. Of course, they won't take no for an answer, but at least they ask first. I felt a little uneasy back there but as long as we don't break any more laws, we shouldn't have any problems with them.

Chapter 74

Back in Bimini, on the docks of the immigration office, two constables were talking about Trevor. "Wasn't that the man that brought the evil fish to the island?"

"You know, I thought I recognized him from somewhere."

Another officer chimed in, "I used to hang out with him, he's a good fellow."

The first officer returned, "He might be, but right know he's responsible for several of our people dying either directly or indirectly. I don't trust him. I think we should keep an eye on him until he returns to the States. Maybe we can keep someone else from perishing while he's here. Grab a patrol boat and let's get going!"

Fortunately Kit had marked the spot where they had previously anchored with the GPS. Within a short time they were back and readying the Whaler for another attempt at capturing the barracuda. Trevor asked Kit about the chemical he had used to sedate the large fish the first time he captured it, "What's that stuff in the syringe?"

"Oh, that's Finquel, an anesthesia for fish—just a little squirt around the gills and they go night night. That big cuda was as harmless as a baby after I gave him a shot of this."

Trevor made sure he remembered the drawer that Kit took the Finquel from just in case he needed some in the future to carry out his plan. A short while later, they kissed the girls goodbye and promised to be careful as they set out for the reef again.

Meanwhile, off the coast of Bimini, an open fisherman boat was speeding along trying to get past the island without stopping at Bahamian customs. John had accomplished what he had set out to do—get ammo for the AK 47. It wasn't easy. He had to go black market and buy the ammo from some crazy Cubans that were stockpiling it to support a dream to take Cuba back from Castro. But as more and more Cubans became rich in the United States, it was hard to find volunteers willing to jeopardize their lifestyle. Hence, they were left with large stockpiles of Russian made guns and ammo that was smuggled to the U.S. after Russia pulled out of Cuba.

Down in the live bait well of the vessel was enough ammo to shoot up a thousand barracudas. Johnny had blown a couple of seagulls away for target practice as they passed through the Gulf Stream. His father smiled with delight as he blew them from the air with a couple of short blasts from the gun. He made him put the gun away as they passed within miles of Bimini just in case any patrol boats were out. They were about an hour away from East Brother's Reef where they planned on carrying out their mission to find and massacre the barracuda.

The Bahamian patrol boat stayed far away from the Black Gold so as not to arouse suspicion. They drifted and watched with high-powered binoculars often used for drug surveillance missions that entailed discretely viewing smugglers from a distance. Kit and Trevor's trek away from the Black Gold did not go unnoticed, but did not look like anything out of the ordinary; however, the officers did find it strange that the men had chosen to go fishing immediately after being interrogated for murder. Didn't they have a conscience? And why did they choose to stay in the Bahamas after going through such an ordeal? These were questions they hoped to get answered by keeping them under surveillance.

Chapter 75

The barracuda's tail had healed from the spear gun wound, but the injury had taken its toll on the aging fish. In addition, his poor eyesight had gotten worse. It was becoming a struggle to find and target its next meal. If it weren't for the abundance of fish on the reef, it probably would have starved.

Its latest attempt at finding food was interrupted by the sound of an outboard motor approaching. When the motor shut off, the fish slowly moved closer to the boat hoping that this would be its chance to eat.

On board the Whaler, Kit and Trevor readied the baits; the attraction devices were turned on and carefully placed inside. Trevor held one up to his ear and said, "I can't hear much coming from mine."

"You won't out of the water, but if you're a fish in the water, the sound is rather loud; they can hear it from probably a hundred yards away. You know how sound travels under water."

The two men placed their baits in the water and held their rods up hoping to feel a tug at the other end. Kit's bait was immediately stripped from the hook before he could react. The fish, a large Wahoo, struck the bait from behind the hook without swallowing the bait; it just tore the meat from the hook. Kit shook his head in amazement when he inspected the bait and said, "Something big just hit this and missed the hook damn it!"

"There are just three more attraction devices in the tackle box. I hope we don't have to do this the old fashioned way," Kit said, disappointed that they had lost another one without catching the cuda. Trevor grabbed another bait and device and began rerigging his rod. Before he could get it back in the water, Kit was screaming with excitement, "I'm hooked with something! I don't know what it is but it's running like O.J. Simpson from the police."

A lumbering mutton snapper, an ancient fish, grabbed the bait and was trying to escape with it; however, the leader and line were selected to capture the barracuda and were much too strong for the fish. After a couple of runs, Kit was steering the fish back towards the boat.

The barracuda hovered below the Whaler watching his next meal approach. The mutton saw the cuda and made one last run knowing death was just around the corner. With a burst of speed the cuda sliced through the midsection of the fish halving it.

Kit almost fell backwards off the boat when the pressure from the end of the line was instantly released. His backward motion flipped the rod back and caused the fish's head to fly on board and slam against the center console with a loud thud. Both men stood in disbelief as they both witnessed the cuda's assault.

"Holy fuck! Did you see that?" Trevor shouted.

"Hell yes! Trevor, get your fucking line in the water quick! This may be our only chance!"

Trevor quickly finished tying the last knot securing the swivel to the monofilament line and tossed the bait into the water. Then men both stood motionless and barely breathing as they watched the water for any signs of the cuda. The fish had moved to the edge of the reef to finish swallowing the tail end of the snapper but was moving slowly back towards the boat hoping to find more food.

Its sensitive hearing was picking up the distress signals of an injured fish. It picked up speed to investigate. Something didn't seem right about the small fish dangling in the water but its need to eat overshadowed any lessons it had learned in the past. The barracuda opened its mouth at the last second and gulped down the fish in one bite.

Kit had hurriedly outfitted Trevor with a gimbal belt hoping that he would need it shortly. When the cuda realized it was hooked, it sped for the open sea. Kit learning his lesson from the last time quickly hit the switch to raise the lower unit of the outboard from the water. In addition, he removed anything that might be sticking up and readied the canvas containment pen by tying it to the cleats so that when they needed it they could just dump it over the side.

Trevor began to sweat as the fish challenged him with a couple of good runs away from the boat. Every time he would take in some line the fish would peel out that much more. "Are you sure this rig is going to hold him?" Trevor asked at one point.

"It did the first time."

All of a sudden the line went slack and Trevor began winding like crazy. "I don't like this!" Trevor said, as his arm turned the crank. Seconds later both men had to duck as they watched the fish speed towards the boat jumping at the last moment and flying through the air chomping its mouth and landing on the opposite side. The line snagged on the fiberglass radio antenna and Kit cursed at himself for not lowering it earlier. As he jumped to try to free the line, it tightened and snapped the antenna off like a kabob stick.

After that maneuver, the old barracuda began to tire. It knew it would soon be giving in to the force tugging at its jaw. With all of the strength it had left, it began tugging but giving in to a wide zigzag pattern that would slowly lead it back to the vessel. "I think it's giving up." Trevor said with excitement.

"I'll get the containment pen in the water. When I lower the outer edge, just lead him inside and I'll give him a dose of Finquel," Kit said, filling the syringe with the drug.

Slowly but surely, Trevor guided the fish towards the canvas containment pen. Like guiding a marlin's spear to a mate's gloved hand, Trevor led the fish alongside the boat into the canvas containment pen trying not to make any quick gestures that would alarm the fish and make it run again.

Kit lowered the syringe into the water next to the fish's gills and released a white cloud of anesthesia to calm the fish before he raised the side of the canvas enclosure. The fish seemed to drop towards the bottom as he raised the exterior canvas wall. He took the lines and tied them securely to the cleats. Both men stood in silence and stared at the majestic fish while its big eyes seemed to rotate up and look back.

Trevor high-fived Kit and moved to the driver's seat at the center console. He lowered the engine and started it up to begin the slow cruise back to the Black Gold.

Fortunately, the yacht was positioned in a manner that kept the Bahamian authorities from seeing them raise the canvas enclosure to the deck. If they had been able to see this, they might have thought it was another body being brought on board.

Carefully, they lifted the enclosure and slid the sleeping fish's body into the live bait well. Kit studied the fish closely to see any indication that he had over anesthetized it. Slowly the fish became more animated and began to rise off the bottom. Kit lowered the lid not wanting to deal with a fully alert seven-foot barracuda.

While stowing the Whaler so they could prepare for the trip to Chub Cay, both men looked up when they heard the whine of outboards heading in their direction. "Shit! I think it's those whackos, John and Johnny, coming back for another visit. Don't let them see anything that will let them know we have the fish. Try to remain cool and collected," Kit said, as he moved to the railing to see what they wanted.

Once again, Johnny was perched on the bow holding the AK-47 with a glazed look in his eyes. John was the first to speak, "You haven't seen that murderous fish lately have you?"

Trevor answered, "No John. Do you think you could have Johnny put the gun away while we speak?"

"Don't worry. He won't shoot you. That is, unless you're lying about the whereabouts of the barracuda."

Kit spoke up, "We're just here to do a little fishing with our girlfriends. That cuda is probably far out to sea after being shot at by you the last time you were here."

"I've thought about it and I still find it funny that you came to this reef to fish considering this is where the last attack took place."

"No, we just came here because the locals told us about the good fishing," Kit said, trying to bluff his way out of a tight situation.

"For some reason I don't believe you. Anyway, I got Johnny enough ammo to blow that creature to kingdom come if we can find him."

Johnny just smiled and nodded his head. With that John cut the wheel and gunned the engines to head to the center of the reef in search of the barracuda. Trevor and Kit continued preparations for the journey, but now working at a quickened pace wanting to be on their way before John senior and junior returned.

A half an hour later, shots could be heard permeating the silence of the reef. Everyone on the Black Gold stopped what he or she was doing and watched as the lunatic son sprayed the ocean with machine gun fire. They weren't the only ones that heard the shots. The captain of the Bahamian gunboat also heard them and ordered the helmsman of the gunboat to investigate the gunfire. The crew of the Black Gold nervously gazed at the Bahamian patrol boat speeding by in pursuit of the men.

John saw them coming and decided to try to outrun them knowing that he may spend some time in a Bahamian jail for being there illegally and with a whole cache of ammo and the AK-47. The

Bahamian patrol boat gave chase for a short time with the commander requesting them to power down over the loudspeaker.

When that didn't work, he ordered the gunner to shoot a couple of rounds from a fifty-caliber machine gun across their bow. John, thinking being alive in jail was better than dying, pulled back on the throttles and killed the engine. What he failed to realize was that his whacked out son was still standing on the bow with an AK-47 aimed at the Bahamian officials.

John stood with his hands up and pleaded with his son, "Johnny, for Christ's sake put down the gun before they shoot you!"

The Bahamian officials made their demands, "Put down the weapon and raise your hands or you will be fired upon!"

John begged his son again, "Johnny put down the gun for me."

Johnny just turned and smiled at his dad and said, "Sorry I can't do that."

Next, he faced the patrol boat and squeezed the trigger on the AK-47 screaming, "Fuck you mother fuckers!"

Bullets sprayed the vessel but were no match for the armored hull. The gunner on the Bahamian vessel didn't wait for any orders to fire. The fifty-caliber shells practically decapitated father and son at such close rage. The rounds made holes the size of baseballs in the fiberglass hull. One of them struck the aluminum tanks holding hundreds of gallons of fuel and the spark ignited the vessel into a gigantic fireball. The commander of the Bahamian vessel ordered the helmsman to back away before their own vessel became a casualty.

"Holy shit!" was all Kit could say as he watched the fireworks.

"I think it's time we hit the road," he said, already on his way to the bridge.

Trevor sprang into action shouting, "I'll check for any loose objects on the deck. And ladies, I think it's best if you stay inside. We don't know what's going to happen if and when the Bahamian officials see us leaving."

The Black Gold pulled away from the reef leaving behind the burning vessel and patrol boat. A lucky shift in the wind caused the thick black smoke of the burning fiberglass hull to mask their departure. The bright flames lit up the darkening sky and stayed visible in the twilight sky for miles. The patrol boat captain eventually realized that they had left the area, but figured he had no real reason to pursue them. And besides, he was going to have to file a report about what had happened with the other American vessel that was now little more than flaming patches of debris. He felt bad for the father, but it was the son who fired first; the gunner would have to be dealt with later for not waiting for orders.

Chapter 76

Kit and Trevor manned the helm during the night taking turns at the wheel. The sun was beginning to rise as they approached the waters of Chub Cay. Kit was at the helm and probably would be for the rest of the trip. Trevor knew that they had already entered the waters where he had originally came into contact with the cuda, but told Kit the area was at least five miles ahead. Making the excuse that he had to use the head, Trevor went to the lab to grab the Finquel that he planned to kill the cuda with. Several minutes later, Trevor returned and said he was going aft to make sure everything was still secure. For some reason Kit didn't believe the excuse Trevor had given for heading aft. He put the boat on automatic pilot and went aft to investigate.

Trevor approached the live bait well cautiously and lifted the lid with the Finquel ready to pour into the tank. As he lifted the lid, Kit showed up from nowhere and shouted, "What the hell are you trying to do?" Trevor, caught red-handed, Finquel ready to pour, dropped the lid in the open position. Kit rushed at him lunging for the chemical, but tripped and managed to knock Trevor backwards into the aft railing. The force of the blow caused Trevor to hit the railing and summersault over into the deep blue waters off Chub Cay. At the same time the barracuda, no longer anesthetized, thrust its tail and flew from the tank and slid across the deck and into the water.

Quickly, Kit ran to the bridge and took the boat off automatic pilot to circle around and rescue Trevor. He shouted to the women below, "Man overboard! I need help ladies!" The women napping in their bunks threw on some clothes and went to the bridge to find out what was going on.

"What's the matter?" Carla said, as she entered the bridge.

"Yeah, what's the commotion?" Ilsa echoed.

"Trevor's fallen overboard and I need you guys to help spot him so we can get him out of the water. Oh, the cuda went overboard. I'll explain later."

"What!" both women said in unison.

Kit slowed the boat down to an idle kicking the engines in and out of gear trying to position the boat as close to Trevor as possible without running him over. Trevor was just a few feet from the dive platform when the girls started screaming, "Trevor! Look out! The cuda is circling you!" Kit, alarmed by their message, ran to the stern and shouted, "Trevor, carefully take off all of your jewelry and put it in your pockets, and then swim to the platform slowly without splashing.

Trevor took off his rings and wristwatch and placed them in his shorts pocket being careful to try and conceal them during the process. He kept treading water slowly making his way to the dive platform watching the cuda as he swam. Kit's theory about the cuda mistakenly attacking people was about to be tested. There were no longer any shiny objects for it to see and no fish smell or fish-like movements were being made. It was now that Trevor actually hoped that Kit was right about the fish. If he made it safely back to the boat, he would be glad that his plans to kill it had been thwarted.

The cuda was still dazed from the Finquel and disoriented from the plunge back into the sea. It suddenly noticed a large object swimming not too far from where it landed. It had been several hours since it had eaten, but other than the object nothing had aroused its senses. The cuda decided to take a closer look but maintained a safe distance not knowing if the object was another predator that might do it harm.

Trevor watched as the fish circled at a distance watching to see if it showed any signs of aggression. The fish's big eyes seemed to follow his every movement as he made his way to the dive platform. He breathed a sigh of relief as he hopped up and swung his legs out of the water. Carla watched in panic thinking about what the cuda had done to her during the same move.

Kit made his way to the railing at the stern and extended his hand to help Trevor over. Trevor hesitated for a moment not sure how he felt about what just happened, but stuck his hand out and accepted the help in the end. "I'm sorry about shoving you so hard. I didn't mean to send you overboard," Kit offered.

"Well, I guess you were justified in your actions this time. I was trying to kill the cuda and you stopped me. Apology accepted. It appears you were right about the barracuda; if it wanted to attack me, it had the opportunity, but it didn't."

Ilsa came up to Trevor and hugged him with no concern about his drenched clothes. Carla wandered over and grabbed Kit's hand. Both couples walked to the railing on the port side and looked down into the blue waters of Chub Cay.

Below them the ancient fish seemed to stare back up thanking them for bringing it home. A school of peanut sized dolphin, attracted to the drifting boat, schooled around the vessel long enough to attract the attention of the cuda. They were no match for the cuda as it cut and slashed its way through the teaming school gorging itself on the succulent young fish's flesh.

Satisfied that they had completed their mission, Kit went to the bridge to begin the journey home. Trevor and Ilsa went below to change their wet clothes.

After grabbing some dry clothes, Ilsa asked, "Would you like to shower together?"

"The shower in the head is awful small."

"I know. Won't that be exciting?"

Trevor just smiled and made his way to the shower. They both removed their clothes and stepped into the small space allotted to the shower. Their breathing was heavy now excited by the feel of skin on skin. Trevor placed his mouth on hers pulling her tightly against his body.

After a couple of minutes of intense French kissing, he reached up and turned on the shower just long enough to wet their bodies. He took the soap and started washing her breasts first. Gently he squeezed and caressed her soft full breasts. Next, he slipped his hand between her legs and washed her warm feminine areas. Ilsa suddenly grabbed the soap from him and began washing his hairy chest. She worked her way down to his stomach and then gently cleansed his manhood.

Trevor turned the water on once more to rinse the soap from their bodies. Ilsa wet her hair, handed Trevor the shampoo and turned her back to him. He became highly aroused as he lathered her hair with shampoo.

Her round cheeks pressed against his stiff member. She reached back and spread them so that he could enter her from behind. His penis slid in easily due to her excited feelings for him. They took a second to rinse the shampoo from her hair, and then Trevor began to nibble on the side of her neck driving her crazy. Forcefully he smacked his groin into her rear until both of them practically collapsed from an intense orgasm.

With their legs still shaking, they cleaned up once more and dried off. Ilsa turned to Trevor and asked, "I know this isn't how it's supposed to go, but will you marry me?"

Taken by surprise, Trevor replied, "Excuse me?"

"You heard me and I'm not going to ask again. Will you, Trevor Callaway, marry me?"

Overcome by emotion, Trevor began to weep. He knew from the past that this is happening too fast. His previously failed marriages began the same way—great sex and then reality hits; however, this time something seemed different. They both worked in the literary industry. They both loved to fish. And another woman had once told him, "You must find a woman who loves you as much as you love her or she will someday leave you." He felt that Ilsa loved him in this way and so with a little hesitation he answered, "I would love to be your husband!"

They stood embracing each other for several minutes until Ilsa blurted out, "Let's get dressed and share the good news with Kit and Carla!"

When the couple entered the stateroom holding hands, Carla new something was up. Kit had put the boat on autopilot and was enjoying a sandwich and beer. Ilsa made the announcement, "Hey guys, I have some good news! Trevor and I are getting married!" Carla's jaw dropped not sure how to take the news. Thoughts of her and Trevor on the beach swam around inside her head until she asked, "I'm happy for you, but this is kind of quick isn't it?"

Trevor answered, "Maybe so, but I've never felt about anybody like I feel about Ilsa."

Feeling relieved that he would no longer have to worry about Carla and Trevor becoming an item, Kit said, "Congratulations!"

Carla had an idea and threw it out there for the others, "What if we have a double wedding when we get back to Key West?"

Ilsa and Trevor looked at each other with a shrug.

Kit considered the proposal and said, "Why not!"

"We could get married at Mallory Square as the sun sets on the ocean. And maybe we can rent part of Sloppy Joes for a reception with a few of our friends," Ilsa offered.

The rest of the trip was uneventful. Both couples stood in the bridge as the yacht approached Key West passing by the Southernmost Point Marker. They watched to the west, as a large orange fireball seemed to drench itself into the ocean with purple and blue clouds hovering above the spectacle. Everyone realized that not long from now, they would be watching this scene over, but with promises of love and commitment that were supposed to be as enduring as the setting sun.

About The Author

Brent Story is a fourth generation Floridian. He lives with his wife, Laura, in Cooper City, Florida. This book is the result of many years of work. It includes quitting his job of twenty-five years in retail grocery and returning to college to earn a bachelors degree in English. The story came from life experienced living in a state surrounded by water.

www.ingramcontent.com/pod-product-compliance
Lightning Source LLC
Chambersburg PA
CBHW021949170626
46808CB00001B/75